中文详注剑桥莎士比亚精选

李尔王

原版创始主编：[英] 瑞克斯·吉布森（Rex Gibson）
原版主编：[英] 瑞查德·安褚斯（Richard Andrews）
　　　　　[英] 维姬·维南德（Vicki Wienand）
原版编注：[英] 埃尔斯佩思·贝恩（Elspeth Bain）
　　　　　[英] 尼克·艾米（Nic Amy）
总主编：陈国华
分册主编：彭宇

社图号 21149

Cambridge School Shakespeare: King Lear [Third edition] [978-1-107-61538-0] was first published by Cambridge University Press in 2015. All rights reserved.

This annotated Chinese edition for the People's Republic of China is published by arrangement with the Press Syndicate of the University of Cambridge, Cambridge, United Kingdom.

© Cambridge University Press & Beijing Language and Culture University Press 2021.

This book is in copyright. No reproduction of any part may take place without the written permission of Cambridge University Press or Beijing Language and Culture University Press.

本书版权由剑桥大学出版社和北京语言大学出版社共同所有。本书任何部分之文字及图片，如未获得出版者书面同意，不得用任何方式抄袭、节录或翻印。

This edition is for sale in the People's Republic of China (excluding Hong Kong SAR, Macao SAR and Taiwan Province) only. 此版本仅限在中华人民共和国境内销售。

北京市版权局著作权合同登记图字：01-2020-4096 号

图书在版编目（CIP）数据

中文详注剑桥莎士比亚精选. 李尔王 / 陈国华总主编；彭宇分册主编. -- 北京：北京语言大学出版社，2021.11

书名原文：Cambridge School Shakespeare：King Lear

ISBN 978-7-5619-5975-6

Ⅰ. ①中… Ⅱ. ①陈… ②彭… Ⅲ. ①悲剧-剧本-英国-中世纪 Ⅳ. ①I561.33

中国版本图书馆 CIP 数据核字（2021）第 190134 号

中文详注剑桥莎士比亚精选：李尔王
ZHONGWEN XIANG ZHU JIANQIAO SHASHIBIYA JINGXUAN: LI'ER WANG

项目策划：李 亮		**责任编辑**：孙冠群 李 亮	
封面设计：乔 剑		**排版制作**：北京创艺涵文化发展有限公司	
责任印制：周 燚			

出版发行 北京语言大学出版社
社　　址 北京市海淀区学院路 15 号，100083
网　　址 www.blcup.com
电子信箱 service@blcup.com
电　　话 编辑部　8610-82301019/0178
　　　　　　发行部　8610-82303650/3591/3648
　　　　　　北语书店　8610-82303653
　　　　　　网购咨询　8610-82303908
印　　刷 北京博海升彩色印刷有限公司
版　　次 2021 年 11 月第 1 版　　**印　次** 2021 年 11 月第 1 次印刷
开　　本 787 毫米 × 1092 毫米　1/16　　**印　张** 16.75
字　　数 436 千字
定　　价 99.00 元

PRINTED IN CHINA

序

由于观察角度不同，评判标准不同，关于哪个国家哪位诗人或小说家的成就最大，世人可能难以达成一致；可是说到剧作家，大家的共识是，莎士比亚不仅是英语国家有史以来最伟大的剧作家，也是全世界最伟大的剧作家，在知名度、影响力和传世作品的数量上，没有任何一位剧作家可以与之比肩。正是由于其公认的文学成就和人文精神，在过去400多年里，莎士比亚戏剧的演出在英语国家和许多非英语国家经久不衰，莎剧的阅读和鉴赏已成为这些国家英文教学的必选内容。

莎剧进入中国，已经有100多年历史，莎士比亚全集已经有了四个中文译本。不懂英文的人可以通过译本来欣赏莎士比亚剧作。然而文学作品的语言，尤其是诗歌的语言，具有相当程度的不可译性，而几乎所有莎剧的大部分台词都是素体诗（blank verse）。例如《哈慕雷》（*Hamlet*）里主人公的名言"To be, or not to be, that is the question"，不论怎样译，都难以完全再现原文的深刻内涵和形式特点。要想真正欣赏莎士比亚的语言和戏剧艺术，还得阅读其英文原作。最早由剑桥大学出版社出版的这套莎剧精选，收录了最受读者和观众喜爱的14部剧目，涵盖莎剧的各个类别，以其独具匠心的设计和编排，成为所有英文原版莎剧中最适合英语学习者阅读、最适合戏剧爱好者排演的莎剧选集。

本选集的创始主编瑞克斯·吉布森（Rex Gibson）在本书引言（Introduction）里指出："不论做什么，都要记住，莎士比亚写下他的剧本是为了演出、观看和享受的。"秉承这一宗旨，这一新版莎剧选集有四个鲜明的区别性特点：

一、书的开本和页面的宽高比例特别适合学校的老师和学生以及剧团的导演和演员在排练莎剧时把书打开，拿在手里，随时参阅，而且左边页面上有许多有关排演活动的建议。

二、书中配有大量世界各国莎剧演出的彩色剧照，为莎剧爱好者和剧团排演莎剧提供了灵感。

三、书的正文部分打开后，右页是未经删减、原汁原味的剧本原文，左页是多种不同栏目，包括导演技巧（Stagecraft）、剧中语言（Language in the play）、人物分析（Characters）、主题分析（Themes）、写作练习（Write about it）及词语注释等。每幕之间（本幕回顾）和最后一幕后（本剧回顾）有与剧情相关的各种思考题。

四、在剧本之后有各种针对全剧的专题论述，以《哈慕雷》为例，包括视角与主题（Perspectives and themes）、人物分析（Characters）、《哈慕雷》的语言（The language of *Hamlet*）、《哈慕雷》的演出（*Hamlet* in performance）、笔论莎士比亚（Writing about Shakespeare）、笔论《哈慕雷》（Writing about *Hamlet*），还有一份莎翁年表（William Shakespeare 1564–1616）。

左页上的栏目对于解读和排演莎剧特别有帮助，剧本后面的专题论述对于撰写有关莎士比亚的文章特别有帮助，而参加莎剧排演，背诵台词，撰写论文，又是提高英语水平的极好途径。

为了方便更多的中国读者阅读、欣赏、排演莎士比亚原作，北京语言大学出版社携手剑桥大学出版社，将这套莎剧精选引入中国。我有幸应邀担任这套书的中文版总主编，组织起一个团队，对原版进行一定程度的改编和汉化，以适应中国读者的需求。我们不仅将原版提供的关键注释基本译成了中文，而且针对中国英语学习者和莎剧爱好者阅读理解上的难点，主要做了以下四件事：

一、参考 The Oxford Dictionary of Original Shakespearean Pronunciation (David Crystal 2016)、Oxford Dictionary of Pronunciation for Current English (Clive Upton 2003) 和 Shakespeare's Names: A Pronouncing Dictionary (Helge Kökeritz 1950)，给每个剧本前面人物表里的人名加上了国际音标。为了便于读者识别，我们将第一本发音词典里一般中国读者不认识的个别音标替换成了大家熟悉的近似音标。

二、为左页顶端的剧情简介添加中文译文。

三、左页中以及剧本后面论文部分里有一些具有挑战性的词和术语（如tableau），我们为其中的大部分添加了相应的中文释义。

四、适当增加了原版里没有的词语注释。

给剧中人物的名字加了国际音标之后，我们发现，现有莎剧中文译本里一些人名的中文译名与原文的读音差别较大且互不相同。根据定名不咎、译音循本、音义兼顾、音系对应的原则，我们给出了新译名。根据前两个原则，我们将剧本 Julius Caesar /ˈdʒuːlɪəs ˈsiːzə(r)/ 译成《儒略·恺撒》，而没有采用《尤利/力乌斯·恺撒》《裘利/力斯·凯撒》《居里厄斯·恺撒》等现成译名中的任何一个，因为从公元前1世纪到公元16世纪西方使用的儒略历（Julian calendar）就是以这位 Julius Caesar（拉丁文读音是 /ˈjuːlɪʊs ˈkaesar/）命名的。根据音义兼顾的原则，我们将剧本 Hamlet /ˈ(h)amlət/ 译成《哈慕雷》而不是《哈姆莱特》或《哈姆雷特》，因为"慕雷"比"姆莱"或"姆雷"更适合用来给男子起名，结尾的辅音 /t/ 在实际说话中往往不发音。根据音系对应的原则，我们借鉴了曹禺的译法，将剧本 Romeo and Juliet 译成《柔密欧与茱丽叶》，没有将 Romeo 译成更常见的"罗密欧"，因为"柔 /rou/"比"罗 /luo/"更接近原名 Romeo /ˈroːmɪoː/ 的读音；同时我们将 Juliet /ˈdʒuːlɪət/ 译成"茱丽叶"而不是"朱丽叶"，因为这样做不容易让人误以为这个女孩姓"朱"。

这套经过改编并且带中文注释的《中文详注剑桥莎士比亚精选》不仅可以用作中国高中和大学的英文教材，而且适合中国所有具有较高英语能力的莎剧爱好者阅读和欣赏，将戏剧从书中提升到自己心中，将剧本从课堂搬演到戏台。

相信《中文详注剑桥莎士比亚精选》会带给中国广大英语爱好者一个惊喜。

陈国华

2020年5月于英国剑桥家中

Contents 目录

Introduction 引言	iv
Photo gallery 剧照精选	v
King Lear 《李尔王》	
List of characters 人物表	1
Act 1 第1幕	3
Act 2 第2幕	57
Act 3 第3幕	99
Act 4 第4幕	135
Act 5 第5幕	175
Perspectives and themes 视角与主题	202
The contexts of *King Lear* 《李尔王》的创作背景	209
Characters 人物分析	214
The language of *King Lear* 《李尔王》的语言	222
Critics' forum 评论家论坛	228
The truth and reconciliation commission 真相与调解委员会	230
King Lear in performance 《李尔王》的演出	232
Writing about Shakespeare 笔论莎士比亚	240
Writing about *King Lear* 笔论《李尔王》	242
The Quarto and Folio editions 四开本和对开本	244
William Shakespeare 1564–1616 莎翁年表	250
Acknowledgements 鸣谢	251

Cambridge School Shakespeare

Introduction 引言

This *King Lear* is part of the **Cambridge School Shakespeare** series. Like every other play in the series, it has been specially prepared to help all students in schools and colleges.

The **Cambridge School Shakespeare** *King Lear* aims to be different. It invites you to lift the words from the page and to bring the play to life in your classroom, hall or drama studio. Through enjoyable and focused activities, you will increase your understanding of the play. Actors have created their different interpretations of the play over the centuries. Similarly, you are invited to make up your own mind about *King Lear*, rather than having someone else's interpretation handed down to you.

Cambridge School Shakespeare does not offer you a cut-down or simplified version of the play. This is Shakespeare's language, filled with imaginative possibilities. You will find on every left-hand page: a summary of the action, an explanation of unfamiliar words, and a choice of activities on Shakespeare's stagecraft, characters, themes and language.

Between each act and in the pages at the end of the play, you will find notes, illustrations and activities. These will help to encourage reflection after every act and give you insights into the background and context of the play as a whole.

This edition will be of value to you whether you are studying for an examination, reading for pleasure or thinking of putting on the play to entertain others. You can work on the activities on your own or in groups. Many of the activities suggest a particular group size, but don't be afraid to make up larger or smaller groups to suit your own purposes. Please don't think you have to do every activity: choose those that will help you most.

Although you are invited to treat *King Lear* as a play, you don't need special dramatic or theatrical skills to do the activities. By choosing your activities, and by exploring and experimenting, you can make your own interpretations of Shakespeare's language, characters and stories.

Whatever you do, remember that Shakespeare wrote his plays to be acted, watched and enjoyed.

Rex Gibson
Founding editor

This new edition contains more photographs, more diversity and more supporting material than previous editions, whilst remaining true to Rex's original vision. Specifically, it contains more activities and commentary on stagecraft and writing about Shakespeare, to reflect contemporary interest. The glossary has been enlarged too. Finally, this edition aims to reflect the best teaching and learning possible, and to represent not only Shakespeare through the ages, but also the relevance and excitement of Shakespeare today.

Richard Andrews and Vicki Wienand
Series editors

This edition of *King Lear* uses the text of the play established by Jay L. Halio in **The New Cambridge Shakespeare**.

'Know that we have divided / In three our kingdom'. *King Lear* dramatises the consequences of an elderly British king's decision to give up his power and land – while wanting to keep the title and status of king. Lear's three daughters, Gonerill, Regan and Cordelia, are asked to declare publicly how much they love him before learning how much of his kingdom they will have. In this production, Lear's Fool sits at his feet.

Gonerill and Regan flatter their father and are rewarded with shares of the kingdom. Here, Regan is trying to outdo her older sister Gonerill's flattery.

'What can you say to draw / A third more opulent than your sisters?' Cordelia, the youngest sister and her father's favourite, is the last to speak. She loves Lear deeply but refuses to play his flattery game, claiming only to love her father as a daughter should. Lear, hurt and enraged by her apparent defiance of his authority, publicly disowns and curses her.

'What wouldst thou do, old man?' The plain-speaking Earl of Kent intervenes on Cordelia's behalf and is rewarded with banishment. Although the Duke of Burgundy rejects the disgraced and disinherited Cordelia, the King of France – another of her suitors – willingly accepts her as his wife.

▶ 'Edgar I nothing am.' The Duke of Gloucester, a shocked witness of events, also has family problems. His illegitimate son Edmond is secretly plotting to frame his elder brother Edgar and steal his inheritance. Soon, Edgar has to flee for his life, disguising himself as Poor Tom, a madman beggar.

▼ The Earl of Kent (seen here on the right) has not gone into banishment but has also assumed a disguise, obtaining a position as the old king's servant. Lear's Fool (on the left) also remains with Lear.

◀ 'Not only, sir, this, your all-licensed fool, / But other of your insolent retinue / Do hourly carp and quarrel'. Lear plans to live alternately with Gonerill and Regan for six months at a time, but the arrangement soon breaks down. Gonerill is vexed by the king's insistence on retaining one hundred knights, plus his Fool, as his companions.

▼ 'O fool, I shall go mad.' Enraged by Gonerill's suggestion that he reduce the number of his knights, Lear sets off to stay with Regan, meeting up with her at the Duke of Gloucester's castle. Gonerill arrives and both sisters insist that Lear has no real need of any followers. Lear is distraught and fears he will go mad. He leaves the castle accompanied only by his Fool. The night becomes stormy.

▲ 'This tempest in my mind'. As the storm rages, Kent finds the king and his Fool wandering on the heath. There, they also encounter Edgar in his disguise as Poor Tom. Lear's mind gives way completely, but in his madness he develops a new concern and sympathy for the 'poor naked wretches' of this world.

▶ 'Go thrust him out at gates, and let him smell / His way to Dover.' Gloucester helps get Lear to safety in Dover, where Cordelia has landed with a French army. This loyalty to the king enrages Gonerill, Regan and her husband, the Duke of Cornwall, who gouges out Gloucester's eyes in punishment and throws him out into the storm. However, Cornwall is fatally wounded by one of his own servants, who was trying to protect Gloucester.

'Alack, I have no eyes.' Edgar, still acting the part of a madman beggar, meets his blind father and agrees to guide him to Dover, where Gloucester plans to throw himself off a cliff. Edgar, however, has a plan of his own that he hopes will make his father believe his life has been miraculously saved, and so decide to live.

'How fares your majesty?' In the French camp at Dover, Cordelia and Lear are reunited. The king, now calm, recognises his youngest daughter and attempts to kneel before her to ask forgiveness. Cordelia says he must not kneel and asks for his blessing. Meanwhile, at the British camp nearby, Gonerill and Regan are in competition for Edmond, jealously eyeing each other.

'She's gone for ever.' After a battle between the French army and Gonerill and Regan's forces, Lear and Cordelia are captured. Edmond orders their deaths. A disguised Edgar fights his brother in single combat. Edmond, badly wounded, tries to revoke the death sentence he passed on Lear and Cordelia, but the reprieve comes too late for Cordelia. The distraught (发狂) king carries her dead body on to the stage.

'The wonder is he hath endured so long.' Edgar and Kent both watch as Lear struggles to accept Cordelia's death, before dying himself.

'We that are young / Shall never see so much, nor live so long.' Edgar speaks the closing words of the play. Lear and Cordelia lie dead. Edmond has died of wounds sustained in his fight with Edgar. Regan and Gonerill are also dead – Regan has been murdered by Gonerill, and Gonerill has committed suicide.

List of characters 人物表

The Royal House of Britain 不列颠王室

LEAR /liː(r)/ (李尔) king of Britain
GONERILL /ˈgɒnərɪl/ (高娜瑞尔) his eldest daughter
REGAN /ˈriːgən/ (蕊根) his second daughter
CORDELIA /kɒ(r)ˈdiːlɪə/ (考蒂丽叶) his youngest daughter
THE DUKE OF ALBANY /ˈɑːlbənɪ/ (阿尔博尼公爵) married to Gonerill
THE DUKE OF CORNWALL /ˈkɔː(r)nwɑːl/ (康沃尔公爵) married to Regan

The Gloucester family 格劳斯特家族

THE EARL OF GLOUCESTER /ˈglɒstə(r)/ (格劳斯特伯爵)
EDGAR /ˈedgə(r)/ (爱德格) his elder son and heir
EDMOND /ˈedmənd/ (爱德门) his illegitimate son

Other characters in the play 剧中其他角色

FOOL 俳优
THE EARL OF KENT /kent/ (肯特伯爵)
(later disguised as CAIUS /ˈkəɪəs/ [凯耶]) } in the king's service

THE KING OF FRANCE 法兰西王
THE DUKE OF BURGUNDY /ˈbɜː(r)gən͵dəɪ/ (勃艮第公爵) } suitors to Cordelia

OSWALD /ˈɒzwəld/ (奥兹沃尔) Gonerill's steward
CURAN /ˈkʌrən/ (喀润) a courtier
A GENTLEMAN (绅士)
AN OLD MAN (老丈) Gloucester's tenant
A CAPTAIN (军官)
A HERALD (先锋官)
A SERVANT (仆人) in Cornwall's household

Knights, gentlemen, soldiers, attendants, messengers, servants

The action of the play takes place in various parts of the kingdom of Britain.

Discussing King Lear's plan to abdicate and share out his kingdom, Kent and Gloucester are unsure about which of his two sons-in-law Lear favours. Gloucester introduces Edmond, his illegitimate son.

剧情简介：肯特和格劳斯特讨论李尔王退位并分封国土的计划，他们不清楚李尔更偏爱两位女婿中的哪一位。格劳斯特把自己的私生子爱德门介绍给肯特。

Themes 主题分析

Introducing themes (in pairs)

In his opening scene, Shakespeare often suggests the themes that the play will go on to explore.

- Agree on a list of the main three topics of conversation in the script opposite (for example, fathers and children).
- Based on these ideas, and on other clues you can find in the opening lines, talk about how you think the play might develop.

1 Sons (and daughters?) (in pairs)

When discussing the transfer of power to the next generation, Kent and Gloucester refer only to the king's sons-in-law, not his daughters.

a Research the laws of inheritance during Shakespeare's time. How did attitudes towards women and power differ from those today?

b Find out more about Queen Elizabeth I, and about Mary, Queen of Scots (whose son James ruled England and Scotland at the time the play was written). Discuss how perceptions of their reigns could have influenced attitudes to female rule. (For more information, see 'The contexts of *King Lear*', pp. 209–13.)

c Some productions have omitted these opening lines and started with the king's entrance. What would be lost by doing this? If you were a director, would you keep or cut this scene?

2 Gloucester gossips, Edmond listens (in threes)

Edmond hears himself described as the result of one of his father's sexual adventures, as a 'knave' and a 'whoreson'. He learns that he will soon be sent away again.

a Take parts and speak lines 7–28. Read them once as though Gloucester is joking and showing real affection for his illegitimate son. Then read them again as though he is being insensitive and deliberately cruel.

b Talk together about the following:
- your impressions of Gloucester and which of the two ways of reading the lines you would prefer in performance
- what Edmond may be thinking about his father's conversation and how an actor might show him reacting
- how Kent might react at line 13 to cause Gloucester to ask 'Do you smell a fault?'

1　affected　喜欢
2　qualities are so weighed　他俩的品格半斤八两
3　curiosity … moiety　无论怎样考量，都无法让你舍此取彼（curiosity：精打细算；moiety：二等份之一）
4　breeding　抚养
5　that … brazed to't　对此我的脸皮已经很厚了
6　conceive　理解；怀孕（肯特是前一个意思，格劳斯特是后一个意思，因此后面按这个意思解释）
7　ere = before
8　issue　所结之果；所生之子
9　proper　堂堂正正；英俊
10　by order of law　合法
11　some year elder　大概年长一岁
12　knave　臭小子，无赖（玩笑口吻）
13　whoreson　野种（玩笑口吻）
14　sue　请求
15　study deserving　不负厚望
16　out　离家；出门在外或在国外

The Tragedy of King Lear

Act 1 Scene 1
King Lear's palace

Enter KENT, GLOUCESTER, *and* EDMOND

KENT I thought the king had more affected[1] the Duke of Albany than Cornwall.

GLOUCESTER It did always seem so to us: but now in the division of the kingdom, it appears not which of the dukes he values most, for qualities are so weighed[2] that curiosity in neither can make choice of either's moiety[3].

KENT Is not this your son, my lord?

GLOUCESTER His breeding[4], sir, hath been at my charge. I have so often blushed to acknowledge him, that now I am brazed to't[5].

KENT I cannot conceive[6] you.

GLOUCESTER Sir, this young fellow's mother could; whereupon she grew round wombed, and had indeed, sir, a son for her cradle ere[7] she had a husband for her bed. Do you smell a fault?

KENT I cannot wish the fault undone, the issue[8] of it being so proper[9].

GLOUCESTER But I have a son, sir, by order of law[10], some year elder[11] than this, who yet is no dearer in my account; though this knave[12] came something saucily to the world before he was sent for, yet was his mother fair, there was good sport at his making, and the whoreson[13] must be acknowledged. Do you know this noble gentleman, Edmond?

EDMOND No, my lord.

GLOUCESTER My lord of Kent; remember him hereafter as my honourable friend.

EDMOND My services to your lordship.

KENT I must love you and sue[14] to know you better.

EDMOND Sir, I shall study deserving[15].

GLOUCESTER He hath been out[16] nine years, and away he shall again. The king is coming.

Lear intends to divide Britain between his daughters. He sets them a test: whoever expresses the greatest love will be given the largest portion. Gonerill voices limitless love for him and wins a share.

剧情简介：李尔打算把不列颠分给女儿们。他对她们进行测验：谁向他表达的爱最多，分到的土地就最多。高娜瑞尔向他表达了无尽的爱，于是赢得了她的那一份。

1 Enter King Lear

Imagine you are planning to direct a performance of *King Lear*. Start your own Director's Journal to record your ideas as you go through the play. Remember that costume, props (道具), ceremonious behaviour and the deportment of the actor are important – not only to convey Lear's status, but also to explain the way others treat him. Consider the following:

- How might the entrance of Lear, his daughters and the members of the court be staged? Describe what kinds of effects you can create by staging it in different ways.
- How will it be clear to the audience which figure is the king?
- Will it be obvious what sort of king he is?
- Will it be obvious what sort of father he is?

When you have finished making notes, look again at the images of Lear throughout this book. How closely do your ideas resemble those of other directors?

Language in the play 剧中语言

'our darker purpose' (in pairs)

Lear makes a formal, public declaration of his plans to give his land and power to his daughters and their husbands.

a Share a reading of lines 31–49 with your partner and find examples of Lear using the language of power:
   - the use of imperatives (orders)
   - the 'royal we' – the use of the plural 'we' and 'our', rather than 'I' or 'mine' (why does he do this?)
   - forceful, determined language.

   Re-read the lines to each other, emphasising all these dominant and regal (王权) elements of his language.

b Talk together about the effect Lear's language might have on the audience.

c Lear's desire to 'crawl toward death' without the burdens of kingship seems oddly humble in such an apparently grand and self-important speech. Discuss why he makes this apparently modest statement and how sincere you think he is.

1 *Sennet* 吹小号（表示显赫人物上场）
2 *we … purpose* 朕要说出朕的私密意图（we和our是御用复数，以复数形式指代单个人，表示庄严和权威）
3 *fast intent* 坚定的意愿
4 *shake* 摆脱
5 *Conferring* 赋予
6 *son* 女婿（英文里son可以用来直接称呼女婿，甚至还可以当"小伙子"来使用）
7 *constant will* 恒定不变的意愿
8 *several dowers* 各自的嫁妆
9 *made their amorous sojourn* 为求婚而客居或暂住
10 *divest us both of* 卸下朕所有的（us也是王室口吻；both当时可以指代两个以上事物）
11 *Interest of territory* 领土拥有权
12 *bounty* 奖赏
13 *nature doth with merit challenge* 天性（指父女亲情）与贤能对阵
14 *word can wield the matter* 字词能传达意思（这里是wield的一种隐喻用法）
15 *breath* 语言
16 *bounds* 边界，地界
17 *champains* 平原
18 *wide-skirted meads* 广阔的草滩（meads = meadows）
19 *issues* 子孙，后代

King Lear Act 1 Scene 1
李尔王

Sennet[1]. *Enter* KING LEAR, CORNWALL, ALBANY, GONERILL, REGAN, CORDELIA, *and Attendants*

LEAR	Attend the lords of France and Burgundy, Gloucester.		
GLOUCESTER	I shall, my lord.	*Exit*	30
LEAR	Meantime we shall express our darker purpose[2].		
	Give me the map there. Know, that we have divided		
	In three our kingdom, and 'tis our fast intent[3]		
	To shake[4] all cares and business from our age,		
	Conferring[5] them on younger strengths while we		35
	Unburdened crawl toward death. Our son[6] of Cornwall,		
	And you, our no less loving son of Albany,		
	We have this hour a constant will[7] to publish		
	Our daughters' several dowers[8], that future strife		
	May be prevented now. The princes, France and Burgundy,		40
	Great rivals in our youngest daughter's love,		
	Long in our court have made their amorous sojourn[9],		
	And here are to be answered. Tell me, my daughters		
	(Since now we will divest us both of[10] rule,		
	Interest of territory[11], cares of state),		45
	Which of you shall we say doth love us most,		
	That we our largest bounty[12] may extend		
	Where nature doth with merit challenge[13]? Gonerill,		
	Our eldest born, speak first.		
GONERILL	Sir, I love you more than word can wield the matter[14],		50
	Dearer than eyesight, space, and liberty;		
	Beyond what can be valued, rich or rare,		
	No less than life, with grace, health, beauty, honour;		
	As much as child e'er loved, or father found;		
	A love that makes breath[15] poor, and speech unable;		55
	Beyond all manner of so much I love you.		
CORDELIA	[*Aside*] What shall Cordelia speak? Love, and be silent.		
LEAR	Of all these bounds[16] even from this line, to this,		
	With shadowy forests and with champains[17] riched		
	With plenteous rivers and wide-skirted meads[18],		60
	We make thee lady. To thine and Albany's issues[19]		
	Be this perpetual. What says our second daughter,		
	Our dearest Regan, wife of Cornwall?		

剧情简介： 蕊根声称她最大的快乐来自父亲的爱。李尔封给她的国土与封给高娜瑞尔的那份不相上下。考蒂丽叶拒绝参与爱的检验，说她只不过以一个女儿对父亲应有的方式来爱父亲。

1 How to say 'Nothing' (in pairs)

Lear seems to suggest that he favours Cordelia in the division of the kingdom (line 81). However, she refuses to join her sisters in flattering her father, answering his request for a declaration of love with 'Nothing' – a word that will be used repeatedly in the rest of the play.

a How should Cordelia speak the word 'Nothing'? Discuss this in your pairs.

b How does Lear respond – with instant rage or with embarrassed patience? In one production the king and his courtiers thought Cordelia was joking and laughed indulgently at her words. (See below, pp. vi top and 55 for different stagings of this scene.) Take parts and speak lines 80–102 in different ways to discover which interpretation you prefer.

c Keep a record of uses of the word 'nothing' during the rest of the play. You could do this in your Director's Journal or on a poster.

▼ The division of the kingdom. In many productions, a clear ceremonial pattern – followed in turn by Gonerill and Regan – is established before Cordelia breaks it by saying: 'Nothing.'

1 self-mettle 同一种金属（mettle = metal）
2 prize me at her worth 自我评价与她同样值钱
3 names … love 道出了我的孝敬之心
4 short 简短
5 most precious square of sense 感官最珍贵之处
6 felicitate 幸福，快乐
7 ponderous 有分量
8 thine hereditary 你的继承人
9 ever = forever
10 validity = value（价值）
11 be interested (to) 对……享有权利，声索对……的权利
12 draw 抽取，赢得
13 opulent 富饶
14 bond （子女对父母的）义务
15 mar 毁掉
16 begot 生
17 bred 养
18 take my plight 接受我的（结婚）誓言（plight = pledge）

REGAN	I am made of that self-mettle[1] as my sister	
	And prize me at her worth[2]. In my true heart	65
	I find she names my very deed of love[3].	
	Only she comes too short[4], that I profess	
	Myself an enemy to all other joys	
	Which the most precious square of sense[5] possesses,	
	And find I am alone felicitate[6]	70
	In your dear highness' love.	
CORDELIA	[*Aside*] Then poor Cordelia,	
	And yet not so, since I am sure my love's	
	More ponderous[7] than my tongue.	
LEAR	To thee and thine hereditary[8] ever[9]	
	Remain this ample third of our fair kingdom,	75
	No less in space, validity[10], and pleasure	
	Than that conferred on Gonerill. Now our joy,	
	Although our last and least, to whose young love	
	The vines of France and milk of Burgundy	
	Strive to be interessed[11]. What can you say to draw[12]	80
	A third more opulent[13] than your sisters? Speak.	
CORDELIA	Nothing, my lord.	
LEAR	Nothing?	
CORDELIA	Nothing.	
LEAR	Nothing will come of nothing, speak again.	85
CORDELIA	Unhappy that I am, I cannot heave	
	My heart into my mouth: I love your majesty	
	According to my bond[14], no more nor less.	
LEAR	How, how, Cordelia? Mend your speech a little,	
	Lest you may mar[15] your fortunes.	
CORDELIA	Good my lord,	90
	You have begot[16] me, bred[17] me, loved me. I	
	Return those duties back as are right fit,	
	Obey you, love you, and most honour you.	
	Why have my sisters husbands, if they say	
	They love you all? Happily, when I shall wed,	95
	That lord whose hand must take my plight[18] shall carry	
	Half my love with him, half my care and duty.	
	Sure, I shall never marry like my sisters.	
LEAR	But goes thy heart with this?	
CORDELIA	Ay, my good lord.	

Enraged, Lear disowns Cordelia and divides her inheritance between Gonerill and Regan. He proposes that he and his one hundred knights live with Gonerill and Regan in turn. Kent protests.

 剧情简介：李尔大怒，与考蒂丽叶断绝了父女关系，将她应继承的国土分给了高娜瑞尔和蕊根。他提议自己和一百名骑士今后轮流住在高娜瑞尔和蕊根家。肯特上前劝谏。

1 A father's curse (in large groups)

In lines 102–14, Lear invokes ancient beliefs to curse and reject Cordelia. He is bitterly angry at her unwillingness to declare unqualified love for him. This activity will help you explore the force of Lear's furious words and their effect on Cordelia.

- One person (volunteer only!) plays Cordelia. The others, who all represent Lear, stand in a circle around her.
- Each 'Lear' chooses a short section of the king's words that they feel conveys his rejection of Cordelia. This extract can be as short as five or six words, or as much as three lines.
- In turn, speak the words you have chosen. When you have spoken your words, turn your back on Cordelia.
- Repeat the activity, adding gestures to emphasise your words.
- Cordelia can try ways of gesturing and speaking lines from earlier in the script to respond to these attacks, but may not leave the circle.

After you have tried several versions of the activity, talk together about the way in which the words and ideas express Lear's feelings, and the effect they have on Cordelia.

Stagecraft 导演技巧

Reaction (in pairs)

The court assembled expecting a formal ceremony in which the kingdom would be divided. Afterwards there would probably have been celebrations of Cordelia's betrothal (订婚) to one of her suitors. By this point, however, things are clearly not going as expected. In some productions (particularly film versions), the court is represented by many actors. In others, only the named characters appear on stage.

a Talk together about how the onlookers should react and behave. Lear's words at line 120 suggest that some people at least are frozen in shock. It is important that minor characters do not draw the audience's attention from the main action. How could these 'extras' convey a reaction without being a distraction? Make notes in your Director's Journal suggesting how to handle this.

b How would you advise Gonerill and Regan to react?

c Work with another pair to create a tableau (定格；活人画) showing the reactions of Gonerill, Regan and the court. Members of another pair should interpret and comment on the tableau.

1 **Hecate** 赫柯媂（希腊神话中一位掌管天、地、海的女神，通常被塑造成三身一体的形象，手持火炬、钥匙和毒蛇）

2 **operation of the orbs** 命运之星的运行

3 **Propinquity and property of blood** 血缘的亲属和财产关系

4 **Scythian** 斯基泰人（古希腊人对被称为斯基提亚 [Scythia] 的黑海和小亚细亚周边地区游牧民族的总称，野蛮人的典型代表）

5 **makes his generation messes** 以自己的后代为食（messes = meals）

6 **neighboured** 得到邻居帮衬

7 **sometime** 昔日

8 **my liege** 陛下

9 **nursery** 照料

10 **be my grave my peace** = let my grave be my peace（愿我不进坟墓不得安宁）

11 **Who stirs?** 哪位动一动？（众人被他的震怒吓呆）

12 **Pre-eminence** 崇高地位

13 **large … majesty** 伴随王位而来的大量荣耀

14 **by monthly course** 按月

15 **addition** 头衔，荣誉

16 **sway** 统治权

17 **Revenue** 岁入（重读第二个音节）

18 **execution of the rest** 其他一切政务

19 **coronet** 王冠

20 **make from the shaft** 避开（我）射出的箭

8

LEAR	So young, and so untender?	100
CORDELIA	So young, my lord, and true.	
LEAR	Let it be so, thy truth then be thy dower.	

            For by the sacred radiance of the sun,
            The mysteries of Hecate[1] and the night,
            By all the operation of the orbs[2]   105
            From whom we do exist and cease to be,
            Here I disclaim all my paternal care,
            Propinquity and property of blood[3],
            And as a stranger to my heart and me
            Hold thee from this forever. The barbarous Scythian[4],   110
            Or he that makes his generation messes[5]
            To gorge his appetite, shall to my bosom
            Be as well neighboured[6], pitied, and relieved,
            As thou my sometime[7] daughter.

KENT   Good my liege[8] –

LEAR   Peace, Kent,   115
            Come not between the dragon and his wrath.
            I loved her most, and thought to set my rest
            On her kind nursery[9]. Hence and avoid my sight!
            So be my grave my peace[10], as here I give
            Her father's heart from her. Call France. Who stirs?[11]   120
            Call Burgundy. – Cornwall and Albany,
            With my two daughters' dowers digest the third.
            Let pride, which she calls plainness, marry her.
            I do invest you jointly with my power,
            Pre-eminence[12], and all the large effects   125
            That troop with majesty[13]. Ourself by monthly course[14],
            With reservation of an hundred knights
            By you to be sustained, shall our abode
            Make with you by due turn; only we shall retain
            The name and all th'addition[15] to a king: the sway[16],   130
            Revenue[17], execution of the rest[18],
            Beloved sons, be yours; which to confirm,
            This coronet[19] part between you.

KENT   Royal Lear,
            Whom I have ever honoured as my king,
            Loved as my father, as my master followed,   135
            As my great patron thought on in my prayers –

LEAR   The bow is bent and drawn, make from the shaft[20].

Kent challenges Lear's decisions. Kent states his loyalty, but continues to criticise the king's actions. Lear warns Kent to stop his protest on pain of death. Lear is outraged, and begins to declare Kent's punishment.

剧情简介：肯特质疑李尔的决定，说自己忠于王上，但是继续批评国王的行为。李尔警告肯特休得劝谏，否则就要处死他。盛怒之下，李尔开始宣布对肯特的惩罚。

Language in the play 剧中语言
Kent's plain speaking (in pairs)

In lines 138–48, Kent accuses Lear of madness, criticises Gonerill's and Regan's empty flattery, urges Lear to hold on to power and defends Cordelia's sincerity. He addresses Lear as 'thou' – an inappropriately intimate and casual term for a subject to use to his monarch, who would expect the courtesy of the plural 'you' in such a public conversation.

a One of you speaks Kent's lines. The other, in role as Lear, moves around the room, changing direction as often as they want. Kent must keep reading aloud, following Lear as closely as possible to make him listen. Lear must stop and turn round whenever Kent says something that has a big impact on his feelings as a king and father.

b Talk together about which of Kent's remarks you think Lear would find the most hurtful.

1. fork （叉形）箭头
2. To plainness honour's bound = Honour is bound to plainness（忠信必定直白）
3. Reserve thy state 保留你的君权
4. Reverb no hollowness 不回响着空洞（从 Nor 开始的这半句话是负负得正的双重否定）
5. wage 下注；冒险
6. blank 靶心（箭靶中心的白圈，如同瞳孔）
7. by Apollo 向阿波罗发誓（阿波罗是希腊和罗马神话中的太阳神，善于射箭，目光明亮）
8. vassal 奴才
9. Miscreant 混账东西
10. forbear 息怒
11. bestow 赠予
12. Revoke 撤回
13. Or 否则
14. vent clamour 发声抗议
15. recreant 逆贼
16. durst = dare
17. strained 勉强
18. betwixt = between
19. sentence 决定
20. nor … nor = neither … nor
21. Our potency made good 朕的权力已得到维护

Lear delivers his verdict (裁决) on Kent. Which line from the script opposite do you think is being said at this moment?

KENT	Let it fall rather, though the fork[1] invade
	The region of my heart. Be Kent unmannerly
	When Lear is mad. What wouldst thou do, old man? 140
	Think'st thou that duty shall have dread to speak
	When power to flattery bows? To plainness honour's bound[2],
	When majesty falls to folly. Reserve thy state[3],
	And in thy best consideration check
	This hideous rashness. Answer my life, my judgement: 145
	Thy youngest daughter does not love thee least,
	Nor are those empty-hearted whose low sounds
	Reverb no hollowness[4].
LEAR	Kent, on thy life no more.
KENT	My life I never held but as a pawn
	To wage[5] against thine enemies, ne'er feared to lose it, 150
	Thy safety being motive.
LEAR	Out of my sight!
KENT	See better, Lear, and let me still remain
	The true blank[6] of thine eye.
LEAR	Now by Apollo[7] –
KENT	Now by Apollo, king,
	Thou swear'st thy gods in vain.
LEAR	O vassal[8]! Miscreant[9]! 155
ALBANY, CORNWALL	Dear sir, forbear[10].
KENT	Kill thy physician, and thy fee bestow[11]
	Upon the foul disease. Revoke[12] thy gift,
	Or[13] whilst I can vent clamour[14] from my throat,
	I'll tell thee thou dost evil.
LEAR	Hear me, recreant[15], 160
	On thine allegiance hear me.
	That thou hast sought to make us break our vows,
	Which we durst[16] never yet; and with strained[17] pride,
	To come betwixt[18] our sentence[19] and our power,
	Which nor our nature nor[20] our place can bear, 165
	Our potency made good[21], take thy reward.
	Five days we do allot thee for provision
	To shield thee from disasters of the world,

Lear banishes Kent from Britain, threatening execution if he remains. Kent praises Cordelia's honesty, and urges Gonerill and Regan to fulfil their words of love. Lear offers Cordelia in marriage to Burgundy, without a dowry.

 剧情简介：李尔放逐肯特，并威胁说他如果不走就会被处死。肯特赞扬了考蒂丽叶的诚实，力劝高娜瑞尔和蕊根履行自己爱戴父亲的诺言。李尔把考蒂丽叶许配给勃艮第公爵，但是没有嫁妆。

Write about it 写作练习

Kent's parting words

Enraged by Kent's plain speaking, Lear banishes him and threatens him with a death sentence should he return. Before he says farewell, Kent addresses Lear, Cordelia and her sisters in turn, speaking each time in **rhyming couplets** (押韵二行连句；对偶句) (two lines of the same length that rhyme at the end). Couplets are often used in the play to indicate the end of a scene or that a character is about to leave the stage. They are also used to draw attention to a moment of significant emotion or to a proverbial statement or 'moral'.

a Why do you think Shakespeare gave Kent rhyming couplets here? What effect does it have on the audience? Write down your ideas.

b In rhyming couplets, write responses to Kent for Lear, Cordelia, Gonerill and Regan. Use what you have learnt so far of their characters, mood and language to help you with the style and tone of their replies.

1 trunk 身躯
2 By Jupiter 向朱庇特发誓（朱庇特是罗马神话中的众神之主）
3 large speeches 大话，漂亮话
4 adieu 告辞；永别
5 shape his old course 依旧我行我素
6 *Flourish* 奏花腔
7 address toward you 向您明言
8 rivalled 竞争（向考蒂丽叶求婚）
9 present dower 现成嫁妆
10 tender 给予
11 aught = anything
12 little seeming substance 不起眼的小东西
13 pieced 加上
14 fitly like 称心如意
15 infirmities she owes 她的缺点（或缺陷）

1 Who speaks line 182? (in pairs)

A director has to decide whether or not to alter a script in performance. *King Lear* presents several options for variations, as it has survived in two slightly different versions – the Quarto (四开本) and the Folio (对开本) (see pp. 244–9). This is also why the spelling of some characters' names varies between copies of the play (for example, Edmond and Gonerill are often Edmund and Goneril in other editions).

In this scene, line 182 is attributed to different characters in the two versions of the script. There are three possible speakers. In the Quarto edition, the line is given to 'Glost' (Gloucester, who has escorted the two suitors into the king's presence). The Folio edition gives the line to 'Cor', which could mean either Cordelia or Cornwall.

a Talk to your partner about which speaker you would choose to deliver the line. Give reasons for your choices and record them in your Director's Journal.

b Looking at the pictures on pages v, vi and 55 will give you an idea of the different ways this scene can be staged. Experiment with ways in which line 182 in particular could be delivered. In the light of your experiments, note down any advice you would give to the actor on his or her body language and tone of voice.

	And on the sixth to turn thy hated back	
	Upon our kingdom; if on the tenth day following	170
	Thy banished trunk[1] be found in our dominions,	
	The moment is thy death. Away! By Jupiter[2],	
	This shall not be revoked.	
KENT	Fare thee well, king, since thus thou wilt appear,	
	Freedom lives hence, and banishment is here.	175
	[*To Cordelia*] The gods to their dear shelter take thee, maid,	
	That justly think'st and hast most rightly said.	
	[*To Gonerill and Regan*] And your large speeches[3] may your deeds approve,	
	That good effects may spring from words of love.	
	Thus Kent, O princes, bids you all adieu[4],	180
	He'll shape his old course[5] in a country new. *Exit*	

Flourish[6]. *Enter* GLOUCESTER *with* FRANCE *and* BURGUNDY [*and*]
Attendants

CORDELIA	Here's France and Burgundy, my noble lord.	
LEAR	My lord of Burgundy,	
	We first address toward you[7], who with this king	
	Hath rivalled[8] for our daughter. What in the least	185
	Will you require in present dower[9] with her,	
	Or cease your quest of love?	
BURGUNDY	Most royal majesty,	
	I crave no more than hath your highness offered,	
	Nor will you tender[10] less?	
LEAR	Right noble Burgundy,	
	When she was dear to us, we did hold her so,	190
	But now her price is fallen. Sir, there she stands.	
	If aught[11] within that little seeming substance[12],	
	Or all of it, with our displeasure pieced[13]	
	And nothing more, may fitly like[14] your grace,	
	She's there, and she is yours.	
BURGUNDY	I know no answer.	195
LEAR	Will you with those infirmities she owes[15],	
	Unfriended, new adopted to our hate,	
	Dowered with our curse, and strangered with our oath,	
	Take her, or leave her?	

Burgundy declines Lear's conditions. Lear advises France to reject Cordelia. France is amazed at Lear's sudden rejection of his favourite. Cordelia insists that she has been condemned for speaking honestly.

 剧情简介：勃艮第公爵拒绝了李尔的条件。李尔建议法兰西王不要考虑考蒂丽叶。法兰西王对李尔突然厌弃自己最爱的女儿感到吃惊。考蒂丽叶坚持说自己是因为说真心话而受到惩罚。

1 A different royal voice (in pairs)

France is faced with a very difficult personal and diplomatic situation. Burgundy has chosen to say little and to focus on the 'deal' he thought he had brokered (协商，斡旋) with Lear. France focuses on Cordelia, although his words are addressed to the king.

- Read aloud France's words in lines 207–17. Notice how he tries to keep the peace without agreeing with Lear's view of Cordelia. What might France be hoping to achieve by his measured approach? Talk about this in your pairs.

Characters 人物分析

Cordelia speaks up (in groups of four to six)

Apart from the disputed line 182, Cordelia has not spoken since line 101. She remains silent as she is disinherited by her father and offered as a bride to Burgundy.

- Stand in a circle and read Cordelia's lines 218–28, switching speaker at the end of each line or at every punctuation mark.
- After the first reading, talk about what you have learnt about Cordelia's character in the scene so far.
- Before reading the lines again, decide on an appropriate style for their delivery. For example, is she smug (自鸣得意) and priggish (一本正经)? Would you emphasise her dignity and honesty? Or do you think some other tone is appropriate?

2 'Better thou / Hadst not been born' (in pairs)

Lear rejects his daughter in words that seem excessively brutal and cruel (lines 228–9). In the seventeenth century, when women usually relied on the protection and support of a family, this rejection may have seemed even more threatening than it does to a modern audience.

a Experiment with various ways of delivering these lines. Lear could be:
  - speaking quietly to Cordelia alone
  - making a formal public announcement
  - saying the lines in some other way.

b Talk together about what you have learnt from this experiment and then make a note in your Director's Journal, indicating whether you want the audience to feel sympathy for Lear's stupidity, anger at his cruelty or some other response.

---

1 Election makes not up 没□的选择
2 stray 背离，偏离
3 beseech 恳请
4 T'avert 转移
5 best object 掌上明珠（莎剧中的object常用来表示言者喜爱或厌恶之人或物）
6 argument 主题
7 balm 药膏（指安慰）
8 dismantle 剥夺
9 monsters it 使之变成魔鬼
10 fore-vouched 原先信誓旦旦的
11 Fall into taint 变味儿；变得不可信
12 reason … me 只有奇迹才能让我相信
13 vicious blot 丑恶的污点
14 foulness 龌龊，不道德
15 still-soliciting eye 时刻乞求恩宠的眼光（still = always）

BURGUNDY	Pardon me, royal sir,

Election makes not up[1] in such conditions. 200

LEAR　　　　　Then leave her, sir, for by the power that made me,
I tell you all her wealth. [*To France*] For you, great king,
I would not from your love make such a stray[2]
To match you where I hate; therefore beseech[3] you
T'avert[4] your liking a more worthier way 205
Than on a wretch whom nature is ashamed
Almost t'acknowledge hers.

FRANCE　　　　　　　　This is most strange,
That she whom even but now was your best object[5],
The argument[6] of your praise, balm[7] of your age,
The best, the dearest, should in this trice of time 210
Commit a thing so monstrous to dismantle[8]
So many folds of favour. Sure, her offence
Must be of such unnatural degree
That monsters it[9], or your fore-vouched[10] affection
Fall into taint[11]; which to believe of her 215
Must be a faith that reason without miracle
Should never plant in me[12].

CORDELIA　　I yet beseech your majesty –
If for I want that glib and oily art,
To speak and purpose not, since what I well intend, 220
I'll do't before I speak – that you make known
It is no vicious blot[13], murder, or foulness[14],
No unchaste action or dishonoured step
That hath deprived me of your grace and favour,
But even for want of that for which I am richer – 225
A still-soliciting eye[15], and such a tongue
That I am glad I have not, though not to have it,
Hath lost me in your liking.

LEAR　　　　　　　　Better thou
Hadst not been born than not t'have pleased me better.

Burgundy offers to marry Cordelia if Lear will guarantee the previously promised dowry. Lear refuses, and Burgundy rejects Cordelia. France takes her as his wife. Lear disowns Cordelia, and vows never to see her again.

 剧情简介：勃艮第公爵提出，如果李尔兑现之前承诺的陪嫁，他还会娶考蒂丽叶。李尔拒绝，于是勃艮第公爵抛弃了考蒂丽叶，法兰西王却要与她结为夫妻。李尔断绝了与考蒂丽叶的亲情，并发誓再也不见她。

Language in the play 剧中语言

A king and future queen (in pairs)

France describes the strange way that Cordelia's fortunes are working out (lines 245–56). These words – the first he speaks directly to Cordelia – contain seven or eight **antitheses** (对偶) (oppositions or paradoxes, such as 'rich'/'poor', 'losest'/'find', see p. 222).

a   Identify the antitheses in the script opposite. Prepare a presentation of the lines, with one person reading and the other miming. For example, the first mime represents 'rich' changing into 'poor'.

b   At line 249, France switches from speaking in unrhymed **blank verse** (无韵诗；素体诗) (see p. 227) to rhyming couplets. Rhymes can sound more poetic, but they are also much more obviously artificial than blank verse. Talk together about why Shakespeare may have used rhyme at this point.

c   The use of antitheses and rhyme contributes to the controlled, even tone of France's words. Read his lines again, sharing the words between you. Try to emphasise his reassuring tone. How might France's use of language affect the way the audience responds to this character?

1 Cordelia's fortunes (in small groups)

Look back over this scene to track Cordelia's rapidly changing fortunes.

a   Find and note down short quotations describing Cordelia from: Lear before he disowns her; Lear after he disowns her; Kent; Burgundy; and France.

b   Some productions show Cordelia and Lear entering together at the start of the scene, happy and relaxed in each other's company. If that is the case, at what point do you think she realises conflict with her father is inevitable?

c   Plot Cordelia's fortunes on a graph, indicating her changing status and her varying mood.

d   Cordelia says very little during the part of the scene involving France and Burgundy. Why do you think this is? Does it indicate something about her character or about the status of women at the time?

e   Write a few lines for Cordelia in which she accepts France as her husband. They should fit between lines 254 and 255 and can be in blank verse or in couplets.

1 tardiness in nature 生性迟钝，生性迟疑
2 history 心迹，想法
3 regards 算计，考虑
4 Aloof from th'entire point 与最重要的事情（爱情）无关
5 respect and fortunes 尊崇和财富
6 seize upon 占据，抓住
7 Be it = If it be
8 kindle 点燃
9 inflamed respect 炽热的仰慕
10 thrown to my chance 有幸把她投掷到我身边（以掷骰子为比喻）
11 waterish （地方）湿漉，（人）平淡乏味
12 unprized 未被估价；无价
13 unkind 不讲亲情
14 benison 祝福
15 *Exeunt* （两个以上演员）退场，下场

FRANCE	Is it but this? A tardiness in nature¹,	230
	Which often leaves the history² unspoke
	That it intends to do? My lord of Burgundy,
	What say you to the lady? Love's not love
	When it is mingled with regards³ that stands
	Aloof from th'entire point⁴. Will you have her?	235
	She is herself a dowry.
BURGUNDY	Royal king,
	Give but that portion which yourself proposed,
	And here I take Cordelia by the hand,
	Duchess of Burgundy.
LEAR	Nothing, I have sworn; I am firm.	240
BURGUNDY	I am sorry then, you have so lost a father
	That you must lose a husband.
CORDELIA	Peace be with Burgundy;
	Since that respect and fortunes⁵ are his love,
	I shall not be his wife.
FRANCE	Fairest Cordelia, that art most rich being poor,	245
	Most choice forsaken, and most loved despised,
	Thee and thy virtues here I seize upon⁶.
	Be it⁷ lawful I take up what's cast away.
	Gods, gods! 'Tis strange, that from their cold'st neglect
	My love should kindle⁸ to inflamed respect⁹.	250
	Thy dowerless daughter, king, thrown to my chance¹⁰,
	Is queen of us, of ours, and our fair France.
	Not all the dukes of waterish¹¹ Burgundy
	Can buy this unprized¹² precious maid of me.
	Bid them farewell, Cordelia, though unkind¹³;	255
	Thou losest here a better where to find.
LEAR	Thou hast her, France, let her be thine; for we
	Have no such daughter, nor shall ever see
	That face of hers again. Therefore be gone,
	Without our grace, our love, our benison¹⁴.	260
	Come, noble Burgundy.

*Flourish. Exeunt*¹⁵ [*Lear, Burgundy, Cornwall, Albany, Gloucester, Edmond, and Attendants*]

| FRANCE | Bid farewell to your sisters. |

Cordelia asks her sisters to care for Lear. They reject her words and criticise her behaviour. Left together, Gonerill and Regan speak about Lear's erratic judgement and plan to work together to control him.

剧情简介：考蒂丽叶要姐姐们照顾好李尔。她们不听，反而批评了她的做法。高娜瑞尔和蕊根一起离开，边走边议论李尔乖张无常的判断力，商量联手操控父亲。

▲ Cordelia and France prepare to leave. What do you feel should be the tone of her leave-taking from her sisters – bitingly critical, sorrowfully rebuking, or something else?

1 washed eyes 充满泪水的双眼（或泪水洗过的明亮眼睛）
2 loath ... named 不情愿点明你们的缺点是什么
3 professèd bosoms 自诩的孝敬
4 commit 托付
5 study 目的；操心
6 At fortune's alms 作为命运施舍的礼物
7 scanted 欠缺
8 well ... wanted 活该越是缺少的越是得不到（即父爱和嫁妆）
9 plighted = pleated （打褶的，喻指隐藏的）
10 Who ... derides 文过饰非之人终将颜面尽失
11 nearly appertains 与……密切相关
12 hence = go hence（离开）
13 grossly 明显
14 long-engraffed 根深蒂固，积习难改
15 choleric 暴躁易怒
16 unconstant starts 喜怒无常的发作
17 compliment 仪式
18 this last surrender 他最近放弃君权的行为
19 i'th'heat 趁早（趁热打铁）

1 Princesses in private (in fours)

The departure of France and Cordelia leaves Gonerill and Regan alone to review the unexpected outcome of their father's declaration.

a Two of you read aloud Gonerill and Regan's private conversation (lines 277–98). Talk together about how to make the differences between their characters as clear as possible.

b Select six different critical comments that Gonerill and Regan make about Lear in these lines. When you have made your selection, sketch outlines of the two sisters and add speech bubbles showing the words of flattery they used earlier in the scene, and then thought clouds showing what they really think, as expressed in the script opposite.

c Gonerill and Regan may be calculating and insincere, but what do you think of their assessment of their father? In your groups, choose four criticisms they make of his conduct and character. Are these supported or contradicted by Lear's behaviour during this scene?

CORDELIA	The jewels of our father, with washed eyes[1]	
	Cordelia leaves you. I know you what you are,	
	And like a sister am most loath to call	
	Your faults as they are named[2]. Love well our father:	265
	To your professèd bosoms[3] I commit[4] him.	
	But yet, alas, stood I within his grace,	
	I would prefer him to a better place.	
	So farewell to you both.	
REGAN	Prescribe not us our duty.	
GONERILL	Let your study[5]	270
	Be to content your lord, who hath received you	
	At fortune's alms[6]. You have obedience scanted[7],	
	And well are worth the want that you have wanted[8].	
CORDELIA	Time shall unfold what plighted[9] cunning hides;	
	Who covers faults, at last with shame derides[10].	275
	Well may you prosper.	
FRANCE	Come, my fair Cordelia.	

Exeunt France and Cordelia

GONERILL Sister, it is not little I have to say of what most nearly appertains[11] to us both. I think our father will hence[12] tonight.

REGAN That's most certain, and with you; next month with us.

GONERILL You see how full of changes his age is; the observation we have made of it hath not been little. He always loved our sister most, and with what poor judgement he hath now cast her off appears too grossly[13]. 280

REGAN 'Tis the infirmity of his age; yet he hath ever but slenderly known himself. 285

GONERILL The best and soundest of his time hath been but rash; then must we look from his age to receive not alone the imperfections of long-engraffed[14] condition, but therewithal the unruly waywardness that infirm and choleric[15] years bring with them. 290

REGAN Such unconstant starts[16] are we like to have from him as this of Kent's banishment.

GONERILL There is further compliment[17] of leave-taking between France and him. Pray you, let us sit together. If our father carry authority with such disposition as he bears, this last surrender[18] of his will but offend us. 295

REGAN We shall further think of it.

GONERILL We must do something, and i'th'heat[19].   *Exeunt*

Edmond questions why he is regarded as inferior because his parents were not married. He is planning to replace his brother, Edgar, as his father's heir. Gloucester expresses concern about the events at court.

 剧情简介：爱德门质疑为什么自己这个非婚生子就低人一等。他打算取代兄长爱德格，做父亲的继承人。格劳斯特对朝堂上发生的事情忧心忡忡。

Characters 人物分析

Edmond revealed (in pairs)

Lines 1–22 are a **soliloquy** (独白) – a speech either made by a character alone on stage or unheard by anyone else present. The theatrical convention is that a soliloquy expresses what the character really thinks and feels. Here, Edmond complains about his treatment as a 'bastard' or illegitimate child. There was a considerable stigma (耻辱，丢脸) attached to children born outside marriage in Shakespeare's day, especially amongst the nobility. Edmond chooses to reject the social customs that condemn him as inferior and to take Nature as his deity (神) or 'goddess'. What does Edmond reveal about himself?

a Make a list of Edmond's grievances and talk together about what he wishes to achieve.

b What impression of Edmond do you gain from this soliloquy? Suggest four or five adjectives to describe his character.

c Look at the photographs of Edmond in this book, such as those on pages 22 and 28. Which image do you find most interesting, and why?

1 Talking to yourself: how to soliloquise
(in groups of four or five)

An actor and director can decide whether Edmond should address the audience directly or whether he should speak as though he is thinking aloud.

- Share two group readings, taking turns to speak the words by changing readers at each punctuation mark or after each sentence.
- In the first reading, speak as though you are addressing the audience directly, suggesting that Edmond is aware of entertaining and shocking them – almost making them his co-conspirators.
- In the second reading, make the words sound like private musings, putting Edmond's innermost thoughts into words.
- In your group, discuss which reading seems most appropriate. This may be affected by the judgements you made about Edmond's character as a result of the 'Characters' box above.

1 **Wherefore** = Why
2 **in the plague of custom** 遭受世俗的折磨
3 **permit … me** 任凭吹毛求疵的国人剥夺我（的权利）
4 **moonshines** 月
5 **Lag of** 比……出生晚
6 **base** 低贱
7 **dimensions** 身材比例
8 **well compact** 相貌堂堂
9 **generous** 慷慨大度
10 **true** 堂堂正正
11 **honest madam's issue** 贞洁女子所生
12 **in … nature** 在情欲高涨的偷情之时
13 **take … quality** 获得更好的身体的构造和精神特征
14 **fops** 蠢货
15 **'tween** = between
16 **speed** 奏效
17 **choler** 愤怒
18 **Prescribed** 限制
19 **Confined to exhibition?** 仅限于生活津贴？
20 **Upon the gad?** 如此突然？
21 **how now?** = how is it going?

Act 1 Scene 2
The Earl of Gloucester's castle

Enter EDMOND

EDMOND   Thou, Nature, art my goddess; to thy law
My services are bound. Wherefore[1] should I
Stand in the plague of custom[2] and permit
The curiosity of nations to deprive me[3]?
For that I am some twelve or fourteen moonshines[4]   5
Lag of[5] a brother? Why 'bastard'? Wherefore 'base'[6]?
When my dimensions[7] are as well compact[8],
My mind as generous[9], and my shape as true[10]
As honest madam's issue[11]? Why brand they us
With 'base'? with 'baseness'? 'bastardy'? 'base, base'?   10
Who in the lusty stealth of nature[12] take
More composition and fierce quality[13]
Than doth within a dull, stale, tired bed
Go to th'creating a whole tribe of fops[14]
Got 'tween[15] a sleep and wake? Well then,   15
Legitimate Edgar, I must have your land.
Our father's love is to the bastard, Edmond,
As to th'legitimate. Fine word, 'legitimate'.
Well, my legitimate, [*Takes out a letter*] if this letter speed[16]
And my invention thrive, Edmond the base   20
Shall to th'legitimate. I grow; I prosper;
Now gods, stand up for bastards!

Enter GLOUCESTER

GLOUCESTER   Kent banished thus? and France in choler[17] parted?
And the king gone tonight? Prescribed[18] his power,
Confined to exhibition?[19] All this done   25
Upon the gad?[20] Edmond, how now?[21] What news?

Edmond tricks Gloucester into reading a letter which he claims is from Edgar. The letter suggests that Edgar is seeking his father's death in order to inherit his wealth. Edmond lies about the origin of the letter.

剧情简介：爱德门设计让格劳斯特读一封信，声称此信是爱德格所写。信中暗示爱德格为了继承家产要陷害父亲。爱德门在信的来源上撒了谎。

Themes 主题分析

'if it be nothing, I shall not need spectacles'

Once again, the word 'nothing' is used (see p. 6).

a Add this to the list of uses in your Director's Journal. Start adding suggestions about how each use should be presented. For example, would you choose to use a dramatic device or a repeated sound effect to highlight each time the word appears?

b You will find out later in the play that Gloucester's words are horrifically ironic. Look out for further references to sight and blindness as the play progresses. Begin a new list of these references in your Director's Journal.

1 *Putting up* 藏起来
2 *terrible dispatch* 急忙处理
3 *quality* 性质，特点
4 *o'erread* 读完
5 *perused* 细读
6 *o'erlooking* 查看
7 *essay or taste of my virtue* 考验我的品性（essay = assay，taste = test）
8 *policy and reverence of age* 尊老敬老的规矩（policy也指"老奸巨猾"）
9 *best of our times* 我们最好的青春岁月
10 *idle and fond bondage* 无用而荒唐的束缚
11 *sways … suffered* 他们能统治（sways）不是通过权力，而是因为我们容忍（suffers）
12 *the casement of my closet* 我房间的窗户
13 *character* 笔迹
14 *fain* 情愿

1 Expressing uncertainty (in pairs)

Gloucester's language in this scene is full of questions, which suggests a troubled and uncertain mood. This seems to leave him vulnerable to Edmond's manipulation.

a One person reads out all the questions Gloucester asks in lines 23–58, pausing after each question. In the pause, the other comments as a member of the audience. Remember, the audience has an advantage over Gloucester, having witnessed not only the whole of the first scene (from which Gloucester is largely absent) but also Edmond's soliloquy.

b Talk about whether the language in this scene suggests that the actor playing Gloucester should present him as a dignified but deceived man, as extremely gullible (轻信) or in some other way.

▶ Edmond is working hard to manipulate and control his father. How might the actor's movements and body language suggest this?

EDMOND   So please your lordship, none. [*Putting up¹ the letter*]

GLOUCESTER   Why so earnestly seek you to put up that letter?

EDMOND   I know no news, my lord.

GLOUCESTER   What paper were you reading?

EDMOND   Nothing, my lord.

GLOUCESTER   No? What needed then that terrible dispatch² of it into your pocket? The quality³ of nothing hath not such need to hide itself. Let's see. Come, if it be nothing, I shall not need spectacles.

EDMOND   I beseech you, sir, pardon me; it is a letter from my brother that I have not all o'erread⁴; and for so much as I have perused⁵, I find it not fit for your o'erlooking⁶.

GLOUCESTER   Give me the letter, sir.

EDMOND   I shall offend either to detain or give it. The contents, as in part I understand them, are to blame.

GLOUCESTER   Let's see, let's see.

EDMOND   I hope for my brother's justification he wrote this but as an essay or taste of my virtue⁷.

[*Gives him the letter*]

GLOUCESTER   *Reads* 'This policy and reverence of age⁸ makes the world bitter to the best of our times⁹, keeps our fortunes from us till our oldness cannot relish them. I begin to find an idle and fond bondage¹⁰ in the oppression of aged tyranny, who sways not as it hath power but as it is suffered¹¹. Come to me, that of this I may speak more. If our father would sleep till I waked him, you should enjoy half his revenue forever and live the beloved of your brother. Edgar.' Hum! Conspiracy! 'Sleep till I waked him, you should enjoy half his revenue.' My son Edgar, had he a hand to write this? a heart and brain to breed it in? When came you to this? Who brought it?

EDMOND   It was not brought me, my lord; there's the cunning of it. I found it thrown in at the casement of my closet¹².

GLOUCESTER   You know the character¹³ to be your brother's?

EDMOND   If the matter were good, my lord, I durst swear it were his: but in respect of that, I would fain¹⁴ think it were not.

Gloucester curses Edgar, but Edmond develops the deception further by protesting that his brother cannot be a villain and by advising caution. Edmond proposes to talk to Edgar where their father can overhear them.

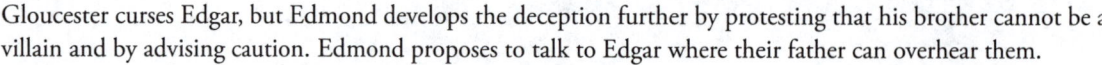 剧情简介：格劳斯特诅咒爱德格，但是爱德门继续编谎话，说自己的兄长不可能是坏人，劝父亲小心行事。爱德门提出要与爱德格谈话，让格劳斯特在一旁偷听。

Language in the play 剧中语言
Edmond the deceiver (in pairs)

The following activity explores the way in which Shakespeare uses language to characterise Edmond, especially in the way he exploits his father's uncertainty and manipulates his feelings between lines 27 and 90. Record your ideas and conclusions on a photocopy of the script using different colours to highlight different features.

- Pick out examples of lies that Edmond tells his father.
- Find three words or phrases of Edmond's that are probably intended to enrage his father.
- Find three or four other words and phrases that he uses to suggest his own honesty and loyalty.
- Pick out examples of sinister hints and worrying suggestions that introduce questions and anxieties to Gloucester's troubled mind.

Characters 人物分析
Edmond: evil incarnate (化身) or anti-hero? (in small groups)

An audience in Shakespeare's day would probably have seen a connection between Edmond and the character of Vice or Machiavel in medieval plays. This was a comic but evil figure who spoke confidentially to the audience, almost making them complicit in his villainy. A modern director can choose to interpret Edmond in this way or take a completely different approach. Discuss the questions below, then make notes in your Director's Journal.

- How should the actor playing Edmond try to engage the audience's sympathy and admiration? This could involve bold, confident behaviour and an obvious enjoyment of risk-taking.
- Edmond can be seen as a potentially attractive 'anti-hero', unwilling to accept his position as an outsider and prepared to do anything to be master of his own fate. Do you agree?
- How far should the scene be played for comic effect? Getting the audience to laugh at his jokes is one way the actor could make them feel involved in his wrongdoing.
- Do you think Edmond is immoral (breaking accepted moral codes while having a conscience) or amoral (having no moral sense at all)? Does your answer to this question change your views on how he should be portrayed?

1 sounded you 探您的口风
2 oft = often
3 sons at perfect age 儿子到了成年
4 Abhorred 可恶
5 sirrah 小子（地位高的人对地位低的男性的称呼）
6 Abominable 没人性
7 testimony of his intent 他意图的证据
8 should run a certain course 应该稳妥行事
9 pawn down 担保；打赌
10 writ = written
11 pretence of danger 恶意；凶险的目的
12 meet 合适
13 an auricular assurance 亲耳听到的真凭实据
14 wind me into him 帮我诓出他的真心话来
15 Frame the business 安排好这件事
16 unstate … resolution 哪怕放弃地位和财产也要查个水落石出
17 presently 立刻
18 convey 小心操办
19 withal = therewith（随后）

GLOUCESTER　It is his.

EDMOND　It is his hand, my lord, but I hope his heart is not in the contents.

GLOUCESTER　Has he never before sounded you[1] in this business?

EDMOND　Never, my lord. But I have heard him oft[2] maintain it to be fit that, sons at perfect age[3], and fathers declined, the father should be as ward to the son, and the son manage his revenue.

GLOUCESTER　O villain, villain – his very opinion in the letter! Abhorred[4] villain, unnatural, detested, brutish villain – worse than brutish! Go, sirrah[5], seek him: I'll apprehend him. Abominable[6] villain, where is he?

EDMOND　I do not well know, my lord. If it shall please you to suspend your indignation against my brother till you can derive from him better testimony of his intent[7], you should run a certain course[8]; where if you violently proceed against him, mistaking his purpose, it would make a great gap in your own honour and shake in pieces the heart of his obedience. I dare pawn down[9] my life for him that he hath writ[10] this to feel my affection to your honour and to no other pretence of danger[11].

GLOUCESTER　Think you so?

EDMOND　If your honour judge it meet[12], I will place you where you shall hear us confer of this and by an auricular assurance[13] have your satisfaction, and that without any further delay than this very evening.

GLOUCESTER　He cannot be such a monster. Edmond, seek him out: wind me into him[14], I pray you. Frame the business[15] after your own wisdom. I would unstate myself to be in a due resolution[16].

EDMOND　I will seek him, sir, presently[17], convey[18] the business as I shall find means, and acquaint you withal[19].

Gloucester sees Edgar's treachery as part of a breakdown in society foretold by the recent eclipses of the sun and moon. Edmond rejects such superstitious belief in astrology. He prepares to trick his brother, Edgar.

剧情简介：格劳斯特认为爱德格的背叛行为是社会堕落的一部分，近期发生的日食和月食就是预兆。爱德门不迷信占星术的这种说法。他准备设计陷害哥哥爱德格。

Write about it 写作练习

Fears for the future?

Gloucester seems to have been greatly troubled by recent events, and he sees a horrifying pattern of collapse and decay in the world.

a Using Gloucester's list of disasters in lines 94–100, write a brief account of the world he predicts and the events that he fears. Then add a paragraph discussing which of these events have already started to come true in the play.

b Write another account, this time describing the world as Gloucester would wish it to be. What does he see as the 'natural order'?

Themes 主题分析

What lies behind the words? (In fives)

This activity will help you explore what Scene 2 contributes to the development of some of the play's themes.

- One group member is the reader and the other four each take on one of the following themes: the natural order; human compassion; justice; appearance versus reality. Write your theme on a piece of card.
- The reader speaks the lines in the script opposite. Each time someone feels their theme is referred to, they hold up their card.
- Go through the lines once with no interruptions and then repeat the activity, pausing to agree or disagree each time a theme card is raised. Which theme do you think is most important here?

1 Edmond the manipulator (in threes)

Divide the script opposite into three sections: lines 91–103, 104–16 and 117–19.

- Talk together about exactly what is happening in each of these sections, then write down one sentence summarising each section.
- For each section, suggest how Edmond should be behaving on stage. Experiment with ways of making him seem more or less cynical and manipulative, especially in the way he responds while Gloucester speaks.

1 **late … moon** 最近的日食和月食（据记载月食发生于1605年9月，日食发生于同年10月）
2 **sequent effects** 接踵而至的后果
3 **'twixt = between**
4 **bias of nature** 大自然的倾向
5 **Machinations** 阴谋诡计
6 **hollowness** 伪善
7 **excellent foppery** 愚蠢至极
8 **surfeits** 荒唐，放肆
9 **heavenly compulsion** 天体运行的影响
10 **treachers** 忤逆；叛徒
11 **spherical predominance** 星辰的影响
12 **divine thrusting on** 天意强加
13 **whoremaster** 色鬼，淫荡之人
14 **lay … star** 把他的淫荡本性归罪在一颗星星上
15 **compounded** 交合
16 **Dragon's tail** 天龙座的尾巴（这里说的the Dragon即the constellation Draco，Draco是dragon的拉丁文形式。该星座位于北半球天空，围绕北极星旋转，是公元2世纪天文学家托勒密列举的48个星座之一，并且仍是现代天文学认定的88个星座之一，北半球的人全年都可以看到。构成该星座的17颗星弯弯曲曲像一条龙，又像阿拉伯数字2，2的起笔处是龙尾，收笔处是龙头；龙头由排成矩形的4颗星组成，最前面比较亮的两颗星是龙眼。希腊和罗马神话里的好几条龙都与该星座有关，包括看守金苹果的巨龙拉冬 [Ladon]。）

（下接28页）

GLOUCESTER These late eclipses in the sun and moon[1] portend no good to us. Though the wisdom of nature can reason it thus and thus, yet nature finds itself scourged by the sequent effects[2]. Love cools, friendship falls off, brothers divide. In cities, mutinies; in countries, discord; in palaces, treason; and the bond cracked 'twixt[3] son and father. This villain of mine comes under the prediction: there's son against father. The king falls from bias of nature[4], there's father against child. We have seen the best of our time. Machinations[5], hollowness[6], treachery, and all ruinous disorders follow us disquietly to our graves. Find out this villain, Edmond, it shall lose thee nothing. Do it carefully. And the noble and true-hearted Kent banished; his offence, honesty. 'Tis strange. *Exit*

EDMOND This is the excellent foppery[7] of the world, that when we are sick in fortune, often the surfeits[8] of our own behaviour, we make guilty of our disasters the sun, the moon, and stars; as if we were villains on necessity, fools by heavenly compulsion[9], knaves, thieves, and treachers[10] by spherical predominance[11], drunkards, liars, and adulterers by an enforced obedience of planetary influence; and all that we are evil in, by a divine thrusting on[12]. An admirable evasion of whoremaster[13] man, to lay his goatish disposition on the charge of a star[14]! My father compounded[15] with my mother under the Dragon's tail[16], and my nativity was under *Ursa major*[17], so that it follows, I am rough and lecherous. I should have been that I am had the maidenliest star in the firmament[18] twinkled on my bastardising.

Enter EDGAR

Pat[19]: he comes, like the catastrophe of the old comedy[20]. My cue[21] is villainous melancholy[22], with a sigh like Tom o'Bedlam[23]. – O these eclipses do portend these divisions. Fa, sol, la, me[24].

EDGAR How now, brother Edmond, what serious contemplation are you in?

Edmond warns Edgar that Gloucester has turned against him, and he is now in great danger. Edmond tells Edgar to hide, saying that he is on his side. Alone on stage, Edmond looks forward to succeeding by trickery.

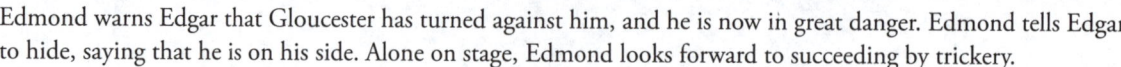
剧情简介：爱德门警告爱德格，格劳斯特已经不信任他了，还说爱德格现在有危险。爱德门让爱德格躲起来，并且表示自己会站在他这边。爱德门一人在戏台上，他期待骗局成功。

Write about it 写作练习
The Gloucester family

Scene 2 develops the characters of Gloucester and Edmond, and introduces Edgar. The illegitimate son dominates the scene and succeeds in his plan to deceive his brother and his father.

- Explore Edgar's gullibility and Edmond's cunning by writing from Edgar's point of view a detailed description of his half-brother's personality and attitudes. Include evidence up to the end of this scene. You could begin: 'I am about a year older than my half-brother Edmond …'

1 Extra dialogue – extra insight?

The Quarto version of the play (see p. 244) includes six extra lines after 'unhappily' in lines 125–6 opposite.

> … as of unnaturalness between the child and the parent, death, dearth, dissolutions of ancient amities, divisions in state, menaces and maledictions (诅咒) against king and nobles, needless diffidences (怀疑), banishment of friends, dissipation (瓦解) of cohorts, nuptial breaches, and I know not what.
>
> EDGAR   How long have … you been a sectary astronomical (星相学迷)?
> EDMOND   Come, come, …

a What do these additional lines suggest about the personalities of Edmond and Edgar? ('diffidences' = doubts, 'dissipation of cohorts' = disbanding armies, 'sectary astronomical' = believer in astrology.)

b As a director, would you include these extra lines or not? Why? Try it both ways before you decide.

Edgar is often shown on stage as a studious, rather unworldly character, in stark contrast to Edmond. How would you portray Edgar?

1 countenance 举止
2 forbear 躲避，避开
3 qualified 减轻，缓和
4 with … allay 把您打个半死不活也难以平息他的怒火
5 have a continent forbearance 克制忍耐
6 ye = you
7 stir abroad 外出
8 anon 很快，马上
9 credulous 轻信
10 practices 计谋
11 wit 小聪明
12 All … fit 只要达到我的目的，什么手段都行

（上接26页）

17 Ursa major 大熊星座（据说该星座下出生的人生性粗野、淫荡）
18 firmament 天空
19 Pat 时机正好
20 catastrophe of the old comedy 老式喜剧的突发灾难（在老式喜剧里，剧情的转折常是某种突发灾难造成的；这里暗指爱德格来得恰到好处）
21 cue 戏台提示
22 villainous melancholy 可怜的忧郁
23 Tom o'Bedlam 贝德兰医院来的汤姆（当时伦敦的乞丐往往声称自己是这家精神病院的病人，见第47页）
24 Fa, sol, la, me （音阶唱名；爱德门这里在唱歌，伴装没注意爱德格走来）

EDMOND   I am thinking, brother, of a prediction I read this other day, what should follow these eclipses.
EDGAR   Do you busy yourself with that?
EDMOND   I promise you, the effects he writes of succeed unhappily. When saw you my father last?
EDGAR   The night gone by.
EDMOND   Spake you with him?
EDGAR   Ay, two hours together.
EDMOND   Parted you in good terms? Found you no displeasure in him by word nor countenance[1]?
EDGAR   None at all.
EDMOND   Bethink yourself wherein you may have offended him, and at my entreaty forbear[2] his presence until some little time hath qualified[3] the heat of his displeasure, which at this instant so rageth in him that with the mischief of your person it would scarcely allay[4].
EDGAR   Some villain hath done me wrong.
EDMOND   That's my fear. I pray you have a continent forbearance[5] till the speed of his rage goes slower; and as I say, retire with me to my lodging, from whence I will fitly bring you to hear my lord speak. Pray ye[6], go; there's my key. If you do stir abroad[7], go armed.
EDGAR   Armed, brother?
EDMOND   Brother, I advise you to the best. I am no honest man, if there be any good meaning toward you. I have told you what I have seen and heard – but faintly, nothing like the image and horror of it. Pray you, away.
EDGAR   Shall I hear from you anon[8]?
EDMOND   I do serve you in this business.

Exit [Edgar]

A credulous[9] father and a brother noble,
Whose nature is so far from doing harms
That he suspects none; on whose foolish honesty
My practices[10] ride easy. I see the business.
Let me, if not by birth, have lands by wit[11].
All with me's meet that I can fashion fit[12].   *Exit*

Gonerill complains about the unreasonable and unruly behaviour of her father and his knights. She instructs Oswald that he and the other servants should show Lear less courtesy and respect.

 剧情简介：高娜瑞尔抱怨父亲及其骑士不讲道理、不守规矩，她要求奥兹沃尔和其他手下对李尔不要那么毕恭毕敬。

1 'I'll not endure it' (in pairs)

Two weeks have passed since Gonerill was last seen with her sister, Regan, in Scene 1. Lear has put his plan into effect and has been staying with Gonerill – to her increasing annoyance and dismay. She complains of her household being disturbed by what she alleges to be the disorderly behaviour of Lear and his one hundred knights.

a   Look back at Gonerill's flattering words in Scene 1 (lines 50–6). Choose one phrase that you both feel is a good example of her extravagant hypocrisy. One of you then reads Gonerill's lines 6–11 opposite, pausing at the end of each line to allow the other person to read the chosen phrase from Scene 1. Continue like this through Gonerill's speech. You can choose whether to repeat the flattering line in an earnest and sincere way or with bitter irony. Swap roles and read through the lines again.

b   Discuss what sort of person you feel Shakespeare shows Gonerill to be in this scene.

1	chiding 斥责
2	He … other 他闯下这样那样的大祸
3	at odds 不和
4	upbraids 责骂，训斥
5	trifle 鸡毛蒜皮
6	come slack of former services 不如以前一样殷勤守礼
7	answer 负责，承担
8	*Horns within* 幕后响起号声
9	weary negligence 爱搭不理的样子
10	come to question 挑事儿
11	distaste 不喜欢
12	straight 马上
13	hold my course 与我一致

Stagecraft 导演技巧

A short scene

At just twenty-two lines, this is a very short scene. Shakespeare did not specify where scenes should be set in his plays; the suggestions at the start of each scene have been made by the play's editors over the years.

Such a short scene would have presented few problems in the Globe Theatre in Shakespeare's day, when one scene flowed into the next with little effort to suggest any change of location. However, some productions, especially in the nineteenth century, attempted a detailed realistic setting – and short scenes like this were sometimes cut to simplify and streamline a production. Directors have another option – they can extend the scene slightly by using the following lines, which the Quarto version gives to Gonerill after line 16:

> Not to be overruled. Idle old man,
> That still would manage those authorities
> That he hath given away! Now, by my life,
> Old fools are babes again, and must be used
> With checks (责备) as flatteries when they are seen abused.

- Note down in your Director's Journal whether or not you would use these lines. Explain your decision.

Act 1 Scene 3
The castle of Albany and Gonerill

Enter GONERILL *and her steward* OSWALD

GONERILL Did my father strike my gentleman for chiding[1] of his fool?
OSWALD Ay, madam.
GONERILL By day and night, he wrongs me; every hour
He flashes into one gross crime or other[2]
That sets us all at odds[3]. I'll not endure it.
His knights grow riotous, and himself upbraids[4] us
On every trifle[5]. When he returns from hunting,
I will not speak with him. Say I am sick.
If you come slack of former services[6],
You shall do well; the fault of it I'll answer[7].

[*Horns within*[8]]

OSWALD He's coming, madam, I hear him.
GONERILL Put on what weary negligence[9] you please,
You and your fellows: I'd have it come to question[10].
If he distaste[11] it, let him to my sister,
Whose mind and mine I know in that are one.
Remember what I have said.
OSWALD Well, madam.
GONERILL And let his knights have colder looks among you:
What grows of it no matter. Advise your fellows so.
I'll write straight[12] to my sister to hold my course[13].
Prepare for dinner.

Exeunt

Kent hopes that his disguise as a poor man will enable him to re-enter Lear's service. In response to Lear's questions, Kent says he wants to serve the king.

 剧情简介：肯特装扮成穷人，希望借此重新为李尔效力。在回答李尔的问题时，肯特说他想为国王效劳。

1 Kent in disguise (in pairs)

This scene begins with a soliloquy, just as Act 1 Scene 2 does, but in marked contrast to Edmond, Kent states that he is motivated by 'good intent'.

a Talk together about what you think motivates Kent to risk his life by not going into exile.

b Choose one or two phrases from Kent's soliloquy (lines 1–7) and one or two from Edmond's soliloquy (Act 1 Scene 2, lines 1–17) that you feel reflect their strongly contrasting beliefs and characters.

c Apparently impenetrable (识不破的) disguises were a convention of the theatre in Shakespeare's time. Talk together about how a reasonably convincing disguise could be achieved in a modern production. Remember, Kent has to make his plan clear to the audience in lines 1–4; otherwise the disguise might be too good and the audience may not recognise him.

d Read the conversation between Lear and Kent (lines 9–38) aloud. Then talk about the persona (表象人格) you think Kent wishes to convey while in his disguise as Caius. Write down six words that could be used to describe Caius. How many of them could be applied to Kent as he appeared in the first scene?

e Finally, discuss what advantages there might be for Shakespeare in having this character in disguise as the play develops.

Language in the play 剧中语言

A borrowed accent (in small groups)

Kent hopes that he can successfully disguise his voice as well as his appearance. He is often shown on stage using a rustic, West Country accent once he starts playing the part of Caius. However, an actor has several other options. Consider the following questions:

- What other accents could be used in a stage production? What elements of these accents might make them more or less suitable?
- How difficult would it be for Kent, a high-ranking nobleman, to establish and maintain his disguise?
- How does Kent's language during his exchange with Lear contrast with that in his initial soliloquy? Why do you think he changes his language?

1 **defuse** 混淆
2 **intent** 意图
3 **full issue** 圆满的结果
4 **razed my likeness** 刮去我原来的模样（razed可能指刮掉头发和胡须）
5 **full of labours** 尽心尽力
6 **stay a jot** 等一会儿
7 **dinner** 午餐（在莎士比亚时代，dinner指一天中的正餐）
8 **What dost thou profess?** 你的职业是什么？
9 **converse** 交往
10 **fear judgement** 害怕末日审判（因此不作恶）
11 **eat no fish** 不吃鱼（三层含义：① 是个体面人，不吃鱼这种劣等肉；② 是新教徒，不是天主教徒，因为后者星期五斋戒，禁吃肉和鱼；③ 不玩弄女人）
12 **countenance** 表情，神情

Act 1 Scene 4
The Great Hall of the castle of Albany and Gonerill

Enter KENT *(disguised)*

KENT If but as well I other accents borrow
That can my speech defuse[1], my good intent[2]
May carry through itself to that full issue[3]
For which I razed my likeness[4]. Now, banished Kent,
If thou canst serve where thou dost stand condemned,   5
So may it come thy master, whom thou lov'st,
Shall find thee full of labours[5].

Horns within. Enter LEAR, *[Knights,] and Attendants*

LEAR Let me not stay a jot[6] for dinner[7]. Go, get it ready.
[*Exit an Attendant*]
How now, what art thou?

KENT A man, sir.   10

LEAR What dost thou profess?[8] What wouldst thou with us?

KENT I do profess to be no less than I seem, to serve him truly that will put me in trust, to love him that is honest, to converse[9] with him that is wise and says little, to fear judgement[10], to fight when I cannot choose, and to eat no fish[11].   15

LEAR What art thou?

KENT A very honest-hearted fellow, and as poor as the king.

LEAR If thou be'st as poor for a subject as he's for a king, thou art poor enough. What wouldst thou?

KENT Service.   20

LEAR Who wouldst thou serve?

KENT You.

LEAR Dost thou know me, fellow?

KENT No, sir; but you have that in your countenance[12], which I would fain call master.   25

LEAR What's that?

KENT Authority.

LEAR What services canst thou do?

33

Lear decides to employ Kent. Oswald pointedly ignores a command from Lear. A knight comments on the growing disrespect being shown to the king. Lear says that he, too, has noticed the lack of courtesy.

剧情简介：李尔决定雇用肯特。奥兹沃尔对李尔的命令故意充耳不闻。一骑士说众人明显对国王越来越不恭敬，李尔说自己也注意到了这种怠慢。

1 'So please you' (in threes)

Oswald has been told by Gonerill to adopt a 'weary negligence' towards Lear.

- In your groups, talk about why you think Gonerill issues this order – and why Oswald agrees to it. Then try out ways in which Oswald could behave and speak during his brief appearance in order to antagonise (与……敌对) the king.

Characters 人物分析

'But where's my fool?'

The Fool is not specifically named as appearing on stage until later in this scene, although he is sometimes shown playing a silent role in Scene 1 (see p. v). In one production he was gagged (被塞着嘴) for the opening scene, presumably to prevent him from interrupting the ceremony of the division of the kingdom.

Fools were once employed by the wealthy to provide entertainment. They would normally be able to sing in a wide variety of styles as well as supplying jokes and witty banter (打趣，逗乐). There was a tradition that allowed a Fool to get away with saying things that no one else would dare to say to his master. Their relationship could be closer and more personal than the relationship between most servants and masters.

- What does the audience learn about the Fool and about Lear's relationship with him before he appears at line 81? Look at lines 60–5 and remember, Gonerill has already mentioned the Fool when she was complaining to Oswald (Act 1 Scene 3, lines 1–2).

1	keep honest counsel	保守正当秘密
2	curious	情节复杂
3	diligence	勤勉
4	knave	侍童（有时带有侮辱性质）
5	hither	= to this place
6	So please you	= If you please（请您原谅 [我忙着呢]）
7	clotpoll	蠢货，笨蛋
8	mongrel	杂种
9	slave	奴才
10	the roundest	最直截了当
11	ceremonious affection	符合礼仪的爱戴
12	were wont	= used to be（以往那样）
13	abatement	减少
14	the general dependants	全体家眷和仆人
15	conception	觉察
16	jealous curiosity	狐疑的挑剔
17	very pretence and purpose	实际意图和目的；存心，故意
18	pined away	憔悴

The king with some of his followers. Do you feel this production wanted them to appear 'riotous', as Gonerill says, or well behaved, as Lear later claims?

KENT   I can keep honest counsel¹, ride, run, mar a curious² tale in telling it, and deliver a plain message bluntly. That which ordinary men are fit for, I am qualified in, and the best of me is diligence³.

LEAR   How old art thou?

KENT   Not so young, sir, to love a woman for singing, nor so old to dote on her for anything. I have years on my back forty-eight.

LEAR   Follow me; thou shalt serve me, if I like thee no worse after dinner. I will not part from thee yet. Dinner, ho, dinner! Where's my knave⁴? my fool? Go you and call my fool hither⁵.

[*Exit an Attendant*]

Enter OSWALD

You, you sirrah, where's my daughter?

OSWALD So please you⁶ –   *Exit*

LEAR   What says the fellow there? Call the clotpoll⁷ back.

[*Exit a Knight*]

Where's my fool? Ho, I think the world's asleep.

[*Enter* KNIGHT]

How now? Where's that mongrel⁸?

KNIGHT He says, my lord, your daughter is not well.

LEAR   Why came not the slave⁹ back to me when I called him?

KNIGHT Sir, he answered me in the roundest¹⁰ manner, he would not.

LEAR   He would not?

KNIGHT My lord, I know not what the matter is, but to my judgement your highness is not entertained with that ceremonious affection¹¹ as you were wont¹². There's a great abatement¹³ of kindness appears as well in the general dependants¹⁴ as in the duke himself also, and your daughter.

LEAR   Ha? Sayest thou so?

KNIGHT I beseech you pardon me, my lord, if I be mistaken, for my duty cannot be silent when I think your highness wronged.

LEAR   Thou but rememberest me of mine own conception¹⁵. I have perceived a most faint neglect of late, which I have rather blamed as mine own jealous curiosity¹⁶ than as a very pretence and purpose¹⁷ of unkindness. I will look further into't. But where's my fool? I have not seen him these two days.

KNIGHT Since my young lady's going into France, sir, the fool hath much pined away¹⁸.

Lear strikes Oswald for his rudeness. Kent joins in the assault. The Fool warns Kent about the dangers of following a king who shows such lack of wisdom in dealing with his daughters.

剧情简介：李尔因奥兹沃尔对自己无礼而打了他，肯特也跟着动了手。俳优警告肯特，国王在处理女儿的问题上缺乏智慧，因此跟着这样一个国王很危险。

1 'who am I, sir?' (in small groups)

Lear presumably intends his question to be answered in a respectful way, which recognises his rank and status. Ironically, it raises doubts about his own identity. He is no longer the all-powerful king that he was at the start of the play, and he is becoming aware of his changed status.

a Suggest three or four replies that Lear might have expected in response to his question, 'who am I, sir?' (line 67)

b Why does Oswald's plain-spoken reply (line 68) anger Lear so much?

c Invent three or four alternative insults that Oswald could use to reply to Lear instead of his deliberately disrespectful 'My lady's father.'

d Kent was the last man to challenge Lear and give unwanted and unexpected responses – and he was banished for it. How does Oswald's behaviour differ from Kent's in Scene 1?

Stagecraft 导演技巧

'Enter FOOL'

a The role of a fool may be unfamiliar to audiences today. As a result, directors may try to give the character a more modern context. The Fool has been played as a stand-up (单口) comedian, a nurse and a drag artist (a male stage performer dressed as a woman).

- Look at the photographs in this book showing how the Fool has been presented in different productions. Pick out some of these variations, as well as any others you can find.
- What other roles might the Fool adopt that could fit in with a modern production of the play?

b The Fool is sometimes played as a man the same age as his master. Lear calls him 'boy', but this could simply be a term of address to an inferior. Sometimes, however, the Fool is a very young man and, occasionally, he has been played by a woman. The actor playing Cordelia has been known to double as the Fool. They never appear on stage together, and in Shakespeare's theatre female roles were played by young men or boys, so a young actor could well have played both parts.

- Consider any similarities or parallels between Cordelia and the Fool. What factors in their relationships with Lear might make doubling up the roles an interesting choice?
- Would you double up the roles of these characters? Make notes explaining your reasons in your Director's Journal.

1 **cur** 狗东西
2 **bandy looks** 回瞪眼（bandy 原指来回击球，这里指相互瞪眼）
3 **base football player** （在莎士比亚时代，踢足球是下等人的运动，不像网球般高雅）
4 **lubber** 傻大个儿
5 **tarry** 等着，别动
6 **go to** = come, come （好了，行了，够了）
7 **earnest** 酬劳
8 **coxcomb** 鸡冠帽（俳优或小丑戴的滑稽帽子）
9 **and thou ... shortly** 你要是不会留意风向（望风使舵），很快就会着凉（遭殃）
10 **nuncle** = mine uncle （老爷子，俳优对主人的典型称呼）

LEAR	No more of that, I have noted it well. Go you and tell my daughter I would speak with her.	65

               [*Exit an Attendant*]

    Go you, call hither my fool.

               [*Exit an Attendant*]

         Enter OSWALD

    Oh, you, sir, you, come you hither, sir, who am I, sir?

OSWALD	My lady's father.	
LEAR	'My lady's father'? My lord's knave, you whoreson dog, you slave, you cur[1]!	70
OSWALD	I am none of these, my lord, I beseech your pardon.	
LEAR	Do you bandy looks[2] with me, you rascal?	

          [*Strikes him*]

OSWALD	I'll not be strucken, my lord.	
KENT	[*Tripping him*] Nor tripped neither, you base football player[3].	
LEAR	I thank thee, fellow. Thou serv'st me, and I'll love thee.	75
KENT	Come, sir, arise, away, I'll teach you differences. Away, away. If you will measure your lubber's[4] length again, tarry[5]; but away, go to[6]! Have you wisdom?	

         [*Pushes Oswald out*]

    So.

LEAR	Now, my friendly knave, I thank thee; there's earnest[7] of thy service.	80

         [*Gives Kent money*]

          Enter FOOL

FOOL	Let me hire him, too; here's my coxcomb[8].	

         [*Offers Kent his cap*]

LEAR	How now, my pretty knave, how dost thou?	
FOOL	[*To Kent*] Sirrah, you were best take my coxcomb.	
LEAR	Why, my boy?	85
FOOL	Why? For taking one's part that's out of favour. [*To Kent*] Nay, and thou canst not smile as the wind sits, thou'lt catch cold shortly[9]. There, take my coxcomb; why, this fellow has banished two on's daughters and did the third a blessing against his will; if thou follow him, thou must needs wear my coxcomb. How now, nuncle[10]? Would I had two coxcombs and two daughters.	90

In spite of Lear's threat of a whipping, the Fool continues to be critical of him. In a series of jokes and rhymes, the Fool chides Lear for disowning Cordelia and giving away his kingdom.

  剧情简介：尽管李尔威胁要鞭打俳优，俳优还是继续对他冷嘲热讽，说了一连串玩笑和打油诗，嘲讽李尔与小女儿断绝关系并放弃自己的江山的做法。

1 More 'nothing'

a Kent uses the word 'nothing' at line 113 and the Fool then repeats it and taunts Lear with it. Add this to your list in your Director's Journal.

b How should Lear speak line 116? Should he speak defiantly, or with a growing realisation of his mistakes, recalled by the word 'nothing'?

▶ What do you think is the purpose behind the Fool's pointed comments on recent events?

1 Take heed 当心，提防
2 kennel 把……关进狗舍
3 Lady Brach 母布拉狗（暗指高娜瑞尔和蕊根）
4 pestilent gall 恶毒挖苦
5 owest = own
6 goest = walk
7 Learn more than thou trowest 多听少信
8 Set less than thou throwest 下的注要少于掷的骰子（不能孤注一掷）
9 thou ... score 你的二十就会不止两个十（即"你就会发家致富"）
10 breath 讲话（引申为"辩护"）
11 unfeed lawyer 没有收到费用的律师（不会替你辩护）
12 Prithee = I pray thee（请你，求你）
13 two crowns 两顶王冠（一个鸡蛋从中间切开，吃掉蛋白和蛋黄后形成的两半空蛋壳与王冠形状相似）
14 meat 瓤儿
15 clovest 劈开
16 thou ... dirt 你就等于背着你的驴走在土路上（bor'st = bore；《伊索寓言》里的一位老者为了让每个人都满意，把原本驮着他的驴背在自己背上去市场）
17 bald crown 秃瓢
18 foppish 愚蠢，糊涂
19 apish 跟猿猴一样；沐猴而冠

Stagecraft 导演技巧

Sweet or bitter fool?

If you were putting on a production of the play, why might you choose to include or omit the lines below, from the Quarto version, after line 119?

FOOL   Dost thou know the difference, my boy, between a bitter fool and a sweet one?

LEAR   No, lad; teach me.

FOOL   That lord that counselled thee
To give away thy land,
Come place him here by me,
Do thou for him stand;
The sweet and bitter fool
Will presently appear,
The one in motley (小丑彩衣) here,
The other found out there.

LEAR   Dost thou call me fool, boy?

FOOL   All thy other titles thou hast given away; that thou wast born with.

KENT   This is not altogether (完全) fool, my lord.

FOOL   No, faith; lords and great men will not let me. If I had a monopoly (垄断) out, they would have part on't; and ladies too – they will not let me have all the fool to myself; they'll be snatching (争抢).

LEAR	Why, my boy?	
FOOL	If I gave them all my living, I'd keep my coxcombs myself. There's mine; beg another of thy daughters.	95
LEAR	Take heed[1], sirrah, the whip.	
FOOL	Truth's a dog must to kennel[2]. He must be whipped out, when the Lady Brach[3] may stand by th'fire and stink.	
LEAR	A pestilent gall[4] to me.	
FOOL	Sirrah, I'll teach thee a speech.	100
LEAR	Do.	
FOOL	Mark it, nuncle:	

> Have more than thou showest,
> Speak less than thou knowest,
> Lend less than thou owest[5],   105
> Ride more than thou goest[6],
> Learn more than thou trowest[7],
> Set less than thou throwest[8],
> Leave thy drink and thy whore,
> And keep in-a-door,   110
> And thou shalt have more,
> Than two tens to a score[9].

KENT	This is nothing, fool.	
FOOL	Then 'tis like the breath[10] of an unfeed lawyer[11]; you gave me nothing for't. Can you make no use of nothing, nuncle?	115
LEAR	Why, no, boy; nothing can be made out of nothing.	
FOOL	[*To Kent*] Prithee[12], tell him so much the rent of his land comes to; he will not believe a fool.	
LEAR	A bitter fool.	
FOOL	Nuncle, give me an egg, and I'll give thee two crowns[13].	120
LEAR	What two crowns shall they be?	
FOOL	Why, after I have cut the egg i'th'middle and eat up the meat[14], the two crowns of the egg. When thou clovest[15] thy crown i'th'middle and gav'st away both parts, thou bor'st thine ass on thy back o'er the dirt[16]. Thou hadst little wit in thy bald crown[17] when thou gav'st thy golden one away. If I speak like myself in this, let him be whipped that first finds it so.	125

> [*Sings*] Fools had ne'er less grace in a year,
>   For wise men are grown foppish[18],
>   And know not how their wits to wear,   130
>   Their manners are so apish[19].

LEAR	When were you wont to be so full of songs, sirrah?

The Fool marvels at the contrasting treatment he receives from Lear and from Lear's daughters. Lear reproaches Gonerill for her sour expression. Gonerill criticises Lear's attendants for their loutish behaviour.

剧情简介： 俳优受到李尔及其女儿们截然不同的对待，感到十分惊奇。李尔责备高娜瑞尔言语刻薄，而高娜瑞尔批评李尔的随从行为粗野。

Write about it 写作练习
The Fool's-eye view

The Fool jokes about a topsy-turvy (乱七八糟) world where wise men become foolish, and he describes Lear as a child being punished by his daughters. Court fools were allowed great freedom to mock and criticise (Gonerill calls Lear's Fool 'all-licensed'). However, they had to judge carefully just how far to take their gibes (讥讽) to avoid being punished.

a List the criticisms the Fool makes in lines 82–155 about Lear and his behaviour, but do so by stating them directly rather than using the upside-down jesting with which the Fool feels safe.

b Afterwards, write a brief speech for the Fool (possibly an **aside** [旁白] only intended to be heard by the audience), criticising Lear by using these direct, frank comments.

1 Gonerill makes her case (in fours)

In lines 160–73, Gonerill, speaking in formal blank verse, mounts a powerful attack on the conduct of Lear's followers, accusing the king of encouraging their riotous behaviour ('put it on / By your allowance') and threatening, for the good of the state, to take drastic measures ('redresses') to deal with the situation, even if this causes offence and brings shame to her father.

- Take parts as Gonerill, Lear, the Fool and Kent. As Gonerill speaks lines 160–73, give her a respectful and quiet hearing.
- Gonerill reads the lines a second time, and the listeners respond more actively – perhaps giggling, busying themselves with eating or drinking, or whispering words from the Fool's songs.
- On a third reading, the listeners use phrases selected from the lines spoken by their characters earlier in the scene to heckle (起哄) and interrupt. Gonerill should try to complete her speech despite the interruptions of her onstage audience.

1 used it 习惯了
2 gav'st … breeches 把手杖交给她们（李尔的女儿们）并脱下你自己的裤子（等着挨打）
3 bo-peep （一种躲猫猫类游戏，现在称为peekaboo或peek-a-boo）
4 And = If
5 pared 削，劈
6 frontlet 额饰，额带（这里指额头上的皱纹，即愁容 [frowning]）
7 O without a figure 前面什么数都没有的零（什么都不是）
8 forsooth 确实，的确
9 Mum 闭嘴
10 He … some 面包皮和面包瓤儿都不留，早晚会为自身生计发愁
11 shelled peascod 剥去了豆子的豌豆荚（徒有虚名）
12 all-licensed 没有规矩，为所欲为
13 insolent retinue 傲慢无理的侍从
14 carp 找碴儿，挑刺儿
15 rank 讨厌，可恶
16 safe redress 妥善的改正办法
17 too late 最近
18 put it on 纵容，鼓励
19 censure 责难

FOOL	I have used it[1], nuncle, e'er since thou mad'st thy daughters thy mothers; for when thou gav'st them the rod and put'st down thine own breeches[2],
[*Sings*] Then they for sudden joy did weep,
And I for sorrow sung,
That such a king should play bo-peep[3],
And go the fools among.
Prithee, nuncle, keep a schoolmaster that can teach thy fool to lie. I would fain learn to lie.
LEAR	And[4] you lie, sirrah, we'll have you whipped.
FOOL	I marvel what kin thou and thy daughters are: they'll have me whipped for speaking true, thou'lt have me whipped for lying, and sometimes I am whipped for holding my peace. I had rather be any kind o'thing than a fool, and yet I would not be thee, nuncle; thou hast pared[5] thy wit o'both sides and left nothing i'th'middle. Here comes one o'the parings.

Enter GONERILL

LEAR	How now, daughter! What makes that frontlet[6] on? You are too much of late i'th'frown.
FOOL	Thou wast a pretty fellow when thou hadst no need to care for her frowning; now thou art an O without a figure[7]. I am better than thou art now; I am a fool, thou art nothing. [*To Gonerill*] Yes, forsooth[8], I will hold my tongue, so your face bids me, though you say nothing.
[*Sings*] Mum[9], mum:
He that keeps nor crust, nor crumb,
Weary of all, shall want some[10].
That's a shelled peascod[11].
GONERILL	Not only, sir, this, your all-licensed[12] fool,
But other of your insolent retinue[13]
Do hourly carp[14] and quarrel, breaking forth
In rank[15] and not-to-be-endurèd riots. Sir,
I had thought by making this well known unto you
To have found a safe redress[16], but now grow fearful,
By what yourself too late[17] have spoke and done,
That you protect this course, and put it on[18]
By your allowance; which if you should, the fault
Would not 'scape censure[19], nor the redresses sleep;

Gonerill wishes that Lear would behave wisely. Lear questions both his own identity and Gonerill's. She criticises the debauchery of Lear's followers, and demands that he reduce their number.

剧情简介：高娜瑞尔希望李尔做事明智些。李尔质疑自己和高娜瑞尔的身份。高娜瑞尔批评李尔的随从纵情声色，要求李尔减少随从的人数。

1 'Does any here know me?' (in small groups)

Gonerill's criticism of Lear's moody and irrational behaviour (lines 179–82), the Fool's barbed comments and the king's own awareness of a general lack of respect all seem to make him very angry. In his lines here, Lear speaks like someone affected by dementia (痴呆) – he seems confused and uncertain.

a Discuss whether you think Lear is genuinely troubled about his identity or whether he is just enraged by his treatment and is complaining about it in a way intended to make Gonerill apologise.

b Talk together about how much our sense of identity and self-worth depends on how we are treated by others.

c Look back at 'who am I, sir?' in line 67 of this scene. How does Lear's state of mind opposite compare with his response there?

2 'Whoop, Jug, I love thee!' (in threes)

'Whoop, Jug, I love thee!' (line 183–4) is a difficult line. It may be mere nonsense or an echo of a popular song of the time. It can be played on stage as a reaction to a blow or threat from Gonerill. The word 'jug' sometimes meant a prostitute, so this could be an insult, with the declaration of love an ironic echo of her words to her father in Scene 1.

a Take parts as Gonerill, Lear and the Fool. Read lines 174–90 and experiment with ways of staging this exchange. How much attention should Gonerill and Lear pay to the Fool? Does he play to the audience?

b After his words at line 190 the Fool says nothing until line 270. Experiment with ways of playing this switch to silence. Is it the result of instructions from Gonerill or Lear? Or does it come from the Fool's own sense of appropriate behaviour?

1 **tender of a wholesome weal** 为国家利益着想
2 **discreet proceeding** 审慎的行动
3 **hedge-sparrow** 篱雀
4 **are fraught** 具备
5 **dispositions** 习性
6 **transport you** 让您性情大变
7 **notion** 头脑，见解
8 **discernings / Are lethargied** 智力减弱，或辨别力迟钝
9 **admiration** （故作）惊讶
10 **much o'th'savour** 很有……的特点 / 特性
11 **pranks** 恶作剧
12 **deboshed = debauched** （放荡，放纵）
13 **epicurism** 大吃大喝；享乐主义
14 **lust** 纵情玩乐
15 **disquantity your train** 减少您的随从人数（train: 随从）
16 **besort** 适合
17 **know themselves and you** 明白他们自己和您的身份

Language in the play 剧中语言

Gonerill's ultimatum (最后通牒) (in pairs)

In lines 192–207, Gonerill continues to criticise the behaviour of Lear's knights and Lear's reaction to her complaints. Highlight the following in different colours on a copy of the script opposite:

- respectful language, which an actor may choose to make sound sincere or not
- language emphasising how little Gonerill is asking
- words suggesting childish behaviour
- words or phrases recalling Lear's age.

	Which in the tender of a wholesome weal¹	170
	Might in their working do you that offence	
	Which else were shame, that then necessity	
	Will call discreet proceeding².	
FOOL	For you know, nuncle,	
	The hedge-sparrow³ fed the cuckoo so long,	175
	That it's had it head bit off by it young.	
	So out went the candle, and we were left darkling.	
LEAR	Are you our daughter?	
GONERILL	I would you would make use of your good wisdom,	
	Whereof I know you are fraught⁴, and put away	180
	These dispositions⁵, which of late transport you⁶	
	From what you rightly are.	
FOOL	May not an ass know when the cart draws the horse? Whoop, Jug, I love thee!	
LEAR	Does any here know me? This is not Lear:	
	Does Lear walk thus? speak thus? Where are his eyes?	185
	Either his notion⁷ weakens, his discernings	
	Are lethargied⁸ – Ha! Waking? 'Tis not so!	
	Who is it that can tell me who I am?	
FOOL	Lear's shadow.	190
LEAR	Your name, fair gentlewoman?	
GONERILL	This admiration⁹, sir, is much o'th'savour¹⁰	
	Of other your new pranks¹¹. I do beseech you	
	To understand my purposes aright:	
	As you are old and reverend, should be wise.	195
	Here do you keep a hundred knights and squires,	
	Men so disordered, so deboshed¹² and bold,	
	That this our court, infected with their manners,	
	Shows like a riotous inn; epicurism¹³ and lust¹⁴	
	Makes it more like a tavern or a brothel	200
	Than a graced palace. The shame itself doth speak	
	For instant remedy. Be then desired	
	By her, that else will take the thing she begs,	
	A little to disquantity your train¹⁵,	
	And the remainders that shall still depend	205
	To be such men as may besort¹⁶ your age,	
	Which know themselves and you¹⁷.	

Lear furiously declares that he will go to Regan. He attacks Gonerill's ingratitude, and defends his followers' honour. He expresses anguish at his treatment of Cordelia. Puzzled, Albany tries to soothe Lear.

剧情简介：李尔大怒，宣布要到蕊根家去住。他指责高娜瑞尔忘恩负义，接着替自己的随从说话，然后表达了自己因与考蒂丽叶断绝关系而感受的痛苦。阿尔博尼感到迷惑，试图安慰李尔。

Language in the play 剧中语言

'Darkness and devils!' (in threes)

Lear has only spoken a few lines since Gonerill entered, and at this point in the scene his pent-up (被压抑) feelings may get the better of him, or he may suddenly find he can articulate his rage. His fragmented words are full of exclamations, questions and sudden shifts in who he is addressing. This is all in sharp contrast to Gonerill's stately (庄重) (if threatening) lines 192–207.

- Read through lines 217–26 and decide who is being addressed at each line. Experiment with ways of reading the lines. For example, you may choose to switch reader each time there is a change of audience.
- Read through the lines again, this time with a real focus on body language and adopting a change of tone in the various sections.
- Think about the effect Lear's changing language here might have on an audience. When do we feel most sympathy for him?

1 rabble 乌合之众
2 Woe = Woe to him （让……不得好死）
3 kite 鸢（一种猛禽，性格凶菅残忍）
4 parts 品德
5 exact regard 事事处处
6 support ... name 维护他们自身的荣誉
7 engine 杠杆或撬棍之类的器械
8 frame of nature 五脏六腑
9 gall 怨恨；痛苦

1 'Lear, Lear, Lear!'

Lines 221–7 seem to be the first indication that Lear is growing aware of the terrible mistake he made in rejecting Cordelia. However, the lines are not completely clear, and this may reflect his state of mind.

- What do you think he means in these lines?
- Why is he thinking of Cordelia at this moment?

2 A confused host (in pairs)

Albany appears to be baffled when he enters to find his father-in-law raging against his wife. He seems genuinely grieved at Lear's distress, even though the Knight who spoke to Lear about his treatment in lines 49–53 suggested that Albany and Gonerill were equally inattentive (不经心). Later in the scene, it is clear that Albany and Gonerill are at odds over how to deal with the situation.

a Come up with three questions that Albany might want to ask different witnesses to the events that occurred prior to his arrival.

b During the remainder of this scene, Gonerill does not speak to her father at all. Talk together about how Albany's presence may affect her behaviour.

LEAR	Darkness and devils!
	Saddle my horses; call my train together. –
	Degenerate bastard, I'll not trouble thee;
	Yet have I left a daughter. 210
GONERILL	You strike my people, and your disordered rabble¹
	Make servants of their betters.

Enter ALBANY

LEAR	Woe² that too late repents!
	Is it your will? Speak, sir. Prepare my horses.
	Ingratitude! Thou marble-hearted fiend,
	More hideous when thou show'st thee in a child 215
	Than the sea-monster.
ALBANY	Pray, sir, be patient.
LEAR	[*To Gonerill*] Detested kite³, thou liest!
	My train are men of choice and rarest parts⁴,
	That all particulars of duty know,
	And in the most exact regard⁵ support 220
	The worships of their name⁶. O most small fault,
	How ugly didst thou in Cordelia show!
	Which, like an engine⁷, wrenched my frame of nature⁸
	From the fixed place, drew from my heart all love,
	And added to the gall⁹. O Lear, Lear, Lear! 225
	Beat at this gate that let thy folly in
	And thy dear judgement out. Go, go, my people.
ALBANY	My lord, I am guiltless as I am ignorant
	Of what hath moved you.

Lear curses Gonerill with childlessness or unloving children. He leaves, but returns having discovered Gonerill's dismissal of fifty of his followers. Lear weeps and again curses Gonerill, claiming that Regan will welcome him.

剧情简介：李尔诅咒高娜瑞尔无后，即使有后，后代也会忤逆不孝，然后离开，回来后却发现高娜瑞尔已经把自己的五十名随从打发走了。李尔痛哭，咒骂高娜瑞尔，又说蕊根会欢迎他。

Themes 主题分析

A father's curse (in pairs)

Lear has already called Gonerill 'Degenerate bastard' (line 209), and now he brings down a curse of childlessness upon her. Both these attacks seem quite disturbing, coming from a father to a child, and connect with the theme of the disruption of the natural order (here seen in the context of a family).

a One partner speaks Lear's lines 230–44, while the other plays Gonerill and experiments with ways of reacting to what Lear says.

b Talk together about Lear's language. What makes it so powerful and distressing?

1 sterility 不孕不育
2 increase 生育
3 derogate = degenerate （下贱）
4 teem 生孩子
5 Create her child of spleen 让她生个脾气暴躁的孩子（脾[spleen] 当时被视为暴躁脾气的来源）
6 thwart disnatured 乖戾，不近人情
7 cadent 掉落
8 fret 冲蚀出
9 Never … it 别自寻烦恼追问原因了
10 let … scope 让他由着性子闹
11 As dotage gives it 他老糊涂了（As = That）
12 at a clap 一下子，一举
13 Within a fortnight 两周之内（在短短两周时间里）
14 perforce 情不自禁
15 untented woundings 无法包扎的伤口
16 fond 愚蠢，傻
17 cast … clay 把你们俩，连同你们洒下的泪水，丢到土里，和成泥
18 comfortable 给人慰藉
19 flay thy wolvish visage 撕破你那张狼一样的脸
20 resume … forever 恢复你以为我永远放弃了的王位

▲ Gonerill talks to her father. The Fool (dressed as a woman) is next to Kent. Which line from the script opposite do you think is being spoken at this moment?

1 Lear's changing mood (in pairs)

In order to see how Lear's mood and feelings change over the course of this scene, go back and look at each page of script from the beginning of Scene 4.

- For each page, write down a few words describing Lear's apparent mood and likely feelings.
- Talk together about what your notes reveal about how Lear's mood develops. You will see how, over the course of this scene, his state of mind changes from an apparently cheerful, relaxed man home from a day's hunting, to a person in deep distress, issuing terrible curses and reduced to planning a journey in the dark to get away.
- Create a 'mood graph', giving a visual representation of your findings about Lear's increasing anxiety, anger and vulnerability.

LEAR   It may be so, my lord.
　　　　　　Hear, Nature, hear, dear goddess, hear: 230
　　　　　　Suspend thy purpose, if thou didst intend
　　　　　　To make this creature fruitful.
　　　　　　Into her womb convey sterility[1],
　　　　　　Dry up in her the organs of increase[2],
　　　　　　And from her derogate[3] body never spring   235
　　　　　　A babe to honour her. If she must teem[4],
　　　　　　Create her child of spleen[5], that it may live
　　　　　　And be a thwart disnatured[6] torment to her.
　　　　　　Let it stamp wrinkles in her brow of youth,
　　　　　　With cadent[7] tears fret[8] channels in her cheeks,   240
　　　　　　Turn all her mother's pains and benefits
　　　　　　To laughter and contempt, that she may feel
　　　　　　How sharper than a serpent's tooth it is
　　　　　　To have a thankless child. Away, away!
　　　　　　　　　　　Exeunt [Lear, Kent, Knights, and Attendants]

ALBANY   Now, gods that we adore, whereof comes this?   245
GONERILL Never afflict yourself to know more of it[9],
　　　　　　But let his disposition have that scope[10]
　　　　　　As dotage gives it[11].

　　　　　　　　　　　Enter LEAR

LEAR   What, fifty of my followers at a clap[12]?
　　　　　　Within a fortnight[13]?
ALBANY   What's the matter, sir?   250
LEAR   I'll tell thee. [*To Gonerill*] Life and death! I am ashamed
　　　　　　That thou hast power to shake my manhood thus,
　　　　　　That these hot tears, which break from me perforce[14],
　　　　　　Should make thee worth them. Blasts and fogs upon thee!
　　　　　　Th'untented woundings[15] of a father's curse   255
　　　　　　Pierce every sense about thee. Old fond[16] eyes,
　　　　　　Beweep this cause again, I'll pluck ye out
　　　　　　And cast you with the waters that you loose
　　　　　　To temper clay[17]. Ha! Let it be so.
　　　　　　I have another daughter,   260
　　　　　　Who I am sure is kind and comfortable[18].
　　　　　　When she shall hear this of thee, with her nails
　　　　　　She'll flay thy wolvish visage[19]. Thou shalt find
　　　　　　That I'll resume the shape which thou dost think
　　　　　　I have cast off forever[20].   *Exit*

Gonerill fears the dangers posed by Lear and his knights. She believes it is better to be suspicious than trusting, and sends Oswald to warn Regan. Gonerill hints that Albany's gentle nature is a weakness in a ruler.

剧情简介：高娜瑞尔害怕李尔及其骑士会对自己不利，认为宁可怀疑他们也不能信任他们，并派奥兹沃尔去警告蕊根。高娜瑞尔暗示阿尔博尼性格软弱，不宜统治国家。

1 'the fool follows after' (in groups of three or four)

The Fool, who has been silent since line 190, speaks in a mixture of sense and nonsense between lines 270 and 275, and it can be difficult to work out exactly what he means. The actor playing the Fool must somehow make these words significant to the audience.

a   Discuss what you think the Fool means. What is the effect of having these puzzling lines here?

b   Experiment with ways in which the Fool could convincingly deliver lines 270–5 just before he follows Lear off the stage. Think about who he may be speaking to, and whether gestures would make his attitude clear.

c   If you were directing the play, what would you have the Fool do during his long silence?

2 Husband and wife (in pairs)

Gonerill interrupts Albany as he talks of his love for her at line 267. She speaks to him sarcastically about allowing Lear to keep a hundred knights, then challenges his judgement and strength of character.

a   Take parts and speak everything Gonerill and Albany say to each other in lines 265–302. Then talk together about how you think they really feel about each other.

b   At this point in the play, how might the actors suggest to the audience what Albany would regard as a satisfactory outcome to the 'Lear problem' and what Gonerill would regard as satisfactory?

1   partial   偏心
2   halter   缰绳；绞索
3   counsel   判断
4   politic   谨慎
5   At point   时刻准备着；武装待命
6   buzz   谣言
7   enguard   保护
8   particular   私密；具体
9   compact   强化
10 milky gentleness and course   优柔寡断
11 ataxed   受责怪，受非议
12 harmful mildness   有害的宽仁

Themes 主题分析

A scene about identity? (in pairs)

There are many references to identity in this scene. It begins with Kent disguising himself and then being asked questions about who he is by the king. Lear questions his own identity. He usually fails to win the reassurance he seeks, but is drawn into further questioning about his role and status. The many insults aimed at Oswald can also be seen as attacks on identity, drawing his response: 'I am none of these, my lord.'

- In pairs, look back at the scene and pick out the references to identity. Note down one short quotation that you feel illustrates this theme most dramatically.
- Make a list of characters whose sense of identity is covered in this scene. Do you think identity is a new theme introduced here, or was it foreshadowed in Scenes 1 and 2?

GONERILL Do you mark that?

ALBANY I cannot be so partial[1], Gonerill,
To the great love I bear you —

GONERILL Pray you, content.
What, Oswald, ho!
You, sir, more knave than fool, after your master.

FOOL Nuncle Lear, nuncle Lear, tarry, take the fool with thee.
    A fox, when one has caught her,
    And such a daughter,
    Should sure to the slaughter,
    If my cap would buy a halter[2];
    So the fool follows after. *Exit*

GONERILL This man hath had good counsel[3]. A hundred knights?
'Tis politic[4] and safe to let him keep
At point[5] a hundred knights? Yes, that on every dream,
Each buzz[6], each fancy, each complaint, dislike,
He may enguard[7] his dotage with their powers
And hold our lives in mercy. Oswald, I say!

ALBANY Well, you may fear too far.

GONERILL Safer than trust too far.
Let me still take away the harms I fear,
Not fear still to be taken. I know his heart.
What he hath uttered I have writ my sister:
If she sustain him and his hundred knights
When I have showed th'unfitness —

Enter OSWALD

How now, Oswald?
What, have you writ that letter to my sister?

OSWALD Ay, madam.

GONERILL Take you some company and away to horse.
Inform her full of my particular[8] fear,
And thereto add such reasons of your own
As may compact[9] it more. Get you gone,
And hasten your return.
    [*Exit Oswald*]
    No, no, my lord,
This milky gentleness and course[10] of yours,
Though I condemn not, yet under pardon
You are much more ataxed[11] for want of wisdom,
Than praised for harmful mildness[12].

Albany decides to wait for whatever happens. Lear sends Kent with letters to Regan. The Fool predicts that Regan's treatment of Lear will be the same as Gonerill's. Lear recalls his mistreatment of Cordelia.

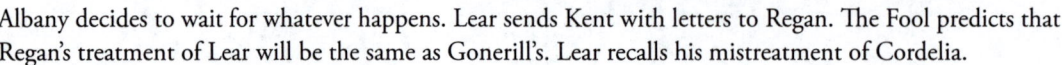

剧情简介：阿尔博尼决定顺其自然。李尔派肯特给蕊根送信。俳优预计蕊根会和高娜瑞尔一样对待李尔。李尔又回忆起他对考蒂丽叶的不公。

Write about it 写作练习

Letters to Regan

Two messengers and two letters are on their way to Regan. Oswald has written on Gonerill's behalf, telling Regan how things stand and urging her not to accept her father's hundred knights; Lear has written to Regan saying he is coming to stay with her.

a Write the two contrasting letters, as if they had been scrawled (潦草写成) in haste. Use only a few sentences for each one. It might help to look back at Gonerill's instructions to Oswald in Act 1 Scene 4, lines 290–4 and at what Lear says to his messenger, Kent/Caius, in Act 1 Scene 5, lines 1–4.

b Write two or three sentences to explain why you think Gonerill and Lear give such different instructions to their messengers.

1 th'event 走着瞧（阿尔博尼无意再争辩下去）
2 your diligence be not speedy 你不加紧办差
3 afore = before
4 kibes 冻疮
5 thy … slipshod 你的脑子不需要拖鞋（因为你没有脑子）（slipshod：穿拖鞋）
6 kindly 像亲人；像同类（即她姐姐）
7 crab 沙果，海棠果（一种野果，形似苹果，味酸）
8 either side's nose = on both sides of the nose

1 A king and his Fool (in pairs)

The Fool and Lear are alone on stage for much of Scene 5. The mood sharply contrasts with that of Scene 4, where there were other people present both as participants and observers. Lear seems increasingly reflective and turned in upon himself. His instructions to Kent are purposeful, but after that he no longer seems combative or even angry.

The Fool directs a series of barbed jokes at Lear in this scene (lines 6–36). Sometimes Lear appears to respond, but at other times he seems to be lost in his own thoughts about Cordelia or about revenge against Gonerill. In one production of the play, the lines were played as though the two characters were a comedy double act. Each 'punchline' was accompanied by appropriate gestures and stamping of feet. In another production, the Fool was barely able to attract Lear's attention.

- Discuss whether or not you would emphasise the humour or the pathos of this scene, and how you might demonstrate both.
- Then take parts and experiment with different styles of performing all the exchanges between Lear and the Fool in Scene 5. Make clear by Lear's tone of voice or body language whether or not he is really listening to the Fool.
- Should line 20 ('I did her wrong') be emphasised in any way?

ALBANY	How far your eyes may pierce I cannot tell; Striving to better, oft we mar what's well.	300
GONERILL	Nay then –	
ALBANY	Well, well, th'event[1].	

Exeunt

Act 1 Scene 5
Outside the castle of Albany and Gonerill

Enter LEAR, KENT *(disguised), and* FOOL

LEAR	Go you before to Gloucester with these letters. Acquaint my daughter no further with anything you know than comes from her demand out of the letter. If your diligence be not speedy[2], I shall be there afore[3] you.	
KENT	I will not sleep, my lord, till I have delivered your letter.	5

Exit

FOOL	If a man's brains were in's heels, were't not in danger of kibes[4]?	
LEAR	Ay, boy.	
FOOL	Then, I prithee, be merry; thy wit shall not go slipshod[5].	
LEAR	Ha, ha, ha.	10
FOOL	Shalt see thy other daughter will use thee kindly[6], for though she's as like this as a crab's[7] like an apple, yet I can tell what I can tell.	
LEAR	What canst tell, boy?	
FOOL	She will taste as like this as a crab does to a crab. Thou canst tell why one's nose stands i'th'middle on's face?	15
LEAR	No.	
FOOL	Why, to keep one's eyes of either side's nose[8], that what a man cannot smell out, he may spy into.	
LEAR	I did her wrong.	20

剧情简介：俳优继续他的冷嘲热讽，但是李尔心不在焉，因为他心里想的是高娜瑞尔的忘恩负义，以及自己如何夺回王权。李尔害怕自己会发疯。俳优开着色情玩笑下场。

Themes 主题分析

'O let me not be mad' (in pairs)

a What do you think is going on in Lear's mind at lines 20, 27, 32 and 37–8? Write down your ideas, then compare them with your partner's. Are any of your ideas the same?

b Lear seems very anxious to discover that he is no longer in control of events. In your Director's Journal, write about whether you would portray this moment of self-doubt as the first sign of madness, or whether you would emphasise the king's erratic (不稳定) misjudgements in Act 1 Scene 1, his outrage at his treatment or his extreme reaction to Gonerill's behaviour in Act 1 Scene 4.

c Discuss how the development of suspense and tension in the play would be altered by having this moment give the first hint of mental breakdown, rather than an emphasis on the earlier 'unconstant starts' that Gonerill and Regan comment on at the end of Scene 1.

1 **leave … case** 使得他头上的角都没地方藏（这是俳优在开下流玩笑，horns指男人被戴绿帽子后头上会长角）
2 **asses** 蠢驴（指李尔的仆人）
3 **mo** = more
4 **To take't again perforce** 用暴力再夺回来
5 **in temper** 理智
6 **maid** 处女，少女

1 Last words

Some critics claim that the Fool's final words are a warning to the audience to take what they are watching seriously. This may be true, but these lines clearly contain a sexual innuendo (暗示). Actors often emphasise the phallic (阴茎的) joke with graphic gestures.

- Make a list of possible reasons why Shakespeare chose to end the first act on this sexual note and with words from the Fool.

FOOL	Canst tell how an oyster makes his shell?	
LEAR	No.	
FOOL	Nor I neither; but I can tell why a snail has a house.	
LEAR	Why?	
FOOL	Why, to put 's head in, not to give it away to his daughters, and leave his horns without a case[1].	25
LEAR	I will forget my nature. So kind a father! Be my horses ready?	
FOOL	Thy asses[2] are gone about 'em. The reason why the seven stars are no mo[3] than seven is a pretty reason.	
LEAR	Because they are not eight.	30
FOOL	Yes, indeed, thou wouldst make a good fool.	
LEAR	To take't again perforce[4]. Monster ingratitude!	
FOOL	If thou wert my fool, nuncle, I'd have thee beaten for being old before thy time.	
LEAR	How's that?	35
FOOL	Thou shouldst not have been old till thou hadst been wise.	
LEAR	O let me not be mad, not mad, sweet heaven! Keep me in temper[5], I would not be mad.	

[*Enter* GENTLEMAN]

	How now, are the horses ready?	
GENTLEMAN	Ready, my lord.	40
LEAR	Come, boy.	
FOOL	She that's a maid[6] now, and laughs at my departure, Shall not be a maid long, unless things be cut shorter.	

Exeunt

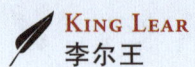

King Lear
李尔王

Looking back at Act 1　第1幕回顾
Activities for groups or individuals

1 An interrupted ceremony

The play opens on a royal court awaiting the start of the ceremony to finalise the division of the kingdom. Directors have staged this in various ways, including as a tense political meeting, a series of public declarations recorded for broadcasting and a spectacular royal event of great pomp (盛况) and grandeur (气派). Despite all expectations, however, the ceremony is never completed. The play's tragic events all stem from this interruption. It also creates a strong sense of there being 'unfinished business' – the audience, as well as those involved in the story, seek a resolution to the situation.

- Use a detailed sketch map of the stage to plan the ceremonial of the first scene – where actors should stand, how they should behave and whether any props are to be used – in addition to the map and the coronet that are mentioned in the script. (See opposite, and pp. vi and 18 for how different productions have staged this scene.)

2 The bond

Cordelia declares that she loves her father according to her 'bond' and Gloucester fears a world with 'the bond cracked 'twixt son and father'. One of the meanings of 'bond' is a legal document or contract.

- Draw up a 'family bond' that states the duties and obligations of a modern father and teenage child towards each other.
- Then draw up the bond that you feel either Lear or Gloucester would believe existed between them and their children. In Gloucester's case, the bond may well be different for his legitimate and his illegitimate sons. Lear might also differentiate between his daughters. Of course, their children may not share their parents' view of 'rights and obligations'.
- Compare your modern and old bonds. In what respects have family obligations remained the same over 400 years?

3 Lear's 'authority'

When Kent, in disguise, seeks employment with Lear, he says he wishes to serve a man who has such a look of 'authority'.

- In pairs, talk about whether Kent is a reliable witness. If so, how could the actor playing Lear make this line credible? Comment on how he should convey authority not only in the formality of the first scene but also at the start of Scene 4, when he is in a more relaxed situation.

4 Lear's folly

During Act 1, Kent, Gonerill and the Fool all accuse Lear of grave failures of judgement.

- Write three short statements in which each character lists specific misjudgements, and then comments on them. Try to make the style of each statement appropriate to the character concerned.
- Read your statements out to a partner and see if they can guess which character is making each accusation.

5 Different perspectives

Retell the events of Act 1 in two or more of the following forms:

- a family saga (家族传奇) dramatising the problems of jealousy and inheritance
- a drama showing a struggle to take or hold on to political power in a state, or to seize control of a large corporation
- a feminist story – retold from a woman's point of view (for example, there has been a play retelling the story from the point of view of the princesses' nanny)
- a fairy story for very young children.

Curan informs Edmond of Cornwall and Regan's imminent arrival, and of the growing tension between Cornwall and Albany. Edmond tries to persuade the innocent Edgar to flee his father's castle.

剧情简介：喀润通知爱德门，康沃尔和蕊根马上就来，还报告说康沃尔和阿尔博尼关系日益紧张。爱德门试图劝说无辜的爱德格逃离父亲的城堡。

1 Rumour and danger (in pairs)

The act opens with a conversation between Edmond and Curan, a courtier, who mentions rumours and gossip circulating, following the division of the kingdom. Curan describes a growing rift (不和) and 'likely wars' between Cornwall and Albany, although there is no other evidence for this and he admits it is but 'whispered'. At a time when accurate news was hard to come by, rumour was a significant danger and a rather more threatening concept than it might seem today – a cause of uncertainty, fear and anxiety.

a Taking parts, read lines 1–13, experimenting with ways of creating a tense and unsettled atmosphere.

b In your Director's Journal, make notes about how movement and gesture could add to the sense of danger and fear.

2 'the good advantage of the night'

In modern theatres this scene is usually played on a fairly dark stage, but in Shakespeare's time performances took place in daylight. Notice that in the script opposite there are several references to 'night'. This was so that the audience understood that events were happening under cover of darkness.

- Act 2 covers the events of only a few hours, so you will find there are regular references to the dark. Make a note of these as you read on.

Language in the play 剧中语言

Edmond sets to work (in pairs)

In lines 14–27, Edmond begins his plan to discredit Edgar. He uses **personification** (拟人) (giving human attributes to non-human things), appealing to Briefness and Fortune to help him seize his opportunity. His lines to Edgar are full of short, sharp statements, commands and questions. He exploits the rumour of tension between Albany and Cornwall in order to further frighten his brother.

- Read aloud lines 19–27, changing over at each punctuation mark. Bring out the urgency of the way in which Edmond manipulates Edgar, persuading him to run away.
- Re-read this section, with one partner reading Edmond's lines, pausing at the end of each line to allow the other person, as Edgar, to express his fears.

---

1 **severally** 分别
2 **Save thee** 上帝保佑你
3 **news abroad** 到处流传的消息
4 **whispered ones** 小道消息
5 **ear-kissing arguments** 交头接耳的议论
6 **pray you** 请问
7 **toward** 即将发生
8 **The better, best** 那再好不过了
9 **perforce** 务必，无论如何
10 **of a queasy question** 棘手，难办
11 **Intelligence** 信息，消息
12 **Upon his party** 站在他（康沃尔）这边
13 **Advise yourself** 您仔细考虑
14 **on't** = of it

Act 2 Scene 1
The Great Hall of Gloucester's castle, at night

Enter EDMOND *and* CURAN, *severally*[1]

EDMOND Save thee[2], Curan.
CURAN And you, sir. I have been with your father and given him notice that the Duke of Cornwall and Regan his duchess will be here with him this night.
EDMOND How comes that?
CURAN Nay, I know not. You have heard of the news abroad[3]? I mean the whispered ones[4], for they are yet but ear-kissing arguments[5].
EDMOND Not I; pray you[6], what are they?
CURAN Have you heard of no likely wars toward[7] 'twixt the Dukes of Cornwall and Albany?
EDMOND Not a word.
CURAN You may do then in time. Fare you well, sir. *Exit*
EDMOND The duke be here tonight! The better, best[8].
This weaves itself perforce[9] into my business.
My father hath set guard to take my brother,
And I have one thing of a queasy question[10]
Which I must act. Briefness and Fortune, work!
Brother, a word, descend; brother, I say!

Enter EDGAR

My father watches: O sir, fly this place.
Intelligence[11] is given where you are hid;
You have now the good advantage of the night.
Have you not spoken 'gainst the Duke of Cornwall?
He's coming hither, now i'th'night, i'th'haste,
And Regan with him. Have you nothing said
Upon his party[12] 'gainst the Duke of Albany?
Advise yourself[13].
EDGAR I am sure on't[14], not a word.

Edmond stages a mock skirmish with Edgar, and deliberately wounds himself. Edgar flees, and Gloucester sends servants to pursue him. Edmond lies about Edgar's wicked intentions towards him and his father.

剧情简介：爱德门和爱德格假装打斗，爱德门故意弄伤了自己。爱德格逃跑，格劳斯特命仆人去追。爱德门谎称爱德格要伤害他和父亲。

1 Shouts and whispers (in small groups)

Edmond hears his father coming and quickly devises a plan to pretend to fight Edgar. Edmond wants to disorientate his brother and to convince his father that Edgar is a dangerous traitor. In lines 28–36, Edmond intends some of his words to be heard by Edgar alone, and some by the guards and Gloucester. Edmond speaks other sections to himself (or perhaps to the audience).

- Explore different ways of speaking lines 28–36, with one person reading Edmond's words and the others representing possible 'hearers' for each line. For example, the person playing Edgar could raise their hand when they think a line is directed at them.
- Go through the lines again, but this time the people representing the 'hearers' speak the words addressed to them.

Themes 主题分析

Appearance and reality (in pairs)

Act 2 opened with references to rumour and all its dangerous deceits. By now, the audience is well aware of Edmond's duplicity (两面三刀) and Edgar's innocence.

a Look at lines 43–55. Find four examples of Edmond creating a convincing 'appearance' to disguise the 'reality' of the situation.

b Look out for more examples of characters and events that are deceitful or misinterpreted as the events of this act unfold.

1 In cunning 作为计策
2 quit you well 好好演
3 beget … endeavour 让人觉得我曾拼命反抗
4 conjuring the moon 召唤月神（即Hecate）
5 stand auspicious mistress 做佑护神
6 parricides 弑父者
7 bend 瞄准（比作射箭）
8 manifold 多方面，多种多样
9 in fine 总之
10 loathly opposite 极力反对
11 in fell motion 拼命一刺
12 charges home 直接对准
13 unprovided 毫无防护；手无寸铁
14 latched 抓住
15 best alarumed spirits 旺盛的斗志
16 ghasted 吓破胆

KING LEAR ACT 2 SCENE 1
李尔王

EDMOND   I hear my father coming. Pardon me,
In cunning¹, I must draw my sword upon you.
Draw, seem to defend yourself. Now, quit you well².   30
[*Shouting*] Yield! Come before my father! – Light ho, here! –
Fly, brother! – Torches, torches! – so, farewell.

Exit Edgar

Some blood drawn on me would beget opinion
Of my more fierce endeavour³.
[*Wounds his arm*]
                              I have seen drunkards
Do more than this in sport. Father, father!   35
Stop, stop! No help?

Enter GLOUCESTER, *and Servants with torches*

GLOUCESTER   Now, Edmond, where's the villain?
EDMOND   Here stood he in the dark, his sharp sword out,
Mumbling of wicked charms, conjuring the moon⁴
To stand auspicious mistress⁵.
GLOUCESTER   But where is he?
EDMOND   Look, sir, I bleed.
GLOUCESTER   Where is the villain, Edmond?   40
EDMOND   Fled this way, sir, when by no means he could –
GLOUCESTER   Pursue him, ho! Go after.

[*Exeunt Servants*]

                   'By no means' what?
EDMOND   Persuade me to the murder of your lordship,
But that I told him the revenging gods
'Gainst parricides⁶ did all the thunder bend⁷,   45
Spoke with how manifold⁸ and strong a bond
The child was bound to th'father; sir, in fine⁹,
Seeing how loathly opposite¹⁰ I stood
To his unnatural purpose, in fell motion¹¹
With his prepared sword he charges home¹²   50
My unprovided¹³ body, latched¹⁴ mine arm;
And when he saw my best alarumed spirits¹⁵
Bold in the quarrel's right, roused to th'encounter,
Or whether ghasted¹⁶ by the noise I made,
Full suddenly he fled.

Gloucester declares that Edgar must be caught and executed. Edmond continues to lie about Edgar. Convinced of Edgar's villainy, Gloucester plans to reward Edmond with his brother's inheritance.

剧情简介：格劳斯特说一定要逮住并处死爱德格。爱德门继续造爱德格的谣。格劳斯特深信爱德格为人险恶，打算把爱德格的继承权赏给爱德门。

1 Edmond begins his ascent (in pairs)

Edmond has already convinced his father of Edgar's villainy, backed up by his own apparent wounding. He has also delayed the search party long enough for Edgar to make his escape (Edmond is presumably uncertain that his story would withstand close scrutiny [推敲]). He now reports an alleged conversation with his brother that he hopes will stop Gloucester from brooding on his elder son, and instead consider making Edmond himself heir to his fortune. Edmond uses contemporary prejudice against bastard children to his own advantage.

a Take turns to read aloud lines 66–76, in which Edmond imitates his brother. Try a variety of styles: mocking, sincere, deliberately exaggerated, and so on. Which do you think will work best to persuade Gloucester? Why might Gloucester be willing to let Edmond's words go unquestioned?

b Parents and children – and other family members – can sometimes be blind to the truth because of strong emotions. Talk about the emotions Gloucester may be experiencing here.

c Together, look back at Act 1 Scene 1. What similarities and what differences can you find between Lear's behaviour in that scene and Gloucester's behaviour in the script opposite? Share your findings with other pairs.

1 dispatch 处死
2 arch and patron 大主公
3 stake 行刑场
4 He that conceals him, death 谁要是把他藏起来，死罪
5 pight 决心
6 discover 揭发
7 unpossessing 一无所有（私生子无继承权）
8 reposal 安置
9 faithed 可信
10 character 亲笔信
11 practice 阴谋诡计
12 thou ... world 你一定把世人都当成了笨蛋 (dullard: 笨蛋)
13 pregnant and potential spirits 强而有力的动机
14 Tucket 进军号
15 strange 违背人性；伤天害理
16 fastened 冥顽不化
17 natural 孝顺
18 capable 有继承权

Themes 主题分析

Naturally ...

Gloucester describes Edmond as 'Loyal and natural'. Ideas of 'nature' and what is 'natural' run through the play, and the words are used to cover a range of meanings. When Gloucester calls Edmond 'natural', he connects two of the themes of the play – appearance and reality and the natural order. There is also an element of wordplay here, as 'natural' was applied to children born outside marriage, like Edmond.

a Consider Gloucester's and Edmond's behaviour in this scene. Whose is 'natural' and whose is 'unnatural'? Who decides what is 'natural'?

b During the rest of this act, look out for references to 'nature', 'natural' and 'unnatural'. For each one, consider what the speaker means and whether their judgement is reliable. Record these uses in a table in your Director's Journal.

GLOUCESTER	Let him fly far,	55

Not in this land shall he remain uncaught;
And found, dispatch[1]. The noble duke my master,
My worthy arch and patron[2], comes tonight.
By his authority I will proclaim it,
That he which finds him shall deserve our thanks, 60
Bringing the murderous coward to the stake[3];
He that conceals him, death[4].

EDMOND When I dissuaded him from his intent
And found him pight[5] to do it, with cursed speech
I threatened to discover[6] him. He replied, 65
'Thou unpossessing[7] bastard, dost thou think,
If I would stand against thee, would the reposal[8]
Of any trust, virtue, or worth in thee
Make thy words faithed[9]? No; what I should deny
(As this I would, ay, though thou didst produce 70
My very character[10]) I'd turn it all
To thy suggestion, plot, and damnèd practice[11];
And thou must make a dullard of the world[12],
If they not thought the profits of my death
Were very pregnant and potential spirits[13] 75
To make thee seek it.'

Tucket[14] within

GLOUCESTER O strange[15] and fastened[16] villain!
Would he deny his letter, said he?
Hark, the duke's trumpets. I know not why he comes.
All ports I'll bar, the villain shall not 'scape;
The duke must grant me that. Besides, his picture 80
I will send far and near, that all the kingdom
May have due note of him; and of my land,
Loyal and natural[17] boy, I'll work the means
To make thee capable[18].

Regan blames Lear's ill-disciplined knights for encouraging Edgar to murder Gloucester. Cornwall praises Edmond's efforts in thwarting Edgar's plans, and takes Edmond into his service.

 剧情简介：蕊根责怪李尔的骑士粗野无礼，说他们教唆爱德格谋杀格劳斯特。康沃尔赞扬爱德门挫败了爱德格的阴谋，让爱德门为他效力。

Language in the play 剧中语言
Different people, different language (in pairs)

What characters say and how they say it often depends upon the status of the person they are addressing. After the Duke of Cornwall's arrival, the language of Gloucester and Edmond undergoes a significant change.

- Take parts as Edmond and Gloucester and speak lines 63–84, followed by Edmond's lines 96, 105 and 116–17 and Gloucester's lines 89, 92 and 95. Identify the contrasts between the way they speak before and after Cornwall and Regan enter.

1 Reading Regan

This is only the second scene in which Regan appears, and the first where the audience sees her without her older sister.

a Look closely at lines 90–1. Why do you think she uses the words 'my father' twice in such quick succession?

b In lines 93–4, Regan asks whether Edgar had kept company with her father's riotous knights. Why do you think she does so? Note that this information comes from Edmond – should we believe it?

Characters 人物分析
Cornwall assesses Edmond (in small groups)

Cornwall praises Edmond's dutiful service to his father ('childlike office'). He also acknowledges Edmond's 'virtue and obedience' and his possession of a nature of 'deep trust'. All three of Cornwall's assessments are dangerously mistaken. This is an example of **dramatic irony** (戏剧反讽) – when the audience knows more than the characters. In your groups, discuss the following:

- How do you think Edmond feels, hearing such unmerited praise from this powerful man?
- Consider each of Cornwall's judgements in turn. How could the words be altered to provide an accurate assessment of Edmond's character?
- What judgements can you make about Cornwall, given his behaviour in this scene and his comments about Edmond?

1 How dost = How are you
2 tended upon 侍奉
3 of that consort 那一伙的
4 ill affected 受到不良影响
5 put him on 教唆他
6 sojourn 逗留，暂住
7 child-like office 孩子般的孝心
8 bewray 揭发，揭露
9 strength 权力及资源
10 seize on 合法占有（法律用语；这里指让爱德门任公职为其服务）

Enter CORNWALL, REGAN, *and Attendants*

CORNWALL How now, my noble friend, since I came hither, 85
Which I can call but now, I have heard strange news.
REGAN If it be true, all vengeance comes too short
Which can pursue th'offender. How dost[1], my lord?
GLOUCESTER O madam, my old heart is cracked, it's cracked.
REGAN What, did my father's godson seek your life? 90
He whom my father named, your Edgar?
GLOUCESTER O lady, lady, shame would have it hid.
REGAN Was he not companion with the riotous knights
That tended upon[2] my father?
GLOUCESTER I know not, madam; 'tis too bad, too bad. 95
EDMOND Yes, madam, he was of that consort[3].
REGAN No marvel, then, though he were ill affected[4].
'Tis they have put him on[5] the old man's death,
To have th'expense and waste of his revenues.
I have this present evening from my sister 100
Been well informed of them, and with such cautions,
That if they come to sojourn[6] at my house,
I'll not be there.
CORNWALL   Nor I, assure thee, Regan.
Edmond, I hear that you have shown your father
A child-like office[7].
EDMOND   It was my duty, sir. 105
GLOUCESTER He did bewray[8] his practice, and received
This hurt you see, striving to apprehend him.
CORNWALL Is he pursued?
GLOUCESTER Ay, my good lord.
CORNWALL If he be taken, he shall never more 110
Be feared of doing harm. Make your own purpose
How in my strength[9] you please. For you, Edmond,
Whose virtue and obedience doth this instant
So much commend itself, you shall be ours;
Natures of such deep trust we shall much need; 115
You we first seize on[10].
EDMOND   I shall serve you, sir,
Truly, however else.
GLOUCESTER   For him I thank your grace.
CORNWALL You know not why we came to visit you?

Regan speaks of her hazardous night journey. She tells Gloucester that she urgently needs his advice. In Scene 2, Kent, in disguise, picks a quarrel with Oswald by insulting him.

 剧情简介：蕊根说她冒险摸黑来访，是迫切需要格劳斯特为她出主意。在第二场中，乔装改扮的肯特辱骂奥兹沃尔，挑起了一场争斗。

1 Insulting Oswald (in large groups)

Kent and Oswald were both sent to deliver letters to Regan – Kent by the king and Oswald by Gonerill. In lines 124–5, Regan refers to the messengers awaiting replies, so they have presumably followed her to Gloucester's castle at her request.

In Act 2 Scene 2, lines 13–21, Kent mounts a passionate attack on Oswald. His language bristles with energetic, extravagant and inventive insults. On stage, the actor playing Kent sometimes makes a point of delivering these lines at great speed, without drawing breath.

- One person plays Oswald (a volunteer only). The other group members stand in a circle around Oswald, and take turns to speak as Kent. Change the speaker at each punctuation mark. Keep pauses between speakers to a minimum.
- Decide in your group whether to make Kent grow increasingly angry or to make him sound icily calm, as if he is merely making a factual analysis of Oswald's character.
- Repeat the activity, with each Kent adding movement and gesture to their insult, without slowing down the pace.
- Experiment to find out how Oswald's body language can add to the impact of the scene. Afterwards, discuss why he does not interrupt Kent during this verbal attack.

Characters 人物分析

Understanding Oswald (in pairs)

Oswald is Gonerill's steward – the manager of her household and a man with a senior and responsible role. He would therefore be comfortable in the company of the aristocrats he serves.

- It is easy to go along with Kent's attitude to Oswald, but review carefully what you know of Oswald so far. What does his behaviour in Act 1 Scene 4 and in this scene tell you? Be scrupulously (审慎) fair to Oswald.
- Now look at Kent's insults in lines 13–21 and decide which ones are justified by the evidence you have collected and which are exaggerated.
- What is your impression of Kent at this point in the play? What might be his motivation here?

---

1 **threading dark-eyed night** 摸黑来到
2 **prize** 重要性
3 **answer from our home** 回答说不在家
4 **attend dispatch** 等着（带着回复）上路
5 **craves the instant use** 要求立刻采取行动
6 **I'th'mire** 在烂泥里
7 **Lipsbury pinfold** 双唇布瑞镇的牲口栏（Lipsbury是个臆造的镇名）
8 **use** 对待
9 **broken meats** 残羹剩菜
10 **three-suited, hundred-pound** 身穿三件套，年薪一百镑（一百镑在当时是 笔不小的财产，一般仆人的全部家当也不及这个数）
11 **worsted-stocking** 羊毛袜（仆人所穿；上流社会流行穿丝袜）
12 **lily-livered** 胆小鬼（字面意思是"百合肝"，当时人们认为胆小是由于肝缺血，没有血色的肝跟百合一样白）
13 **action-taking** 只会告状（挨了打也不敢反抗）
14 **glass-gazing** 爱照镜子；顾盼自雄
15 **superserviceable** 超级殷勤
16 **finical** 爱挑剔，吹毛求疵
17 **one-trunk-inheriting** 仅够装一个衣箱的继承财产
18 **bawd** 鸨母
19 **pander** 拉皮条的
20 **addition** 称号

REGAN	Thus out of season, threading dark-eyed night[1]?
	Occasions, noble Gloucester, of some prize[2], 120
	Wherein we must have use of your advice.
	Our father he hath writ, so hath our sister,
	Of differences, which I best thought it fit
	To answer from our home[3]. The several messengers
	From hence attend dispatch[4]. Our good old friend, 125
	Lay comforts to your bosom and bestow
	Your needful counsel to our businesses,
	Which craves the instant use[5].
GLOUCESTER	 I serve you, madam;
	Your graces are right welcome. *Exeunt. Flourish*

Act 2 Scene 2
The entrance to Gloucester's castle

Enter KENT *(disguised) and* OSWALD, *severally*

OSWALD	Good dawning to thee, friend. Art of this house?
KENT	Ay.
OSWALD	Where may we set our horses?
KENT	I'th'mire[6].
OSWALD	Prithee, if thou lov'st me, tell me. 5
KENT	I love thee not.
OSWALD	Why, then I care not for thee.
KENT	If I had thee in Lipsbury pinfold[7], I would make thee care for me.
OSWALD	Why dost thou use[8] me thus? I know thee not. 10
KENT	Fellow, I know thee.
OSWALD	What dost thou know me for?
KENT	A knave, a rascal, an eater of broken meats[9], a base, proud, shallow, beggarly, three-suited, hundred-pound[10], filthy worsted-stocking[11] knave; a lily-livered[12], action-taking[13], whoreson glass-gazing[14], superserviceable[15], finical[16] rogue; one-trunk-inheriting[17] slave; one that wouldst be a bawd[18] in way of good service, and art nothing but the composition of a knave, beggar, coward, pander[19], and the son and heir of a mongrel bitch, one whom I will beat into clamorous whining if thou deniest the least 20
	syllable of thy addition[20].

Kent insults Oswald again, and draws his sword. Oswald calls for help. Kent threatens Edmond, and Cornwall demands an explanation. Kent further insults Oswald, who seizes the chance to get his own back.

剧情简介：肯特再次辱骂奥兹沃尔，并拔出剑；奥兹沃尔呼救。肯特威胁爱德门，康沃尔要求他们解释为何如此。肯特继续侮辱奥兹沃尔，奥兹沃尔抓住机会报复。

Stagecraft 导演技巧

Kent versus Oswald (in pairs)

The exchanges between Kent and Oswald are often presented as very comic, but stage-fighting needs a great deal of planning to make it appear spontaneous in performance, and to ensure it is safe.

a In your pairs, work out what advice you would give to the actors in lines 22–37. Read the lines and decide between you:
- how Oswald responds to Kent drawing his sword (line 28)
- how Oswald responds to Kent's threats (lines 30, 35 and 37)
- whether or not Oswald feels in real danger
- at what point Oswald recognises Kent as the man who previously assaulted him
- the effect of Cornwall's entrance on the combatants.

b By line 42, Cornwall has forced Kent and Oswald to stop fighting. He then tries to find out what happened, but is baffled by Kent's lively vocabulary and elaborate insults. Oswald revives and tries to explain the argument, but he gets little opportunity to develop his story before Kent launches into a further tirade (长篇大论).
- Make notes in your Director's Journal describing how you would want the exchanges between Cornwall, Kent and Oswald to take place to highlight Cornwall's confusion.

1 rail on   辱骂
2 brazen-faced varlet   厚颜无耻的恶棍
3 make … you   叫您变成一片浸了水的白面包（即"打得您爬不起来"）
4 cullionly   泼皮一样的
5 barber-monger   理发店常客；油头粉面的家伙（纨绔子弟）
6 Vanity the puppet's part   "虚荣"这一傀儡角色（中世纪道德剧中一般有"虚荣"这一女性角色；这里是对高娜瑞尔的蔑称）
7 carbonado your shanks   把您的小腿划烂（准备烧烤）
8 neat   整整齐齐，人模狗样
9 goodman boy   浑小子
10 I'll flesh ye   我先给你比画两下（侮辱对方不知道怎么打斗）
11 so bestirred your valour   您的斗志如此昂扬
12 disclaims in thee   与你撇清关系
13 a tailor made thee   裁缝造的你（继续讽刺他人模狗样的打扮）
14 at suit of   看在……的分儿上

▶ Often the actor playing Kent is bearded in Act 1 but reappears as a clean-shaven 'Caius'. One production showed him with elaborate facial tattoos to conceal his appearance.

66

OSWALD   Why, what a monstrous fellow art thou, thus to rail on[1] one that is neither known of thee nor knows thee!

KENT   What a brazen-faced varlet[2] art thou to deny thou knowest me! Is it two days since I tripped up thy heels and beat thee before the king? Draw, you rogue! For though it be night, yet the moon shines. I'll make a sop o'th'moonshine of you[3], [*Drawing his sword*] you whoreson cullionly[4] barber-monger[5], draw!

OSWALD   Away, I have nothing to do with thee.

KENT   Draw, you rascal. You come with letters against the king, and take Vanity the puppet's part[6] against the royalty of her father. Draw, you rogue, or I'll so carbonado your shanks[7] – draw, you rascal, come your ways!

OSWALD   Help, ho, murder, help!

KENT   Strike, you slave! Stand, rogue! Stand, you neat[8] slave, strike!

OSWALD   Help, ho, murder, murder!

Enter EDMOND, CORNWALL, REGAN, GLOUCESTER, *Servants*

EDMOND   How now, what's the matter? Part!

KENT   With you, goodman boy[9], if you please; come, I'll flesh ye[10]; come on, young master.

GLOUCESTER   Weapons? Arms? What's the matter here?

CORNWALL   Keep peace, upon your lives; he dies that strikes again. What is the matter?

REGAN   The messengers from our sister and the king?

CORNWALL   What is your difference – speak!

OSWALD   I am scarce in breath, my lord.

KENT   No marvel, you have so bestirred your valour[11], you cowardly rascal. Nature disclaims in thee[12]: a tailor made thee[13].

CORNWALL   Thou art a strange fellow – a tailor make a man?

KENT   A tailor, sir, a stone-cutter, or a painter could not have made him so ill, though they had been but two years o'th'trade.

CORNWALL   Speak yet, how grew your quarrel?

OSWALD   This ancient ruffian, sir, whose life I have spared at suit of[14] his grey beard –

Kent is enraged by Oswald's lie, and attacks the sycophantic, dishonest nature of great men's servants. Kent says that he dislikes Oswald's face, then insults Cornwall, Regan and the others.

 剧情简介：肯特被奥兹沃尔的谎言激怒，抨击王公贵族的侍从们谄媚、欺诈的本性，说自己厌恶奥兹沃尔这副嘴脸，然后又骂了康沃尔、蕊根和其他人一通。

1 No time for flatterers (in pairs)

Kent claims that his anger against Oswald comes from a loathing of flattery and insincerity. He attacks the dishonesty of such 'smiling rogues', saying that they are villains who undermine marriages and families. Oswald is a flatterer who follows the moods of his master, inflaming his passions ('Being oil to fire') or feeding his melancholy ('colder moods') with further depression. A flatterer is like a kingfisher (翠鸟) ('halcyon'), which was reputed to have a beak that always pointed in the direction of the wind. Kent ends with an assault on Oswald's inane smiling (傻笑) ('epileptic visage'), which may be a hint to the actor playing Oswald to try to look unconvincingly relaxed when he is really terrified.

a What connections can you make between Kent's remarks on flatterers and the events that have taken place so far?

b Discuss how Kent's attitude links with the theme of appearance versus reality in the play.

c There have been many attempts to explain the lines about Camelot and cackling geese, but their meaning remains uncertain. What do you think Shakespeare meant by these lines?

Stagecraft 导演技巧

''tis my occupation to be plain' (in fours)

Kent says that he despises Oswald for his looks. Cornwall questions the validity of such a judgement, and Kent then widens his criticism, saying that he has a poor opinion of the looks of everyone standing before him. On stage, this moment can be both amusing and very dramatic, as the 'noble' characters take in the meaning of Kent's insult.

a Take parts as Cornwall, Regan, Edmond and Gloucester. Experiment with different reactions to Kent's lines 82–5 for each character. When you have chosen your favourites, present a tableau for the rest of the class to comment on.

b Talk together about whether you think Kent is needlessly exposing himself to danger by insulting the nobles in this way. Is he making an important point about his plain-speaking personality or about their vanity?

1 **zed** 人渣（字母表里最后一个字母Z；拉丁文里没有这个字母，莎士比亚时代的英文也很少用这个字母，喻指无足轻重的人）
2 **leave** 许可，同意
3 **unbolted** 没有门闩的（缺乏男子气）
4 **jakes** 厕所，茅房
5 **wagtail** 摇尾巴的鹡鸰（行进时尾巴上下摆动）
6 **holy cords** 神圣的纽带（维系婚姻和亲情）
7 **a-twain** = into two（断为两截）
8 **too intrince t'unloose** 结为一体，牢不可破
9 **smooth** 放纵，纵容
10 **in ... rebel** 根据其老爷的喜怒好恶
11 **Renege** 否认
12 **halcyon beaks** 翠鸟的喙（当时人们相信把这种鸟死后倒挂起来，其喙就会迎风转向；这里喻指望风使舵的小人）
13 **gall and vary** 风向转变（gall = gale，这里用了重言法）
14 **naught** = nothing
15 **epileptic** 发羊痫风
16 **Smile** 笑话
17 **Goose ... Camelot** 笨鹅，我要是在塞润平原上遇上您，就会把您撵得嘎嘎叫着回到堪穆崂（Sarum是英国索尔兹伯里市 [Salisbury] 的旧称，塞润平原在温彻斯特市 [Winchester] 附近，英语中"温彻斯特鹅 [Winchester goose]"是妓女的别称；Camelot是传说中亚瑟王 [King Arthur] 的城堡）
18 **antipathy** 反感，厌恶
19 **His countenance likes me not** 我不喜欢他那张脸
20 **perchance** = perhaps

KENT   Thou whoreson zed[1], thou unnecessary letter! My lord, if you   55
                will give me leave[2], I will tread this unbolted[3] villain into mortar
                and daub the wall of a jakes[4] with him. Spare my grey beard,
                you wagtail[5]?
CORNWALL   Peace, sirrah.
                You beastly knave, know you no reverence?   60
KENT   Yes, sir, but anger hath a privilege.
CORNWALL   Why art thou angry?
KENT   That such a slave as this should wear a sword,
                Who wears no honesty. Such smiling rogues as these,
                Like rats, oft bite the holy cords[6] a-twain[7],   65
                Which are too intrince t'unloose[8]; smooth[9] every passion
                That in the natures of their lords rebel[10],
                Being oil to fire, snow to the colder moods,
                Renege[11], affirm, and turn their halcyon beaks[12]
                With every gall and vary[13] of their masters,   70
                Knowing naught[14], like dogs, but following.
                A plague upon your epileptic[15] visage!
                Smile[16] you my speeches, as I were a fool?
                Goose, if I had you upon Sarum Plain,
                I'd drive ye cackling home to Camelot[17].   75
CORNWALL   What, art thou mad, old fellow?
GLOUCESTER   How fell you out? Say that.
KENT   No contraries hold more antipathy[18]
                Than I and such a knave.
CORNWALL   Why dost thou call him knave?
                What is his fault?
KENT   His countenance likes me not[19].   80
CORNWALL   No more perchance[20] does mine, nor his, nor hers.
KENT   Sir, 'tis my occupation to be plain.
                I have seen better faces in my time
                Than stands on any shoulder that I see
                Before me at this instant.

Cornwall criticises Kent's blunt speaking. Kent uses exaggerated, courteous language, then claims truth in bluntness. Oswald lists Kent's actions against him. Cornwall decides to punish Kent in the stocks.

剧情简介：康沃尔攻击肯特说话粗鲁，肯特于是改用浮夸而彬彬有礼的语言，然后又声称粗鲁的话里有真理。奥兹沃尔历数肯特对他的种种攻击。为惩罚肯特，康沃尔决定把他铐在足枷上示众。

1 Blunt language, false language (in pairs)

Cornwall says that Kent pretends to be rough and rude well in excess of his true character. The duke mocks such plain speaking. He suspects that Kent's bluntness is a mask, concealing more evil intentions than any number of flattering, anxious-to-please attendants.

In lines 95–8, Kent deliberately mocks the insincere, deceitful language of false flatterers. He uses pompous terms that parody (戏仿) polite speech. In lines 99–102, however, he reverts to his customary plain manner of speaking, and uses prose (散文；散体) instead of verse (韵文；诗体).

a Speak both sets of Kent's lines, making the contrast between them as pronounced as you can by altering his tone and accent.

b Talk about possible reasons for the switch from poetry to prose here.

Write about it 写作练习

Cornwall's justice

- Write a description of the events from Cornwall's entrance at line 38 up to his order at line 114, from the point of view of a flattering courtier, eager to please his master, who will make everything he says cast Cornwall in the best possible light. (You may feel that Oswald fits this description but do not write from his point of view – he is too involved in the events.)
- This piece of writing does not need to be very long, but it should be very, very flattering. Remember, Cornwall has said he trusts flatterers more than people who claim to be 'honest' and 'plain'.

2 Ajax – the final insult?

Kent's reference to Ajax may be what finally triggers Cornwall's anger, leading to his decision to put Kent in the stocks. Ajax was a mythological Greek warrior, and the line may mean 'Such cowards manage to make fools of heroes'. However, the reference is also a pun on a 'jakes', meaning toilet – a word used by Kent earlier in this scene.

- Some actors deliver the line as a direct insult; others say it as an aside that Kent did not really mean to be heard. Which style would you choose? Can you suggest another way to say this line?

---

1 **saucy roughness** 粗鲁无礼
2 **constrains ... nature** 强装一副有违本性的样子（garb: 装扮）
3 **more corrupter ends** 更变态的目的（用双重比较级和最高级表示强调的用法在莎士比亚时代很常见）
4 **silly-ducking observants** 傻乎乎点头哈腰的奴才
5 **stretch their duties nicely** 尽心竭力地侍奉
6 **in sincere verity** 精诚相待（与前面的in good faith同义，这里故意说话矫揉造作）
7 **Under ... aspect** 有您伟大容颜的容许（这是在模仿阿谀的口吻）
8 **Phoebus' front** 福玻斯的前额（Phoebus是罗马神话中太阳神阿波罗的别名，意思是"光明"，这里指太阳）
9 **dialect** 说话方式
10 **beguiled** 蒙骗
11 **plain knave** 纯粹的奴才
12 **though ... to't** 哪怕您要我当而我不当会惹您不高兴
13 **very late** 最近
14 **misconstruction** 误解，误会
15 **compact** 与……一伙
16 **deal of man** 爷们儿气概
17 **For ... self-subdued** 因为他打一个自我克制不还手的人
18 **fleshment** 初战告捷的兴奋

CORNWALL	This is some fellow	85

                Who, having been praised for bluntness, doth affect
                A saucy roughness[1], and constrains the garb
                Quite from his nature[2]. He cannot flatter, he;
                An honest mind and plain, he must speak truth.
                And they will take it, so; if not, he's plain.   90
                These kind of knaves I know, which in this plainness
                Harbour more craft and more corrupter ends[3]
                Than twenty silly-ducking observants[4]
                That stretch their duties nicely[5].

KENT   Sir, in good faith, in sincere verity[6],   95
                Under th'allowance of your great aspect[7],
                Whose influence like the wreath of radiant fire
                On flick'ring Phoebus' front[8] –

CORNWALL   What mean'st by this?

KENT   To go out of my dialect[9], which you discommend so much. I know, sir, I am no flatterer. He that beguiled[10] you in a plain accent was a plain knave[11], which for my part I will not be, though I should win your displeasure to entreat me to't[12].   100

CORNWALL   What was th'offence you gave him?

OSWALD   I never gave him any.
                It pleased the king his master very late[13]   105
                To strike at me upon his misconstruction[14],
                When he, compact[15], and flattering his displeasure,
                Tripped me behind; being down, insulted, railed,
                And put upon him such a deal of man[16]
                That worthied him, got praises of the king   110
                For him attempting who was self-subdued[17],
                And in the fleshment[18] of this dread exploit
                Drew on me here again.

KENT   None of these rogues and cowards
                But Ajax is their fool.

CORNWALL   Fetch forth the stocks!
                You stubborn, ancient knave, you reverend braggart,   115
                We'll teach you.

1 An explanation of the stocks

Cornwall insists that Kent should be put in the stocks as punishment. Kent objects, saying that as the king's messenger he deserves more respect. The lines below, taken from the Quarto edition (see p. 244), explain in more detail why Gloucester is worried and feels the punishment is not appropriate.

> His fault is much, and the good King his master
> Will check him for't. Your purpos'd low correction (下三烂的惩罚)
> Is such as basest and contemned'st wretches
> For pilf'rings (小偷小摸) and most common trespasses
> Are punish'd with.
>
> (basest = lowest, trespasses = minor offences)

- As a director, would you want to include these lines in your production, to help explain to a modern audience the fact that the stocks were for minor offences and a humiliating punishment? Or would you leave out these lines as unnecessary to the progression of the storyline? Write your decision and your reasons for it in your Director's Journal.

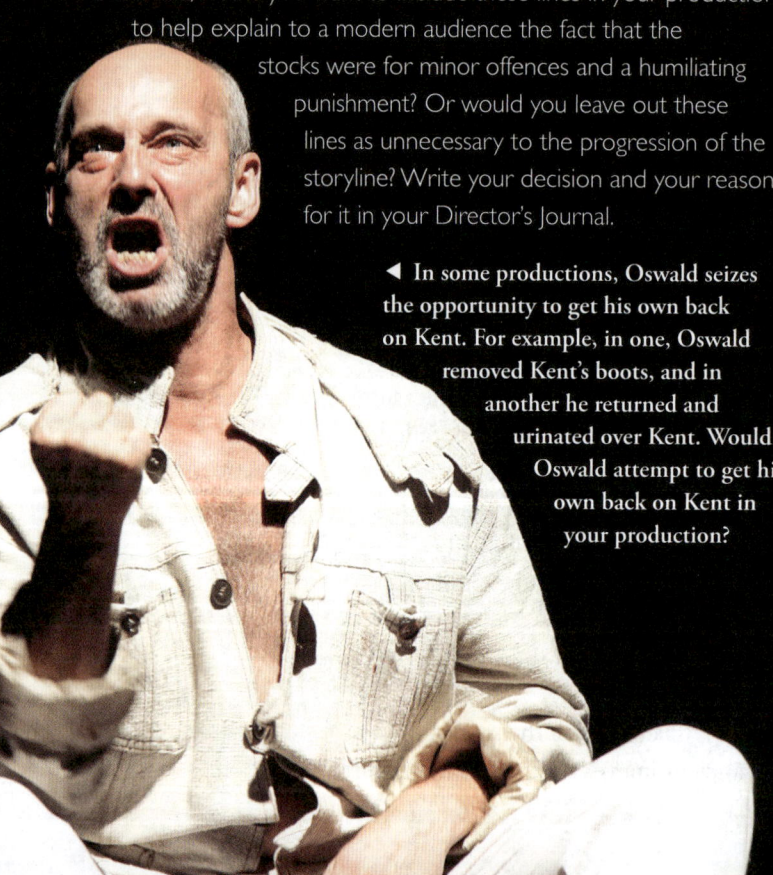

◀ In some productions, Oswald seizes the opportunity to get his own back on Kent. For example, in one, Oswald removed Kent's boots, and in another he returned and urinated over Kent. Would Oswald attempt to get his own back on Kent in your production?

1. **do small respect** 不给什么面子
2. **grace and person** 君王颜面以及做人的尊严
3. **selfsame colour** 同一种性格或德行
4. **bring away** 快拿来
5. **slightly valued** 轻视，蔑视
6. **rubbed** 受阻，受挫
7. **entreat** 央求
8. **watched** 没合眼
9. **A good … heels** 一个好人的运气说不定会从脚后跟长出来（**out at heels**原义为"鞋跟穿破"，表示境遇潦倒；肯特此时被锁在足枷上，是一种自我调侃的说法）
10. **Give you good morrow =** May God give you a good morning

KENT	Sir, I am too old to learn:
	Call not your stocks for me. I serve the king,
	On whose employment I was sent to you.
	You shall do small respects¹, show too bold malice
	Against the grace and person² of my master,
	Stocking his messenger.
CORNWALL	Fetch forth the stocks!
	As I have life and honour, there shall he sit till noon.
REGAN	Till noon? Till night, my lord, and all night too.
KENT	Why, madam, if I were your father's dog,
	You should not use me so.
REGAN	Sir, being his knave, I will.

Stocks brought out

CORNWALL	This is a fellow of the selfsame colour³
	Our sister speaks of. Come, bring away⁴ the stocks.
GLOUCESTER	Let me beseech your grace not to do so.
	The king his master needs must take it ill
	That he, so slightly valued⁵ in his messenger,
	Should have him thus restrained.
CORNWALL	I'll answer that.
REGAN	My sister may receive it much more worse
	To have her gentleman abused, assaulted.

[*Kent is put in the stocks*]

CORNWALL	Come, my lord, away.

[*Exeunt all but Gloucester and Kent*]

GLOUCESTER	I am sorry for thee, friend; 'tis the duke's pleasure,
	Whose disposition all the world well knows
	Will not be rubbed⁶ nor stopped. I'll entreat⁷ for thee.
KENT	Pray do not, sir. I have watched⁸ and travelled hard.
	Some time I shall sleep out, the rest I'll whistle.
	A good man's fortune may grow out at heels⁹.
	Give you good morrow¹⁰.
GLOUCESTER	The duke's to blame in this; 'twill be ill taken. *Exit*

Line numbers: 120, 125, 130, 135, 140

In the stocks Kent reads a letter from Cordelia in which she promises to right all wrongs. Wearied, he sleeps. In Scene 3, Edgar plans to disguise himself as a mad beggar in an attempt to escape capture.

  剧情简介：肯特被铐在足枷里，读一封考蒂丽叶写给他的信，信中考蒂丽叶承诺要纠正一切错误。肯特筋疲力尽，睡着了。在第三场中，爱德格打算扮成一个疯癫的乞丐，试图逃避追捕。

1 Cordelia's letter

Kent reads a letter he has received from Cordelia. She has been informed of Kent's disguise and of his actions, and tells him she hopes to restore order to the country. This is one of many letters in the play. They help characters keep up with events occurring at a distance. They also offer opportunities for deception.

- Write Cordelia's letter.

Stagecraft 导演技巧

Kent in the stocks

At the Globe Theatre in Shakespeare's day, Kent would have remained on stage in the stocks while Edgar disguised himself to escape capture by his pursuers. Today, directors can use lighting to make Kent very unobtrusive (不引人注目).

- How would you present Kent in a production of your own? Would you make him virtually invisible or keep him in plain sight, showing the two men together on stage – both unjustly cast out and in disguise?

2 Edgar as Tom o'Bedlam

In Shakespeare's time, some mentally ill people were sent to Bethlem Royal Hospital ('Bedlam') in London. When they were discharged, if unable to make a living, they might take up begging on the streets and wandering the countryside, often sticking sharp objects into their flesh, either as a result of their illness or in order to attract attention and charity. Such beggars were given the generic name 'Tom o'Bedlam', having either lost any clear sense of their own identity or being regarded as dehumanised and, therefore, not worthy of an individual name.

Edgar plans to reduce himself to an almost animal-like existence, tangling his hair and wearing only a loin-cloth (缠腰布，遮羞布). In some productions, he removes his clothes and covers himself with filth as he talks.

a How would you stage lines 1–21 to highlight the ways in which Edgar plans to adopt a new personality?

b Edgar is assuming a new identity. His 'Poor Turlygod!' (line 20) is his first attempt at using the nonsensical language of a mad beggar. How might an actor playing Edgar use voice and actions to emphasise the theme of appearance and reality here?

---

1 saw = saying（成语）
2 Thou … sun 刚脱离天恩，又晒到艳阳
3 beacon 灯塔（指早晨的太阳）
4 Nothing … misery 只有苦难中才能遇见奇迹
5 obscurèd course 乔装的现状
6 enormous state 恶劣的境地
7 give / Losses their remedies 把损失弥补回来
8 o'er-watched 极其困乏
9 Take vantage 抓住机会
10 turn thy wheel 转动你的轮子（在对命运女神 [Fortune] 的描述中，她转动手中命运之轮，司掌人的生老病死和吉凶苦乐）
11 proclaimed 被通缉
12 happy hollow 恰好遇见的洞
13 vigilance 警戒
14 attend my taking 随时准备缉拿我
15 bethought 决心
16 penury in contempt of man 贬低或羞辱人的贫困
17 Blanket my loins 用毯子裹腰（遮羞）
18 elf 缠绕
19 presented 暴露，展示
20 outface 勇敢面对
21 proof and precedent 证据和例证
22 numbed and mortifièd 麻木无知觉
23 sprigs 嫩枝

King Lear Act 2 Scene 3
李尔王

KENT Good king, that must approve the common saw[1],
Thou out of heaven's benediction com'st
To the warm sun[2].   145
Approach, thou beacon[3] to this under globe,
That by thy comfortable beams I may
Peruse this letter. Nothing almost sees miracles
But misery[4]. I know 'tis from Cordelia,
Who hath most fortunately been informed   150
Of my obscurèd course[5], and shall find time
For this enormous state[6], seeking to give
Losses their remedies[7]. All weary and o'er-watched[8],
Take vantage[9], heavy eyes, not to behold
This shameful lodging. Fortune, goodnight,   155
Smile once more, turn thy wheel[10]. [*He sleeps*]

Act 2 Scene 3
Open countryside near Gloucester's castle

Enter EDGAR

EDGAR I heard myself proclaimed[11],
And by the happy hollow[12] of a tree
Escaped the hunt. No port is free, no place
That guard and most unusual vigilance[13]
Does not attend my taking[14]. Whiles I may 'scape   5
I will preserve myself, and am bethought[15]
To take the basest and most poorest shape
That ever penury in contempt of man[16]
Brought near to beast. My face I'll grime with filth,
Blanket my loins[17], elf[18] all my hairs in knots,   10
And with presented[19] nakedness outface[20]
The winds and persecutions of the sky.
The country gives me proof and precedent[21]
Of Bedlam beggars, who with roaring voices
Strike in their numbed and mortified[22] arms,   15
Pins, wooden pricks, nails, sprigs[23] of rosemary;

Lear wonders why Cornwall and Regan were not at home to receive him. Seeing Kent in the stocks, the Fool mocks him, but Lear refuses to believe that Cornwall and Regan were responsible for such punishment.

剧情简介：李尔想知道康沃尔和蕊根为何没在府中迎接自己。俳优看见肯特戴着枷锁，于是对他冷嘲热讽，但是李尔不相信康沃尔和蕊根会如此惩罚肯特。

'Edgar I nothing am' says Edgar as he conceals his identity in his disguise as Poor Tom. The word 'nothing' has been spoken at least ten times in the play so far. Find these references and talk in pairs about possible connections and contrasts.

1 pelting 微不足道
2 lunatic bans 疯狂的咒骂
3 Enforce their charity 逼人施舍
4 Poor Turlygod! 可怜的好人！（Turlygod的意思从未得到令人信服的解释，这里根据上下文译出）
5 remove 改换住处
6 Mak'st … pastime? 你受此羞辱还开玩笑？
7 garters 袜带（指足枷）
8 overlusty at legs 腿脚的欲望太强
9 nether-stocks 短袜
10 place 官职；身份
11 son = son-in-law
12 Juno 朱诺（罗马神话里的天后，朱庇特之妻）

1 The king's entrance (in threes)

In contrast to his arrival in Act 1 Scene 1, where the whole court assembled and there was a fanfare and solemn ceremonial behaviour, Lear enters now accompanied only by one Gentleman and the Fool. Initially, he seems distracted by thoughts of Regan's absence from home, but then he discovers his messenger in the stocks.

a Take parts as Lear, the Fool and Kent, and read lines 4–19. Experiment with ways of delivering these lines, first to suggest that the Fool and Kent are trying to play things down so as not to worry Lear, and then as though they are being deliberately blunt and direct, to force him to acknowledge how insulting it is to put his messenger in the stocks. Which way of delivering the lines seems to be most effective?

b Talk together about Lear's state of mind and what Kent and the Fool might be feeling about their master's situation.

And with this horrible object, from low farms,
Poor pelting[1] villages, sheep-cotes, and mills,
Sometimes with lunatic bans[2], sometime with prayers,
Enforce their charity[3]. 'Poor Turlygod![4] Poor Tom!' 20
That's something yet: Edgar I nothing am.   *Exit*

Act 2 Scene 4
The entrance to Gloucester's castle

Enter LEAR, FOOL, *and* GENTLEMAN

LEAR 'Tis strange that they should so depart from home
And not send back my messenger.

GENTLEMAN   As I learned,
The night before there was no purpose in them
Of this remove[5].

KENT [*Waking*] Hail to thee, noble master.

LEAR Ha! 5
Mak'st thou this shame thy pastime?[6]

KENT   No, my lord.

FOOL Ha, ha, he wears cruel garters[7]. Horses are tied by the heads, dogs and bears by th'neck, monkeys by th'loins, and men by th'legs: when a man's overlusty at legs[8], then he wears wooden nether-stocks[9]. 10

LEAR What's he that hath so much thy place[10] mistook
To set thee here?

KENT   It is both he and she,
Your son[11] and daughter.

LEAR No.

KENT Yes. 15

LEAR No, I say.

KENT I say, yea.

LEAR By Jupiter, I swear no.

KENT By Juno[12], I swear ay.

Lear, angered by Kent's punishment, asks him to explain. Kent describes his cold reception and his recent clash with Oswald. The Fool speaks ominously of fortune favouring the wealthy.

 剧情简介：李尔因肯特受罚而大发雷霆，要肯特解释是怎么回事。肯特描述他受到的冷遇和他最近与奥兹沃尔的冲突。俳优语出不祥，说运气更喜欢有钱人。

Write about it 写作练习

Kent tells his story

Kent describes the events leading up to his punishment in the stocks. The audience learns new information about his reception at Regan and Cornwall's castle. Kent also admits that his reaction to Oswald was a result of 'Having more man than wit about me'. Lear allows Kent to speak at length with no interruption, but he is clearly becoming increasingly angry and distressed, leading to an outburst at lines 52–5.

- Imagine you are Lear and write an account of your feelings. Begin with your arrival at Gloucester's castle, and focus on how your feelings change as you discover Kent in the stocks and hear his account of events. You could write this in a stream-of-consciousness (意识流) style, beginning: 'All bones aching. Lights, servants. Gloucester's castle. Where is Regan?', or in a style more like a diary entry, beginning: 'By the time we drew near Gloucester's castle, I was exhausted and melancholy …'

1 Resolve me 跟我说清楚
2 modest haste 尽量简洁
3 Coming from us 朕派来的人
4 commend 递呈
5 reeking post 汗流浃背的信使
6 panting forth 气喘吁吁上前
7 spite of intermission 尽管打断了我
8 On those contents 读完信的内容
9 meiny 随从，扈从
10 Displayed so saucily 表现得如此无礼
11 Having more man than wit 有勇无智
12 trespass 罪过
13 Winter's … way 假如大雁还往那边飞，冬天仍没有过去（暗指还有更多麻烦）
14 bear bags 带着钱袋子（意思是"有钱"）
15 arrant 十足；坏透
16 dolours 悲伤（与dollars［银币］谐音）
17 tell 算清，数清

At this point in the play, Lear has to deal with the fact that he can no longer command unquestioning obedience. Would you advise an actor to rage or to seem subdued and baffled?

LEAR   They durst not do't:
They could not, would not do't. 'Tis worse than murder, 20
To do upon respect such violent outrage.
Resolve me[1] with all modest haste[2] which way
Thou mightst deserve or they impose this usage,
Coming from us[3].

KENT   My lord, when at their home
I did commend[4] your highness' letters to them, 25
Ere I was risen from the place that showed
My duty kneeling, came there a reeking post[5],
Stewed in his haste, half breathless, panting forth[6]
From Gonerill, his mistress, salutations;
Delivered letters spite of intermission[7], 30
Which presently they read. On those contents[8]
They summoned up their meiny[9], straight took horse,
Commanded me to follow and attend
The leisure of their answer, gave me cold looks;
And meeting here the other messenger, 35
Whose welcome I perceived had poisoned mine –
Being the very fellow which of late
Displayed so saucily[10] against your highness –
Having more man than wit[11] about me, drew.
He raised the house with loud and coward cries. 40
Your son and daughter found this trespass[12] worth
The shame which here it suffers.

FOOL   Winter's not gone yet, if the wild geese fly that way[13].
    Fathers that wear rags
        Do make their children blind, 45
    But fathers that bear bags[14]
        Shall see their children kind.
    Fortune, that arrant[15] whore,
        Ne'er turns the key to th'poor.
But for all this, thou shalt have as many dolours[16] for thy 50
daughters as thou canst tell[17] in a year.

Lear feels hysteria rising. He goes to find Regan. Kent asks why Lear has come with so few followers. The Fool speaks of the way in which men desert unsuccessful leaders, but claims he will remain faithful.

 剧情简介：李尔怒不可遏，去找蕊根。肯特问李尔为什么只带这么几个随从。俳优谈到人们如何抛弃失败的头领，但说自己会继续尽忠。

1 'Mother' – a 'climbing sorrow'

Hysteria was believed to be primarily a female disease originating in the uterus – hence Lear's reference to 'this mother' in line 52 – and then rising through the body, affecting one part after another. (Lear calls it 'climbing sorrow' in line 53.)

- As you read on through Act 2, think about the way in which Lear's rising anger and potential madness might be conveyed through the actor's movements and body language, or through the design of the set. Keep a note of your ideas in your Director's Journal.

Themes 主题分析

The wheel of fortune (in large groups)

In lines 62–70, the Fool tells Kent of the folly of following a leader in decline. He says that Kent could learn the folly of pointless labour from the proverbial ant, which will not try to seek food in the winter when there is none about. A calculating person will follow the 'great wheel' as it moves upwards and their fortunes improve, but they will know when to get off, and leave their master, as it spins downhill. The Fool's image is derived from the traditional wheel of Fortune. Kent referred to this earlier ('Fortune, goodnight, / Smile once more, turn thy wheel.') The following activity will help you understand different characters' positions on the wheel of Fortune:

- In your groups, each person takes on the role of a main character in the play.
- Sit in a circle. Decide where the top and bottom of your wheel are and whether it moves clockwise or anti-clockwise. Then position the characters in the appropriate place – those who are ascending, those who have reached the top or bottom, and those who are on the way down.
- Aim to have very reasonable discussions rather than fierce arguments: 'I feel Kent is going down and Oswald up because …'
- Record the positions you have agreed on in a diagram. You can return to this activity later in the play to see how the fate of various characters has changed.

1 **mother** 歇斯底里（古时人们认为这种疾病多见于女性，生自子宫或小腹的一股气，由下自上发展，在胃部形成疝气，冲入人的头脑，让人头昏目眩）
2 *Hysterica passio!* 歇斯底里！（拉丁文，即上文的 **mother**）
3 **element** 位置；领域
4 **How chance** 为什么
5 **school** 学习
6 **We'll … i'th'winter** 我们应该送你去向蚂蚁讨教，让它教你冬天不用忙活（夏天食物充足之时才需要囤足食物以备过冬；故事出自《伊索寓言》）
7 **stinking** 发臭（指失败和倒霉，暗指李尔）
8 **sir** 先生（指李尔的手下）
9 **for form** 做做样子
10 **perdy** 向天发誓
11 **fetches** 伎俩（也可解读为"回避"）
12 **revolt and flying off** 背叛和当逃兵

LEAR	O how this mother[1] swells up toward my heart!	
	Hysterica passio![2] Down, thou climbing sorrow,	
	Thy element's[3] below. Where is this daughter?	
KENT	With the earl, sir, here within.	
LEAR	Follow me not, stay here.	55

Exit

GENTLEMAN	Made you no more offence but what you speak of?	
KENT	None.	
	How chance[4] the king comes with so small a number?	
FOOL	And thou hadst been set i'th'stocks for that question, thou'dst well deserved it.	60
KENT	Why, fool?	
FOOL	We'll set thee to school[5] to an ant, to teach thee there's no labouring i'th'winter[6]. All that follow their noses are led by their eyes but blind men, and there's not a nose among twenty but can smell him that's stinking[7]. Let go thy hold when a great wheel runs down a hill, lest it break thy neck with following. But the great one that goes upward, let him draw thee after. When a wise man gives thee better counsel, give me mine again; I would have none but knaves follow it, since a fool gives it.	65 70
	That sir[8] which serves and seeks for gain	
	And follows but for form[9],	
	Will pack when it begins to rain	
	And leave thee in the storm.	
	But I will tarry, the fool will stay,	75
	And let the wise man fly;	
	The knave turns fool that runs away,	
	The fool no knave, perdy[10].	
KENT	Where learned you this, fool?	80
FOOL	Not i'th'stocks, fool.	

Enter LEAR *and* GLOUCESTER

LEAR	Deny to speak with me? They are sick, they are weary,	
	They have travelled all the night? Mere fetches[11],	
	The images of revolt and flying off[12].	
	Fetch me a better answer.	

Gloucester tries to excuse Cornwall's refusal to speak to Lear. At first Lear is angry, then hesitant, but finally he demands that Regan and Cornwall appear. He fears the onset of madness.

剧情简介：康沃尔拒绝与李尔说话，格劳斯特试图给康沃尔找借口。李尔起初很生气，然后是迟疑，但最后他要求蕊根和康沃尔来见他。他害怕自己疯病发作。

1 Lear's changing moods (in pairs)

To understand Lear's changing moods, try one or more of the following activities based on lines 88–114.

a Take parts as Lear and Gloucester. The person playing Lear reads the lines while walking around the room, changing direction at every punctuation mark. Gloucester should try to keep up and to make his lines sound soothing and conciliatory (缓和).

b One person reads all Lear's lines aloud. After each punctuation mark, the other, in role as director, says 'calmer' or 'angrier' to indicate Lear's changing emotions.

c Decide what movements or gestures Lear could use to accompany his words to emphasise his emotions.

Write about it 写作练习

Lear in a rage

At this stage in the play, Lear is struggling to control his feelings and his thoughts.

- Write a short essay about how Lear's unhappiness, anger and anxiety are conveyed to the audience. Activity 1 above will give you some ideas about his changeable tone, but you should also refer to the content of his words and to aspects of his language, such as his use of repetition, exclamations, questions and imperatives (orders). You could conclude your essay with some suggestions about how an actor could best portray these feelings on stage.

2 'Down, wantons, down' (in pairs)

Lear struggles to control his growing agitation by saying 'down' (line 114). The Fool uses this as an excuse to relate a story about a kind cook who couldn't bear to kill the eels before cooking them, but when they tried to escape from the pie, she hit them on their heads, saying 'Down, wantons, down!'

- Talk together about why the Fool chooses to tell the story at this particular point in the play. Is he trying to cheer Lear up, to remind him of his folly, to paint a picture of a world going mad? Or is he simply telling a story with a punch-line mimicking the word Lear has just used?

---

1 quality 性情
2 Infirmity … bound 疾病总是令人无法尽忠职守
3 forbear 克制，忍耐
4 fallen … will 与我的刚愎任性决裂
5 sickly fit 有病
6 Death on my state! 让死亡降临本王！（李尔的王国 [state] 实际上已亡）
7 remotion 疏远，远离
8 practice only 仅是个策略
9 cockney did to the eels 考克尼人对待鳗鱼那样（考克尼人是伦敦本地人，考克尼女人杀鳗鱼时，击打鳗鱼头的动作太慢，无法将之杀死）
10 paste 面糊（杀鳗鱼时把鳗鱼放在面糊里，使之行动缓慢）
11 knapped'em o'th'coxcombs 击打鳗鱼的头顶
12 wantons 调皮鬼
13 buttered his hay 在其草料上抹黄油（马不爱油腻，因此这是好心做傻事）

GLOUCESTER	My dear lord,	
	You know the fiery quality[1] of the duke,	85
	How unremovable and fixed he is	
	In his own course.	
LEAR	Vengeance, plague, death, confusion!	
	'Fiery'? What 'quality'? Why Gloucester, Gloucester,	
	I'd speak with the Duke of Cornwall and his wife.	90
GLOUCESTER	Well, my good lord, I have informed them so.	
LEAR	'Informed them'? Dost thou understand me, man?	
GLOUCESTER	Ay, my good lord.	
LEAR	The king would speak with Cornwall, the dear father	
	Would with his daughter speak! Commands – tends – service!	95
	Are they 'informed' of this? My breath and blood!	
	'Fiery'? The 'fiery duke'? Tell the hot duke that –	
	No, but not yet; maybe he is not well:	
	Infirmity doth still neglect all office	
	Whereto our health is bound[2]. We are not ourselves	100
	When nature, being oppressed, commands the mind	
	To suffer with the body. I'll forbear[3],	
	And am fallen out with my more headier will[4],	
	To take the indisposed and sickly fit[5]	
	For the sound man. – Death on my state![6] Wherefore	105
	Should he sit here? This act persuades me	
	That this remotion[7] of the duke and her	
	Is practice only[8]. Give me my servant forth.	
	Go tell the duke and's wife I'd speak with them,	
	Now, presently: bid them come forth and hear me,	110
	Or at their chamber door I'll beat the drum	
	Till it cry sleep to death.	
GLOUCESTER	I would have all well betwixt you. *Exit*	
LEAR	Oh me, my heart! My rising heart! But down.	
FOOL	Cry to it, nuncle, as the cockney did to the eels[9] when she put	115
	'em i'th'paste[10] alive; she knapped 'em o'th'coxcombs[11] with a stick	
	and cried, 'Down, wantons[12], down!' 'Twas her brother that in	
	pure kindness to his horse buttered his hay[13].	

Kent is freed from the stocks. Lear criticises Gonerill's treatment of him. Regan defends her sister, and says that Lear needs guidance in old age. Lear mocks the suggestion that he should apologise to Gonerill.

剧情简介：肯特被从足枷上解救下来。李尔指责高娜瑞尔待他不好，蕊根为其姐辩护，说李尔年纪大了需要引导。蕊根提议李尔向高娜瑞尔道歉，李尔对此冷嘲热讽。

1 An awkward meeting

After the cautious formality of their greetings in lines 119–20, Lear seems to lay aside his rage at Kent's punishment, and at Regan's initial refusal to come out and meet him. He now addresses her with great affection. In his only reference to his dead queen in the play, Lear says that if Regan had not been pleased to see him, it would prove her mother had been unfaithful to Lear (in other words, Regan's tender feelings are a direct result of Lear being her father). It soon becomes clear, however, that family bonds do not make Regan kind or sympathetic.

- Even very short sentences contain a wealth of possibilities for actors to interpret and perform. Using only lines 119–20, stage the entrance of Cornwall and Regan and the greetings they exchange with Lear.

Language in the play 剧中语言
Father and daughter (in pairs)

a In lines 121–9, Lear uses Regan's name four times. You will find that he continues to use it many times later in the scene. Do you think this indicates that he has recovered a sense of affection for her, or is there another explanation?

b Pick out words or phrases from the script opposite that show how Regan maintains a rather chilly courtesy whilst not accepting Lear's version of events.

c Observe Regan's use of an imperative (order) to her father in line 150. Why is this an important detail in terms of their relationship?

1 **Sepulch'ring an adultress** 埋葬着一个奸妇（咒骂蕊根是她母亲与人通奸所生）
2 **naught** 心肠坏，邪恶
3 **vulture** 秃鹰（希腊神话中的天神普罗米修斯看到人类生活困苦，从奥林波斯山 [Mount Olympus] 盗出天火给人类使用，因此触怒宙斯；宙斯将普罗米修斯锁在悬崖上，派秃鹰去吃他的肝，又让他的肝重新长出，使他日复一日承受被恶鹰啄食之苦）
4 **depraved** 腐败；邪恶
5 **You … duty** 是您低估了她的品德，而不是她缺少孝心
6 **confine** 期限（暗指死期）
7 **some discretion** 某个有判断力的人
8 **becomes the house** 合乎王室礼数；符合家庭利益
9 **vouchsafe** 赐予，赏给
10 **raiment** 衣物

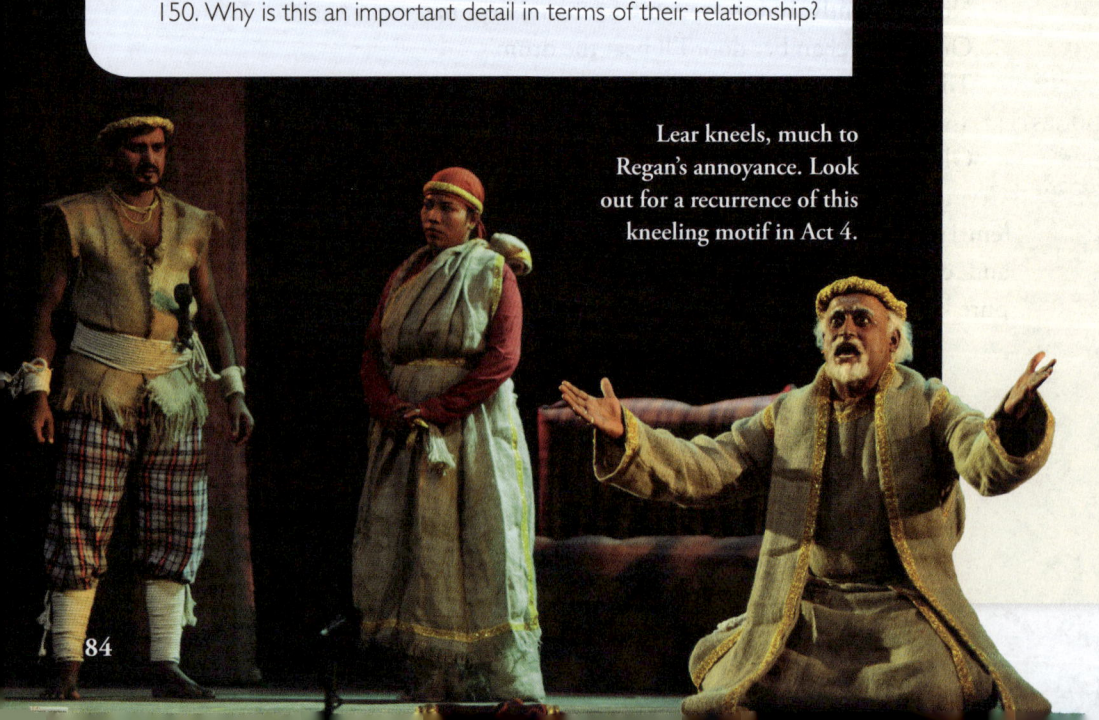

Lear kneels, much to Regan's annoyance. Look out for a recurrence of this kneeling motif in Act 4.

Enter CORNWALL, REGAN, GLOUCESTER, [*and*] SERVANTS

LEAR Good morrow to you both.
CORNWALL   Hail to your grace.
Kent here set at liberty
REGAN I am glad to see your highness.
LEAR Regan, I think you are. I know what reason
I have to think so. If thou shouldst not be glad,
I would divorce me from thy mother's tomb,
Sepulch'ring an adultress[1]. [*To Kent*] O are you free?
Some other time for that. Belovèd Regan,
Thy sister's naught[2]. Oh Regan, she hath tied
Sharp-toothed unkindness, like a vulture[3] here –
I can scarce speak to thee – thou'lt not believe
With how depraved[4] a quality – oh Regan!
REGAN I pray you, sir, take patience. I have hope
You less know how to value her desert
Than she to scant her duty[5].
LEAR   Say? How is that?
REGAN I cannot think my sister in the least
Would fail her obligation. If, sir, perchance
She have restrained the riots of your followers,
'Tis on such ground and to such wholesome end
As clears her from all blame.
LEAR   My curses on her.
REGAN O sir, you are old,
Nature in you stands on the very verge
Of his confine[6]. You should be ruled and led
By some discretion[7] that discerns your state
Better than you yourself. Therefore I pray you
That to our sister you do make return;
Say you have wronged her.
LEAR   Ask her forgiveness?
Do you but mark how this becomes the house[8]?
[*Kneels*] 'Dear daughter, I confess that I am old;
Age is unnecessary: on my knees I beg
That you'll vouchsafe[9] me raiment[10], bed, and food.'
REGAN Good sir, no more: these are unsightly tricks.
Return you to my sister.

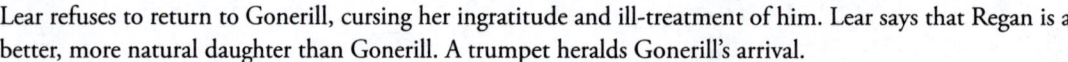

Lear refuses to return to Gonerill, cursing her ingratitude and ill-treatment of him. Lear says that Regan is a better, more natural daughter than Gonerill. A trumpet heralds Gonerill's arrival.

剧情简介：李尔拒绝回到高娜瑞尔那里，大骂她忘恩负义，虐待自己，还说蕊根是个比高娜瑞尔有孝心的孩子。号声响起，宣告高娜瑞尔的到来。

Language in the play 剧中语言

Calculating love (in pairs)

Lear's language shows how selfishly he quantifies and calculates his love. In Act 1 he demanded of his daughters, 'Which of you shall we say doth love us most?' setting up a competitive test. Now his hatred of Gonerill (described in lines 150–6) comes, at least in part, from his belief that in halving his numbers of followers, she has failed to fulfil her debt of love to him. Even his softer language to Regan, whom he says he will never curse, expresses the arithmetic of love ('grudge', 'cut', 'scant', 'offices', 'bond', 'effects', 'dues', 'half').

a Read lines 166–74 (from ''Tis not …') to each other, emphasising words or phrases that express Lear's calculating view of love.

b Talk about what impression Lear's numerical language might have on the audience.

c Note down any numerical and mathematical imagery that you find during the rest of this act. You could do this as a chart or list of your own, or as a group poster.

1 abated 剥夺
2 Looked black upon me 对我没好脸色
3 top 头
4 young bones 腹中的骨肉
5 taking airs 要命的气体；毒气
6 fen-sucked fogs 沼泽里冒出的雾气
7 blister 起水疱
8 tender-hefted 温柔
9 scant my sizes 削减我的津贴
10 oppose the bolt 插上门闩
11 offices of nature 亲情孝道
12 Effects of courtesy 礼节的表示
13 endowed 赐予
14 to th'purpose 说重点
15 approves 确认，证实

1 Regan's reply: appearance versus reality

When we hear Lear's flattering words to Regan in lines 163–74, we know that even if Lear himself believes his words to be true, they are in fact terribly mistaken. Regan proves this by cutting across her father impatiently – 'Good sir, to th'purpose.'

- Experiment with ways of speaking Regan's five words to show how her superficial politeness masks a cold and steely determination.

2 Where does power lie now?

Read the whole of the script opposite. In some ways, Lear sounds powerful and in control: he calls down curses on Gonerill and expresses his preference for Regan with her 'tender-hefted nature'. But does he command the attention and respect of his onstage audience?

- Look at the way he is interrupted, ignored and contradicted. Consider how these discourtesies could be made more obvious through staging.
- His response to Regan's 'Good sir, to th'purpose' is to ask who put Kent in the stocks. Is that really his 'purpose'? Why does he say it?
- Do you feel his words show a man struggling to regain control or someone in such mental distress that they cannot make rational decisions?

LEAR	[*Rising*]　　　　　　Never, Regan.	150

　　　　　She hath abated[1] me of half my train,
　　　　　Looked black upon me[2], struck me with her tongue
　　　　　Most serpent-like upon the very heart.
　　　　　All the stored vengeances of heaven fall
　　　　　On her ingrateful top[3]! Strike her young bones[4], 155
　　　　　You taking airs[5], with lameness.

CORNWALL　　　　　　　　　　　Fie, sir, fie.

LEAR　　You nimble lightnings, dart your blinding flames
　　　　　Into her scornful eyes! Infect her beauty,
　　　　　You fen-sucked fogs[6], drawn by the powerful sun
　　　　　To fall and blister[7]. 160

REGAN　　O the blessed gods! So will you wish on me
　　　　　When the rash mood is on.

LEAR　　No, Regan, thou shalt never have my curse.
　　　　　Thy tender-hefted[8] nature shall not give
　　　　　Thee o'er to harshness. Her eyes are fierce, but thine 165
　　　　　Do comfort and not burn. 'Tis not in thee
　　　　　To grudge my pleasures, to cut off my train,
　　　　　To bandy hasty words, to scant my sizes[9],
　　　　　And in conclusion, to oppose the bolt[10]
　　　　　Against my coming in. Thou better know'st 170
　　　　　The offices of nature[11], bond of childhood,
　　　　　Effects of courtesy[12], dues of gratitude.
　　　　　Thy half o'th'kingdom hast thou not forgot
　　　　　Wherein I thee endowed[13].

REGAN　　　　　　　　　　　Good sir, to th'purpose[14].

LEAR　　Who put my man i'th'stocks?

Tucket within

CORNWALL　　　　　　　What trumpet's that? 175

REGAN　　I know't, my sister's. This approves[15] her letter
　　　　　That she would soon be here.

Enter OSWALD

　　　　　　　　Is your lady come?

Lear is shaken by Regan's warm greeting of Gonerill. Regan advises Lear to return to Gonerill, reducing his followers by half. Lear lists the hardships and ignominies that he would rather endure.

剧情简介：李尔对蕊根热情迎接高娜瑞尔感到震惊。蕊根奉劝李尔减少一半随从，回到高娜瑞尔那儿去。李尔表示他情愿忍受列举出的种种艰难和羞辱，也不愿回去。

1 Lear's isolation

The entrance of Gonerill means that most of the main characters are on stage again together as they were in Act 1 Scene 1. A director can decide whether to echo the first scene in some way, or whether to highlight the differences in the way this one is staged. There are certainly strong contrasts in the way Gonerill and Regan address their father.

- How do you think the staging of this scene, including the grouping of the characters, could emphasise Lear's growing isolation? Regan, Gonerill and Cornwall are clearly united against him. Regan takes Gonerill by the hand in a show of friendship. Gonerill chooses her words carefully to give offence to Lear, referring to his 'indiscretion' and 'dotage'. Kent, the Gentleman, the Fool and Gloucester – all possible allies of Lear – are on stage but do not speak.

1	easy-borrowed	轻易得来
2	varlet	恶棍，流氓
3	sway	影响
4	indiscretion	不慎
5	dotage	老糊涂
6	O ... tough!	我这胸膛太结实！（怎么还没气炸！）
7	disorders ... advancement	胡作非为应得到少得多的奖励（反话）
8	abjure	发誓放弃
9	wage ... o'th'air	与狂风暴雨抗争
10	Necessity's sharp pinch	饥寒交迫的刺骨折磨
11	hot-blooded	血气方刚
12	knee	跪在……面前
13	squire-like	像奴才似的
14	keep base life afoot	让这卑贱的生活维持下去
15	sumpter	拉货或驮物的驴马

Write about it 写作练习

Kent's perspective

From the entrance of the king at line 81 to his exit at line 279, Kent is a silent observer of all that takes place. Yet his loyalty to Lear has been paramount, and it must hurt to witness his master's torment.

- Write his version of events, including how he responds to what he witnesses and giving reasons for his silence, as you read through to the end of the scene. Remember that Kent the plain-speaker will not mince his words.

2 Lear struggles to accept the truth (in pairs)

a Lear's words in this part of the scene show how his thoughts are darting from one topic to another, distracted by Oswald's and then Gonerill's entrances.

- Look at lines 181–7. For each sentence, decide who Lear is talking to: someone on stage, himself or the gods?

b He goes on to say he would rather live a life like the wolf and the owl, suffering from exposure to the elements, than return to live with Gonerill. His image in line 204 is of physical pain ('pinch') inflicted upon him by another of his grim, cruel companions, 'Necessity' (the most bare existence).

- As you read on, make notes on the ways in which Lear's imagined ordeal here becomes a reality.

LEAR	This is a slave whose easy-borrowed[1] pride	
	Dwells in the sickly grace of her he follows.	
	Out, varlet[2], from my sight!	
CORNWALL	What means your grace?	180

Enter GONERILL

LEAR	Who stocked my servant? Regan, I have good hope	
	Thou didst not know on't. Who comes here? O heavens!	
	If you do love old men, if your sweet sway[3]	
	Allow obedience, if you yourselves are old,	
	Make it your cause; send down and take my part.	185
	[*To Gonerill*] Art not ashamed to look upon this beard?	
	O Regan, will you take her by the hand?	
GONERILL	Why not by th'hand, sir? How have I offended?	
	All's not offence that indiscretion[4] finds,	
	And dotage[5] terms so.	
LEAR	O sides, you are too tough![6]	190
	Will you yet hold? How came my man i'th'stocks?	
CORNWALL	I set him there, sir; but his own disorders	
	Deserved much less advancement[7].	
LEAR	You? Did you?	
REGAN	I pray you, father, being weak, seem so.	
	If till the expiration of your month	195
	You will return and sojourn with my sister,	
	Dismissing half your train, come then to me.	
	I am now from home and out of that provision	
	Which shall be needful for your entertainment.	
LEAR	Return to her? and fifty men dismissed?	200
	No, rather I abjure[8] all roofs and choose	
	To wage against the enmity o'th'air[9],	
	To be a comrade with the wolf and owl,	
	Necessity's sharp pinch[10]. Return with her?	
	Why, the hot-blooded[11] France, that dowerless took	205
	Our youngest born – I could as well be brought	
	To knee[12] his throne and, squire-like[13], pension beg	
	To keep base life afoot[14]. Return with her?	
	Persuade me rather to be slave and sumpter[15]	
	To this detested groom.	
GONERILL	At your choice, sir.	210

Lear curses Gonerill and renounces her. He decides to stay with Regan with his hundred followers. Regan gives her reasons for rejecting Lear's proposal, and says that she will accept only twenty-five knights.

剧情简介：李尔咒骂高娜瑞尔，宣布与她断绝关系，并决定与他的百名随从住在蕊根家。蕊根说出她拒绝李尔提议的理由，说她只能接受25名骑士。

Stagecraft 导演技巧

'Thou art a boil' (in pairs)

Lear describes Gonerill in lines 214–18 using the language of bodily corruption and disease.

a Read the lines as though Lear is wildly angry and relishes the appalling comparisons with diseased flesh. Then read the same lines as though Lear is calm – sad and insistent rather than enraged. How appropriate is each of these readings?

b Talk together about how body language and movement could reveal the feelings of the characters as they listen to Lear's words. For example, how might Gonerill react on hearing herself described as a disease? How might this reaction change depending on the way the lines are delivered?

c How do you think an audience would respond to these lines? With sympathy for Gonerill or for Lear? Or neither of them?

1 boil 疖子
2 plague-sore 瘟疫疮
3 embossèd carbuncle 鼓起的肿瘤
4 thunder-bearer 手持霹雳者（即朱庇特）
5 shoot 用雷劈
6 mingle reason with your passion 理性地思考您大动肝火的行为
7 avouch it 保证，确认
8 sith = since
9 charge 开销
10 slack ye 怠慢您
11 in ... it 也是该给我们的时候了
12 depositaries 托管人

1 Family likeness (in threes)

Just as Lear's love is measured and calculating, so his sense of self-esteem seems to be in direct proportion to the number of knights in his retinue. Now he is experiencing the consequences of his arithmetical way of judging value. Regan and Gonerill cruelly pay their father back in kind – by also measuring their love for him in numbers.

- Take parts and speak lines 223–56, emphasising all words connected with numbers. Then talk together about any other similarities you have found between this father and his two elder daughters.

2 'I gave you all' (in pairs)

Lear's four simple words at line 243 carry huge emotional weight.

- Try different ways of speaking the line in order to capture a variety of Lear's possible moods. For example, he could be furious, despairing, astonished, disbelieving or full of pathos.
- Regan's crisp reply can also be delivered in many different ways. Is she brusque and ruthless, amused or disgusted? Alternatively, should the actor aim to convey more than one reaction?
- Try out various combinations of ways to deliver the line and the reply. Talk about which works best and why you think this is.

LEAR	I prithee, daughter, do not make me mad.	
	I will not trouble thee, my child. Farewell.	
	We'll no more meet, no more see one another.	
	But yet thou art my flesh, my blood, my daughter,	
	Or rather a disease that's in my flesh,	215
	Which I must needs call mine. Thou art a boil[1],	
	A plague-sore[2], or embossèd carbuncle[3]	
	In my corrupted blood. But I'll not chide thee;	
	Let shame come when it will, I do not call it.	
	I do not bid the thunder-bearer[4] shoot[5],	220
	Nor tell tales of thee to high-judging Jove.	
	Mend when thou canst, be better at thy leisure;	
	I can be patient, I can stay with Regan,	
	I and my hundred knights.	
REGAN	Not altogether so.	
	I looked not for you yet, nor am provided	225
	For your fit welcome. Give ear, sir, to my sister,	
	For those that mingle reason with your passion[6]	
	Must be content to think you old, and so –	
	But she knows what she does.	
LEAR	Is this well spoken?	
REGAN	I dare avouch it[7], sir. What, fifty followers?	230
	Is it not well? What should you need of more?	
	Yea, or so many, sith[8] that both charge[9] and danger	
	Speak 'gainst so great a number? How in one house	
	Should many people under two commands	
	Hold amity? 'Tis hard, almost impossible.	235
GONERILL	Why might not you, my lord, receive attendance	
	From those that she calls servants, or from mine?	
REGAN	Why not, my lord? If then they chanced to slack ye[10],	
	We could control them. If you will come to me	
	(For now I spy a danger) I entreat you	240
	To bring but five and twenty; to no more	
	Will I give place or notice.	
LEAR	I gave you all.	
REGAN	And in good time you gave it[11].	
LEAR	Made you my guardians, my depositaries[12],	
	But kept a reservation to be followed	245
	With such a number. What, must I come to you	
	With five and twenty? Regan, said you so?	

Lear engages in the arithmetic of love once again, but his daughters' reductive calculations devastate him. He deliberates on humanity's basic needs, and swears revenge against his daughters. He fears for his sanity.

剧情简介：李尔再次做起爱的算术题，但是女儿的减法让他痛不欲生。他认真思考人类的基本需要，发誓要报复女儿们。他很怕自己会发疯。

1 'What need one?' (in groups of three or four)

Regan and Gonerill continue their downward haggling over the number of followers they will permit their father to have. Lear agrees to go and live with Gonerill (who he has just called an 'embossèd carbuncle' and earlier cursed with sterility) because she will allow more followers than Regan. A logical conclusion is reached with Regan undercutting Gonerill with a final offer, 'What need one?'

a Experiment with ways of reading the lines to emphasise the number countdown. The Fool could mime reactions; a sound or gesture could be repeated at each use of a number; or the numbers could be voiced very loudly or very softly. Discuss what would work best on stage.

b Suggest a gesture or movement for Regan to use as she says 'What need one?' at line 256.

1 **Stands … praise** 倒值得夸赞了
2 **tend** 伺候
3 **Our … superfluous** 在朕的治下，哪怕最卑贱的乞丐也有些他不完全需要的东西
4 **unnatural hags** 伤天害理的女妖
5 **flaws** 碎片

Characters 人物分析

'O reason not the need!' (in groups of five or six)

Lear's final lines before leaving Gloucester's castle can be seen to fall into four sections:

- **Lines 257–63** He says that human need cannot be determined by precise calculation. If our requirements are no more than the very basic necessities, then a human life is worth no more than an animal's. Regan's fine clothes are superfluous to her natural needs.
- **Lines 264–71** Pleading for patience, Lear calls upon the gods to inspire him to noble and manly anger against his daughters.
- **Lines 271–5** Lear issues a terrifying but confused threat against his daughters.
- **Lines 275–9** Lear claims that nothing will make him weep. He fears that he will go mad.

a Decide to whom Lear is addressing individual lines (to both sisters, only one sister, the gods, the Fool?).

b Lear identifies his prime need as patience. Share your ideas about his most pressing need at this moment.

c Look at each of the four parts of Lear's final outburst and decide what it tells the audience about his character.

d Has Lear changed at all from the king we saw dividing his kingdom at the start of the play? If so, in what ways?

REGAN	And speak't again, my lord. No more with me.
LEAR	Those wicked creatures yet do look well-favoured
	When others are more wicked. Not being the worst 250
	Stands in some rank of praise¹. [*to Gonerill*] I'll go with thee;
	Thy fifty yet doth double five and twenty,
	And thou art twice her love.
GONERILL	Hear me, my lord:
	What need you five and twenty? ten? or five?
	To follow in a house where twice so many 255
	Have a command to tend² you?
REGAN	What need one?
LEAR	O reason not the need! Our basest beggars
	Are in the poorest thing superfluous³.
	Allow not nature more than nature needs,
	Man's life is cheap as beast's. Thou art a lady; 260
	If only to go warm were gorgeous,
	Why nature needs not what thou gorgeous wear'st,
	Which scarcely keeps thee warm. But for true need –
	You heavens, give me that patience, patience I need.
	You see me here, you gods, a poor old man, 265
	As full of grief as age, wretched in both;
	If it be you that stirs these daughters' hearts
	Against their father, fool me not so much
	To bear it tamely. Touch me with noble anger,
	And let not women's weapons, water drops, 270
	Stain my man's cheeks. No, you unnatural hags⁴,
	I will have such revenges on you both
	That all the world shall – I will do such things –
	What they are, yet I know not, but they shall be
	The terrors of the earth! You think I'll weep; 275
	No, I'll not weep,

Storm and tempest

I have full cause of weeping, but this heart
Shall break into a hundred thousand flaws⁵
Or ere I'll weep. O fool, I shall go mad.

Exeunt [Lear, Gloucester, Kent, Gentleman, and Fool]

Regan and Gonerill agree that they will welcome Lear, but not his followers. Gloucester fears for Lear's well-being. Regan and Cornwall insist that Gloucester close his doors against Lear and the storm.

 剧情简介：蕊根和高娜瑞尔达成一致，她们欢迎李尔，但是不欢迎他的随从。格劳斯特担心李尔的安危。门外狂风暴雨，蕊根和高娜瑞尔坚持要格劳斯特把李尔关在门外。

Themes 主题分析

Nature: ''tis a wild night' (in pairs)

a The storm is an example of **pathetic fallacy** (借物喻情), a device often used in storytelling in which the weather is made to mirror human feelings or experience. The storm, a great disruption in nature, seems to represent the disruption in Lear's kingdom, family and mind. In its harshness, it can also be seen to reflect the unnatural cruelty of the people who force the 'old man' out on to the heath.

- List five other examples of pathetic fallacy from plays, poems or films, and talk about how this device adds to the emotional experience for the reader or audience in each case.

b In the Globe Theatre in Shakespeare's day, the one special effect available was the sound of thunder, made by rolling cannon balls around in the loft above the canopy over the stage.

- Discuss and then make notes in your Director's Journal about different ways in which the noise could be produced in a modern production, to show how nature is in uproar.

Characters 人物分析

Regan, Cornwall and Gonerill

By the end of this scene, the audience has learned much more about Regan, Cornwall and Gonerill.

a Do you think that:
- their characters are consistent, but simply becoming much clearer as we learn more
- power has released qualities within them that existed already
- power has actually changed them?

b Had Lear once been right in thinking Regan 'tender-hefted' but she has simply grown out of it – or was he wrong all along?

1 Gloucester: divided loyalty?

Although Gloucester initially follows Lear out into the storm, he quickly returns to his own castle with news of the king's distress.

- Study his lines opposite and consider what makes his situation so difficult. Where do his loyalties lie?

1 bestowed   安置
2 put himself from rest   自己放着清福不享
3 For his particular   就他个人而言
4 but … whither   但是我不知道他想去哪儿
5 Alack   哎呀，天啊（表示悲伤或遗憾）
6 ruffle   （风）怒吼
7 desperate train   肆意妄为的跟班
8 incense   挑唆
9 apt … abused   惯于让他听信谗言的误导

CORNWALL	Let us withdraw; 'twill be a storm.	280
REGAN	This house is little. The old man and's people	
	Cannot be well bestowed[1].	
GONERILL	'Tis his own blame; hath put himself from rest[2]	
	And must needs taste his folly.	
REGAN	For his particular[3], I'll receive him gladly,	285
	But not one follower.	
GONERILL	So am I purposed.	
	Where is my lord of Gloucester?	
CORNWALL	Followed the old man forth.	

Enter GLOUCESTER

	He is returned.	
GLOUCESTER	The king is in high rage.	
CORNWALL	Whither is he going?	
GLOUCESTER	He calls to horse, but will I know not whither[4].	290
CORNWALL	'Tis best to give him way; he leads himself.	
GONERILL	My lord, entreat him by no means to stay.	
GLOUCESTER	Alack[5], the night comes on, and the high winds	
	Do sorely ruffle[6]; for many miles about	
	There's scarce a bush.	
REGAN	O sir, to wilful men,	295
	The injuries that they themselves procure	
	Must be their schoolmasters. Shut up your doors.	
	He is attended with a desperate train[7],	
	And what they may incense[8] him to, being apt	
	To have his ear abused[9], wisdom bids fear.	300
CORNWALL	Shut up your doors, my lord; 'tis a wild night,	
	My Regan counsels well: come out o'th'storm.	

Exeunt

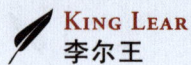

KING LEAR
李尔王

Looking back at Act 2 第2幕回顾
Activities for groups or individuals

1 Different generations

Gonerill and Regan find their father's erratic behaviour perplexing and demanding. They are greatly irritated by Lear's capricious and unpredictable ways, and he is appalled by their lack of respect and affection.

a Working in groups of four, talk together about the challenges, difficulties and rewards of relationships between young and older people.

b Take roles as Lear, Gonerill, Regan and a family guidance counsellor. The counsellor's task is to interview father and daughters about the disagreements and tensions between them.

2 Glimpses of goodness

The forces of evil seem to gather momentum in Act 2, although a few signs of hope flicker, suggesting that 'goodness' is still at work in Lear's Britain.

- Find at least one example of goodness – the hope of a better future – in each of the four scenes. What do these examples signify?

3 The Fool's jingles

Choose any of the Fool's songs or jingles from Act 2. Decide which aspects you want to emphasise, rehearse it, and present it appropriately. In your performance, try to make sense of what you can, but also look for ways to make the nonsense entertaining for the audience.

4 A well-informed audience

In many plays, the audience knows more about what is going on than most of the characters (dramatic irony).

Look briefly at the major characters in this act and pick out something significant about their situation that the audience knows but they do not. Who seems to be best informed or most realistic, and who are the most deceived? How has this changed from Act 1?

5 Place and time

Unlike Act 1, which was set in various places and covered a period of about two weeks, Act 2 is set in one place, in and around Gloucester's castle, and appears to cover only a few hours. Events almost appear to unfold in real time, only taking as long as the performance itself. This can give the act an intense and uncomfortable feel. From the start, the audience knows that there is very little chance of the situation improving.

- In a stage production, what could be done to heighten this sense of claustrophobic intensity? Consider how you could use staging and lighting and how you could manage the pace of the action and the transitions between scenes.

6 Sisters

Some critics have claimed that Gonerill and Regan are very much alike and that, just as in Act 1 Scene 1, Regan is simply trying to match her sister's behaviour.

a How distinct are their personalities in Act 2? How could you use costume and body language to distinguish between them?

b There are references to Regan's tender feminine nature. Would you stress these in a production?

c One major difference between the sisters lies in the character of their husbands. What does the audience know about Cornwall by the end of Act 2? Compare this with what we know about Albany from Act 1.

7 What happens next?

At this point in the play, the audience is bound to have many questions about what will happen next.

- Make a list of at least six questions about a range of characters in the play. Talk with other students about which questions are likely to be uppermost in the audience members' minds.

97

The Gentleman describes Lear raging at the storm. Kent recounts the French spies' reports of growing rivalry between Albany and Cornwall. Kent gives the Gentleman a ring to show to Cordelia.

 剧情简介：绅士描述李尔向暴风雨发怒的样子。肯特叙述法国暗探报告的阿尔博尼和康沃尔之间日益紧张的关系。肯特给了绅士一枚指环，让他拿给考蒂丽叶看。

1 Who knows what? (in pairs)

One of the dramatic functions of this scene is to convey important information to the audience. In *King Lear*, Shakespeare does this in different ways: sometimes the audience watches actions unfold on stage; at other times anonymous characters such as the Gentleman, the Knight and the Captain make brief appearances and tell the audience about things that are happening off stage. In this short scene, we hear news and speculation about Lear, the rivalry between Cornwall and Albany, and about servants who are actually French spies.

a Working with a partner, make three short lists of all the milestone events up to this point in the play that:

- we have seen or heard ourselves on stage
- we have been informed about by characters such as the Gentleman
- you think might have happened off stage, but which we haven't found out about yet.

b Compare your notes with another pair, or share your key ideas with the class as a whole.

2 Kent and Cordelia (in pairs)

Kent tells the Gentleman that he will 'see Cordelia – / As fear not but you shall' (lines 25–6). Shakespeare invites the audience to imagine scenes taking place beyond the onstage action, in order to convey a sense of the world at large.

a Imagine the scene in which the Gentleman meets Cordelia. Take parts and improvise the conversation between these two characters. Consider:

- how Cordelia will react when the Gentleman shows her Kent's ring (as proof that he brings genuine information)
- what information the Gentleman will give Cordelia
- what questions Cordelia might ask the Gentleman.

b Feed back to the class on your findings, focusing particularly on the effects of this scene and what the audience might imagine in response to the conversation.

---

1 **Contending with the fretful elements** 与狂暴的自然元素搏斗（古时欧洲人认为世界由水、火、土、气这四种元素组成；这里指狂风［气］、暴雨［水］和闪电［火］，接下来骑士提到土）
2 **curlèd waters** 惊涛骇浪
3 **main** = mainland, shore
4 **labours to out-jest** 努力拿……开玩笑
5 **upon … note** 以我对您的观察保证
6 **Commend … you** 拜托您一件要事
7 **mutual cunning** 互相使诈
8 **their … high** 他们福星高照，获得王权富贵
9 **speculations / Intelligent of …** 密探密报……的情况
10 **snuffs and packings** 怨恨和算计
11 **hard rein** 严厉的控制
12 **furnishings** 外部表象
13 **out-wall** 外表；外衣
14 **Fie on** 呸

Act 3 Scene 1
Near Gloucester's castle

Storm still. Enter KENT *(disguised) and a* GENTLEMAN, *severally*

KENT Who's there, besides foul weather?
GENTLEMAN One minded like the weather, most unquietly.
KENT I know you. Where's the king?
GENTLEMAN Contending with the fretful elements[1];
Bids the wind blow the earth into the sea, 5
Or swell the curlèd waters[2] 'bove the main[3],
That things might change or cease.
KENT   But who is with him?
GENTLEMAN None but the fool, who labours to out-jest[4]
His heart-struck injuries.
KENT   Sir, I do know you,
And dare upon the warrant of my note[5] 10
Commend a dear thing to you[6]. There is division,
Although as yet the face of it is covered
With mutual cunning[7], 'twixt Albany and Cornwall,
Who have – as who have not, that their great stars
Throned and set high[8]? – servants, who seem no less, 15
Which are to France the spies and speculations
Intelligent of[9] our state. What hath been seen,
Either in snuffs and packings[10] of the dukes,
Or the hard rein[11] which both of them hath borne
Against the old kind king; or something deeper, 20
Whereof, perchance, these are but furnishings[12] –
GENTLEMAN I will talk further with you.
KENT   No, do not.
For confirmation that I am much more
Than my out-wall[13], open this purse and take
What it contains. If you shall see Cordelia – 25
As fear not but you shall – show her this ring,
And she will tell you who that fellow is
That yet you do not know. Fie on[14] this storm!
I will go seek the king.

Kent and the Gentleman separate to find Lear. Lear rages furiously with the storm, demanding that it destroy humankind. He ignores the Fool's request for shelter, and accuses the storm of joining forces with his daughters.

  剧情简介：肯特和绅士分头去找李尔。李尔对着暴风雨发怒，要求暴风雨摧毁人类。俳优请求他找地方避雨，他没有理睬，还指责暴风雨与他的两个女儿为伍。

Characters 人物分析

Lear in the storm (in small groups)

Lear is an old man in an exposed place facing a terrible storm. Although he seems to be a vulnerable victim of the weather, his words in lines 1–9 are actually a defiant sequence of commands. He is telling the storm to become even more violent, and encouraging the elements to bring about mass destruction. In your groups, take turns to read Lear's lines in the script opposite one sentence at a time.

- Emphasise the words you think are the most important in conveying Lear's anger.
- Think about how your performance might be enhanced by movement and actions.
- Do you think this is the point at which Lear begins his descent into madness? Change your tone to indicate where you think this might be happening.

1. to effect 在重要性上
2. your pain 有劳您
3. Holla 呼喊
4. cataracts and hurricanoes 瀑布大雨和排山海啸
5. cocks 风信鸡（公鸡样子的风向标）
6. thought-executing fires 随思想而行的天火（即闪电）
7. Vaunt-couriers 先驱，先行者
8. oak-cleaving 劈裂橡树
9. Singe 烧焦
10. thick rotundity o'th'world 世界（即地球）的浑圆肚子
11. nature's moulds 造化的模具
12. germens 种子
13. spill 撒掉
14. court holy water 奉承话
15. tax 指控，责怪
16. subscription 忠诚，顺从
17. servile ministers 奴颜婢膝的家臣
18. pernicious 恶毒
19. high-engendered battles 天兵天将

GENTLEMAN	Give me your hand. Have you no more to say?	30
KENT	Few words, but to effect[1] more than all yet:	
	That when we have found the king – in which your pain[2]	
	That way, I'll this – he that first lights on him	
	Holla[3] the other.	

Exeunt

Act 3 Scene 2
The heath near Gloucester's castle

Storm still. Enter LEAR *and* FOOL

LEAR	Blow, winds, and crack your cheeks! Rage, blow,	
	You cataracts and hurricanoes[4], spout	
	Till you have drenched our steeples, drowned the cocks[5]!	
	You sulph'rous and thought-executing fires[6],	
	Vaunt-couriers[7] of oak-cleaving[8] thunderbolts,	5
	Singe[9] my white head; and thou all-shaking thunder,	
	Strike flat the thick rotundity o'th'world[10],	
	Crack nature's moulds[11], all germens[12] spill[13] at once	
	That makes ingrateful man.	
FOOL	O nuncle, court holy water[14] in a dry house is better than this rain-water out o'door. Good nuncle, in, ask thy daughters blessing. Here's a night pities neither wise men nor fools.	10
LEAR	Rumble thy bellyful; spit, fire; spout, rain!	
	Nor rain, wind, thunder, fire are my daughters.	
	I tax[15] not you, you elements, with unkindness.	15
	I never gave you kingdom, called you children.	
	You owe me no subscription[16]. Then let fall	
	Your horrible pleasure. Here I stand your slave,	
	A poor, infirm, weak, and despised old man;	
	But yet I call you servile ministers[17],	20
	That will with two pernicious[18] daughters join	
	Your high-engendered battles[19] 'gainst a head	
	So old and white as this. O, ho! 'tis foul.	

The Fool sings of the foolishness of sexual excess. Kent fears for Lear's safety in this worst-ever storm. Lear calls on the gods to use the storm to reveal all hidden crimes.

 剧情简介：俳优用歌谣嘲笑纵欲过度的愚蠢。肯特担心李尔在这场可怕暴风雨中的安全。李尔呼吁天神用这场暴风雨揭露所有隐藏的罪恶。

Language in the play 剧中语言

'Nothing'

Lear says 'No, I will be the pattern of all patience. / I will say nothing' (lines 35–6). The word 'nothing' is important in the play, and is repeated on several occasions.

a On page 6, you began a list or a poster of occurrences of 'nothing' in *King Lear*. Look at this list now and remind yourself how often and in what ways the word is used. What is the effect of repeating 'nothing' so frequently?

b Draw a mind map summarising your ideas about how and why the word 'nothing' is used in the play. Then write a paragraph, using embedded quotations, about the importance of this word. You should consider:

- what the characters are thinking when they say 'nothing'
- what effect the word has on other characters on stage
- why 'nothing' is repeated immediately by other characters in some instances and so often in the play as a whole.

Themes 主题分析

Justice and kingship

At the end of his speech to Kent, Lear says: 'I am a man / More sinned against than sinning' (lines 57–8). Throughout the play so far, Lear has made several decisions in which he might be accused of 'sinning' (such as banishing Cordelia). He has also been treated harshly by others (been 'sinned against').

a By yourself, make a note of all the ways in which you think Lear has 'sinned' and all the ways in which he has been 'sinned against' so far.

b In pairs, one of you claims that Lear is the victim and the other that it is his sinful actions that have led him to be caught in the storm on the heath. Hold a debate in which you try to convince each other of your side of the case. Give examples from the play to support your arguments.

c After your debate, feed back to the class which side of the argument you feel is most convincing. Is Lear more sinning or sinned against?

1 **He … head-piece** 一个人有了房子，把自己的头装进去才算有个好脑瓜
2 **The codpiece … louse** 头还没有房，阴兜就想入房，头和人必将长虱子（codpiece 指古代男性马裤裆部鼓起的阴兜，转指阴茎；louse 喻指染上性病）
3 **beggars marry many** 乞丐娶妻多
4 **The man … make** 把本应放在心头的人踩在脚底下
5 **Shall … woe** = Shall cry woe of a corn（必将饱受鸡眼之苦）
6 **made mouths in a glass** 对着镜子搔首弄姿
7 **grace and a codpiece** 陛下和阴兜（codpiece 也可喻指傻子或俳优）
8 **wrathful** 狂怒，激愤
9 **Gallow** 恐吓
10 **affliction** 痛苦
11 **pudder** 骚动，喧嚣
12 **undivulgèd** 未暴露
13 **perjured** 发假誓
14 **simular of virtue** 伪君子
15 **incestuous** 乱伦
16 **Caitiff** 卑鄙小人
17 **convenient seeming** 适合（达到目的）的虚伪外表
18 **practised on** 密谋损害
19 **pent-up** 被藏匿
20 **Rive your concealing continents** 撕开你们的藏匿之所
21 **cry / These dreadful summoners grace** 向可怕的天庭传令官（指风雨雷电）求饶

FOOL   He that has a house to put 's head in has a good head-piece¹.
        [*Sings*] The codpiece that will house
                Before the head has any,
            The head and he shall louse²;
                So beggars marry many³.
            The man that makes his toe
                What he his heart should make⁴,
            Shall of a corn cry woe⁵,
                And turn his sleep to wake.
        For there was never yet fair woman but she made mouths in a glass⁶.

                    Enter KENT [*disguised*]

LEAR   No, I will be the pattern of all patience.
        I will say nothing.

KENT   Who's there?

FOOL   Marry, here's grace and a codpiece⁷; that's a wise man and a fool.

KENT   Alas, sir, are you here? Things that love night
        Love not such nights as these. The wrathful⁸ skies
        Gallow⁹ the very wanderers of the dark
        And make them keep their caves. Since I was man
        Such sheets of fire, such bursts of horrid thunder,
        Such groans of roaring wind and rain I never
        Remember to have heard. Man's nature cannot carry
        Th'affliction¹⁰ nor the fear.

LEAR   Let the great gods,
        That keep this dreadful pudder¹¹ o'er our heads,
        Find out their enemies now. Tremble, thou wretch,
        That hast within thee undivulgèd¹² crimes
        Unwhipped of justice. Hide thee, thou bloody hand,
        Thou perjured¹³ and thou simular of virtue¹⁴
        That art incestuous¹⁵. Caitiff¹⁶, to pieces shake,
        That under covert and convenient seeming¹⁷
        Has practised on¹⁸ man's life. Close pent-up¹⁹ guilts,
        Rive your concealing continents²⁰ and cry
        These dreadful summoners grace²¹. I am a man
        More sinned against than sinning.

Kent urges Lear to rest in a nearby hovel. Kent plans to return to the castle to ask for shelter for the king. The Fool's prophecy promises mixed fortunes for Britain.

 剧情简介：肯特催促李尔在附近的茅舍休息，打算自己回到城堡为国王求个栖身之所。俳优的预言暗示了不列颠吉凶未卜的命运。

1 'My wits begin to turn' (in pairs)

In line 65, Lear claims 'My wits begin to turn'. He feels that he is losing his grip on sanity. In contrast, the Fool is a 'professional madman', employed to speak as if he is insane.

a Take parts and read Lear and the Fool's exchange in lines 65–76. Repeat it several times, changing the reading each time so it appears:
 - as if Lear is sane and the Fool is mad
 - as if Lear is mad and the Fool is serious and totally sane
 - as if both characters are mad
 - with each character saying some of his lines as if he is sane and some as if he is mad.

b Afterwards, talk with your partner about which performance you thought was most successful and which approach to Lear's character you would adopt if you were directing this play.

Stagecraft 导演技巧

A Fool's prophecy (in small groups)

At the end of this scene the Fool, alone on stage, makes a strange prophecy. He predicts that Britain ('Albion') will suffer from an age of corruption and unhappiness, but then things will take a turn for the better and all evils will be reversed.

a In your groups, discuss the significance of the Fool's prophecy at this point in the play.

b Take turns to perform this short speech in different ways – sad, ironic, serious or comic.

c Discuss what you liked about each performance, which you felt was the most successful reading, and why.

d Make notes in your Director's Journal about how you would direct the Fool to deliver the last line of this speech: 'This prophecy Merlin shall make, for I live before his time.'

---

1 **bare-headed** 光着头（国王在位时，头上一般会戴王冠；国王退位后，头上一般会戴帽子。暴风雨中的李尔光着头，十分不寻常）
2 **hard ... hovel** 这附近有一间茅舍
3 **hard house** 狠心家族
4 **demanding after you** 代您打听
5 **scanted courtesy** 欠缺的礼数
6 **wits** 理智
7 **brave** 美好
8 **cool a courtesan** 给娼妓（的热辣）降温
9 **more in word than matter** 说得多，做得少
10 **mar their malt** 损害其麦芽酒
11 **heretics** 异教徒
12 **Albion** 阿尔比恩（不列颠的旧称）
13 **squire** 扈从
14 **slanders** 谎言；诽谤
15 **cutpurses** 扒手，小偷
16 **throngs** 人群
17 **usurers ... i'th'field** 放高利贷者在大庭广众数其金币
18 **That ... feet** 走路还要靠双脚（一切都会回归正常）
19 **Merlin** 梅林（传说中亚瑟王时期的一名巫师）

King Lear Act 3 Scene 2

李尔王

KENT   Alack, bare-headed[1]?
Gracious my lord, hard by here is a hovel[2].
Some friendship will it lend you 'gainst the tempest.
Repose you there, while I to this hard house[3] –
More harder than the stones whereof 'tis raised,
Which even but now, demanding after you[4],
Denied me to come in – return and force
Their scanted courtesy[5].

LEAR   My wits[6] begin to turn.
Come on, my boy. How dost, my boy? Art cold?
I am cold myself. – Where is this straw, my fellow?
The art of our necessities is strange,
And can make vile things precious. Come, your hovel. –
Poor fool and knave, I have one part in my heart
That's sorry yet for thee.

FOOL   [*Sings*] He that has and a little tiny wit,
        With heigh-ho, the wind and the rain,
     Must make content with his fortunes fit,
        Though the rain it raineth every day.

LEAR   True, boy. – Come, bring us to this hovel.
                                       [*Exeunt Lear and Kent*]

FOOL   This is a brave[7] night to cool a courtesan[8]. I'll speak a prophecy ere I go:
    When priests are more in word than matter[9];
    When brewers mar their malt[10] with water;
    When nobles are their tailors' tutors,
    No heretics[11] burned, but wenches' suitors,
    Then shall the realm of Albion[12]
    Come to great confusion.
    When every case in law is right;
    No squire[13] in debt nor no poor knight;
    When slanders[14] do not live in tongues,
    Nor cutpurses[15] come not to throngs[16];
    When usurers tell their gold i'th'field[17],
    And bawds and whores do churches build,
    Then comes the time, who lives to see't,
    That going shall be used with feet[18].
This prophecy Merlin[19] shall make, for I live before his time.
                                                  Exit

Gloucester has been forbidden to help Lear. He tells of a secret letter about an armed invasion to support the king, and proposes to go to Lear. But the treacherous Edmond plans to betray his father.

剧情简介：格劳斯特得到命令不得帮助李尔。他提及一封密信，内容是一支武装部队要入侵不列颠以支持国王。他提议到李尔那里去。但是奸诈的爱德门打算背叛他父亲。

Language in the play 剧中语言

Edmond's irony (by yourself)

Gloucester uses the word 'unnatural' in the first line to mean 'against natural feeling', or something that is not in accord with kinship. Edmond then knowingly repeats this word, ironically playing with the idea that 'natural' also means 'illegitimate'. There is dramatic irony here – the audience knows that Edmond cannot be trusted. Edmond's speech is ironic because he does not want Gloucester to know his real motives. But what do you think Edmond is really thinking here?

- Design a comic strip that captures Edmond's thoughts during this scene. Use thought bubbles to record what Edmond is thinking when Gloucester speaks, as well as what actions he might be considering in response to Gloucester's news.

Themes 主题分析

Fathers and children (in pairs)

The relationship between fathers and their children is a key theme in *King Lear*. Here, the relationship between the father, Gloucester, and the son, Edmond, is deeply troubled. Gloucester trusts Edmond, but his son is plotting against him. In performance, the actors need to find a way of conveying Gloucester's ignorance and naivety as well as Edmond's cunning.

a Take parts and read this scene together. Consider the following:
  - What tone will you adopt for each character?
  - Which words will each man stress? For example, will Edmond emphasise 'unnatural' when he repeats it?
  - When Gloucester leaves after line 17, and Edmond begins talking while alone, he switches from prose to verse. How will you perform this section differently?

b Write two paragraphs about how the theme of fathers and their children has developed up to this point in the play.

1 unnatural dealing 不近人情的做法（指两个女儿对待老国王的做法）
2 leave 许可
3 perpetual 永久
4 sustain 接济
5 home 彻底
6 footed 登陆（有的版本这里为landed）
7 incline 倾向
8 look = look for
9 privily 暗中，秘密地
10 of = by
11 perceived 注意，觉察
12 toward 将发生
13 This courtesy, forbid thee 这一善事（指接济李尔），禁止你做
14 deserving 奖赏
15 draw me 带给我

Act 3 Scene 3
A room in Gloucester's castle

Enter GLOUCESTER *and* EDMOND

GLOUCESTER Alack, alack, Edmond, I like not this unnatural dealing[1]. When I desired their leave[2] that I might pity him, they took from me the use of mine own house, charged me on pain of perpetual[3] displeasure neither to speak of him, entreat for him, or any way sustain[4] him. 5

EDMOND Most savage and unnatural!

GLOUCESTER Go to, say you nothing. There is division between the dukes, and a worse matter than that. I have received a letter this night – 'tis dangerous to be spoken – I have locked the letter in my closet. These injuries the king now bears will be 10 revenged home[5]. There is part of a power already footed[6]. We must incline[7] to the king. I will look[8] him and privily[9] relieve him. Go you and maintain talk with the duke, that my charity be not of[10] him perceived[11]. If he ask for me, I am ill and gone to bed. If I die for it – as no less is threatened me – the king my old master 15 must be relieved. There is strange things toward[12], Edmond; pray you be careful. *Exit*

EDMOND This courtesy, forbid thee[13], shall the duke
Instantly know, and of that letter too.
This seems a fair deserving[14], and must draw me[15] 20
That which my father loses: no less than all.
The younger rises when the old doth fall. *Exit*

Kent urges Lear to shelter in a hovel. Lear refuses, saying that he cannot feel the storm because the mental pain caused by his daughters is more severe. He insists the Fool goes in before him.

 剧情简介：肯特催李尔到茅舍去避雨，李尔拒绝去，说自己感受不到暴风雨，因为女儿们给自己带来的精神痛苦更厉害。他坚持要俳优优先进茅舍。

Stagecraft 导演技巧

Lear's suffering in the storm (in small groups)

In lines 6–21, Lear explains why the storm does not torment him as much as the hurt caused by his daughters' 'filial ingratitude'. He is so obsessed by the extent of their hostility and disrespect that he is numb to the effects of the 'contentious storm'. Lear believes that only someone who doesn't have things to worry about is sensitive to the discomfort of the body ('When the mind's free, / The body's delicate').

a The activity below will help you to explore Lear's feelings at this point in the play.

- One student plays Kent. All the others represent Lear and stand in a circle around him.
- Kent asks each Lear to enter, speaking line 22 ('Good my lord, enter here').
- Each Lear refuses, using any one of the remarks from lines 6–22.
- The Lears should vary their tone and add gestures, deciding whether they reply to Kent, address an imaginary Gonerill and/or Regan, or speak to the storm.

b At the end of the exercise, discuss which of these different audiences you think is uppermost in Lear's mind when he is making this speech.

c In your Director's Journal, record your ideas about how you would stage Lear's suffering in this scene.

1 tyranny 暴虐
2 open night 露天之夜
3 Wilt = Will you
4 contentious 狂暴
5 malady 疾病，痛苦
6 fixed 扎根
7 scarce 几乎不
8 shun 躲避
9 flight 逃跑路线
10 i'th'mouth 直面
11 free 无牵无挂
12 delicate 敏感
13 filial ingratitude 子女不孝
14 frank 慷慨
15 ease 休息之处
16 leave ... more 允许我继续回想伤心事

Write about it 写作练习

Shakespeare's imagery

Consider lines 9–11. Write a short paragraph explaining the effects of this image of the bear and the sea. Aim to comment on:

- the comparison between fighting a bear and 'escaping' into the sea
- the particular effects of Shakespeare's choices of individual words, such as the verb 'shun' and the adjective 'roaring'
- what the imagery tells the audience about Lear's state of mind.

Act 3 Scene 4
Outside a hovel on the heath

Enter LEAR, KENT *(disguised), and* FOOL

KENT   Here is the place, my lord. Good my lord, enter.
The tyranny[1] of the open night's[2] too rough
For nature to endure.

Storm still

LEAR   Let me alone.
KENT   Good my lord, enter here.
LEAR   Wilt[3] break my heart?
KENT   I had rather break mine own. Good my lord, enter.   5
LEAR   Thou think'st 'tis much that this contentious[4] storm
Invades us to the skin: so 'tis to thee.
But where the greater malady[5] is fixed[6],
The lesser is scarce[7] felt. Thou'dst shun[8] a bear,
But if thy flight[9] lay toward the roaring sea,   10
Thou'dst meet the bear i'th'mouth[10]. When the mind's free[11],
The body's delicate[12]. This tempest in my mind
Doth from my senses take all feeling else,
Save what beats there: filial ingratitude[13].
Is it not as this mouth should tear this hand   15
For lifting food to't? But I will punish home.
No, I will weep no more. In such a night
To shut me out? Pour on, I will endure.
In such a night as this! O Regan, Gonerill,
Your old kind father, whose frank[14] heart gave all –   20
O that way madness lies; let me shun that;
No more of that.
KENT   Good my lord, enter here.
LEAR   Prithee, go in thyself, seek thine own ease[15].
This tempest will not give me leave to ponder
On things would hurt me more[16]; but I'll go in.   25
In, boy, go first. You houseless poverty –
Nay, get thee in; I'll pray, and then I'll sleep.

Exit [Fool]

Lear prays for the homeless and starving, whose plight he has previously ignored. The Fool rushes from the hovel, frightened and crying for help. Edgar, as Poor Tom, speaks madly of being tormented by the devil.

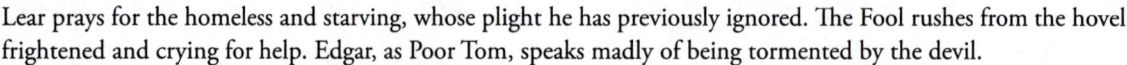

剧情简介：李尔为无家可归、饥肠辘辘的苦命人祈祷，忏悔之前忽视了他们的困苦。俳优从茅舍飞奔而出，惊慌失措，高喊救命。爱德格伪装成可怜的汤姆，胡言乱语说自己受到魔鬼折磨。

Themes 主题分析

Madness (in pairs)

Act 3 Scene 4 features three characters who are either mad, going mad or acting as though they were mad. The Fool is a professional madman, Edgar is feigning insanity and Lear is slowly losing his wits. Recognising the absurdity of the situation in which they find themselves, the Fool declares: 'This cold night will turn us all to fools and madmen.' In fact, none of the characters is as he appears. Remember that Kent is also in disguise, as Caius.

a For each character, find and make a note of two quotations which, on the surface at least, make them appear to be insane. Then find one or two quotations that show them making sense or where there is 'Reason, in madness'.

b Talk together about how Shakespeare uses the babble of 'mad' voices to achieve interesting dramatic effects. Then write a paragraph about these effects, using embedded quotations to back up your points.

Language in the play 剧中语言

Poor Tom's mad words (in small groups)

As 'Poor Tom', pretending madness, Edgar uses language that mixes sense and nonsense. You do not have to understand it all (critics cannot agree on what 'do, de, do, de, do de' means, for example). Tom's dislocated language adds to the chaotic atmosphere, and his appearance may shock the audience. Lear assumes that 'Tom' must have given everything away to his daughters to be reduced to such a state. In lines 49–58, Edgar begs for charity and describes how he has been tempted and tormented by a devilish 'foul fiend'. He could be addressing his words to a specific character on stage, to Lear, Kent and the Fool as a group, or to an imaginary person.

a Take a part each and decide amongst yourselves to whom Edgar is addressing each sentence and the kind of reaction he gets. Present your version to the rest of the class.

b Discuss what you think the effect of Edgar's language is on the other characters in this scene.

1 **naked wretches** 身无分文的苦命人
2 **wheresoe'er** = wherever
3 **bide** 忍受
4 **pelting** 打击
5 **sides** 身体
6 **looped and windowed** 千疮百孔
7 **ta'en** = taken
8 **physic** 药（指泻药）
9 **pomp** 权贵
10 **shake the superflux** 散尽多余的财物
11 **Fathom and half** 一英寻半（fathom为计量水深的单位，1英寻合6英尺或1.8米）
12 **spirit** 鬼
13 **Away** 躲开
14 **bog and quagmire** 泥潭和沼泽
15 **halters in his pew** 在教堂长椅上放置绞索
16 **set ratsbane by his porridge** 在他的燕麦糊里下耗子药
17 **ride … bridges** 骑一匹枣红马在四英寸宽的桥上狂奔
18 **five wits** 五智（中世纪欧洲人认为人有五智：常识 [common wit]、想象 [imagination]、幻觉 [fantasy]、判断 [estimation] 和记忆 [memory]）
19 **star-blasting, and taking** 灾星降临，疾病缠身
20 **vexes** 纠缠，折磨

Poor naked wretches[1], wheresoe'er[2] you are
That bide[3] the pelting[4] of this pitiless storm,
How shall your houseless heads and unfed sides[5],   30
Your looped and windowed[6] raggedness defend you
From seasons such as these? O I have ta'en[7]
Too little care of this. Take physic[8], pomp[9],
Expose thyself to feel what wretches feel,
That thou mayst shake the superflux[10] to them   35
And show the heavens more just.

Enter FOOL

EDGAR   [*Within*] Fathom and half[11]; fathom and half; poor Tom!
FOOL   Come not in here, nuncle! Here's a spirit[12]! Help me, help me!
KENT   Give me thy hand. Who's there?   40
FOOL   A spirit, a spirit! He says his name's Poor Tom.
KENT   What art thou that dost grumble there i'th'straw? Come forth.

[*Enter* EDGAR, *disguised as a madman*]

EDGAR   Away[13], the foul fiend follows me. Through the sharp hawthorn blow the winds. Humh! Go to thy bed and warm thee.   45
LEAR   Didst thou give all to thy daughters? And art thou come to this?
EDGAR   Who gives anything to Poor Tom, whom the foul fiend hath led through fire and through flame, through ford and whirlpool, o'er bog and quagmire[14]; that hath laid knives under his pillow and halters in his pew[15]; set ratsbane by his porridge[16]; made him proud of heart to ride on a bay trotting-horse over four-inched bridges[17], to course his own shadow for a traitor. Bless thy five wits[18], Tom's a-cold! O do, de, do, de, do de. Bless   55
thee from whirlwinds, star-blasting, and taking[19]. Do Poor Tom some charity, whom the foul fiend vexes[20]. There could I have him now, and there, and there again, and there.   50

Storm still

Lear assumes that Tom's madness has been caused by unkind daughters. Tom offers a mangled version of the ten commandments, and then parodies the seven deadly sins in his story of his past life as a lustful serving-man.

 剧情简介：李尔认定汤姆发疯是他不孝的女儿们造成的。汤姆胡乱编了一个摩西十诫的版本，然后讲了他自己当仆人时纵欲的事，戏仿七宗致命罪过。

1 Edgar's disjointed thoughts (in small groups)

Directors and actors can be very creative with Edgar's disjointed thoughts in lines 77–90. Some critics suggest that 'Tom' is imitating the sound of the wind at 'suum' and 'mun', and pretending to ride an imaginary horse at 'Dauphin … cessez!' But these lines are open to interpretation, and they can be read very differently.

Nevertheless, the story 'Tom' tells is certainly dramatic, and it helps to illuminate the themes and situations in the play. He appears to be alluding to the biblical ten commandments (Exodus 20:2–17 and Deuteronomy 5:6–21) and the seven deadly sins: lust, gluttony, greed, sloth, wrath, envy and pride.

- Prepare a series of tableaux to illustrate some of the tales Edgar tells as 'Poor Tom', in lines 82 ('Wine loved I dearly') to line 88.
- One person reads these lines aloud, pausing frequently for the others to guess which words accompany the different tableaux.

▼ Edgar (as Poor Tom) in the storm with Lear, Kent and the Fool.

1 pass 窘况
2 Nay … shamed 不，他留了一条毯子，不然我们都会没脸见人了
3 pendulous air 高悬在空中
4 fated 注定（要堕落）
5 light 降落在
6 subdued nature 压制本性
7 Judicious 明断，公正
8 pelican 鹈鹕（莎士比亚时代的人们以为小鹈鹕以母鹈鹕的血肉为生，故用鹈鹕比喻忘恩负义的子女）
9 Pillicock （俚语，表示"阴茎"；后文的Pillicock Hill指女阴）
10 alow, alow, loo, loo （拟声词，相当于hello；或在模仿吆喝狗去追猎物）
11 commit … array 不要与有夫之妇通奸，也不要给你的心上人华衣美服
12 did the act of darkness 干那夜里干的事
13 out-paramoured 情人多过……
14 the Turk 土耳其苏丹（以妻妾和情妇众多而闻名）
15 light of ear 耳根子软；容易轻信流言
16 sloth 懒惰
17 plackets 裙缝（暗指女阴）
18 thy pen from lender's books 你的笔远离放债人的账簿（不在上面签字）
19 suum, mun, nonny （前两个词是模仿风声，第三个词常用在歌谣中作副歌叠句；这里爱德格故意疯言疯语，不知所云）
20 Dauphin 道芬（从上下文看，应当是一匹马的名字）
21 cessez! 停下！（法语）

LEAR	What, has his daughters brought him to this pass[1]?	
	Couldst thou save nothing? Wouldst thou give 'em all?	60
FOOL	Nay, he reserved a blanket, else we had been all shamed[2].	
LEAR	Now all the plagues that in the pendulous air[3]	
	Hang fated[4] o'er men's faults, light[5] on thy daughters!	
KENT	He hath no daughters, sir.	
LEAR	Death, traitor! Nothing could have subdued nature[6]	65
	To such a lowness but his unkind daughters.	
	Is it the fashion that discarded fathers	
	Should have thus little mercy on their flesh?	
	Judicious[7] punishment: 'twas this flesh begot	
	Those pelican[8] daughters.	70
EDGAR	Pillicock[9] sat on Pillicock Hill; alow, alow, loo, loo[10].	
FOOL	This cold night will turn us all to fools and madmen.	
EDGAR	Take heed o'th'foul fiend, obey thy parents, keep thy words' justice, swear not, commit not with man's sworn spouse, set not thy sweet heart on proud array[11]. Tom's a-cold.	75
LEAR	What hast thou been?	
EDGAR	A servingman, proud in heart and mind, that curled my hair, wore gloves in my cap, served the lust of my mistress' heart, and did the act of darkness[12] with her. Swore as many oaths as I spake words, and broke them in the sweet face of heaven. One that slept in the contriving of lust and waked to do it. Wine loved I dearly, dice dearly, and in woman outparamoured[13] the Turk[14]. False of heart, light of ear[15], bloody of hand; hog in sloth[16], fox in stealth, wolf in greediness, dog in madness, lion in prey. Let not the creaking of shoes nor the rustling of silks betray thy poor heart to woman. Keep thy foot out of brothels, thy hand out of plackets[17], thy pen from lender's books[18], and defy the foul fiend. Still through the hawthorn blows the cold wind, says suum, mun, nonny[19]. Dauphin[20], my boy, boy, *cessez!*[21] let him trot by.	80 85 90
	Storm still	

Lear believes that poor naked Tom represents humankind's essential nature and tries to remove his own clothes in imitation. Edgar, as Tom, speaks of demons and nightmares, and tells Gloucester of his suffering.

剧情简介：李尔相信赤身裸体的可怜人汤姆代表人类的基本天性，并要脱掉自己的衣服来模仿汤姆。伪装成汤姆的爱德格说起了魔鬼和噩梦，并告诉格劳斯特他所遭受的痛苦。

1 'the thing itself' (in pairs)

Lear, in his madness, continues to be preoccupied by 'Tom', and begins to regard him as a sage or philosopher. At the start of the play, Lear refuses to listen to well-intentioned advice from Kent; as part of his reversal, he is now desperate to hear wisdom from the mouths of others. Lear believes that Tom, 'the thing itself', demonstrates humanity's fundamental nature. 'Unaccommodated man' (that is, man stripped of the material trappings of life) is just a 'poor, bare, forked animal'.

- Take turns to speak lines 91–7 to each other. Then suggest why the traumatised (精神受伤) king might wish to remove his clothes, and how you imagine the other characters would react to Lear's attempts to undress.

Stagecraft 导演技巧

Performing 'Poor Tom' (in small groups)

Shakespeare probably borrowed much of Tom's language from Samuel Harsnett's 1603 book on witchcraft, *A Declaration of Egregious Popish Impostures* (see p. 212). For example, Edgar calls Gloucester 'Flibbertigibbet' – a dancing devil that stalks the Earth at night, spreading disease and deformity. He chants about St Swithin meeting 'the nightmare', a female monster who suffocated her victims. St Swithin orders her to 'alight' (get off), makes her 'troth plight' (promise not to do it again) and tells her 'aroint thee' (clear off).

a Working in small groups, prepare a performance of lines 102–25. During your preparations, consider the following questions:

- What facial expressions and/or gestures might Edgar use to accompany his discussion of the various creatures?
- To whom might Edgar address the various lines? Will some of the lines be aimed at different people?
- How might Lear, Kent and Gloucester react to Edgar's lines? Do they listen attentively, ignore him or respond in some other way?

b Perform your version of the scene to the class. After all the groups have done so, hold a discussion about the effectiveness of each performance. List the strongest aspects and consider how each might be improved further.

1 answer 遭遇
2 ow'st = owe
3 hide 兽皮
4 cat 麝猫（其肛门囊体里提取出来的分泌物可做香料）
5 on's = of us
6 sophisticated 老于世故（不再单纯）
7 Unaccommodated 赤条条
8 forked 双腿行走
9 lendings 借来之物（指衣服）
10 naughty （天气）恶劣
11 old lecher 老色鬼
12 on's = of his
13 Flibbertigibbet 弗立博提吉比（Samuel Harsnett于1603年出版的 *A Declaration of Egregious Popish Imposture*［《一份关于天主教恶劣欺诈行为的报告》］中一个魔鬼的名字）
14 curfew 晚钟；宵禁
15 first cock 鸡叫头遍（破晓）
16 web and the pin 白内障
17 squints 使斜视
18 mildews the white wheat 让黄了的麦子生霉
19 creature 众生灵
20 Swithold footed thrice the wold 圣威特侯三次踏上荒丘（Swithold 或许 = St Withold，传说这位圣人能让鬼怪发誓不害人）
21 nightmare 梦魇女妖（夜里侵扰熟睡者，导致其在噩梦中窒息；mare又指母马）
22 ninefold 九个马驹（或指梦魇女妖的九个侍从）
23 aroint 走开
24 the wall-newt, and the water 墙上的壁虎和水里的蝾螈
25 mantle （水塘上的一层）浮沫
26 standing pool 死水潭
27 tithing 教区
28 stocked 铐着足枷
29 three … body （三身外套和六件衬衣是一个仆人被限定的衣服件数；这里埃德加回应他之前是一位serving-man）
30 small deer 小动物
31 Smulkin 司玛尔金（一种老鼠模样的小妖精）

KING LEAR ACT 3 SCENE 4
李尔王

LEAR Thou wert better in a grave than to answer¹ with thy uncovered body this extremity of the skies. Is man no more than this? Consider him well. Thou ow'st² the worm no silk, the beast no hide³, the sheep no wool, the cat⁴ no perfume. Ha! Here's three on's⁵ are sophisticated⁶; thou art the thing itself. Unaccommodated⁷ man is no more but such a poor, bare, forked⁸ animal as thou art. Off, off, you lendings⁹! Come, unbutton here. 95

FOOL Prithee, nuncle, be contented; 'tis a naughty¹⁰ night to swim in. Now a little fire in a wild field were like an old lecher's¹¹ heart – a small spark, all the rest on's¹² body cold. Look, here comes a walking fire. 100

Enter GLOUCESTER *with a torch*

EDGAR This is the foul Flibbertigibbet¹³; he begins at curfew¹⁴ and walks till the first cock¹⁵. He gives the web and the pin¹⁶, squints¹⁷ the eye, and makes the harelip; mildews the white wheat¹⁸, and hurts the poor creature¹⁹ of earth. 105
   [*Chants*] Swithold footed thrice the wold²⁰,
      He met the nightmare²¹ and her ninefold²²;
         Bid her alight
         And her troth plight,
      And aroint²³ thee, witch, aroint thee! 110

KENT How fares your grace?
LEAR What's he?
KENT Who's there? What is't you seek?
GLOUCESTER What are you there? Your names?
EDGAR Poor Tom, that eats the swimming frog, the toad, the tadpole, the wall-newt, and the water²⁴; that in the fury of his heart, when the foul fiend rages, eats cowdung for salads, swallows the old rat and the ditch-dog, drinks the green mantle²⁵ of the standing pool²⁶; who is whipped from tithing²⁷ to tithing, and stocked²⁸, punished, and imprisoned; who hath had three suits to his back, six shirts to his body²⁹, 115
      Horse to ride, and weapon to wear; 120
      But mice and rats and such small deer³⁰
      Have been Tom's food for seven long year.
Beware my follower. Peace, Smulkin³¹; peace, thou fiend! 125

Gloucester tries to persuade Lear to leave for a place of safety, but Lear wants to learn wisdom from Poor Tom. Gloucester speaks of his love for Edgar. Lear shows compassion for Poor Tom.

剧情简介：格劳斯特试图劝李尔到安全的地方去，但是李尔想从可怜的汤姆那里学习智慧。格劳斯特谈起他对爱德格的爱。李尔对可怜汤姆的遭遇感到同情。

Write about it 写作练习

The play's philosophers

In line 138, Lear says of 'Tom', 'First let me talk with this philosopher'. Lear also calls him a 'learnèd Theban' and 'Noble philosopher'. Although it is ironic that Lear should look for philosophical consolation from a character who is acting as a madman, it is interesting to compare the various ideas that are touched upon in the play about how best to lead one's life. The brothers, Edmond and Edgar, offer a particularly significant contrast. Some critics have referred to Edmond's philosophy of life as 'Machiavellian', which essentially means that Edmond believes the ends justify the means. On the other hand, Edgar's philosophy has been characterised as selfless or altruistic.

- Write a couple of paragraphs contrasting Edgar and Edmond's philosophical views on life. Try to use quotations to support your ideas. (For example, you might quote Edmond from Act 1 Scene 2 saying 'Thou, Nature, art my goddess' or Edgar from Act 2 Scene 3 saying 'Edgar I nothing am.')

1 Metaphorical (隐喻性) blindness

Lear could not recognise the true nature of his own daughters until they turned on him, and Gloucester displays similar blindness. He laments the loss of Kent and Edgar, but fails to recognise them when they are right in front of him. He remains completely ignorant of Edmond's scheming.

a In groups, discuss the significance of the motif of blindness/not seeing in *King Lear*.

b Four of you take parts as Lear, Kent, Edgar and Gloucester and prepare to read aloud lines 126–60. Any remaining group members should prepare themselves to speak what they think Edgar's and Kent's reactions and private thoughts might be at significant moments. The four character readers should pause at the end of each set of lines to allow the 'other' Edgar and Kent to interject their thoughts and comments on what has been said.

1 **Modo/Mahu** 摩多/玛胡（地狱里两个恶魔长官的名字）
2 **Our ... gets it** 我们的骨肉丧尽天良，恨起了自己的生身父母 (gets = begets)
3 **injunction** 禁令
4 **bar** 闩上（门）
5 **this same learnèd Theban** 这位现世有学问的特拜人（Theban是Thebes的派生词，后者多译作"底比斯"，但这个地名在古希腊文里读作 [tʰéːbai̯]。特拜是希腊神话里位于希腊中部的一座古城，那里出了许多名人和故事。"有学问的特拜人"说的应当是古希腊犬儒学派哲学家第欧根尼 [Diogenes of Sinope]，爱德格的言谈举止与之相似。）
6 **vermin** 害人虫
7 **Importune** 恳求
8 **His wits begin t'unsettle** 他的脑子犯起糊涂了
9 **outlawed from my blood** 断绝血亲关系
10 **cry you mercy** 求您原谅

GLOUCESTER	What, hath your grace no better company?	
EDGAR	The Prince of Darkness is a gentleman. Modo[1] he's called, and Mahu[1].	
GLOUCESTER	Our flesh and blood, my lord, is grown so vile, That it doth hate what gets it[2].	130
EDGAR	Poor Tom's a-cold.	
GLOUCESTER	Go in with me. My duty cannot suffer T'obey in all your daughters' hard commands. Though their injunction[3] be to bar[4] my doors And let this tyrannous night take hold upon you, Yet have I ventured to come seek you out And bring you where both fire and food is ready.	135
LEAR	First let me talk with this philosopher. What is the cause of thunder?	
KENT	Good my lord, take his offer; go into th'house.	140
LEAR	I'll talk a word with this same learnèd Theban[5]. What is your study?	
EDGAR	How to prevent the fiend, and to kill vermin[6].	
LEAR	Let me ask you one word in private.	
KENT	Importune[7] him once more to go, my lord. His wits begin t'unsettle[8].	145
GLOUCESTER	Canst thou blame him?	

Storm still

	His daughters seek his death. Ah, that good Kent, He said it would be thus, poor banished man! Thou sayst the king grows mad; I'll tell thee, friend, I am almost mad myself. I had a son, Now outlawed from my blood[9]; he sought my life But lately, very late. I loved him, friend; No father his son dearer. True to tell thee, The grief hath crazed my wits. What a night's this! I do beseech your grace –	150
LEAR	O, cry you mercy[10], sir. – Noble philosopher, your company.	155
EDGAR	Tom's a-cold.	
GLOUCESTER	In, fellow, there, in t'hovel; keep thee warm.	
LEAR	Come, let's in all.	
KENT	This way, my lord.	
LEAR	With him; I will keep still with my philosopher.	160

The king's party enters the hovel. Edmond shows Cornwall the letter implicating Gloucester in the French invasion plans. Cornwall promises Edmond his father's title and orders him to help in Gloucester's arrest.

剧情简介：国王一行人进入茅舍。爱德门给康沃尔看了封信，信里指控格劳斯特与法国军队的进攻计划有牵连。康沃尔许诺爱德门由他继承父亲格劳斯特的头衔，命令他协助逮捕格劳斯特。

1 Out of the storm

At this point in Act 3, the action moves away from the heath and the storm. Lear and his strange entourage (随从) leave the stage, but the last word is left to an enigmatic (高深莫测) Edgar, who utters the sinister line: 'I smell the blood of a British man.'

a Write a paragraph discussing the effects of this particular line at this point in the play.

b If you were the director, how would you instruct the characters to leave the stage? Write up your notes in your Director's Journal.

2 Tom the story-teller (in pairs)

Edgar's final lines refer to two medieval stories. Child Roland ('Child' here means an untested knight) is the hero of a twelfth-century tale, *Chanson de Roland*, and may also have featured in a version of *Jack the Giant-killer*. The 'dark tower' in Tom's story could be Gloucester's castle. Lines 167–8 are still well known and much used.

- In your pairs, talk about what Edgar's parting words suggest might happen next in the play.
- Decide how and to whom Edgar speaks: to his father, to the audience, or to himself in his own voice?

Characters 人物分析

Edmond as manipulator (in pairs)

In this scene, Edmond deliberately betrays his father under the pretence of feeling torn between family obligation and loyalty to Cornwall.

- Together, compare Edmond's behaviour in this scene with his manipulation of Edgar and Gloucester in Act 1 Scene 2 and Act 2 Scene 1.
- Find all the occasions in the play so far in which Edmond takes on the role of 'manipulator'.
- Briefly describe these occasions in your own words. Order the list in terms of which actions you think are the most cunning.
- Share your judgements with the rest of the class and give each other feedback on the ideas you put forward.

---

1 **soothe** 顺着
2 **Athenian** 雅典人
3 **Child … came** 少年柔兰来到黑暗塔楼前（可能出自一首未流传下来的古代歌谣。柔兰是现存最早法文史诗《柔兰之歌》[*La Chanson de Roland*，创作于11世纪] 的主人公，法兰克国王和西罗马帝国皇帝查理大帝 [Charlemagne，768年—814年在位] 统治时期的一位著名英雄）
4 **word** 暗号
5 **censured** 被说三道四
6 **nature** 亲情，孝心
7 **something fears me** 令我有些害怕
8 **a provoking … himself** 格劳斯特自己的邪恶招致，是他咎由自取
9 **approves … France** 证明他是替法兰西效劳的奸细
10 **apprehension** 逮捕
11 **stuff his suspicion** 坐实了对他（格劳斯特）的怀疑
12 **persever** = **persevere**（坚持到底；此处重读第二个音节）

KENT	Good my lord, soothe¹ him; let him take the fellow.	
GLOUCESTER	Take him you on.	
KENT	Sirrah, come on. Go along with us.	
LEAR	Come, good Athenian².	
GLOUCESTER	No words, no words. Hush.	165
EDGAR	Child Roland to the dark tower came³.	
	His word⁴ was still 'Fie, fo, and fum;	
	I smell the blood of a British man.'	

Exeunt

Act 3 Scene 5
A room in Gloucester's castle

Enter CORNWALL *and* EDMOND

CORNWALL I will have my revenge ere I depart his house.

EDMOND How, my lord, I may be censured⁵, that nature⁶ thus gives way to loyalty, something fears me⁷ to think of.

CORNWALL I now perceive it was not altogether your brother's evil disposition made him seek his death, but a provoking merit set a-work by a reprovable badness in himself⁸.   5

EDMOND How malicious is my fortune, that I must repent to be just! This is the letter which he spoke of, which approves him an intelligent party to the advantages of France⁹. O heavens, that this treason were not, or not I the detector!   10

CORNWALL Go with me to the duchess.

EDMOND If the matter of this paper be certain, you have mighty business in hand.

CORNWALL True or false, it hath made thee Earl of Gloucester. Seek out where thy father is, that he may be ready for our   15
apprehension¹⁰.

EDMOND [*Aside*] If I find him comforting the king, it will stuff his suspicion¹¹ more fully. – I will persever¹² in my course of loyalty, though the conflict be sore between that and my blood.

CORNWALL I will lay trust upon thee, and thou shalt find a dearer   20
father in my love.

Exeunt

Gloucester leaves to find provisions for Lear and his followers. Edgar continues his talk of devils, but briefly drops his disguise. The Fool poses a puzzling question. In his mental anguish, Lear imagines revenge.

剧情简介：格劳斯特离开，去给李尔及其随从找吃的。爱德格继续说他的魔鬼，但是短暂放下了自己的伪装。俳优提了个难解的问题。李尔在精神的极度痛苦中想象复仇。

1 piece out the comfort 弄得舒服些
2 impatience 急躁
3 Frateretto 弗拉特雷托（一个跳舞的魔鬼的名字）
4 Nero 尼禄（罗马帝国第五位皇帝，54年—68年在位，著名的暴君，传说死后被打入地狱）
5 angler 钓鱼者
6 the lake of darkness 幽冥湖（地狱之湖）
7 innocent 呆子，笨蛋（可能在称呼俳优）
8 yeoman 自耕农（地位低于绅士；这里可能是莎士比亚对自己家庭的玩笑）
9 a thousand 一千个恶魔
10 spits 烤肉扦子
11 mar my counterfeiting 毁坏我的伪装

1 A mock trial? (in small groups)

In the Quarto version of the play, Lear stages a mock trial of Gonerill and Regan during this scene. Read this extract on page 245, then carry out the following activities:

a Prepare a performance of the scene in your groups, thinking very carefully about how you would stage it, where the actors would be positioned and how you could create the right atmosphere for a 'mock trial'.

b If you were directing the play, would you include the trial scene in your production? List arguments for and against its inclusion.

Act 3 Scene 6
Inside the hovel on the heath

Enter KENT *(disguised) and* GLOUCESTER

GLOUCESTER Here is better than the open air; take it thankfully. I will piece out the comfort[1] with what addition I can. I will not be long from you.

KENT All the power of his wits have given way to his impatience[2]; the gods reward your kindness!

Exit [Gloucester]

Enter LEAR, EDGAR *[disguised as a madman], and* FOOL

EDGAR Frateretto[3] calls me, and tells me Nero[4] is an angler[5] in the lake of darkness[6]. Pray, innocent[7], and beware the foul fiend.

FOOL Prithee, nuncle, tell me whether a madman be a gentleman or a yeoman[8].

LEAR A king, a king!

FOOL No, he's a yeoman that has a gentleman to his son; for he's a mad yeoman that sees his son a gentleman before him.

LEAR To have a thousand[9] with red burning spits[10]
Come hizzing in upon 'em!

EDGAR Bless thy five wits.

KENT O pity! Sir, where is the patience now
That you so oft have boasted to retain?

EDGAR [*Aside*] My tears begin to take his part so much
They mar my counterfeiting[11].

LEAR The little dogs and all,
Tray, Blanch, and Sweetheart – see, they bark at me.

Tom speaks a verse of warning to all dogs. Lear broods on Regan's ingratitude, then falls asleep. Gloucester warns Kent of a plot to assassinate the king. He urges him to take Lear to safety at Dover.

剧情简介：汤姆为所有的狗念了一首警告的小诗。李尔闷闷不乐地想着蕊根的忘恩负义，然后入睡。格劳斯特警告肯特有人要谋害国王，他催肯特带着李尔躲到多佛去。

1 Tom's rhyme (in pairs)

Lines 22–30 are Tom's response to Lear's vision of his pet dogs.

- Experiment with ways of reading the lines to make them sound like a nursery rhyme, a charm or an incantation (咒语). How do you think Lear would react? Does he 'see' Tom's dogs in the way he seems to have seen his own dogs, Tray, Blanch and Sweetheart, in line 21?
- In pairs, read the lines to each other several times and agree on the best way of performing them. Take turns in reading Edgar's lines and acting Lear's responses.
- Discuss how the meaning or connotations of the lines change each time they are spoken.

Write about it 写作练习

The Fool's last words

'And I'll go to bed at noon' (line 41) are the Fool's last words in the play. It is often thought to be puzzling that the Fool should disappear with two acts still remaining. However, his role has diminished with the arrival of 'Tom' and Lear's shifting perspective. Directors deal with the disappearance of the Fool in different ways. Some productions use wordless stage action later in the play to explain it. One production showed Lear accidentally inflicting a fatal wound at line 33 of this scene. As the king said 'Let them anatomise Regan', he pretended to be carrying out a dissection (解剖) with his sword and unwittingly stabbed the Fool through a cushion that he was holding across his stomach. Other directors have played on the possible link between the Fool and Cordelia, and have had Lear carry the Fool to bed, anticipating the later scene in which he appears with Cordelia in his arms and utters the line: 'And my poor fool is hanged.'

- Decide how you would have the Fool speak his last line and how you would stage this section of the scene.
- Then write a set of detailed notes for the actors to explain both how the line should be delivered and what should be happening on stage at this point. Make sure you justify your decisions.
- When you have finished writing, present your ideas to the class and compare your handling of the scene with that of your fellow students.

1 throw his head （可能指猛摇头做出吓唬的表情）
2 Avaunt 滚
3 Mastiff … him 无论獒、格力犬、凶猛的杂种狗，还是赛犬和猎犬，不管是公是母
4 Bobtail tyke 短尾野狗
5 trundle-tail 卷毛尾巴狗
6 leap the hatch 窜出小门
7 Do, de, de, de （可能是因为寒冷牙齿打战的声音）
8 wakes 维克斯节（英格兰北方和苏格兰的一个基督教节日，为期一周）
9 horn 牛角杯（乞丐乞讨用的）
10 anatomise 解剖
11 entertain 留用，雇用
12 Persian 波斯式的（波斯服饰一般雍容华贵；这里很明显是反讽，因为爱德格衣不蔽体）
13 litter （放在马车上的）轿子或担架
14 dally 耽搁，磨蹭
15 Stand in assurèd loss （命）必将不保
16 that … conduct 那个会快速把你带到有给养的地方去的人

EDGAR	Tom will throw his head¹ at them. – Avaunt², you curs!	
	Be thy mouth or black or white,	
	Tooth that poisons if it bite,	
	Mastiff, greyhound, mongrel grim,	25
	Hound or spaniel, brach or him³,	
	Bobtail tyke⁴ or trundle-tail⁵,	
	Tom will make him weep and wail;	
	For with throwing thus my head,	
	Dogs leap the hatch⁶, and all are fled.	30

EDGAR Do, de, de, de⁷. *Cessez!* Come, march to wakes⁸ and fairs and market towns. Poor Tom, thy horn⁹ is dry.

LEAR Then let them anatomise¹⁰ Regan; see what breeds about her heart. Is there any cause in nature that makes these hard-hearts? [*To Edgar*] You, sir, I entertain¹¹ for one of my hundred, only I do not like the fashion of your garments. You will say they are Persian¹²; but let them be changed.

KENT Now, good my lord, lie here and rest a while.

LEAR Make no noise, make no noise. Draw the curtains: so, so. We'll go to supper i'th'morning. [*He sleeps*]

FOOL And I'll go to bed at noon.

Enter GLOUCESTER

GLOUCESTER Come hither, friend. Where is the king my master?

KENT Here, sir, but trouble him not; his wits are gone.

GLOUCESTER Good friend, I prithee take him in thy arms.
I have o'erheard a plot of death upon him.
There is a litter¹³ ready. Lay him in't
And drive toward Dover, friend, where thou shalt meet
Both welcome and protection. Take up thy master;
If thou shouldst dally¹⁴ half an hour, his life
With thine and all that offer to defend him
Stand in assurèd loss¹⁵. Take up, take up,
And follow me, that will to some provision
Give thee quick conduct¹⁶. Come, come away.

Exeunt

Cornwall reports that the French army has invaded. He instructs Edmond to leave to avoid witnessing his father's harsh punishment. Oswald reports that some of Gloucester's followers have gone to Dover with Lear.

 剧情简介：康沃尔报告说法国军队已经攻入。他命爱德门离开，省得亲眼看着父亲被严惩。奥兹沃尔报告说格劳斯特的一些随从已经和李尔到多佛去了。

1 'Pluck out his eyes'

In Shakespeare's time, punishment depended on rank. A duke guilty of treason could expect to be beheaded rather than hanged, drawn and quartered. Both Regan and Gonerill are keen to say how Gloucester should be punished.

- As you read on, note how quickly and terrifyingly Gonerill's suggestion becomes reality. Note also how the literal blinding she demands fits in with the play's themes of metaphorical sight and blindness.

Language in the play 剧中语言

The language of action (in small groups)

The language of this scene contrasts sharply with the preceding scene on the heath. For example, Cornwall and the two sisters both frequently employ imperatives: they issue instructions and commands. This suggests that they are establishing control and authority over fast-moving events.

a Plan and prepare a reading of lines 1–12 that emphasises this sense of power and activity.

b Experiment with the ways in which lines 4 and 5 could be delivered in order to contrast the characters of Regan and Gonerill.

c Discuss how Cornwall's character is different from Regan's and Gonerill's in this scene. Look carefully at the language he uses.

Characters 人物分析

What is Edmond thinking? (in pairs)

Edmond says nothing in this scene. He has manoeuvred himself into a powerful position and he now hears Cornwall call him 'my lord of Gloucester'.

a Discuss what Edmond might be thinking at various points in this scene.

b One of you is the reader and the other plays Edmond. As the reader reads through the scene aloud, pausing after each character's contribution, Edmond speaks his thoughts.

c Together, write an aside for Edmond that could be inserted after line 12.

1	Post	骑马赶到
2	sister	妻姐
3	beholding	目睹
4	festinate preparation	迅速准备（战斗）
5	bound to the like	必定一样
6	posts	信使
7	intelligent	传递消息
8	lord of Gloucester	（这里指爱德门，高娜瑞尔已经默认其为格劳斯特伯爵；而第14行中的lord of Gloucester仍指爱德门的父亲）
9	Hot questrists	急切的搜寻者们

Act 3 Scene 7
The Great Hall of Gloucester's castle

Enter CORNWALL, REGAN, GONERILL, EDMOND *and Servants*

CORNWALL [*To Gonerill*] Post[1] speedily to my lord your husband; show him this letter. The army of France is landed. – Seek out the traitor Gloucester.

[*Exeunt some Servants*]

REGAN Hang him instantly.
GONERILL Pluck out his eyes.
CORNWALL Leave him to my displeasure. Edmond, keep you our sister[2] company. The revenges we are bound to take upon your traitorous father are not fit for your beholding[3]. Advise the duke, where you are going, to a most festinate preparation[4]: we are bound to the like[5]. Our posts[6] shall be swift and intelligent[7] betwixt us. Farewell, dear sister; farewell, my lord of Gloucester[8].

[*Gonerill and Edmond start to leave*]

Enter OSWALD

How now, where's the king?
OSWALD My lord of Gloucester hath conveyed him hence.
Some five or six and thirty of his knights,
Hot questrists[9] after him, met him at gate,
Who, with some other of the lord's dependants,
Are gone with him toward Dover, where they boast
To have well-armèd friends.
CORNWALL Get horses for your mistress.

[*Exit Oswald*]

Cornwall plans to punish Gloucester without reference to the law. Gloucester is brought in and tied to a chair. He protests that his captors are breaking the customs of hospitality, but his interrogation begins.

 剧情简介：康沃尔打算不依照法律，直接惩罚格劳斯特。格劳斯特被带上来，并被绑在椅子上。他向捉拿他的人抗议说，他们坏了待客之道，但对他的拷问开始了。

1 Power without responsibility

Cornwall seems to be aware that 'in the tender of a wholesome weal', with great power comes great responsibility. In lines 24–7, for example, he admits that he should not execute Gloucester without a proper trial. However, he also knows that no one will stop him acting on his own authority, and he is prepared to let his anger override other considerations ('our power / Shall do a curtsy to our wrath').

- Working on your own or with a partner, make a list of examples from history or from current affairs where the abuse of power has resulted in similar atrocities.
- As a class, discuss the ways in which this theme of power – and the other themes in the play – might be relevant to the world today.

Write about it 写作练习

Interrogation and torture (by yourself)

This scene features the interrogation and torture of Gloucester. Regan and Cornwall – who should show respect to Gloucester as both their host and as a senior member of the aristocracy – instead delight in inflicting cruelty on him. In their language and their harsh actions, Regan and Cornwall demonstrate coldness, cunning and brutal interrogation skills.

- Write two or three analytical paragraphs showing how Regan and Cornwall set about humiliating and trying to extract information from Gloucester.
- Pay particular attention to the language in the scene; make sure that you quote some of the lines the characters say to demonstrate the effectiveness of their language.
- Consider Gloucester's lines, too, and write about how he responds to his ordeal.
- Once you have finished writing, you might discuss with a partner, or with the class as a whole, how you think the various protagonists can be regarded in this scene. Talk about how you think each of the characters will be affected in the long run by the events that have taken place here. For each character, share your ideas about what you think will happen to them and why, basing your predictions on evidence from the play.

1 Pinion 绑起来
2 pass ... justice 不经正式审判就判他死刑
3 do ... wrath 向我们的愤怒表示敬意
4 corky 干瘪
5 foul play 胡来
6 filthy 恶心人
7 ignobly 不光彩
8 ravish 扯，拔
9 quicken 活过来
10 hospitable favours 殷勤款待的面容
11 ruffle 糟践
12 simple-answered 老实回答
13 confederacy 阴谋
14 Late footed = Lately landed（指法军登陆）

GONERILL	Farewell, sweet lord, and sister.
CORNWALL	Edmond, farewell.

                                             [Exeunt Gonerill and Edmond]

                  [*To Servants*]   Go seek the traitor Gloucester.
                  Pinion[1] him like a thief; bring him before us.

                                                 [Exeunt other Servants]

                  Though well we may not pass upon his life
                  Without the form of justice[2], yet our power   25
                  Shall do a curtsy to our wrath[3], which men
                  May blame but not control.

                            Enter GLOUCESTER *and Servants*

                                Who's there – the traitor?

REGAN	Ingrateful fox! 'tis he.
CORNWALL	Bind fast his corky[4] arms.
GLOUCESTER	What means your graces? Good my friends, consider 30 You are my guests. Do me no foul play[5], friends.
CORNWALL	Bind him, I say.
REGAN	Hard, hard! O filthy[6] traitor!
GLOUCESTER	Unmerciful lady as you are, I'm none.
CORNWALL	To this chair bind him. Villain, thou shalt find –

                              [Regan plucks Gloucester's beard]

GLOUCESTER	By the kind gods, 'tis most ignobly[7] done, 35 To pluck me by the beard.
REGAN	So white, and such a traitor?
GLOUCESTER	Naughty lady, These hairs which thou dost ravish[8] from my chin Will quicken[9] and accuse thee. I am your host. With robbers' hands my hospitable favours[10] 40 You should not ruffle[11] thus. What will you do?
CORNWALL	Come, sir, what letters had you late from France?
REGAN	Be simple-answered[12], for we know the truth.
CORNWALL	And what confederacy[13] have you with the traitors Late footed[14] in the kingdom?
REGAN	To whose hands 45 You have sent the lunatic king. Speak.

Gloucester admits that he sent Lear to safety in Dover. He hopes to see Lear's enemies receive just punishment. Cornwall gouges out one of Gloucester's eyes. A servant challenges Cornwall.

剧情简介：格劳斯特承认他把李尔送到多佛的安全地方去了，还说希望看到李尔的敌人得到公正惩罚。康沃尔挖了格劳斯特一只眼睛。一位仆人挑战康沃尔。

1 Gloucester 'tied to th'stake' (in pairs)

The image in line 53 is of the popular Jacobean sport of bear-baiting. Indeed, almost exactly the same image appears at the end of *Macbeth* when Macbeth says: 'They have tied me to a stake; I cannot fly, / But bear-like I must fight the course.' There was a bear-baiting pit next to the Globe Theatre (环球剧场), and a nearby street is still called Bear Gardens.

- Look again at the activity about imagery on page 108. Then find out a bit more about the practice of bear-baiting in Shakespeare's time and discuss with a partner how audiences might have reacted to the use of this image here. What does it tell us about Gloucester's mood and his fears for his safety?

Stagecraft 导演技巧

'Out, vile jelly!' (in small groups)

During this scene, Gloucester's eyes are brutally gouged out. It would appear that Shakespeare intended this vicious act of cruelty to take place in front of the audience. Directors have struggled both with the horror of the scene and with the difficulty of making it seem realistic. Some have decided not to portray it on stage.

- In small groups, consider how you would stage this scene using either no props or only very simple ones and no modern technology.
- Then block your version (work out where characters will be on stage) and perform it, showing how you will make the events happening on stage appear both horrific and believable.

1 **guessingly set down** 根据揣测写下来的
2 **neutral heart** 中立立场
3 **at peril** 冒着（生命）危险
4 **course** 攻击（格劳斯特把自己比喻为被绑在木桩上受群狗攻击的熊；斗熊是莎士比亚时代英格兰常见的娱乐）
5 **anointed flesh** 涂过圣油的圣体（指李尔王在加冕时涂过圣油的身体；欧洲君主加冕时在额头涂抹膏油，因此他们被称为"上帝的受膏者"）
6 **boarish fangs** 野猪那种獠牙
7 **buoyed up** 冉冉升起
8 **stellèd** 星星的
9 **holp** – holpod
10 **stern** 严峻
11 **All cruels else subscribe** （李尔之外）所有其他野兽均可放进来
12 **wingèd vengeance** 天谴报应

128

GLOUCESTER	I have a letter guessingly set down[1],	
	Which came from one that's of a neutral heart[2],	
	And not from one opposed.	
CORNWALL	Cunning.	
REGAN	And false.	
CORNWALL	Where hast thou sent the king?	
GLOUCESTER	To Dover.	50
REGAN	Wherefore to Dover? Wast thou not charged at peril[3] –	
CORNWALL	Wherefore to Dover? Let him answer that.	
GLOUCESTER	I am tied to th'stake, and I must stand the course[4].	
REGAN	Wherefore to Dover?	
GLOUCESTER	Because I would not see thy cruel nails	55
	Pluck out his poor old eyes, nor thy fierce sister	
	In his anointed flesh[5] stick boarish fangs[6].	
	The sea, with such a storm as his bare head	
	In hell-black night endured, would have buoyed up[7]	
	And quenched the stellèd[8] fires.	60
	Yet, poor old heart, he holp[9] the heavens to rain.	
	If wolves had at thy gate howled that stern[10] time,	
	Thou shouldst have said, 'Good porter, turn the key:	
	All cruels else subscribe[11].' But I shall see	
	The wingèd vengeance[12] overtake such children.	65
CORNWALL	See't shalt thou never. Fellows, hold the chair.	
	Upon these eyes of thine I'll set my foot.	
GLOUCESTER	He that will think to live till he be old,	
	Give me some help! – O cruel! O you gods!	
	[*Cornwall puts out one of Gloucester's eyes*]	
REGAN	One side will mock another: th'other, too.	70
CORNWALL	If you see vengeance –	
SERVANT	Hold your hand, my lord.	
	I have served you ever since I was a child,	
	But better service have I never done you	
	Than now to bid you hold.	
REGAN	How now, you dog!	

Regan kills the servant. Cornwall blinds Gloucester's other eye. Regan tauntingly informs Gloucester of Edmond's treachery. She orders Gloucester to be thrown out. Cornwall says he is badly wounded.

 剧情简介：蕊根把仆人杀了，康沃尔弄瞎了格劳斯特另一只眼睛。蕊根嘲弄地告诉格劳斯特，爱德门背叛了他。她下令把格劳斯特扔出去。康沃尔说自己伤得很严重。

Characters 人物分析

'tender-hefted' Regan? (in pairs)

In Act 2 Scene 4, line 164, Lear describes Regan as 'tender-hefted' (soft-hearted or gentle) and she is sometimes portrayed on stage as very feminine. Yet she urges Cornwall on in his barbaric maiming of Gloucester, kills the servant who protests and further tortures Gloucester by telling him that it was Edmond who betrayed him.

- Decide exactly how Regan should be played from the putting out of Gloucester's eyes (line 69) to the end of this scene.
- Do you think the audience should feel any sympathy towards her, or would you characterise her as an out-and-out villain? You could write up your notes in your Director's Journal.

▶ The director of this production chose to show Regan licking the blood from her fingers following Gloucester's blinding. How might an audience react to this in the theatre?

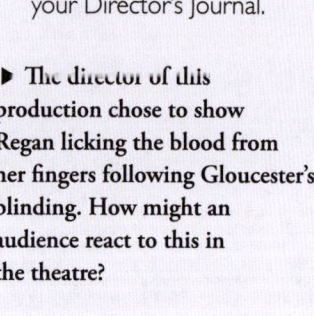

1 If … quarrel 如果您的下巴有胡子（是个男的），我就要跟您决斗
2 villain 坏蛋，恶棍
3 take the chance of anger 领教一下我的愤怒
4 stand up 冒犯，反抗
5 mischief 伤害
6 lustre 光彩
7 enkindle 点燃
8 nature 天良
9 quit 报复
10 made … us 揭露了你背叛我们的阴谋
11 follies 错误
12 abused 被冤枉
13 dunghill 粪堆
14 bleed apace 血流如注
15 hurt 伤口

Themes 主题分析

Sight and blindness (in pairs)

With his exclamation 'O, my follies!' Gloucester finally recognises the truth about his sons. It is, of course, one of the play's ironies that it is only when he is blind that he can 'see' the truth. In the course of the play, several characters are either misread (other characters are 'blind' to the truth) or literally not recognised (as in the case of the disguised Kent or Edgar).

- Make a list of all those characters who are at some stage not recognised or are seriously misunderstood.
- Next to each character you mention, write the names of those characters who are 'blind' to the truth in these situations.

SERVANT	If you did wear a beard upon your chin	75
	I'd shake it on this quarrel¹. What do you mean?	
CORNWALL	My villain²!	
SERVANT	Nay then, come on, and take the chance of anger³.	

[*They draw and fight*]

REGAN   [*To another Servant*] Give me thy sword. A peasant stand up⁴ thus!

Kills him

SERVANT   Oh, I am slain. My lord, you have one eye left   80
To see some mischief⁵ on him. Oh!   [*He dies*]

CORNWALL   Lest it see more, prevent it. Out, vile jelly!
[*He puts out Gloucester's other eye*]
Where is thy lustre⁶ now?

GLOUCESTER   All dark and comfortless. Where's my son Edmond?
Edmond, enkindle⁷ all the sparks of nature⁸   85
To quit⁹ this horrid act.

REGAN   Out, treacherous villain!
Thou call'st on him that hates thee. It was he
That made the overture of thy treasons to us¹⁰,
Who is too good to pity thee.

GLOUCESTER   O, my follies¹¹! Then Edgar was abused¹².   90
Kind gods, forgive me that, and prosper him.

REGAN   Go thrust him out at gates, and let him smell
His way to Dover.

Exit [*a Servant*] *with Gloucester*

How is't, my lord? How look you?

CORNWALL   I have received a hurt. Follow me, lady.
[*To Servants*] Turn out that eyeless villain. Throw this slave   95
Upon the dunghill¹³. Regan, I bleed apace¹⁴.
Untimely comes this hurt¹⁵. Give me your arm.

Exeunt

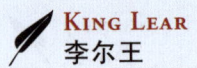
KING LEAR
李尔王

Looking back at Act 3 第3幕回顾
Activities for groups or individuals

1 Staging Act 3

Act 3 presents a number of interesting challenges for directors and producers. First, the heath and the storm are difficult to represent on stage. Although most productions avoid trying to be too realistic, many use sound effects during the storm, and some recent productions have recreated rain in the theatre. Second, the gratuitous (无端) violence depicted on stage – with the gouging out of Gloucester's eyes – can be hard to make realistic. Some might consider it inappropriate.

- Imagine the production meeting that takes place prior to a new performance of this play. Working in a group, take roles as the producer, the director and one or two of the actors playing the key parts, such as Lear. Discuss the important decisions you will need to make for your production. Consider issues of staging, the responses of the audience and the resources at your disposal.
- Write up your decisions in your Director's Journal, explaining carefully the reasons for making them.

2 Signs of goodness

Some hope is provided in Scene 7, in the actions of the brave servant who attempts to defend Gloucester. He is a reminder that goodness could reign again in Lear's kingdom. In the Quarto version of the play, this scene closes with two other servants who decide to assist the blinded Gloucester. They express revulsion (极度厌恶) at Cornwall's and Regan's evil, try to soothe Gloucester's pain ('Til fetch some flax and whites of eggs / To apply to his bleeding face'), and call on heaven to help him. In the theatre, the interval is sometimes placed at the end of this scene.

- Decide whether you would include the two kind servants from the Quarto version to conclude the first half of the play, end it at line 97 as in the Folio version, or place the interval before the blinding scene. Present your final decision to the rest of the class, giving your reasons.

3 Madness

The representation of madness is a key element in Act 3. For large parts of the act, the audience is presented with three characters who are all demonstrating or feigning degrees of madness. Lear is losing his reason, the Fool is a professional madman and Edgar is acting mad as 'Poor Tom'. Some of the words spoken under the guise of madness are the most perceptive and the 'truest' words in the play.

- Re-read the scenes in Act 3 that feature these three characters.
- Pick out two or three lines that you feel best represent the version of madness presented by Edgar, the Fool and Lear.
- Then choose two or three lines from each of these characters that seem to you to be the sanest, clearest ideas that these three people articulate.
- In pairs or groups, discuss the effects Shakespeare achieves by juxtaposing (并置) insanity with clarity and perceptiveness in these scenes from Act 3.

4 Gloucester is blinded

Act 3 ends with Gloucester physically blinded but 'seeing' the truth about his sons. Cornwall is mortally wounded, and Gonerill and Regan are presented as particularly nasty and vindictive (怀恨在心).

- Working on your own, use the clues the play has given you to write a paragraph each on Gloucester, Regan and Gonerill, predicting what will happen to them and what the consequences of their various actions might be.

LOOKING BACK AT ACT 3

Edgar reflects on the advantages of being destitute. He is shocked by the sight of his blinded father. In despair, Gloucester acknowledges his past errors. He regrets his treatment of Edgar.

剧情简介：爱德格思考一贫如洗的好处。他看见被弄瞎双眼的父亲惊愕不已。绝望中格劳斯特承认了自己过去的错误，为曾对待爱德格不公而后悔。

1 New act, new day

The madness, despair and horror of Act 3 are over and the storm has passed. Act 4 opens on a new day and with a contrasting mood, as Edgar reflects on the advantages of his situation.

- In modern productions, this scene often reopens the play after the interval. What effects of lighting or scenery do you feel would be appropriate for this change of mood?
- In Shakespeare's theatre, only limited changes to lighting and staging were available. How could the voice, bearing and body language of the actor suggest the sense of a new beginning?

2 At the bottom of Fortune's wheel? (in small groups)

Edgar refers to the image of the wheel of Fortune (see p. 80), and finds that pretending to be an insane beggar brings advantages. He says he prefers life as a despised outcast, certain of how he is viewed, to a life made insecure by the insincere judgements of others.

- Talk together about why in lines 1–9 he feels safe as 'The low'st' on Fortune's wheel.
- Next read lines 9–12 and discuss how his short-lived sense of calm has been disturbed.
- Read Gloucester's words at lines 19–21. Talk about how they echo Edgar's thinking at the start of the scene.
- Look back at previous acts and consider how both men's attitudes have been changed by events.

Write about it 写作练习

'I stumbled when I saw'

Gloucester expresses regret at his past mistakes.

- As Gloucester, identify the earlier events in the play that you now feel involved stumbling and error. Then, in role, write a paragraph on each of these mistakes, commenting on how suffering has given you new understanding of each event.

1 Yet … flattered 与其（在朝中）表面受人阿谀，暗中遭人鄙视，还不如眼下这般模样（做个乞丐），明明白白地被人嗤之以鼻
2 dejected 受冷落，被抛弃
3 esperance 希望
4 The worst returns to laughter 坏到尽头便转为欢笑（否极泰来）
5 parti-eyed 眼睛流着血
6 But that = Except that
7 mutations 变化无常
8 yield to age 向岁数投降
9 fourscore 八十
10 want 缺少；需要
11 means 财产
12 secure us 令我们盲目自信
13 our mere defects 我们一无所有
14 commodities 好处，优势

Act 4 Scene 1
Near Gloucester's castle

Enter EDGAR *(disguised as a madman)*

EDGAR　　　　Yet better thus, and known to be condemned,
　　　　　　Than still condemned and flattered[1]. To be worst,
　　　　　　The low'st and most dejected[2] thing of fortune,
　　　　　　Stands still in esperance[3], lives not in fear.
　　　　　　The lamentable change is from the best;　　　　　5
　　　　　　The worst returns to laughter[4]. Welcome, then,
　　　　　　Thou unsubstantial air that I embrace:
　　　　　　The wretch that thou hast blown unto the worst
　　　　　　Owes nothing to thy blasts.

Enter GLOUCESTER *and an* OLD MAN

　　　　　　　　　　　　　But who comes here?
　　　　　　My father, parti-eyed[5]? World, world, O world!　　10
　　　　　　But that[6] thy strange mutations[7] make us hate thee,
　　　　　　Life would not yield to age[8].

OLD MAN　　　　　　　　　　O my good lord,
　　　　　　I have been your tenant and your father's tenant
　　　　　　These fourscore[9] –

GLOUCESTER　Away, get thee away; good friend, be gone.　　15
　　　　　　Thy comforts can do me no good at all;
　　　　　　Thee they may hurt.

OLD MAN　　　　　　　　　You cannot see your way.

GLOUCESTER　I have no way, and therefore want[10] no eyes:
　　　　　　I stumbled when I saw. Full oft 'tis seen,
　　　　　　Our means[11] secure us[12], and our mere defects[13]　　20
　　　　　　Prove our commodities[14]. Oh, dear son Edgar,
　　　　　　The food of thy abusèd father's wrath:
　　　　　　Might I but live to see thee in my touch,
　　　　　　I'd say I had eyes again.

OLD MAN　　　　　　　　　　How now? Who's there?

Edgar fears that worse events may follow. Gloucester recalls that Poor Tom reminded him of Edgar, and reflects that humans are the playthings of the gods. He asks if Edgar knows the way to Dover.

剧情简介：爱德格担心还会有更糟糕的事情发生。格劳斯特回忆说，可怜的汤姆令他想起爱德格。他认为人类就是天神的玩物，又问爱德格是否知道去多佛怎么走。

Themes 主题分析

'As flies to wanton boys' (in groups of six or more)

Edgar hears his father say that, just as irresponsible boys might torment and kill flies, so human life merely provides casual entertainment for the gods. Try the following activity to investigate the themes of justice and of compassion in the play.

- Stand or sit in a circle. One person speaks Gloucester's lines 36–7, deciding whether to make him sound desperate, accepting, enraged or depressed.
- The next person in the circle replies with Edgar's words 'How should this be?', varying their tone of voice in response to the tone taken by the first speaker.
- Repeat the activity around the circle until everyone has had the opportunity to speak as both Edgar and Gloucester.
- Discuss Gloucester's attitude to suffering and justice, and how Edgar reacts to it.

1 Deceit and sorrow

Edgar decides to continue deceiving his father into thinking he is both 'Madman and beggar' in spite of criticising such behaviour (lines 38–9).

- Do you think he is justified in choosing to 'play fool to sorrow' with his blind and grief-stricken father? What reasons might he have?
  - What might happen if Edgar chose to be immediately truthful?
  - What benefits can he hope for by deceiving his father?

1. reason　理智
2. scarce　简直算不上，不够
3. wanton　顽皮
4. Bad … others　对着伤心的人装傻，这种做法很不好，我不喜欢，别人也会不喜欢（trade：做法）
5. twain　二
6. ancient love　老交情
7. soul　魂灵；人
8. time's plague　时代的灾祸（整句话暗讽统治者为疯子，愚昧的臣民为瞎子）
9. Above the rest　最要紧的
10. 'parel = apparel（衣服）
11. Come on't what will　无论发生什么
12. daub it further　继续假装下去

EDGAR	[*Aside*] O gods! Who is't can say 'I am at the worst'?	25
	I am worse than e'er I was.	
OLD MAN	'Tis poor mad Tom.	
EDGAR	[*Aside*] And worse I may be yet. The worst is not	
	So long as we can say 'This is the worst.'	
OLD MAN	Fellow, where goest?	
GLOUCESTER	Is it a beggarman?	
OLD MAN	Madman and beggar too.	30
GLOUCESTER	He has some reason[1], else he could not beg.	
	I'th'last night's storm I such a fellow saw,	
	Which made me think a man a worm. My son	
	Came then into my mind, and yet my mind	
	Was then scarce[2] friends with him. I have heard more since.	35
	As flies to wanton[3] boys are we to th'gods;	
	They kill us for their sport.	
EDGAR	[*Aside*] How should this be?	
	Bad is the trade that must play fool to sorrow,	
	Ang'ring itself and others[4]. – Bless thee, master.	
GLOUCESTER	Is that the naked fellow?	
OLD MAN	Ay, my lord.	40
GLOUCESTER	Get thee away. If for my sake	
	Thou wilt o'ertake us hence a mile or twain[5]	
	I'th'way toward Dover, do it for ancient love[6],	
	And bring some covering for this naked soul[7],	
	Which I'll entreat to lead me.	45
OLD MAN	Alack, sir, he is mad.	
GLOUCESTER	'Tis the time's plague[8] when madmen lead the blind.	
	Do as I bid thee; or rather do thy pleasure.	
	Above the rest[9], be gone.	
OLD MAN	I'll bring him the best 'parel[10] that I have,	50
	Come on't what will[11]. *Exit*	
GLOUCESTER	Sirrah, naked fellow.	
EDGAR	Poor Tom's a-cold. [*Aside*] I cannot daub it further[12].	
GLOUCESTER	Come hither, fellow.	
EDGAR	[*Aside*] And yet I must. – Bless thy sweet eyes, they bleed.	
GLOUCESTER	Know'st thou the way to Dover?	55

Gloucester hopes for a more just society. Edgar, as Poor Tom, agrees to guide Gloucester to Dover. Oswald tells Gonerill that Albany welcomes the French invasion and criticises Gonerill's and Edmond's actions.

剧情简介：格劳斯特希望社会更加公平。爱德格继续假扮可怜的汤姆，同意带格劳斯特去多佛。奥兹沃尔禀报高娜瑞尔，说阿尔博尼不但欢迎法国军队的进攻，还指责高娜瑞尔和爱德门的所作所为。

Stagecraft 导演技巧

The naming of fiends

In the Quarto version of the play, Edgar adds these words after line 58:

Five fiends have been in poor Tom at once: of lust, as Obidicut; Hobbididence Prince of dumbness; Mahu, of stealing; Modo, of murder; Flibbertigibbet, of mopping and mowing (做鬼脸), who since possesses chambermaids and waiting-women. So, bless thee, master!

a How do you think these lines should be spoken: comically, threateningly or in some other way?

b Research the significance of the names and the effect they might have had on Shakespeare's audience.

c In your Director's Journal, provide reasons for whether or not you would include the Quarto lines in your own production.

1 Journeys to Dover (in pairs)

The main characters of the play are gradually gathering near Dover, a real place and an important English seaport. Dover stands at the narrowest point of the English Channel, and the French coast is often clearly visible from its distinctive white chalk cliffs. Its position close to the European mainland means Dover has experienced various invasions. It is an obvious destination for Cordelia's French troops.

Lear has been sent to Dover to seek safety under Cordelia's protection. Regan and Gonerill are planning to send their forces to Dover to defend Britain against the invasion. Gloucester, however, is making a similar journey in order to commit suicide by throwing himself from the cliffs.

When referring to the psychological and moral progress and development of characters in plays or novels, critics often speak of the 'character's journey'. The characters in the play are on both literal and metaphorical journeys here.

a List the principal characters and for each one say what you think they hope to achieve by travelling to Dover.

b Who do you think has made the most dramatic and challenging personal journey since the start of the play?

c Try to identify characters who have not changed and have not undertaken a metaphorical journey. What made you choose these people?

1 **goodman's son** 好人自耕农的儿子（假扮可怜汤姆的爱德格的自称）
2 **humbled to all strokes** 忍受各种灾祸
3 **superfluous and lust-dieted man** 挥霍无度、穷奢极欲之人
4 **slaves your ordinance** 让法律满足一己私欲
5 **feel** 同情，感同身受
6 **distribution should undo excess** （上天的干涉）会重新分配财富，消除挥霍
7 **high and bending head** 高高耸立的崖顶
8 **fearfully** 令人胆寒
9 **confinèd deep** 峭壁紧紧环绕的海水（多佛海峡）
10 **sot** 傻瓜
11 **turned the wrong side out** 颠倒黑白（字面意思：把衣服里外反穿）

EDGAR   Both stile and gate, horseway and footpath. Poor Tom hath been scared out of his good wits. Bless thee, goodman's son[1], from the foul fiend.

GLOUCESTER   Here, take this purse, thou whom the heavens' plagues
             Have humbled to all strokes[2]. That I am wretched   60
             Makes thee the happier. Heavens deal so still.
             Let the superfluous and lust-dieted man[3]
             That slaves your ordinance[4], that will not see
             Because he does not feel[5], feel your power quickly.
             So distribution should undo excess[6],   65
             And each man have enough. Dost thou know Dover?

EDGAR   Ay, master.

GLOUCESTER   There is a cliff whose high and bending head[7]
             Looks fearfully[8] in the confinèd deep[9].
             Bring me but to the very brim of it,   70
             And I'll repair the misery thou dost bear
             With something rich about me. From that place
             I shall no leading need.

EDGAR   Give me thy arm.
             Poor Tom shall lead thee.

                                                                    Exeunt

Act 4 Scene 2
A room in the castle of Gonerill and Albany

Enter GONERILL *with* EDMOND *and* OSWALD, *severally*

GONERILL   Welcome, my lord. I marvel our mild husband
           Not met us on the way. – Now, where's your master?

OSWALD   Madam, within; but never man so changed.
           I told him of the army that was landed;
           He smiled at it. I told him you were coming;   5
           His answer was, 'The worse'. Of Gloucester's treachery,
           And of the loyal service of his son
           When I informed him, then he called me sot[10],
           And told me I had turned the wrong side out[11].
           What most he should dislike seems pleasant to him;   10
           What like, offensive.

Gonerill criticises Albany's cowardice and bids Edmond an affectionate farewell. She reflects on how much she prefers Edmond to her husband. Albany and Gonerill exchange vicious insults.

剧情简介： 高娜瑞尔批评阿尔博尼懦弱，然后与爱德门依依不舍地告别。她反省自己喜欢爱德门远甚于喜欢丈夫。阿尔博尼和高娜瑞尔恶语相向。

1 Wife and lover (in pairs)

It is clear in this scene that Gonerill wishes Edmond to be her lover – if he is not already. Edmond, in contrast to Gonerill, is very quiet, uttering only a few words (at line 26).

a Talk together, and then compile a list of reasons why Edmond says so little in this scene.

b Discuss how the actor playing Edmond should perform his role in the script opposite. Should he be a passive listener, be busy making preparations to leave or knowingly wink at the audience, in keeping with his earlier soliloquies? Come up with some other suggestions.

c This very intimate scene – often played in a highly charged and sexually suggestive way – is witnessed by Oswald. What effect might it have on the audience, seeing this apparently passionate couple behaving in such a way in the presence of a third person?

Language in the play 剧中语言

Husband and wife (in pairs)

Edmond leaves the stage just before Albany arrives. Gonerill switches from using denigrating language about her husband in front of her lover, to denigrating him face to face. However, Albany's language has changed dramatically since we last saw him with Gonerill in Act 1 Scene 4. He no longer speaks soothingly to her, but responds in kind.

a Talk about why you think Albany's characterisation has changed at this point.

b Take parts and read lines 31–8. Choose whether this quarrel should be staged in cold rage, in fiery anger or in some other style.

c Try first whispering the words to each other from close by and then shouting them out at each other from further away. Which delivery makes the language seem more effective?

▶ Gonerill with Edmond in Act 4 Scene 2. Which line from the script opposite might she be speaking here?

1. cowish terror 胆小怯懦
2. He'll … answer 面对侮辱，即使必须报复，他都会无动于衷
3. May prove effects 也许最终实现了
4. brother 妹夫
5. musters 招兵买马；集结队伍
6. conduct his powers 统率他的军队
7. change names at home 夫妻互换家庭责任
8. distaff 纺线杆（妻子职责的象征）
9. dare … behalf 胆敢为自己冒险
10. Decline 低下
11. Conceive 理解我
12. My fool usurps my body 我那傻老公强占着我的身子
13. worth the whistle 值得一声（唤狗的）呼哨（来自谚语 "It is a poor dog that is not worth the whistling."）
14. Milk-livered 奶白色的肝（即胆小如鼠；莎士比亚时代人们认为肝司勇气，胆小者的肝会因为缺血而发白）
15. That … wrongs 觍着脸任人抽，伸着头任人砍
16. Proper deformity 正当的畸形

GONERILL [*To Edmond*] Then shall you go no further.
It is the cowish terror[1] of his spirit
That dares not undertake. He'll not feel wrongs
Which tie him to an answer[2]. Our wishes on the way   15
May prove effects[3]. Back, Edmond, to my brother[4].
Hasten his musters[5] and conduct his powers[6].
I must change names at home[7] and give the distaff[8]
Into my husband's hands. This trusty servant
Shall pass between us. Ere long you are like to hear   20
(If you dare venture in your own behalf[9])
A mistress's command. Wear this; spare speech.
Decline[10] your head. This kiss, if it durst speak,
Would stretch thy spirits up into the air.
Conceive[11], and fare thee well.   25

EDMOND Yours in the ranks of death.

GONERILL   My most dear Gloucester.

Exit [Edmond]

Oh, the difference of man and man.
To thee a woman's services are due;
My fool usurps my body[12].

OSWALD Madam, here comes my lord.   [*Exit*]   30

Enter ALBANY

GONERILL I have been worth the whistle[13].

ALBANY   O Gonerill,
You are not worth the dust which the rude wind
Blows in your face.

GONERILL   Milk-livered[14] man,
That bear'st a cheek for blows, a head for wrongs[15];
Who hast not in thy brows an eye discerning   35
Thine honour from thy suffering –

ALBANY   See thyself, devil:
Proper deformity[16] shows not in the fiend
So horrid as in woman.

GONERILL   O vain fool!

A messenger brings news of Cornwall's death and of Gloucester's blinding. Gonerill fears Regan as a rival who could destroy her plans for a life with Edmond. Albany vows to avenge Gloucester's blinding.

剧情简介：一位信使带来了康沃尔死亡和格劳斯特眼瞎的消息。高娜瑞尔想和爱德门一起生活，担心蕊根会成为自己的对手，坏了她的好事。阿尔博尼发誓要为格劳斯特的失明报仇。

Write about it 写作练习
The duke and his duchess

Albany and Gonerill appear to dislike each other instensely, but in very different ways. Think carefully about the expectations of a spouse from a duke and duchess in Gonerill and Albany's positions.

- In role as Gonerill, write an account of her perception of her husband. Add a paragraph that sums up her perception of herself.
- Then write a matching piece from Albany's point of view: give a description of his wife and a description of himself.

(There are some extra lines that may give you more ideas for this activity from the Quarto version on pp. 246–7.)

1 **thrilled with remorse** 出于同情而激愤
2 **bending his sword / To** 持剑刺向
3 **felled him dead** 将他刺倒身亡
4 **plucked him after** 把他也拖着随他而去
5 **nether** 尘世
6 **venge** 遭报应
7 **all … life** 拉倒我梦想中的整座大厦，让我在可憎的生活中煎熬
8 **tart** 糟糕
9 **informed against** 告发

1 Reacting to the news (in threes)

Gonerill and Albany have very different responses to the messenger's news. The activities below will help you explore their reactions. In your groups, swap the parts you read as the activities progress.

a Take parts as Albany, Gonerill and the Messenger and read lines 39–66. Then talk together about what these lines reveal about the relationship between the two men. Experiment with different ways of showing their reactions to the blinding of Gloucester.

b Mime the scene, aiming to show the sequence of emotions and responses. Plan a way that movement and body language could emphasise Albany's lines 47–50 about divine justice. Decide whether Gonerill should be shown to be reacting silently to the news before her lines 52–6 or whether she should instead seem impassive.

c Talk about ways in which Gonerill's reaction contrasts with that of the two men. Note that when she says 'Gloucester' she means Edmond, not his father.

d Discuss what Gonerill means when she says 'One way I like this well' in reference to Cornwall's death. Can you agree on what she might regard as the principal disadvantage of his death?

e Finish with another reading of the lines, incorporating some of the ideas about staging and movement that you have discussed and presented.

Enter a MESSENGER

MESSENGER O my good lord, the Duke of Cornwall's dead,
Slain by his servant going to put out
The other eye of Gloucester.

ALBANY   Gloucester's eyes?

MESSENGER A servant that he bred, thrilled with remorse¹,
Opposed against the act, bending his sword
To² his great master; who, thereat enraged,
Flew on him and amongst them felled him dead³,
But not without that harmful stroke which since
Hath plucked him after⁴.

ALBANY   This shows you are above,
You justicers, that these our nether⁵ crimes
So speedily can venge⁶. But O, poor Gloucester!
Lost he his other eye?

MESSENGER   Both, both, my lord.
This letter, madam, craves a speedy answer:
'Tis from your sister.

GONERILL [*Aside*]   One way I like this well;
But being widow, and my Gloucester with her,
May all the building in my fancy pluck
Upon my hateful life⁷. Another way
The news is not so tart⁸. – I'll read, and answer. *Exit*

ALBANY Where was his son when they did take his eyes?

MESSENGER Come with my lady hither.

ALBANY   He is not here.

MESSENGER No, my good lord; I met him back again.

ALBANY Knows he the wickedness?

MESSENGER Ay, my good lord; 'twas he informed against⁹ him
And quit the house on purpose that their punishment
Might have the freer course.

ALBANY   Gloucester, I live
To thank thee for the love thou showed'st the king,
And to revenge thine eyes. – Come hither, friend.
Tell me what more thou know'st.

Exeunt

Cordelia grieves for Lear's madness. She sends soldiers to search for Lear, who has wandered off wearing a crown of wild flowers. The Gentleman says Lear's sanity can be restored by rest.

 剧情简介： 考蒂丽叶因李尔疯了感到悲痛，派士兵寻找走失的、头戴野花王冠的李尔。绅士说李尔的心智可以靠休息恢复。

Characters 人物分析

Cordelia reappears (in pairs)

In this scene, Cordelia appears again for the first time since her departure with the King of France during Act 1 Scene 1. She speaks about her father's present condition, although she has not yet been reunited with him. She describes what she has been told of the old man wandering the countryside crowned with wild flowers, and orders one hundred soldiers to look for him. In an ironic way, Lear is again a crowned king and again has his hundred knights. However, her words also tell us much about Cordelia herself.

a Take parts as Cordelia and the Gentleman (sometimes portrayed as a doctor) and read lines 1–20. Then discuss which aspects of her character Shakespeare is emphasising for the audience at this point in the play.

b Quickly remind yourselves of what happens to Cordelia in Act 1 Scene 1. Do you feel she is presented in the same way there as she is here in Act 4 Scene 3? Is her characterisation consistent or do you think Shakespeare is showing a different side to her. If so, why?

1 colours 军旗
2 vexed 疯狂
3 idle weeds 杂草
4 Crowned ... corn 头上戴着野花编成的王冠，有怒放的烟堇、地垄的杂草，还有牛蒡、毒参、荨麻、碎米荠、毒麦，以及庄稼地里长的各种没用的杂草
5 century 一百名士兵
6 bereavèd sense 丧失的心智
7 foster-nurse of nature is repose 天然的养生护士是休息
8 simples operative 灵验的单方
9 unpublished virtues 秘不外宣的药草
10 aidant and remediate 有辅助和治疗作用
11 wants ... it 缺乏引导人生的手段
12 hitherward 往这边

1 Cordelia: warlike, saintly, regal (in pairs)

In this scene, directors and designers have an opportunity to emphasise various aspects of Cordelia's role in the play. They may choose to highlight her caring, maternal side (in at least one production she is pregnant at this point). In a production emphasising the theme of justice, she might be dressed as a soldier – visibly enforcing her rights. In one emphasising reconciliation, Cordelia may be presented in saintly white or she may be dressed regally but behave in a humble way.

- Talk about what themes you would choose to emphasise through Cordelia's costume and demeanour. Make notes and sketches demonstrating your ideas in your Director's Journal.
- In the Quarto version of the play, there is an additional scene after Act 4 Scene 2 in which Kent and a Gentleman discuss Cordelia and her mission in Britain. Read through this scene on pages 247–8 to get some more ideas on how Cordelia could be portrayed.

Act 4 Scene 3
The French camp near Dover

Enter with drum and colours[1], CORDELIA, GENTLEMAN,
and Soldiers

CORDELIA Alack, 'tis he: why, he was met even now,
As mad as the vexed[2] sea, singing aloud,
Crowned with rank fumitor and furrow-weeds,
With burdocks, hemlock, nettles, cuckoo-flowers,
Darnel, and all the idle weeds[3] that grow   5
In our sustaining corn[4]. A century[5] send forth.
Search every acre in the high-grown field,
And bring him to our eye.

[Exit an Officer]

What can man's wisdom
In the restoring his bereavèd sense[6]?
He that helps him take all my outward worth.   10

GENTLEMAN There is means, madam.
Our foster-nurse of nature is repose[7],
The which he lacks. That to provoke in him
Are many simples operative[8], whose power
Will close the eye of anguish.

CORDELIA   All blest secrets,   15
All you unpublished virtues[9] of the earth,
Spring with my tears; be aidant and remediate[10]
In the good man's distress. — Seek, seek for him,
Lest his ungoverned rage dissolve the life
That wants the means to lead it[11].

Enter MESSENGER

MESSENGER   News, madam.   20
The British powers are marching hitherward[12].

Cordelia declares that love, not political ambition, makes her fight. In Scene 4, Regan questions Oswald closely, and says that Edmond has gone in search of Gloucester in order to kill him.

剧情简介：考蒂丽叶说，令她投入战斗的是爱而非政治野心。在第四场中，蕊根追问奥兹沃尔，还说爱德门已经去追杀格劳斯特了。

1 Cordelia's mission (in small groups)

At the end of Scene 4, Cordelia claims that she is leading an invading French army to Britain – not out of a desire for power but in order to rescue and support her father. Her lines 23–4 echo words spoken by Jesus in the New Testament (Luke 2:49), suggesting self-sacrifice and devotion.

- Take turns to read lines 22–9. Explore different readings to establish a range of possible states of mind for Cordelia. She could be determined, anxious, tearful or humble.
- Talk together about which reading seems most appropriate. Also look back at your comments in response to Activity 1 on page 144 and think about the ideal combination of costume and behaviour.

Write about it 写作练习
Albany's dilemma

Cordelia has brought a French army to Britain to help her father. Her action has put Albany in a difficult situation – torn between loyalty to his king and the desire to defend Britain from a foreign invasion. Gonerill has criticised Albany for indecisiveness, but such divided loyalties on the part of a man with a keen sense of morality and justice may account for Albany's reluctance (his 'much ado', line 4) to go to war.

- One person takes the part of Albany and the other two play 'War' and 'Peace'. 'War' voices reasons why Albany should go to war against Cordelia's troops. 'Peace' gives reasons why he should not. (For example, 'War' could begin by saying 'Gonerill really needs your help.' 'Peace' could say 'Cordelia is acting in her father's interests!') Albany must debate his decisions with his two inner voices.
- Afterwards, each group member should write a paragraph in which Albany justifies his final decision.

2 Regan's worries (in pairs)

a Take parts and read lines 1–20 of Scene 4. Then talk together about what Regan, recently widowed, is chiefly concerned about at this stage in the play and what this scene suggests about her relationship with her older sister.

b Agree on three words that Oswald might use to describe this conversation with Regan if Gonerill asked him to report back.

1 importuned 再三恳求
2 No … incite 不是膨胀的野心在激励我们拿起武器
3 my brother's powers 我姐夫（阿尔博尼）的军队
4 with much ado 费了不少事
5 import 传达意思
6 posted hence 匆匆策马赶往别处
7 ignorance 愚蠢
8 moves 打动人
9 dispatch 了断，快速解决
10 'nighted 暗无天日（因为失去双眼）
11 descry 探察
12 charged my duty 我得听命于我家夫人

CORDELIA	'Tis known before. Our preparation stands
	In expectation of them. – O dear father,
	It is thy business that I go about:
	Therefore great France	25
	My mourning and importuned[1] tears hath pitied.
	No blown ambition doth our arms incite[2],
	But love, dear love, and our aged father's right.
	Soon may I hear and see him.

Exeunt

Act 4 Scene 4
A room in Gloucester's castle

Enter REGAN *and* OSWALD

REGAN	But are my brother's powers[3] set forth?
OSWALD	Ay, madam.
REGAN	Himself in person there?
OSWALD	Madam, with much ado[4].
	Your sister is the better soldier.	5
REGAN	Lord Edmond spake not with your lord at home?
OSWALD	No, madam.
REGAN	What might import[5] my sister's letter to him?
OSWALD	I know not, lady.
REGAN	Faith, he is posted hence[6] on serious matter.	10
	It was great ignorance[7], Gloucester's eyes being out,
	To let him live. Where he arrives he moves[8]
	All hearts against us. Edmond, I think, is gone,
	In pity of his misery, to dispatch[9]
	His 'nighted[10] life, moreover to descry[11]	15
	The strength o'th'enemy.
OSWALD	I must needs after him, madam, with my letter.
REGAN	Our troops set forth tomorrow. Stay with us.
	The ways are dangerous.
OSWALD	I may not, madam.
	My lady charged my duty[12] in this business.	20

Regan urges Oswald to give her Gonerill's letter, and claims that she should be Edmond's partner. She offers to reward anyone who kills Gloucester. Edgar deceives Gloucester into believing that they are climbing a slope.

剧情简介：蕊根逼奥兹沃尔把高娜瑞尔的信给她，并宣称自己才应该是爱德门的伴侣。她答应不管谁杀死格劳斯特都会受到奖赏。爱德格骗格劳斯特说他们在走上坡。

Stagecraft 导演技巧

'Let me unseal the letter' (in pairs)

Scene 4 is full of eddies and currents of intrigue, veiled accusations, jealousy, betrayal and self-interest.

a Take parts and read the scene through, then change parts for a second reading. Afterwards, talk together about the ways in which Regan and Oswald are trying to manipulate each other.

b Rehearse a presentation of the whole scene ready to be performed to the class. Consider in particular:

- how the actors could play lines 21–4, when Regan appears to keep changing her mind
- whether or not Regan opens and reads the letter (lines 24–5)
- whether 'note' in line 31 refers to a letter or means 'note this carefully'
- what it is that Oswald 'may gather more' of (line 34)
- what Regan gives Oswald at line 35.

c After watching the performances, discuss whether you think Oswald is a match for Regan in manipulative techniques.

1 Belike   或许
2 oeilliads   媚眼
3 of her bosom   是她的心腹（双关，暗指是她的情夫）
4 I speak in understanding   我心知肚明
5 take this note   要注意这一点
6 thus much   我跟你说的这些话
7 call her wisdom to her   请她理智些
8 Preferment   提拔，晋升
9 cuts him off   除掉他

◀ Edgar tries to convince his father that they are climbing a slope towards a cliff edge at Dover.

REGAN	Why should she write to Edmond? Might not you	
	Transport her purposes by word? Belike[1] –	
	Some things – I know not what. I'll love thee much:	
	Let me unseal the letter.	
OSWALD	Madam, I had rather –	
REGAN	I know your lady does not love her husband.	25
	I am sure of that; and at her late being here	
	She gave strange oeilliads[2] and most speaking looks	
	To noble Edmond. I know you are of her bosom[3].	
OSWALD	I, madam?	
REGAN	I speak in understanding[4]. Y'are, I know't.	30
	Therefore I do advise you take this note[5]:	
	My lord is dead; Edmond and I have talked;	
	And more convenient is he for my hand	
	Than for your lady's. You may gather more.	
	If you do find him, pray you give him this;	35
	And when your mistress hears thus much[6] from you,	
	I pray desire her call her wisdom to her[7].	
	So, fare you well.	
	If you do chance to hear of that blind traitor,	
	Preferment[8] falls on him that cuts him off[9].	40
OSWALD	Would I could meet him, madam, I should show	
	What party I do follow.	
REGAN	Fare thee well. *Exeunt*	

Act 4 Scene 5
The countryside near Dover

Enter GLOUCESTER *and* EDGAR *(dressed like a peasant)*

GLOUCESTER	When shall I come to th'top of that same hill?	
EDGAR	You do climb up it now. Look how we labour.	
GLOUCESTER	Methinks the ground is even.	
EDGAR	Horrible steep.	
	Hark, do you hear the sea?	
GLOUCESTER	No, truly.	
EDGAR	Why, then your other senses grow imperfect	5
	By your eyes' anguish.	

Edgar describes the alarming view that he claims to see. Gloucester asks to be set at the very edge of the cliff. Edgar says that he is misleading his father in order to save him from despair.

剧情简介：爱德格描述了自称看见的吓人景象。格劳斯特要求他把自己带到悬崖边。爱德格说他误导父亲是为了让父亲从绝望中解脱出来。

1 Creating an imaginary view (in small groups)

Edgar has made his father believe they have reached the top of the cliff. To convince him they are at the very edge, he describes the imaginary view.

a In your group, practise speaking lines 11–24. Share the words round the group and change speaker at the end of each sentence.

b In lines 20–1, Edgar describes the noise of the waves ('the murmuring surge … chafes'). His words suggest the sound of the sea by using words that echo their meaning in their sound (**onomatopoeia** [拟声]). Read these lines, emphasising the onomatopoeia.

c Notice how Edgar frequently refers to a dramatic contrast in scale – comparing things he can see to much smaller things. Highlight these contrasts by experimenting with making some words louder and some softer, in line with the scale of the thing described.

Write about it 写作练习
Why does Edgar lie?

Gloucester ironically suffers deception at the hands of both his sons. But while Edmond uses deception for evil purposes, Edgar believes his motives are benign. When Edgar first begins to deceive his blinded father he says 'Bad is the trade that must play fool to sorrow' (Act 4 Scene 1, line 38), apparently regretting the necessity of tricking someone so vulnerable and distressed.

Now, in Act 4 Scene 5, Edgar tells an elaborate sequence of lies about what he can see and, in lines 33–4, states his motive for misleading his father (perhaps to reassure the audience as well as himself).

a How do you respond to Edgar's behaviour in this scene?

b Make a list of all the deceptions practised on Gloucester by both his sons.

c Write a paragraph about why it is so disturbing for the audience to witness this. Write another paragraph suggesting reasons why Edgar feels the need to deceive his father.

d Share with other class members the judgement you reach about whether Edgar's apparent cruelty can be justified.

---

1 **phrase and matter** 措辞和风格
2 **choughs** 山鸦
3 **gross** 大
4 **samphire** 海蓬子（海滩上生长的一种耐盐碱多肉绿色植物，有梗无叶，可食用）
5 **yon** 那个
6 **barque** 巴克船（一种小帆船）
7 **Diminished … buoy** 缩小成其壳船，其壳船又缩小成一个浮标（cock = cock-boat，原本写作cog，可能源自法文 coque [壳]，指称大船后面拖着的无龙骨小船）
8 **unnumberd idle pebble chafes** 摩擦那无数无用鹅卵石的声音
9 **turn** 发晕
10 **deficient sight** 眼神不济
11 **Topple down headlong** 从悬崖上一头栽下去
12 **For all beneath the moon** 哪怕给我这月光下的一切
13 **leap upright** 跳得直上直下（落下时不会落偏，落到悬崖下）
14 **Prosper it** 发扬光大（据说仙子们会让隐藏的财富增加）
15 **Why … it** = The reason why I trifle thus with his despair is to cure it （trifle with 的意思是 play with，即"拿……打趣，开玩笑"）

GLOUCESTER	So may it be indeed.	
	Methinks thy voice is altered, and thou speak'st	
	In better phrase and matter[1] than thou didst.	
EDGAR	Y'are much deceived. In nothing am I changed	
	But in my garments.	
GLOUCESTER	Methinks y'are better spoken.	10
EDGAR	Come on, sir, here's the place. Stand still. How fearful	
	And dizzy 'tis to cast one's eyes so low.	
	The crows and choughs[2] that wing the midway air	
	Show scarce so gross[3] as beetles. Half-way down	
	Hangs one that gathers samphire[4], dreadful trade!	15
	Methinks he seems no bigger than his head.	
	The fishermen that walk upon the beach	
	Appear like mice, and yon[5] tall anchoring barque[6]	
	Diminished to her cock; her cock, a buoy[7]	
	Almost too small for sight. The murmuring surge,	20
	That on th'unnumbered idle pebble chafes[8],	
	Cannot be heard so high. I'll look no more,	
	Lest my brain turn[9] and the deficient sight[10]	
	Topple down headlong[11].	
GLOUCESTER	Set me where you stand.	
EDGAR	Give me your hand. You are now within a foot	25
	Of th'extreme verge. For all beneath the moon[12]	
	Would I not leap upright[13].	
GLOUCESTER	Let go my hand.	
	Here, friend, 's another purse: in it, a jewel	
	Well worth a poor man's taking. Fairies and gods	
	Prosper it[14] with thee. Go thou further off.	30
	Bid me farewell, and let me hear thee going.	
EDGAR	Now fare ye well, good sir.	
GLOUCESTER	With all my heart.	
EDGAR	[*Aside*] Why I do trifle thus with his despair	
	Is done to cure it[15].	

Gloucester tells the gods he intends to kill himself. He throws himself forward. Edgar pretends to be someone standing on the beach who saw him fall and land in safety. Gloucester is confused and distressed.

 剧情简介：格劳斯特告诉众神他要自杀。他往前一扑，爱德格假装沙滩上的路人，看见格劳斯特安全落地。格劳斯特感到既困惑又沮丧。

Characters 人物分析

Defiance, patience or despair? (in threes)

Gloucester is determined to kill himself. In Shakespeare's time Christians saw suicide as an unforgivable sin and those who committed suicide were denied Christian burial. Gloucester tells the gods that, even if he continued to endure life ('bear it longer') and did not challenge the destiny the gods had decreed ('great opposeless wills'), his exhausted body would die like a burnt-out candle.

- All three group members read lines 34–40, but in different ways. One reads them despairingly (emphasising Gloucester's helplessness), another defiantly (emphasising his feeling of being in control) and the third patiently (emphasising his humility). Try it with each member reading one sentence, followed by the others reading the same sentence, and so on through the lines.
- Talk about which style of reading you feel most accurately represents Gloucester's character.

Stagecraft 导演技巧

Gloucester's 'leap'

Gloucester, believing that he is at the cliff's edge, throws himself forward, expecting to die. This can be a stunning moment of theatre, and it is often played on a bare stage as it would have been in Shakespeare's day, giving full weight to the suggestive power of the language to sustain the illusion.

- Describe how you would stage this part of the scene. What effects would you seek? What would be the special challenges of playing this scene on film?

1 Edgar – cruel or kind?

This is a painful scene to watch, as Gloucester is so distressed and is being so oddly manipulated by his son. It may seem bad enough that he has been tricked into thinking he is on the cliff edge, but to go on and convince him that he has, in fact, fallen and to draw from him the distraught words 'Alack, I have no eyes' seems excessively cruel.

- Note down in your Director's Journal how you would advise the actor playing Edgar to deliver each of his lines between 41 and 80 in ways that could minimise the audience's unease.

1 **opposeless** 不可抵挡
2 **snuff … nature** 风烛残年和生命的可憎部分
3 **conceit** 幻觉
4 **pass** = pass away（去世）
5 **gossamer** 蛛丝
6 **precipitating** 坠落
7 **shivered** 摔碎
8 **Ten masts at each** 十根桅杆首尾相连
9 **perpendicularly** 垂直
10 **summit of this chalky bourn** 这道白垩边沿的顶上（chalky 指英国东南海岸线多佛一带高耸的白垩悬崖 [White Cliffs]；bourn = boundary ［边界，边缘］）
11 **shrill-gorged** 尖叫
12 **beguile … will** 欺骗独裁者的狂怒，挫败他的高傲意志

KING LEAR ACT 4 SCENE 5
李尔王

GLOUCESTER [*Kneels*]   O you mighty gods! 35
This world I do renounce, and in your sights
Shake patiently my great affliction off.
If I could bear it longer and not fall
To quarrel with your great opposeless¹ wills,
My snuff and loathèd part of nature² should
Burn itself out. If Edgar live, O bless him. 40
Now, fellow, fare thee well.

EDGAR   Gone, sir; farewell.
[*Gloucester throws himself forward and falls*]
[*Aside*] And yet I know not how conceit³ may rob
The treasury of life, when life itself
Yields to the theft. Had he been where he thought,
By this had thought been past. – Alive or dead? 45
Ho, you sir, friend! Hear you, sir? Speak!
[*Aside*] Thus might he pass⁴ indeed. Yet he revives. –
What are you, sir?

GLOUCESTER   Away, and let me die.

EDGAR   Hadst thou been aught but gossamer⁵, feathers, air,
So many fathom down precipitating⁶, 50
Thou'dst shivered⁷ like an egg. But thou dost breathe,
Hast heavy substance, bleed'st not, speak'st, art sound.
Ten masts at each⁸ make not the altitude
Which thou hast perpendicularly⁹ fell.
Thy life's a miracle. Speak yet again. 55

GLOUCESTER But have I fall'n or no?

EDGAR   From the dread summit of this chalky bourn¹⁰.
Look up a-height: the shrill-gorged¹¹ lark so far
Cannot be seen or heard; do but look up.

GLOUCESTER Alack, I have no eyes. 60
Is wretchedness deprived that benefit
To end itself by death? 'Twas yet some comfort
When misery could beguile the tyrant's rage
And frustrate his proud will¹².

EDGAR   Give me your arm.
Up; so. How is't? Feel you your legs? You stand. 65

GLOUCESTER Too well, too well.

Gloucester resolves to endure his suffering. Edgar urges him to feel free of guilt. Lear's disordered talk is of archers, mice and challenges. He acknowledges that flatterers misled him.

剧情简介：格劳斯特下决心忍受痛苦，爱德格劝他不要内疚。李尔说话颠三倒四，提到了射箭手、老鼠和挑战。他承认马屁精们误导了他。

1 Gloucester chooses to 'bear affliction' (in pairs)

Gloucester seems resigned to the will of the gods and Edgar says, 'Bear free and patient thoughts' (line 80).

- Talk together about exactly what Edgar means by this. Do you think that finally achieving this resignation justifies the deceits he has practised on his father in this scene?

Themes 主题分析

Sense and nonsense (in pairs)

It is not only Lear's costume and behaviour (both mentioned by Cordelia in Scene 3) that signal his madness; he also speaks in a jumbled, volatile, distracted manner, his words seeming to gush and tumble out. Sense and nonsense mingle. He refers to commanding troops, archery, the storm, issues of power, a mouse (which may be real or imagined), flattery and deception.

a Prepare two contrasting sets of notes:

- The first should list any references, or possible references, to previous events in the play that you can recognise.
- The second should note any words that connect with the theme of appearance versus reality.

b From your notes, select those words or references you would want the actor to emphasise in performance.

1 whelked and waved 卷曲并且有波纹
2 happy father 幸运的老人家
3 clearest 最英明
4 make … impossibilities 用人类无法完成的奇迹来获得自己的荣耀
5 Bear free and patient thoughts 让头脑自由自在，无忧无虑
6 The safer … thus 稳妥的头脑绝不会让主人陷入这种境地
7 touch me for crying 因为我哭而谴责我
8 side-piercing 利矛穿肋（令人联想到耶稣被钉死在十字架上时，被人用长枪刺穿两肋）
9 press-money （士兵的）饷银
10 crow-keeper 假人或撵乌鸦的人
11 Draw me a clothier's yard 给我把弓拉到一码宽（clothier 的意思是"卖布的"，1码布的长度是90多厘米；把弓拉开到这个程度就等于把它拉满了）
12 gauntlet 护手（中世纪欧洲骑士所穿戴铁甲的一部分。两位骑士相遇，一方如将护手扔在地上，就表示向对方发起挑战。）
13 brown bills 执戟手
14 i'th'clout 正中靶心（李尔想象中的箭射中了靶心）
15 Hewgh! 嗖！（模拟箭射出的声音）
16 marjoram 墨角兰（又叫马郁草，牛至属的一种，有香气，被当时人认为可治疗精神失常）
17 no good divinity 不好的神学（意思是国王享有神权，人们对国王唯唯诺诺）
18 not ague-proof 免不了也有个头疼脑热

154

EDGAR	This is above all strangeness.
	Upon the crown o'th'cliff what thing was that
	Which parted from you?
GLOUCESTER	A poor unfortunate beggar.
EDGAR	As I stood here below, methought his eyes
	Were two full moons. He had a thousand noses,
	Horns whelked and waved[1] like the enragèd sea.
	It was some fiend. Therefore, thou happy father[2],
	Think that the clearest[3] gods, who make them honours
	Of men's impossibilities[4], have preserved thee.
GLOUCESTER	I do remember now. Henceforth I'll bear
	Affliction till it do cry out itself
	'Enough, enough', and die. That thing you speak of,
	I took it for a man. Often 'twould say
	'The fiend, the fiend!' He led me to that place.
EDGAR	Bear free and patient thoughts[5].

Enter LEAR, [*mad*]

	But who comes here?
	The safer sense will ne'er accommodate
	His master thus[6].
LEAR	No, they cannot touch me for crying[7]. I am the king himself.
EDGAR	O thou side-piercing[8] sight!
LEAR	Nature's above art in that respect. There's your press-money[9]. That fellow handles his bow like a crow-keeper[10]. Draw me a clothier's yard[11]. Look, look, a mouse! Peace, peace, this piece of toasted cheese will do't. There's my gauntlet[12]. I'll prove it on a giant. Bring up the brown bills[13]. O well flown bird: i'th'clout[14], i'th'clout! Hewgh![15] Give the word.
EDGAR	Sweet marjoram[16].
LEAR	Pass.
GLOUCESTER	I know that voice.
LEAR	Ha! Gonerill with a white beard? They flattered me like a dog and told me I had the white hairs in my beard ere the black ones were there. To say 'ay' and 'no' to everything that I said 'ay' and 'no' to was no good divinity[17]. When the rain came to wet me once and the wind to make me chatter, when the thunder would not peace at my bidding, there I found 'em, there I smelt 'em out. Go to, they are not men o'their words. They told me I was everything; 'tis a lie, I am not ague-proof[18].

> Gloucester recognises the king's voice. Lear embarks on a frenzied condemnation of women's sexuality. Gloucester asks whether Lear recognises him. The king seems to mock Gloucester's empty eye sockets.
>
> 剧情简介：格劳斯特认出了国王的声音。李尔激烈谴责起女人的淫欲。格劳斯特问李尔能否认出他来，而国王似乎在嘲弄格劳斯特空洞的眼窝。

1 Lear's obsession (in small groups)

Lear's language reflects the disturbance and distress of his mind. At line 103, he switches from prose to poetry, briefly asserts his authority as a king and then begins to speak about sex. He shows an intense fear and loathing of women's sexual desires. Lear seems to be totally disinhibited – ignoring usual social conventions – and obsessive. His mind particularly runs on the way the seeming purity of a woman can mask lust.

a Try different ways of speaking lines 103–27 to bring out Lear's initial haughtiness (傲慢不逊) followed by his deep sexual loathing.

b Work together to devise a reading of the lines that highlights the theme of appearance versus reality that runs through the play.

c Talk about these questions:
- Does Lear's sexual obsession suggest anything about his character, or does it simply indicate that he has a mental illness?
- Do you think this obsession was triggered by events in the play, or is it just introduced to show Lear's derangement (精神错乱)?
- How differently do you think each of Lear's three daughters might react if they heard his words?
- How should the listening Gloucester respond to what he hears?
- What challenges do you think this speech poses for an actor?

Language in the play 剧中语言

Gloucester – more humiliation? (in pairs)

Despite Lear's behaviour, Gloucester wants to show him all the courtesy due to a king by kissing his hand. Lear responds by repeatedly referring to Gloucester's blindness. There are many images in English that derive from blindness and sight, and in a different context Lear's words might seem innocent. Here, however, they are highly charged for Edgar, Gloucester and the audience.

a Read lines 132–48 and pick out words that relate to sight. Then talk together about whether Lear is using language in an obsessive way, just as earlier he talked obsessively of sex.

b Select three or four of Lear's lines and experiment with ways in which they could be performed. Suggest how an audience might react to Lear's apparent lack of concern over Gloucester's distress, and whether in performance a director and actors should seek to make the lines grimly amusing or handle them in a way that remains serious.

---

1 trick 鲜明特征
2 cause 所犯之罪
3 gilded fly 绿豆蝇
4 lecher 交配
5 luxury 淫欲
6 pell-mell 滥交，淫乱
7 simp'ring dame 傻笑的娘儿们
8 face … snow 脸埋在两腿之间，好像冷若冰霜（forks = legs）
9 minces virtue 假装正经
10 hear of pleasure's name 听到荤段子
11 fitchew 臭鼬（俚语：妓女）
12 soilèd horse （吃饱鲜草以致）活泼兴奋的马
13 centaurs 人马（希腊神话中半人半马的怪物，素有淫荡之名）
14 girdle 腰部
15 inherit 拥有
16 burning, scalding, stench, consumption 灼热滚烫，散发恶臭，被火烧毁
17 civet 麝香
18 apothecary 药师
19 smells of mortality 散发出死亡的气味
20 Shall … naught 也会消磨殆尽
21 squiny 眯着眼看
22 challenge 挑战书
23 penning 字体
24 take 相信

GLOUCESTER	The trick[1] of that voice I do well remember.	
	Is't not the king?	
LEAR	Ay, every inch a king.	
	When I do stare, see how the subject quakes.	
	I pardon that man's life. What was thy cause[2]?	105
	Adultery?	
	Thou shalt not die. Die for adultery? No,	
	The wren goes to't, and the small gilded fly[3]	
	Does lecher[4] in my sight.	
	Let copulation thrive: for Gloucester's bastard son	110
	Was kinder to his father than my daughters	
	Got 'tween the lawful sheets.	
	To't, luxury[5], pell-mell[6], for I lack soldiers.	
	Behold yon simp'ring dame[7],	
	Whose face between her forks presages snow[8],	115
	That minces virtue[9], and does shake the head	
	To hear of pleasure's name[10].	
	The fitchew[11] nor the soilèd horse[12] goes to't	
	With a more riotous appetite.	
	Down from the waist they're centaurs[13],	120
	Though women all above.	
	But to the girdle[14] do the gods inherit[15];	
	Beneath is all the fiend's.	
	There's hell, there's darkness, there is the sulphurous pit, burning, scalding, stench, consumption[16]. Fie, fie, fie; pah, pah! Give me an ounce of civet[17], good apothecary[18], sweeten my imagination: there's money for thee.	125
GLOUCESTER	O, let me kiss that hand!	
LEAR	Let me wipe it first; it smells of mortality[19].	
GLOUCESTER	O ruined piece of nature! This great world	130
	Shall so wear out to naught[20]. Dost thou know me?	
LEAR	I remember thine eyes well enough. Dost thou squiny[21] at me?	
	No, do thy worst, blind Cupid, I'll not love.	
	Read thou this challenge[22]; mark but the penning[23] of it.	
GLOUCESTER	Were all thy letters suns, I could not see.	135
EDGAR	[*Aside*] I would not take[24] this from report; it is,	
	And my heart breaks at it.	

Lear condemns the hypocritical and distorted justice exercised by those with power but without morality. He complains that the rich can escape punishment while the poor cannot. Lear recognises Gloucester.

剧情简介：李尔谴责那些有权有势却毫无道德的人所行使的虚伪而扭曲的正义。他控诉说有钱人可以逃避惩罚，而穷人却不能。李尔认出了格劳斯特。

Themes 主题分析

Hypocrisy: appearance versus reality (in small groups)

Lear continues to harp on Gloucester's blindness, but moves on from describing sexual hypocrisy to list other examples of the vice. He condemns several examples of hypocritical behaviour: a beadle whipping a prostitute while wishing he was one of her clients; a powerful money-lender having a minor cheat executed for lesser crimes than his own; and the fact that the sinful rich are protected from justice by their wealth, while the sinful poor are vulnerable.

a Read lines 150–65 several times, changing the speaker at the end of each sentence.

b Experiment with ways of dramatising the examples of hypocrisy, for example, by having one person reading the words while the others mime the scenes described.

c Lear seems to think that the gap between appearance and reality is a particular issue for the rich and powerful. Think about how different his attitude is at this point from the Lear of Act 1. Also, consider whether his ideas have changed since his experiences in the storm in Act 3.

1 case of eyes 眼窝
2 heavy case 悲惨的状态
3 see it feelingly 靠摸索来看这个世界（感觉世界的不公）
4 rails upon 痛骂
5 simple 卑贱
6 handy-dandy 猜猜看（原指猜左右手哪个手里有东西的游戏）
7 beadle 衙役
8 use her in that kind 以同样的方式跟她干那事
9 cozener 骗子
10 Plate sin with gold 给罪孽披上金盔甲
11 pygmy's straw 侏儒的麦秸秆（喻指弱小的武器）
12 I'll able 'em 我会为他们赋能
13 glass eyes 眼镜（不是义眼，因为玻璃义眼在17世纪末才出现）
14 scurvy 卑鄙，狡猾
15 matter and impertinency 正经话和胡说八道
16 wawl 号叫

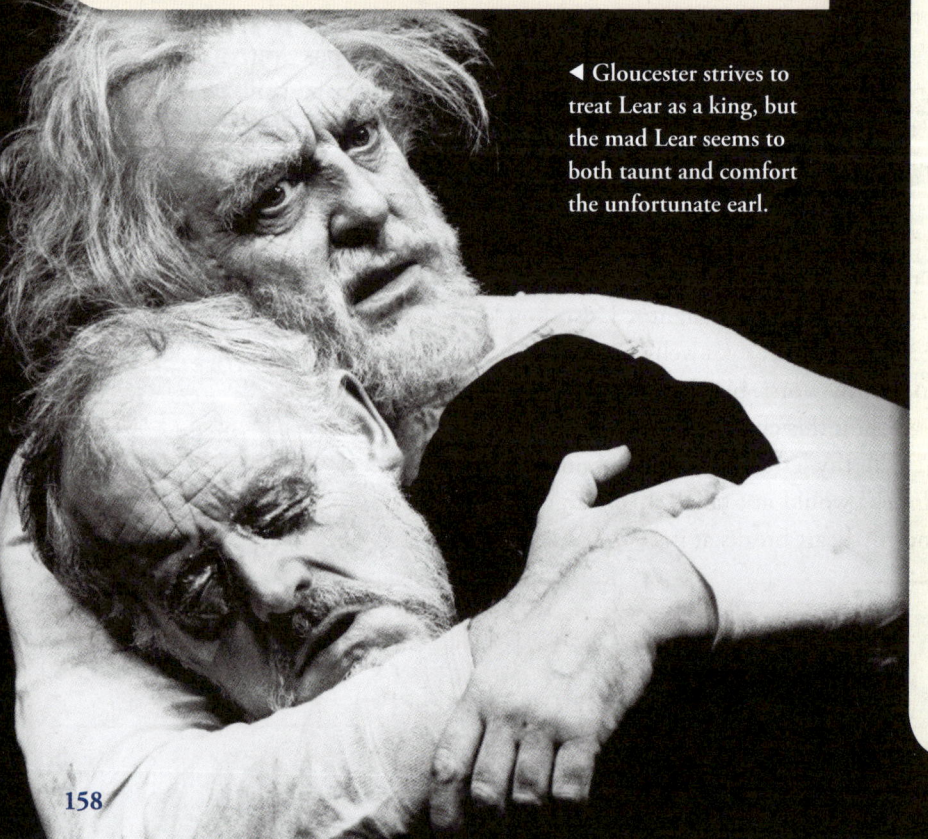

◀ Gloucester strives to treat Lear as a king, but the mad Lear seems to both taunt and comfort the unfortunate earl.

LEAR   Read.

GLOUCESTER   What – with the case of eyes[1]?

LEAR   O ho, are you there with me? No eyes in your head, nor no money in your purse? Your eyes are in a heavy case[2], your purse in a light; yet you see how this world goes.

GLOUCESTER   I see it feelingly[3].

LEAR   What, art mad? A man may see how this world goes with no eyes; look with thine ears. See how yon justice rails upon[4] yon simple[5] thief. Hark in thine ear: change places, and handy-dandy[6], which is the justice, which is the thief? Thou hast seen a farmer's dog bark at a beggar?

GLOUCESTER   Ay, sir.

LEAR   And the creature run from the cur? There thou mightst behold the great image of authority. A dog's obeyed in office.
           Thou rascal beadle[7], hold thy bloody hand.
           Why dost thou lash that whore? Strip thy own back.
           Thou hotly lusts to use her in that kind[8]
           For which thou whip'st her. The usurer hangs the cozener[9].
           Through tattered clothes great vices do appear:
           Robes and furred gowns hide all. Plate sin with gold[10],
           And the strong lance of justice hurtless breaks;
           Arm it in rags, a pygmy's straw[11] does pierce it.
           None does offend, none, I say none. I'll able 'em[12].
           Take that of me, my friend, who have the power
           To seal th'accuser's lips. Get thee glass eyes[13],
           And, like a scurvy[14] politician, seem
           To see the things thou dost not. Now, now, now, now.
           Pull off my boots. Harder, harder! So.

EDGAR   [*Aside*] O matter and impertinency[15] mixed,
           Reason in madness.

LEAR   If thou wilt weep my fortunes, take my eyes.
           I know thee well enough; thy name is Gloucester.
           Thou must be patient. We came crying hither.
           Thou know'st the first time that we smell the air
           We wawl[16] and cry. I will preach to thee: mark.

GLOUCESTER   Alack, alack the day.

Lear imagines revenge on his enemies. He greets the search party enigmatically, then runs away. Edgar learns that the French and British armies will soon meet in battle.

 剧情简介：李尔想象向他的敌人复仇。他用令人费解的方式与找寻他的队伍打招呼，然后跑开。爱德格获悉法国和不列颠的军队很快会遇上并开战。

Stagecraft 导演技巧
'great stage of fools'

In line 172, Lear says that he is going to preach to Gloucester, so lines 174–5 could be the rather grand introduction to a sermon that then seems to peter out (逐渐减少). Lear suggests an explanation for the cry of the new-born baby, already mentioned in lines 171–2. It is a lament for being brought into the world, onto this 'great stage of fools'. Shakespeare commented on life being like a stage in several of his plays.

a In your Director's Journal, write down whether you would choose to have the actor emphasise this image, to draw attention to it in a deliberately theatrical way.

b Can you suggest any reasons why this image is used at this point in the play?

1	delicate stratagem	神机妙算
2	felt	毡
3	put't in proof	检验
4	natural fool	天生的傻瓜
5	seconds	帮手（联系之前李尔胡言乱语提及的要与巨人决斗的事情）
6	man of salt	泪人儿
7	a smug bridegroom	衣冠楚楚的新郎
8	jovial	如乔武（即朱庇特）般庄严快乐
9	Then there's life in't	那就还有些指望
10	an = if	
11	it	（可能指前文的ransom [赎金]）
12	Sa, sa, sa, sa	那儿，那儿（打猎用语，源自法文ça, ça，相当于there, there)
13	twain	那俩人（指高娜瑞尔和蕊根）
14	speed you = God speed you	（上天保佑你成功）
15	sure and vulgar	确定且众所周知
16	on speedy foot	腿脚很快
17	the main … thought	我们随时都可能看到主力部队

1 Making sense of the 'good block' (in pairs)

Many people find Lear's words at line 175 ('This' a good block') puzzling. Some think the block refers to a mounting block for getting on a horse; others believe it is a reference to the block on which a hatter forms a hat. As Edgar said at line 166, Lear's words show 'matter and impertinency mixed'.

- The reference to a block is unclear, as was the earlier line 87 about the mouse. Experiment with ways of delivering lines 87 and 175 so that they do not unduly puzzle or distract the audience. This might involve a mime to explain the line or an emphasis on Lear's madness.

2 Catching the king (in small groups)

Lear quickly emerges from his brief reflective mood in lines 174–5 to imagine taking bloody revenge on his enemies (lines 175–9). Then he seems to be confused and unsettled by the arrival of Cordelia's men and, in a manner that has echoes of a children's pursuit game, he manages to elude them (lines 193–4). Sometimes on stage he gestures that they must kneel before him and, when they do, he makes a run for it.

- Talk together about what might be motivating Lear to run away. Then work out how his escape could be staged. Remember that he is old and frail, and that his pursuers – although probably very fit soldiers – are anxious to deal gently with someone who is both an old man and a king.

LEAR	When we are born, we cry that we are come	
	To this great stage of fools. This' a good block.	175
	It were a delicate stratagem¹ to shoe	
	A troop of horse with felt². I'll put't in proof³,	
	And when I have stol'n upon these son-in-laws,	
	Then kill, kill, kill, kill, kill, kill!	

Enter a GENTLEMAN [*with Attendants*]

GENTLEMAN	O here he is: lay hand upon him. Sir,	180
	Your most dear daughter –	
LEAR	No rescue? What, a prisoner? I am even	
	The natural fool⁴ of fortune. Use me well.	
	You shall have ransom. Let me have surgeons,	
	I am cut to th'brains.	
GENTLEMAN	You shall have anything.	185
LEAR	No seconds⁵? All myself?	
	Why, this would make a man a man of salt⁶,	
	To use his eyes for garden water-pots.	
	I will die bravely, like a smug bridegroom⁷. What?	
	I will be jovial⁸. Come, come, I am a king.	190
	Masters, know you that?	
GENTLEMAN	You are a royal one, and we obey you.	
LEAR	Then there's life in't⁹. Come, an¹⁰ you get it¹¹, you shall get it by running. Sa, sa, sa, sa¹²!	

Exit [*running, Attendants following*]

GENTLEMAN	A sight most pitiful in the meanest wretch,	195
	Past speaking of in a king. Thou hast a daughter	
	Who redeems nature from the general curse	
	Which twain¹³ have brought her to.	
EDGAR	Hail, gentle sir.	
GENTLEMAN	Sir, speed you¹⁴: what's your will?	
EDGAR	Do you hear aught, sir, of a battle toward?	200
GENTLEMAN	Most sure and vulgar¹⁵: everyone hears that,	
	Which can distinguish sound.	
EDGAR	But, by your favour,	
	How near's the other army?	
GENTLEMAN	Near and on speedy foot¹⁶: the main descry	
	Stands on the hourly thought¹⁷.	
EDGAR	I thank you, sir. That's all.	205

Gloucester says that he is no longer suicidal. Edgar, expressing pity, offers to lead him to shelter. Oswald plans to kill Gloucester for the reward. Edgar, speaking as a peasant, defies Oswald. They fight.

剧情简介：格劳斯特说他已经不想自杀了。爱德格表示同情，并愿意把他领到栖身之处。奥兹沃尔计划杀死格劳斯特来获得奖赏。爱德格以农民身份跟奥兹沃尔说话并激怒了他，二人打了起来。

1 'known and feeling sorrows' (in pairs)

Gloucester and Edgar have both suffered. In lines 212–14, Edgar describes himself as a man who has learned the value of pity through his suffering.

a Think back over the play so far and talk about the different 'sorrows' that could have 'educated' Edgar.

b Notice that Edgar's words at this point are strictly true, in contrast to what he said before and after the 'fall' from the cliff. Discuss what an actor should do, if anything, to emphasise this.

Characters 人物分析

Oswald the brave? (in fours)

Edgar's disguise means Oswald is misled by appearances. He soon finds out that appearance and reality can prove to be surprisingly and dangerously different.

- Read Oswald's lines 217–21 and 222–5 around your group, changing speaker at each punctuation mark.
- Which words could be emphasised to highlight Oswald's gloating (沾沾自喜), threatening, over-confident behaviour?
- Look back at Kent's insults to Oswald in Act 2 Scene 2, lines 13–21. Do any of these gibes seem to have been further justified by Oswald's conduct in the play since this point?

2 A voice in (yet another) disguise (in pairs)

Edgar adopts a country accent when he challenges Oswald. Earlier in the play, when Kent says he will 'other accents borrow', how he actually sounds is largely left to the actor. Here, however, Shakespeare has given a phonetic version of words supposedly in a regional accent. You will probably find these words easier to understand if you speak them aloud.

a Take parts and read lines 226–34 in a way that suggests Edgar is anxious to avoid confrontation. Swap parts and then read the same lines in a way that suggests Edgar is trying to provoke or distract Oswald by mocking his courtly, swaggering style. Decide which style would work best on stage.

b Talk about why Edgar has changed his accent yet again.

---

1 special cause 因为特别原因（即照料李尔）
2 worser spirit 邪恶的天使或魔鬼
3 father 老人家
4 tame to 屈服于
5 by … sorrows 借助亲历并感受不幸
6 Am pregnant to good pity 我现在满肚子怜悯！
7 biding 住所
8 bounty and the benison 慷慨和祝福
9 To boot, and boot 降临，降临吧
10 A proclaimed prize! 一颗悬赏通缉的脑袋！
11 most happy! 太幸运了！
12 first framed flesh 头号傻瓜
13 Briefly thyself remember 快快回想罪过（准备受死）
14 Chill 我会（爱德格以农夫身份出现，说的是当时萨默赛特郡的方言；后文的 zir = sir）
15 without vurther 'casion 说不出个一二三（'casion = occasion, reason）
16 go your gait 你走你的路
17 volk = folk（方言发音）
18 And chud = If I could
19 zwaggered = swaggered（唬住）
20 vortnight = fortnight（方言发音）
21 che vor'ye = I warn you（我可警告你）
22 I s' = I shall
23 costard 脑袋（字面义是"苹果"）
24 ballow = baton（棒子）
25 foins 刺（击剑的招数）

GENTLEMAN	Though that the queen on special cause¹ is here, Her army is moved on.	
EDGAR	I thank you, sir.	

Exit [Gentleman]

GLOUCESTER	You ever gentle gods, take my breath from me. Let not my worser spirit² tempt me again To die before you please.	
EDGAR	Well pray you, father³.	210
GLOUCESTER	Now, good sir, what are you?	
EDGAR	A most poor man, made tame to⁴ fortune's blows, Who by the art of known and feeling sorrows⁵ Am pregnant to good pity⁶. Give me your hand; I'll lead you to some biding⁷.	
GLOUCESTER	Hearty thanks; The bounty and the benison⁸ of heaven To boot, and boot⁹.	215

Enter OSWALD

OSWALD	A proclaimed prize!¹⁰ most happy!¹¹ That eyeless head of thine was first framed flesh¹² To raise my fortunes. Thou old, unhappy traitor, Briefly thyself remember¹³: the sword is out That must destroy thee.	220
GLOUCESTER	Now let thy friendly hand Put strength enough to't.	
OSWALD	Wherefore, bold peasant, Dar'st thou support a published traitor? Hence, Lest that th'infection of his fortune take Like hold on thee. Let go his arm.	225
EDGAR	Chill¹⁴ not let go, zir, without vurther 'casion¹⁵.	
OSWALD	Let go slave, or thou di'st.	
EDGAR	Good gentleman, go your gait¹⁶, and let poor volk¹⁷ pass. And chud¹⁸ ha' been zwaggered¹⁹ out of my life, 'twould not ha' been zo long as 'tis by a vortnight²⁰. Nay, come not near th'old man. Keep out, che vor'ye²¹, or I s'²² try whether your costard²³ or my ballow²⁴ be the harder; chill be plain with you.	230
OSWALD	Out, dunghill!	

[They fight]

EDGAR	Chill pick your teeth, zir: come, no matter vor your foins²⁵.	

Oswald, mortally wounded, asks Edgar to deliver his letters to Edmond. Edgar reads a letter from Gonerill urging Edmond to kill Albany and marry her. Edgar plans to take the letter to Albany.

剧情简介：奥兹沃尔受了致命伤，请求爱德格把他的一些信交给爱德门。爱德格读了一封高娜瑞尔写给爱德门的信，信中高娜瑞尔怂恿爱德门杀死阿尔博尼然后娶她。爱德格打算把信交给阿尔博尼。

Stagecraft 导演技巧

'O untimely death' (in pairs)

Oswald believes that he will easily overcome an untrained peasant. Edgar has to fight armed only with a staff. Oswald is often shown on stage to be startled by the ferocity and skill with which Edgar fights.

a Plan how to stage their fight to show Oswald's overconfidence and Edgar's attitude to violence.

b Experiment with how Oswald should speak his final lines (235–9). Decide whether the lines should sound noble or bitter, or strike some other tone.

c Talk about the audience's reaction to Oswald's death. How might your choices about staging this event affect that reaction?

1 serviceable villain 唯命是从的奴才
2 deathsman 刽子手
3 Leave 对不起
4 wax 封蜡
5 reciprocal 你来我往
6 gaol = jail
7 for your labour 作为您出力的奖赏
8 indistinguished 没有边际
9 rake up 埋葬（奥兹沃尔）
10 post unsanctified 不圣洁的信使
11 ungracious paper 邪恶的信件
12 strike 击毁
13 death-practised duke 遭人暗算的公爵（阿尔博尼）

Characters 人物分析

The real Edgar (in large groups)

Edgar's lines after Oswald's death do not involve any pretence on his part (other than a brief word of reassurance to Gloucester). We knew little about Edgar before he pretended madness and hid behind assumed personas.

- Most of the group sit or stand in a circle with one person in the middle. Read Edgar's words round the group, changing reader at each punctuation mark.
- Repeat this process, but this time the person in the middle should interrupt to comment on any evidence of Edgar's character that is revealed by the words being spoken.
- What have you discovered about Edgar's attitudes and personality?

▶ Edgar has killed Oswald. The letter he finds is presumably the one Regan was so eager to open earlier in the play.

King Lear Act 4 Scene 5
李尔王

OSWALD   Slave, thou hast slain me. Villain, take my purse. 235
          If ever thou wilt thrive, bury my body,
          And give the letters which thou find'st about me
          To Edmond, Earl of Gloucester: seek him out
          Upon the English party. O untimely death, death.
                                               [*He dies*]

EDGAR   I know thee well – a serviceable villain¹, 240
          As duteous to the vices of thy mistress
          As badness would desire.

GLOUCESTER   What, is he dead?

EDGAR   Sit you down, father; rest you.
          Let's see these pockets. The letters that he speaks of
          May be my friends. He's dead. I am only sorry 245
          He had no other deathsman². Let us see.
          Leave³, gentle wax⁴; and manners, blame us not:
          To know our enemies' minds, we rip their hearts;
          Their papers is more lawful.
                         Reads the letter

'Let our reciprocal⁵ vows be remembered. You have many 250
opportunities to cut him off. If your will want not, time and
place will be fruitfully offered. There is nothing done, if he
return the conqueror; then am I the prisoner, and his bed my
gaol⁶, from the loathed warmth whereof, deliver me, and supply
the place for your labour⁷. 255
                Your (wife, so I would say)
                       affectionate servant,
                                   Gonerill.'

          O indistinguished⁸ space of woman's will,
          A plot upon her virtuous husband's life – 260
          And the exchange my brother! Here in the sands
          Thee I'll rake up⁹, the post unsanctified¹⁰
          Of murderous lechers; and in the mature time
          With this ungracious paper¹¹ strike¹² the sight
          Of the death-practised duke¹³. For him 'tis well 265
          That of thy death and business I can tell.
                         [*Exit, dragging out the body*]

Gloucester wishes he was insane and could forget his griefs. Edgar plans to take him to safety. Cordelia thanks Kent for his loyalty. She prays that the sleeping Lear will wake to sanity.

剧情简介：格劳斯特希望自己疯掉，这样就可以忘记自己的痛苦。爱德格打算送他到安全的地方。考蒂丽叶感谢肯特的忠诚。她祈祷睡着的李尔醒来就能恢复心智。

1 Gloucester's thoughts on madness (in pairs)

Gloucester is left briefly alone on stage as Edgar drags Oswald's body off stage for burial. Dragging the body off was a practical necessity in Shakespeare's theatre, as otherwise the actor playing the dead character would have to stand up and walk off, destroying the illusion and distracting the audience.

- Read Gloucester's words spoken during his few moments of solitude in lines 267–72. Talk about how Gloucester can see a benefit in madness. What might Edgar's reaction have been, had he heard his father's words?

Language in the play 剧中语言
Edgar says 'father'

In the final line of Scene 5, Edgar uses the word 'father' when addressing Gloucester. This is the fourth time that he has done so (see lines 72, 210 and 243). When the play was written, the word 'father' was used to address any older man, much as the word 'son' may be today to a young man or boy. Clearly, in this context the actors can emphasise the double meaning. Some productions make Gloucester's line 211 hint at a dim sense of recognition.

- What is the effect of using this ambiguous word here?
- Do you think Edgar wants to be recognised?
- Would you advise the actor playing Gloucester to react to any of the uses of 'father'?

2 Cordelia's prayer

Many people in Shakespeare's audience would have had very negative attitudes to madness, believing it was a sign of possession by evil spirits. It may have been to challenge such attitudes that Shakespeare makes Gloucester speak positively about the benefits of madness (see Activity 1 above). Cordelia also makes it clear that she believes recovery is possible. In lines 14–17, Cordelia compares Lear's state of mind to an untuned and discordant musical instrument.

- Read her lines and write down what makes this image optimistic. (You can find out more about seventeenth-century attitudes to madness on pp. 206–7.)

---

1 ingenious 敏锐
2 distract 精神错乱
3 severed 断绝
4 woes by wrong imaginations lose 伤感凭借幻觉就能消失
5 every measure fail me 我无以为报（肯特的善良无法衡量）
6 modest truth 毫不夸张的事实
7 Nor more, nor clipped 既不添油加醋，也不缺枝少叶
8 Be better suited 换件更好的衣服
9 weeds 衣服
10 shortens my made intent 提前暴露我制订的计划
11 boon 请求
12 Th'untuned … up 让他的心智恢复正常（wind up原义为调节琴弦使之发音准确）
13 child-changèd 被自己的孩子改变

GLOUCESTER The king is mad. How stiff is my vile sense,
That I stand up and have ingenious[1] feeling
Of my huge sorrows! Better I were distract[2],
So should my thoughts be severed[3] from my griefs,   270
Drum afar off
And woes by wrong imaginations lose[4]
The knowledge of themselves.

[*Enter* EDGAR]

EDGAR   Give me your hand.
Far off methinks I hear the beaten drum.
Come, father, I'll bestow you with a friend.

Exeunt

Act 4 Scene 6
The French camp near Dover

Enter CORDELIA, KENT (*disguised*) *and* GENTLEMAN

CORDELIA O thou good Kent, how shall I live and work
To match thy goodness? My life will be too short,
And every measure fail me[5].
KENT To be acknowledged, madam, is o'erpaid.
All my reports go with the modest truth[6],   5
Nor more, nor clipped[7], but so.
CORDELIA   Be better suited[8]:
These weeds[9] are memories of those worser hours.
I prithee, put them off.
KENT   Pardon, dear madam.
Yet to be known shortens my made intent[10].
My boon[11] I make it that you know me not   10
Till time and I think meet.
CORDELIA Then be't so, my good lord. — How does the king?
GENTLEMAN Madam, sleeps still.
CORDELIA O you kind gods,
Cure this great breach in his abusèd nature;   15
Th'untuned and jarring senses O wind up[12]
Of this child-changèd[13] father!

The sleeping Lear is carried on stage, dressed in fresh clothes. Cordelia speaks of him with pity and love. On waking, Lear thinks that he may be dead and that Cordelia is an angel.

 剧情简介：睡眠中的李尔被带到了舞台上，穿着新衣服。考蒂丽叶说起他的时候心中充满怜悯和爱。李尔醒来后，觉得自己可能已经死了，考蒂丽叶是个天使。

1 Music and additional lines

In the Quarto version of the play, music is played as Cordelia speaks to Lear. She has four additional lines after line 32:

To stand against the deep dread-bolted thunder?
In the most terrible and nimble stroke
Of quick cross lightning? to watch, poor perdu,
With this thin helm?

('perdu' = lost one, 'thin helm' = uncovered head)

- Decide, giving reasons, whether or not you would include music and these lines in your production. Make a note of your conclusions in your Director's Journal.

Themes 主题分析

'fresh garments' (in pairs)

Nakedness and clothing have been mentioned several times in the play as symbols – real things that represent something abstract. Edgar sheds his clothes to cast off his identity; Lear pulls off his garments in the storm to experience a greater connection with other humans (Act 3 Scene 4); and his costume in Act 4 Scene 5 makes his madness apparent. Now the audience sees him waken in fresh clothes. He can make a fresh start, leave the madness and anxiety behind and resume a calmer life. However, he is not wearing regal garments or a crown. He is restored to full humanity rather than to his kingship. Costume in the play can be used to convey a great deal about roles and status.

a List the different costumes that Lear may have worn so far in the play. (Look at the photographs of Lear in this edition to get some ideas if you need to.)

b What do different costumes demonstrate to the audience about a particular character's progress?

c Talk about how costume could be used to highlight the themes of appearance and reality and of the natural order.

d Make notes in your Director's Journal about one significant costume for a major character. Include an annotated sketch of your design.

---

1 I'th'sway … will 您认为怎样最好就怎样
2 arrayed 穿戴好了
3 Be by 站在近旁
4 temperance 自控力，理性
5 white flakes 白发
6 challenge 要求
7 hovel thee 待在茅棚里
8 rogues forlorn 孤苦伶仃的流浪汉
9 short and musty straw 细碎而发霉的麦秸
10 concluded all 完全消亡
11 bliss 天堂，极乐
12 wheel of fire 火轮（指地狱的煎熬）
13 far wide 太离谱（wide = wide of the mark，指李尔仍然很糊涂）
14 Would … condition 但愿我清楚自己的境况

GENTLEMAN	So please your majesty,	
	That we may wake the king? He hath slept long.	
CORDELIA	Be governed by your knowledge, and proceed	20
	I'th'sway of your own will[1]. Is he arrayed[2]?	

Enter LEAR [*asleep*] *in a chair carried by servants*

GENTLEMAN	Ay, madam: in the heaviness of sleep	
	We put fresh garments on him.	
	Be by[3], good madam, when we do awake him;	
	I doubt not of his temperance[4].	25
CORDELIA	O my dear father, restoration hang	
	Thy medicine on my lips, and let this kiss	
	Repair those violent harms that my two sisters	
	Have in thy reverence made.	
KENT	Kind and dear princess!	
CORDELIA	Had you not been their father, these white flakes[5]	30
	Did challenge[6] pity of them. Was this a face	
	To be opposed against the warring winds?	
	Mine enemy's dog,	
	Though he had bit me, should have stood that night	
	Against my fire. And wast thou fain, poor father,	35
	To hovel thee[7] with swine and rogues forlorn[8]	
	In short and musty straw[9]? Alack, alack,	
	'Tis wonder that thy life and wits at once	
	Had not concluded all[10]. He wakes. Speak to him.	
GENTLEMAN	Madam, do you; 'tis fittest.	40
CORDELIA	How does my royal lord? How fares your majesty?	
LEAR	You do me wrong to take me out o'th'grave.	
	Thou art a soul in bliss[11], but I am bound	
	Upon a wheel of fire[12], that mine own tears	
	Do scald like molten lead.	
CORDELIA	Sir, do you know me?	45
LEAR	You are a spirit, I know. Where did you die?	
CORDELIA	Still, still far wide[13].	
GENTLEMAN	He's scarce awake. Let him alone a while.	
LEAR	Where have I been? Where am I? Fair daylight?	
	I am mightily abused. I should ev'n die with pity	50
	To see another thus. I know not what to say.	
	I will not swear these are my hands. Let's see:	
	I feel this pin prick. Would I were assured	
	Of my condition[14].	

Cordelia asks her father for his blessing. He attempts to kneel before her. Although still confused, he is calm and recognises Cordelia, who expresses total forgiveness. As Lear leaves, he again asks Cordelia for forgiveness.

剧情简介　考蒂丽叶请求父亲祝福她。李尔试图想跪在她面前。此时的李尔尽管仍然困惑，却很平静。他认出了考蒂丽叶，考蒂丽叶表示完全原谅他。李尔离开时，再一次请求考蒂丽叶的原谅。

Finding that Cordelia's tears are real convinces Lear of her sincerity. Cordelia's repeated 'No cause' expresses the unconditional love that she has for her father, which forgives all injuries.

1	benediction	祝福
2	fond	傻
3	deal plainly	坦率地讲
4	mainly	彻底，完全
5	skill	了解；知识
6	abuse	欺骗，耍弄
7	great rage	癫狂
8	settling	平静

Language in the play 剧中语言

Lear's simple words (in pairs)

Lear seems calm, but he is clearly still aware of his own troubled mind and his recent traumatic experiences.

- Take parts as Lear and Cordelia. Read lines 56–74 and Lear's parting words at lines 81–2.
- Now look back to one of the sections when Lear was raving in his madness and to his words in Act 1 Scene 1. List the differences in the way he now expresses his ideas, refers to himself and requests help.

1 Visible reconciliation (in pairs)

This is a calm scene compared to many in the play, but it requires the actors to perform several specific actions.

a List the sequence of movements that can be inferred from the script.

b Lear's kneeling to Cordelia is in dramatic contrast with his kneeling to Regan in Act 2 Scene 4 (see p. 84). Compare the circumstances and effects of his actions in both cases.

c Cordelia offers Lear her support (line 80). Some see this gesture as an echo of Lear with his Fool (Act 3) and Edgar with his father (Act 4). Work with your partner to set up three tableaux showing each of these three relationships at the moment when support is offered. Talk together about why Shakespeare may have included these parallel situations.

King Lear Act 4 Scene 6
李尔王

CORDELIA   O look upon me, sir,
And hold your hand in benediction[1] o'er me.   55
You must not kneel.

LEAR   Pray do not mock me:
I am a very foolish, fond[2] old man,
Fourscore and upward,
Not an hour more nor less; and to deal plainly[3],
I fear I am not in my perfect mind.   60
Methinks I should know you and know this man;
Yet I am doubtful: for I am mainly[4] ignorant
What place this is, and all the skill[5] I have
Remembers not these garments, nor I know not
Where I did lodge last night. Do not laugh at me,   65
For, as I am a man, I think this lady
To be my child Cordelia.

CORDELIA   And so I am: I am.

LEAR   Be your tears wet? Yes, faith. I pray, weep not.
If you have poison for me, I will drink it.   70
I know you do not love me; for your sisters
Have, as I do remember, done me wrong.
You have some cause; they have not.

CORDELIA   No cause, no cause.

LEAR   Am I in France?

KENT   In your own kingdom, sir.   75

LEAR   Do not abuse[6] me.

GENTLEMAN   Be comforted, good madam. The great rage[7]
You see is killed in him. Desire him to go in.
Trouble him no more till further settling[8].

CORDELIA   Will't please your highness walk?   80

LEAR   You must bear with me. Pray you now, forget
And forgive. I am old and foolish.

                                                    Exeunt

KING LEAR 李尔王

Looking back at Act 4 第4幕回顾
Activities for groups or individuals

1 The king and the earl

Act 4 follows the fortunes of two 'old and foolish' men. There are many similarities between their experiences.

- In a written paragraph, summarise what has happened to Lear and Gloucester during this act. Try to establish similarities and differences in their experience.

2 Madness, sight and blindness

There are many moments in Act 4 (particularly in Scene 5) in which the themes of madness, sight and blindness are dramatically explored.

- Make a list of all examples and then write a short essay on the effects created by these images.

3 Edmond

In Act 4, Edmond appears only in Scene 2, where he speaks just one line. Imagine a short soliloquy in which he comments on his progress, his relationships with Regan and Gonerill, his feelings about his father and brother and his hopes for the future.

- Write seven or eight lines for Edmond to deliver as an aside after his one line in Scene 2 (line 26).

4 The absent Fool

The Fool does not appear in Act 4.

- Look back through the scenes in which Lear appears. In small groups, discuss whether the Fool's presence would have added to or detracted from the audience's understanding of the events unfolding.

5 Moving towards a conclusion

At the end of this act, all the main characters are in the Dover area and it is clear that the play is moving towards its conclusion.

- Write a list of questions that could be in the minds of audience members seeing the play for the first time.

6 The 'natural order'

The word 'nature' is used frequently in the play and its meaning is not always consistent – it can be used just a few lines apart to mean different things. However, the theme of the 'natural order' runs through events. Lear disrupts the political order by dividing the kingdom, and goes on to destroy the natural order of his family life.

- In pairs, make a list of examples of the natural order being disturbed, destroyed or restored in Act 4.

7 The Lear sisters

Cordelia, Gonerill and Regan all appear in Act 4 – but not together.

- Consider how these three characters have developed since Act 1 Scene 1, and how their different natures may stem from their upbringing. In small groups, talk about how the sisters might have felt about each other growing up. How long have Regan and Gonerill known that Cordelia was Lear's favourite? Has Gonerill been a dominating older sister? Was Cordelia spoiled by her sisters and by her father?

8 The missing mothers

Lear's queen and Gloucester's wife are completely absent from the play – they are scarcely mentioned, and then only in ribald (下流粗俗) references to conception and birth. They are not given names. A glance at the list of characters of this, or any, Shakespeare play reveals that he wrote far fewer parts for women than for men. This came, at least in part, from the fact that women were played by men or boys in his theatre.

- Discuss the role of the missing mothers in raising their children. Speculate about how the events of the play might have differed had it been written at a time when female characters were fully represented on stage and women were able to act.

Lear and the blinded Gloucester. Find a line from Scene 5 as an appropriate caption for this moment.

Edmond is unsure if Albany still intends to fight the French invaders. Regan jealously warns Edmond not to love Gonerill. Albany brings news that Lear and Cordelia have been joined by British rebels.

剧情简介：爱德门不确定阿尔博尼是否还想与法国入侵军队作战。蕊根心生嫉妒，她警告爱德门不要爱高娜瑞尔。阿尔博尼带来消息，说李尔和考蒂丽叶已经和不列颠叛军会师。

Stagecraft 导演技巧
'Drum and colours'

This final act starts with sounds and sights establishing a military atmosphere, very different from the mood in which Act 4 ended – one of peaceful reconciliation and expressions of love. The drums and flags were a convenient way to indicate an army on Shakespeare's stage.

- Note in your Director's Journal whether you would use drums and flags, or show this change of atmosphere in some other way – through costume, lighting, sound effects, set or stage business. (Notice that the first lines of the scene concern military matters, but Regan is more engrossed in her jealousy and suspicion about Edmond and Gonerill than in battle planning.)

Characters 人物分析
Mistrust and tension (in fours)

It is clear that Albany has continued to struggle with divided loyalties (see p. 146). This, and other issues, has led to strained relations between Albany, Gonerill, Regan and Edmond.

- Take parts and speak lines 15–26, with one group member taking the role of the silent Edmond.
- Read the lines again. This time, each reader should pause at the end of every sentence so that Edmond can state what he thinks is the true meaning behind the words that have been spoken.
- Afterwards, each group member speaks in character, summing up their feelings towards the other three.

1 What's the riddle?

After initially refusing to go with Regan and Albany to attend the council of war, Gonerill changes her mind. Her remark about the riddle (line 26) could refer to a real riddle or could mean 'I can see what you're getting at'.

- What do you think is running through Gonerill's mind here?

1 last purpose hold 坚持原定计划
2 since 近来
3 advised by aught 什么事让他改了主意
4 course 行动计划
5 self-reproving 自我责备
6 constant pleasure 下定的决心
7 Our … miscarried 我姐姐的仆人（奥兹沃尔）肯定遇到了不测
8 'Tis to be doubted 恐怕是这样
9 honoured 光彩；贞洁
10 forfended place 禁地；禁脔（指高娜瑞尔的床或身体）
11 I never shall endure her 我不会容忍她（成为自己的对手）
12 well bemet 幸会
13 rigour of our state 我们国家的严厉手段
14 Forced to cry out 迫使他们发声反对我们
15 Why is this reasoned? 为什么讨论这个？
16 domestic and particular broils 内斗和私下的争吵
17 th'ancient of war 久经沙场的军官
18 proceeding 作战计划

Act 5 Scene 1
The British camp near Dover

Enter with drum and colours, EDMOND, REGAN, OFFICERS *and* SOLDIERS

EDMOND [*To an Officer*] Know of the duke if his last purpose hold[1],
Or whether since[2] he is advised by aught[3]
To change the course[4]. He's full of alteration
And self-reproving[5]. Bring his constant pleasure[6].
[*Exit Officer*]

REGAN Our sister's man is certainly miscarried[7]. 5

EDMOND 'Tis to be doubted[8], madam.

REGAN Now, sweet lord,
You know the goodness I intend upon you.
Tell me but truly, but then speak the truth,
Do you not love my sister?

EDMOND In honoured[9] love.

REGAN But have you never found my brother's way 10
To the forfended place[10]?

EDMOND No, by mine honour, madam.

REGAN I never shall endure her[11]. Dear my lord,
Be not familiar with her.

EDMOND Fear me not.
She and the duke her husband –

Enter with drum and colours, ALBANY, GONERILL, *Soldiers*

ALBANY Our very loving sister, well bemet[12]. 15
Sir, this I heard: the king is come to his daughter,
With others whom the rigour of our state[13]
Forced to cry out[14].

REGAN Why is this reasoned?[15]

GONERILL Combine together 'gainst the enemy;
For these domestic and particular broils[16] 20
Are not the question here.

ALBANY Let's then determine with th'ancient of war[17]
On our proceeding[18].

REGAN Sister, you'll go with us?

GONERILL No.

REGAN 'Tis most convenient. Pray, go with us. 25

GONERILL [*Aside*] O ho, I know the riddle. – I will go.

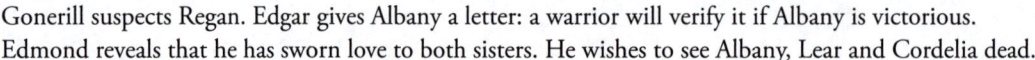
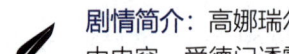

Gonerill suspects Regan. Edgar gives Albany a letter: a warrior will verify it if Albany is victorious. Edmond reveals that he has sworn love to both sisters. He wishes to see Albany, Lear and Cordelia dead.

剧情简介：高娜瑞尔怀疑蕊根。爱德格给了阿尔博尼一封信：如果阿尔博尼胜利了，一名武士会来验证信中内容。爱德门透露，他与两姐妹都曾立下爱的誓言，他想让阿尔博尼、李尔和考蒂丽叶统统去死。

1 Brothers reunited

Edgar and Edmond appear together briefly at lines 27–8. Some directors ignore the stage direction at line 28, choosing to keep Edmond on stage so that he hears Edgar's exchange with Albany.

- Make a list of the advantages and disadvantages of keeping Edmond on stage at this point. What might be the outcome of him overhearing his brother's words? How might he react?

2 'Hear me one word' (in pairs)

Albany is a high-ranking nobleman about to lead his army into battle, yet he pauses to listen to a poor peasant who asks to speak to him.

- Taking parts as Edgar and Albany, first read through lines 27–39 with Edgar acting as a humble peasant, grateful for Albany's attention.
- Then read through the lines again, with Edgar acting in a courteous but self-assured way, as though he were Albany's equal.
- Decide which approach you feel is more appropriate and agree on why this is. Or suggest another way the lines could be performed.

Characters 人物分析

Edmond's future plans (in sixes)

Despite the imminent battle, Edmond pauses to review his prospects (lines 44–58). In rehearsal, actors sometimes use activities like the first one below to bring out the full implications of his soliloquy.

a Take parts as Gonerill, Regan, Albany, Lear and Cordelia and stand in a circle. The sixth person, as Edmond, walks around the space, speaking his lines to each of the characters as they are mentioned and adding gestures where they seem appropriate.

b Discuss whether the audience would find Edmond's words chilling in their ruthlessness or amusing in their exuberance, and whether or not an audience feels comfortable being drawn into the secrets and confidence of so wicked a character.

c Should this rather artificial situation be played realistically (perhaps giving Edmond a practical task to do) or in a deliberately artificial way (possibly with all other characters immobile on stage as Edmond takes time out to think things through and talk to the audience)?

1 overtake you 赶过来
2 ope = open
3 champion 战士
4 miscarry 战败身亡
5 machination 阴谋诡计
6 o'erlook 读一遍
7 guess 估测
8 diligent discovery 详细侦查
9 We will greet the time 我已经迫不及待了（We是御用复数）
10 jealous 猜疑
11 adder 蝰蛇（一种毒蛇）
12 Exasperates 激怒
13 carry out my side 达到我的目的（称王）；履行我（对高娜瑞尔）的承诺
14 countenance 力量，权威
15 taking off 谋杀
16 Shall = They shall
17 state 情形
18 Stands … debate 在于我要落实到行动上，而不是口头上

Enter EDGAR [*dressed like a peasant*]

EDGAR　　　If e'er your grace had speech with man so poor,
　　　　　　Hear me one word.
ALBANY　　[*To the others*]　　I'll overtake you[1].

　　　　　　　　　　　　　　　　　　　Exeunt both the armies
　　　　　　　　　　Speak.
EDGAR　　　Before you fight the battle, ope[2] this letter.
　　　　　　If you have victory, let the trumpet sound　　　　　　30
　　　　　　For him that brought it. Wretched though I seem,
　　　　　　I can produce a champion[3] that will prove
　　　　　　What is avouchèd there. If you miscarry[4],
　　　　　　Your business of the world hath so an end,
　　　　　　And machination[5] ceases. Fortune love you.　　　　35
ALBANY　　Stay till I have read the letter.
EDGAR　　　　　　　　　　　　　I was forbid it.
　　　　　　When time shall serve, let but the herald cry,
　　　　　　And I'll appear again.　　　　　　　　　　　*Exit*
ALBANY　　Why, fare thee well. I will o'erlook[6] thy paper.

Enter EDMOND

EDMOND　　The enemy's in view; draw up your powers.　　　40
　　　　　　Here is the guess[7] of their true strength and forces
　　　　　　By diligent discovery[8]; but your haste
　　　　　　Is now urged on you.
ALBANY　　　　　　　　　We will greet the time[9].　　*Exit*
EDMOND　　To both these sisters have I sworn my love,
　　　　　　Each jealous[10] of the other as the stung　　　　　45
　　　　　　Are of the adder[11]. Which of them shall I take?
　　　　　　Both? one? or neither? Neither can be enjoyed
　　　　　　If both remain alive. To take the widow
　　　　　　Exasperates[12], makes mad her sister Gonerill,
　　　　　　And hardly shall I carry out my side[13],　　　　　50
　　　　　　Her husband being alive. Now then, we'll use
　　　　　　His countenance[14] for the battle, which being done,
　　　　　　Let her who would be rid of him devise
　　　　　　His speedy taking off[15]. As for the mercy
　　　　　　Which he intends to Lear and to Cordelia,　　　　55
　　　　　　The battle done, and they within our power,
　　　　　　Shall[16] never see his pardon; for my state[17]
　　　　　　Stands on me to defend, not to debate[18].　　*Exit*

Edgar leaves Gloucester, but returns with the news that Albany's forces have won. Edgar comforts Gloucester. Edmond orders the imprisonment of Cordelia and Lear. Cordelia expresses compassion for Lear.

剧情简介：爱德格离开了格劳斯特，但是带回了阿尔博尼军队胜利的消息。爱德格安慰格劳斯特。爱德门命人将考蒂丽叶和李尔都监禁起来。考蒂丽叶对李尔表示怜悯。

Stagecraft 导演技巧

The battle at Dover (in pairs)

Shakespeare suggests the battle by having Lear and Cordelia lead their 'army' across the stage. The battle itself is fought off stage ('*within*', line 4), but some productions show glimpses of the fighting or its aftermath. Sometimes directors choose to stage a non-realistic 'symbolic' battle, as though imagined by the blind Gloucester. Others suggest the conflict through sound effects or percussion (打击乐器). Still others have shown the consequences of battle with lines of refugees or prisoners being mistreated by soldiers. Some show nothing at all of the battle, but suggest, through lighting changes, the passage of some hours between lines 4 and 5.

a Talk about the different effects you think each of the above methods of presenting the battle would have on an audience. Note in your Director's Journal what choices you would make.

b The staging may suggest that the battle itself is not of central importance. Discuss what is the principal focus of the action at this stage in the play.

Themes 主题分析

'Ripeness is all' (in pairs)

Gloucester's words 'a man may rot' (line 8) suggest he is again despairing. Edgar tries to lift his father's spirits. Lines 9–11 seem to say that the time of a person's death is chosen by the gods.

a Some people find in Edgar's words a stoic (斯多葛学派，对痛苦和困难泰然处之) acceptance of fate, others a serene acceptance of the natural order and others still a pessimistic resignation in the face of what could, in fact, be changed. What do you think?

b Do you feel this issue (of how much control over their own lives humans should desire) is an important theme in the play? Look back at other situations where the characters have either had to resign themselves to difficult situations or have struggled to oppose them.

c Show your ideas about which characters might also say, 'Ripeness is all', and which definitely would not. You could present this in a table or place them all on a line with 'total resistance' at one end and 'utter resignation' at the other.

1 *Alarum* 号角声
2 *good host* 栖身之所
3 *retreat* 撤退的号角声
4 *ta'en* = taken （被俘）
5 *Ripeness is all* 一切听天由命（只要时机成熟，任何事情上天自有安排）
6 *good guard* 严加看守
7 *their greater pleasures* 上峰的意愿
8 *censure* 判决
9 *meaning* 意图
10 *incurred* 遭受
11 *cast down* 心灰意冷
12 *Myself … frown* 否则我向来对不幸的命运横眉立目（藐视不幸的命运）

Act 5 Scene 2
The countryside near Dover

Alarum[1] within. Enter with drum and colours, LEAR, CORDELIA,
and Soldiers, over the stage, and exeunt

Enter EDGAR, *dressed like a peasant, and* GLOUCESTER

EDGAR Here, father, take the shadow of this tree
For your good host[2]; pray that the right may thrive.
If ever I return to you again
I'll bring you comfort.
GLOUCESTER   Grace go with you, sir.

Exit [Edgar]

Alarum and retreat[3] within. Enter EDGAR

EDGAR Away, old man! Give me thy hand; away! 5
King Lear hath lost, he and his daughter ta'en[4].
Give me thy hand. Come on.
GLOUCESTER No further, sir; a man may rot even here.
EDGAR What, in ill thoughts again? Men must endure
Their going hence even as their coming hither: 10
Ripeness is all[5]. Come on.
GLOUCESTER   And that's true too.

Exeunt

Act 5 Scene 3
The British camp near Dover

Enter in conquest with drum and colours EDMOND; LEAR *and*
CORDELIA, *as prisoners; Soldiers;* CAPTAIN

EDMOND Some officers take them away: good guard[6],
Until their greater pleasures[7] first be known
That are to censure[8] them.
CORDELIA   We are not the first
Who with best meaning[9] have incurred[10] the worst.
For thee, oppressèd king, I am cast down[11], 5
Myself could else outfrown false fortune's frown[12].
Shall we not see these daughters and these sisters?

Lear is joyful to be imprisoned forever with Cordelia. They will mock the petty quarrels of the court. Edmond gives Lear and Cordelia's death warrant to the Captain. He promises promotion and warns against soft-heartedness.

 剧情简介：李尔很高兴跟考蒂丽叶永远监禁在一起。他们将嘲笑朝廷里琐碎的争吵。爱德门把处死李尔和考蒂丽叶的判决书给了军官，宣布奖赏办法，警告行动不要心软。

1 The king's future (in pairs)

- Take the roles of Edmond and Lear. Edmond reads lines 26–35, pausing at each full stop.
- At each pause, Lear speaks a few words taken from his lines 8–25. You could use the same line each time (possibly line 9) or different phrases that seem appropriate.
- Talk about the likely effect of Edmond's lines on an audience that has just heard Lear express his hopes for the future.

Language in the play 剧中语言

Captivity and execution (in small groups)

Edmond arranges for Lear's and Cordelia's executions as soon as they have left the stage to be escorted to prison, promising the Captain promotion if he carries out the orders.

a Look at the language Edmond uses in lines 27–38. Consider his use of imperatives and his short, brisk sentences. His style is very confident and assertive, and he makes it clear that the Captain will be risking a great deal if he does not follow these orders. What does Edmond's language here reveal about his status and his character? Discuss this in your groups.

b Look back at Edmond's language in an earlier act (for example, his soliloquy at the start of Act 1 Scene 2, or his words to his father in Act 2 Scene 1, starting at line 43). Contrast his language there with that in the script opposite.

1 gilded butterflies   金光灿灿的蝴蝶（喻指衣着华丽、朝生暮死的朝臣）
2 poor rogues   可怜虫
3 take … things   担起参透世事奥秘的责任
4 wear out   活的时间长过，熬死
5 packs and sects   宗派团伙（结党营私之徒）
6 The gods themselves throw incense   天神都会亲自（像祭司一样）焚香致敬
7 shall … foxes   需要用天神的火把，像把狐狸从地洞里熏出来那样，才能把我们分开
8 goodyears   凶年；瘟疫
9 flesh and fell   连肉带皮
10 One … thee   我已经给你升了一级
11 men … is   人要会审时度势
12 not become a sword   不配舞刀弄枪
13 Will not bear question   不容多问
14 write 'happy'   交好运

This is how a Russian film version showed Lear's and Cordelia's capture. What mood and atmosphere has the director created here?

LEAR	No, no, no, no! Come, let's away to prison.
	We two alone will sing like birds i'th'cage.
	When thou dost ask me blessing, I'll kneel down 10
	And ask of thee forgiveness: so we'll live,
	And pray, and sing, and tell old tales, and laugh
	At gilded butterflies[1], and hear poor rogues[2]
	Talk of court news, and we'll talk with them too –
	Who loses and who wins; who's in, who's out – 15
	And take upon 's the mystery of things[3],
	As if we were God's spies; and we'll wear out[4]
	In a walled prison packs and sects[5] of great ones
	That ebb and flow by th'moon.
EDMOND	Take them away.
LEAR	Upon such sacrifices, my Cordelia, 20
	The gods themselves throw incense[6]. Have I caught thee?
	He that parts us shall bring a brand from heaven
	And fire us hence like foxes[7]. Wipe thine eyes.
	The goodyears[8] shall devour them, flesh and fell[9],
	Ere they shall make us weep. We'll see 'em starved first. 25
	Come.

Exeunt Lear and Cordelia, guarded

EDMOND	Come hither, captain. Hark.
	Take thou this note. Go follow them to prison.
	One step I have advanced thee[10]; if thou dost
	As this instructs thee, thou dost make thy way 30
	To noble fortunes. Know thou this: that men
	Are as the time is[11]; to be tender-minded
	Does not become a sword[12]. Thy great employment
	Will not bear question[13]: either say thou'lt do't,
	Or thrive by other means.
CAPTAIN	I'll do't, my lord. 35
EDMOND	About it, and write 'happy'[14] when th'hast done.
	Mark, I say, instantly, and carry it so
	As I have set it down.

Exit Captain

Albany demands that Edmond hand over Lear and Cordelia. Edmond delays, provoking Albany to assert Edmond's social inferiority. Regan defends Edmond. Gonerill resents Regan's patronage of Edmond.

剧情简介：阿尔博尼命爱德门交出李尔和考蒂丽叶。爱德门拖延，惹得阿尔博尼说他低人一等。蕊根维护爱德门的名誉。高娜瑞尔憎恨蕊根如此庇护爱德门。

1 The alliance falls apart (in fours)

The tone of this meeting is very different from the touching exchange between the captive Lear and Cordelia, and from Edmond's authoritative commands to the Captain. Now the tensions between the victorious allies come to the surface: Edmond and Albany clash, Regan resents Albany's leadership (which she feels unable to challenge fully without support from a husband) and the two sisters compete for Edmond's favours.

a Take parts and read through lines 39–65, thinking about which character each line is addressed to. Then read the lines again, but this time vary how far you stand from the person you are addressing to suit how angry you feel – the closer, the angrier.

b How carefully do you think Gonerill and Regan follow the earlier part of this discussion?

Language in the play 剧中语言

Blindness (in pairs)

There have been many references to sight and blindness in the play, one of the first being Gonerill's declaration in Act 1 Scene 1 that Lear was 'dearer than eyesight'. Here, Edmond expresses concern that sympathy for Lear and Cordelia might turn the British conscripted pikemen against their leaders. However, the language he uses (in line 49) means literally that they might turn and blind them with their pikes. In line 66, Gonerill accuses Regan of not seeing clearly because of her jealousy. Gonerill's words, 'That eye that told you so, looked but asquint', are probably based on the proverb 'Love, being jealous, makes a good eye look asquint'.

a Why do you think Shakespeare chose to use imagery of distorted perception here?

b Develop the notes you have already made on blindness in the play, looking both at imagery and at the theme of damaged sight or moral blindness.

c As you read to the end of the play, make a note of further references to damaged sight.

1 **strain** 品质
2 **their merits and our safety** 他们应有的惩罚和我们的安全
3 **equally determine** 公平决断（如何处置）
4 **retention** 拘押，收监
5 **Whose … it** 他的年迈会令人同情
6 **common bosom** 民众的爱戴
7 **impressed lances** 所征新兵的投枪
8 **session** 审讯
9 **by your patience** 恕我直言
10 **I … brother** 在这一仗中我只把您看作我的下属，而非妹夫
11 **we list to grace him** 本宫选择给他论功行赏（we是御用复数）
12 **Bore … person** 委任他代表本宫的身份和地位
13 **The which immediacy** 和本宫的这种直接关系
14 **your addition** 您授予他的（尊荣）
15 **invested** 授予
16 **compeers** 与……平起平坐
17 **Holla, holla!** 哎哟，哎哟！（引起他人注意的叫声）

Flourish. Enter ALBANY, GONERILL, REGAN, [*Officers,*] *Soldiers*

ALBANY   Sir, you have showed today your valiant strain[1],
And fortune led you well. You have the captives
Who were the opposites of this day's strife.
I do require them of you, so to use them
As we shall find their merits and our safety[2]
May equally determine[3].

EDMOND   Sir, I thought it fit
To send the old and miserable king
To some retention[4] and appointed guard,
Whose age had charms in it[5], whose title more,
To pluck the common bosom[6] on his side
And turn our impressed lances[7] in our eyes
Which do command them. With him I sent the queen:
My reason all the same, and they are ready
Tomorrow, or at further space, t'appear
Where you shall hold your session[8].

ALBANY   Sir, by your patience[9],
I hold you but a subject of this war,
Not as a brother[10].

REGAN   That's as we list to grace him[11].
Methinks our pleasure might have been demanded
Ere you had spoke so far. He led our powers,
Bore the commission of my place and person[12],
The which immediacy[13] may well stand up
And call itself your brother.

GONERILL   Not so hot.
In his own grace he doth exalt himself
More than in your addition[14].

REGAN   In my rights,
By me invested[15], he compeers[16] the best.

ALBANY   That were the most if he should husband you.

REGAN   Jesters do oft prove prophets.

GONERILL   Holla, holla![17]
That eye that told you so, looked but asquint.

Regan betrothes herself to Edmond. Albany forbids the marriage, accusing Edmond and Gonerill of treason and adultery. Albany challenges Edmond to a duel. He accepts. Regan falls ill, poisoned by Gonerill.

剧情简介：蕊根将自己许配给了爱德门。阿尔博尼禁止这桩婚姻，指控爱德门和高娜瑞尔犯了叛国罪和通奸罪。阿尔博尼向爱德门提出决斗，爱德门接受了。高娜瑞尔给蕊根下毒，蕊根中毒。

Write about it 写作练习
Edmond reacts as Regan stakes her claim

Edmond could not decide between the two sisters in Act 5 Scene 1, lines 44–54. Now, Regan announces publicly that he is to be her husband and says that she surrenders everything to him, like a city at the end of a siege ('the walls is thine').

- Write a short soliloquy for Edmond to show his response to this very public declaration. (You can look back at Edmond's last soliloquy on p. 177 for ideas.)

1 Throwing down the gauntlets (in fours)

Albany has read the letter Edgar took from Oswald and consequently arrests Edmond for treason, announcing that he also knows of Gonerill's guilt. Because Edmond is now Earl of Gloucester, Albany allows him the aristocratic right to defend his honour in single combat. He pledges to challenge Edmond himself if no one else is prepared to do so.

- Take parts as the four characters and read lines 84–95.
- Decide what movements and gestures each character could make. Consider in particular how differently each of the four might react when the two gauntlets are thrown down.
- Regan is suffering the effects of some sort of slow poison in this scene. Consider how the actor should show this on stage.
- Be prepared to share your scene with other groups and then to discuss the differences in interpretation.

Language in the play 剧中语言
Gonerill, the 'gilded serpent'?

Animal imagery is used frequently in the play, often as an unflattering comparison. Lear called Gonerill a 'detested kite' (Act 1 Scene 4) and Gloucester referred to her 'boarish fangs' (Act 3 Scene 7).

a What image does Albany's insulting description of his wife (line 78) conjure up in your mind?

b During this scene, Gonerill watches her sister showing the first effects of poisoning. Decide how serpent-like her behaviour should be and how she could behave when delivering her cynical aside at line 90, with its snake-like sibilance (hissing sounds).

1 a full-flowing stomach 一肚子火
2 patrimony 继承的遗产
3 the walls is thine 城堡是你的了（即"我接受你的处置"；蕊根想象自己是投降的城堡）
4 let-alone 干涉权
5 Half-blooded 半血亲（上流人家的私生子）
6 attaint 指控
7 subcontracted 以身相许
8 banns 婚事预告
9 make … bespoke 向我求婚吧，因为我夫人已经（与爱德门）有婚约了
10 An interlude! 好一场闹剧！
11 heinous 罪大恶极
12 manifest 昭然若揭
13 pledge 挑战的保证（扔下一只护手或手套）
14 medicine 毒药

REGAN   Lady, I am not well, else I should answer
          From a full-flowing stomach[1]. [*To Edmond*] General,
          Take thou my soldiers, prisoners, patrimony[2].
          Dispose of them, of me; the walls is thine[3].   70
          Witness the world that I create thee here
          My lord and master.
GONERILL   Mean you to enjoy him?
ALBANY   The let-alone[4] lies not in your good will.
EDMOND   Nor in thine, lord.
ALBANY   Half-blooded[5] fellow, yes.
REGAN   [*To Edmond*] Let the drum strike, and prove my title thine.   75
ALBANY   Stay yet, hear reason. Edmond, I arrest thee
          On capital treason, and in thy attaint[6]
          This gilded serpent. For your claim, fair sister,
          I bar it in the interest of my wife.
          'Tis she is subcontracted[7] to this lord,   80
          And I, her husband, contradict your banns[8].
          If you will marry, make your love to me,
          My lady is bespoke[9].
GONERILL   An interlude![10]
ALBANY   Thou art armed, Gloucester; let the trumpet sound.
          If none appear to prove upon thy person   85
          Thy heinous[11], manifest[12], and many treasons,
          There is my pledge[13]!
                    [*Throws down a glove*]
                            I'll make it on thy heart,
          Ere I taste bread, thou art in nothing less
          Than I have here proclaimed thee.
REGAN   Sick, O sick!
GONERILL [*Aside*] If not, I'll ne'er trust medicine[14].   90
EDMOND   There's my exchange!
                    [*Throws down a glove*]
                            What in the world he is
          That names me traitor, villain-like he lies.
          Call by the trumpet: he that dares, approach;
          On him, on you – who not? – I will maintain
          My truth and honour firmly.

Albany has dismissed Edmond's soldiers, so Edmond must fight alone. Regan, sick, is taken to Albany's tent. At the third trumpet call Edgar appears, disguised and armed. Refusing to give his name, he challenges Edmond.

 剧情简介：阿尔博尼解散了爱德门的士兵，因此爱德门只好与阿尔博尼单打独斗。病倒的蕊根被带到了阿尔博尼的营帐中。第三声号声响起，乔装打扮、全副武装的爱德格出现了。他不肯透露自己的姓名，挑战爱德门。

Write about it 写作练习
Waiting for a challenger

The audience has to wait for the arrival of Edgar. The ritual language and ceremonial behaviour suggest that traditional rules of chivalry are now at work, governing the deadly encounter of two knights.

- Write a few paragraphs about the way Shakespeare builds the tension here. Comment on the effect of the repeated trumpet calls and on the attitudes of the various witnesses at this moment of uncertainty. Describe how this sense of tension could be developed by the way Edgar makes his entrance and conclude by commenting on the effect of Edgar's mysterious answer (lines 111–14) to the Herald's questions.

1. thy single virtue 你一个人的本事
2. levied 征召
3. Took their discharge 把他们解散了
4. quality or degree 出身或地位高贵
5. lists 花名册
6. manifold 作恶多端
7. bare-gnawn 被啃光
8. canker-bit 被蚕食
9. adversary 对手
10. cope 决战

1 'my name is lost' (in pairs)

Edgar refuses to give his name, saying it has been devoured 'by treason's tooth'. When he first disguised himself as Poor Tom he said: 'Edgar I nothing am.'

a List all the various assumed identities that Edgar has undertaken in the play and his motives for each pretence. You may want to include sketches of costume and notes on body language.

b Do you think that Edgar simply does not want Edmond to know who he is fighting, or is there some other explanation for his refusal to give his name? Talk about this in your pairs.

▼ Edgar and Edmond before their duel. Edgar's costume at this point varies: he may be shown in gleaming armour, pure white, or – as in this image – still dressed as a poor man. How would you portray him?

ALBANY	A herald, ho!	95

Enter a HERALD

Trust to thy single virtue¹, for thy soldiers,
All levied² in my name, have in my name
Took their discharge³.

REGAN My sickness grows upon me.
ALBANY She is not well. Convey her to my tent.

[*Exit Regan, led by an Officer*]

Come hither, herald. Let the trumpet sound, 100
And read out this.

A trumpet sounds

HERALD *Reads* 'If any man of quality or degree⁴ within the lists⁵ of the army will maintain upon Edmond, supposed Earl of Gloucester, that he is a manifold⁶ traitor, let him appear by the third sound of the trumpet. He is bold in his defence.' 105

First trumpet

Again.

Second trumpet

Again.

Third trumpet

Trumpet answers within. Enter EDGAR, *armed*

ALBANY Ask him his purposes, why he appears
Upon this call o'th'trumpet.
HERALD What are you?
Your name, your quality, and why you answer 110
This present summons?
EDGAR Know, my name is lost,
By treason's tooth bare-gnawn⁷ and canker-bit⁸.
Yet am I noble as the adversary⁹
I come to cope¹⁰.
ALBANY Which is that adversary?
EDGAR What's he that speaks for Edmond, Earl of Gloucester? 115
EDMOND Himself. What sayst thou to him?

Edgar proclaims Edmond's treachery. Edmond denies his guilt. Edmond is fatally wounded in the fight. Albany shows Gonerill's letter to Edmond. Gonerill attempts to seize it, claiming to be ruler and law-maker.

 剧情简介：爱德格公布爱德门的背叛行为，爱德门否认自己有罪，在打斗中受了致命伤。阿尔博尼给爱德门看了高娜瑞尔写的信。高娜瑞尔企图抢过来，说她才是国君和制定法律的人。

Characters 人物分析

The adversaries (in fours)

Edgar makes a formal statement denouncing Edmond. The following activities will help you decide on the appropriate tone for his words.

a Take parts as Edgar, Edmond and Albany. Edgar reads lines 116–31 slowly and clearly, while the fourth group member points at whoever is being mentioned, including 'I' and 'thee'. Swap roles and read again.

b Discuss how Edgar should deliver these lines. Remember that he is making specific accusations about Edmond but not identifying himself as a victim. How neutral and disinterested or detached, is Edgar's statement? At which point in his words do you feel he shows most anger against his brother? Is he taking on yet another persona, or is this the 'real' Edgar?

c The laws of chivalry meant that a knight could refuse a challenge from a social inferior, so Edmond says he takes a risk in agreeing to the fight with a nameless, unknown combatant. What does his choice to accept the challenge tell us about his character?

1 Maugre 尽管
2 place 地位
3 eminence 显赫身份
4 fire-new fortune 炙手可热的好运（所获的头衔和打胜仗）
5 high illustrious prince 高贵显赫的亲王（指阿尔博尼）
6 toad-spotted 烙上癞蛤蟆印
7 bent 下定决心
8 some say of breeding 有几分高贵
9 safe and nicely 合理合法，中规中矩
10 hell-hated lie 如地狱一般可恨的谎言
11 give them instant way 立刻给它们让路
12 vanquished 被打败
13 cozened and beguiled 遭人设局蒙骗
14 arraign 控告

Stagecraft 导演技巧

The fight (in pairs)

The duel between Edgar and Edmond is described by just a few words of stage directions, but it usually takes up some time on stage.

- Decide what motivates and drives on each of the adversaries.
- Make some suggestions about how the fight should be staged. Presumably the bouts are controlled in some way by the Herald, but how? Are the brothers equally matched?
- Discuss appropriate styles of fighting. The swordplay could be delicate, like fencing, or brutal and murderous. The two men could fight in similar or very different styles, as might befit their different characters. The style of fighting may change as the fight progresses.
- Talk about what the audience can judge about each character from their conduct in the duel.

EDGAR	Draw thy sword,
	That if my speech offend a noble heart
	Thy arm may do thee justice. Here is mine.
	Behold, it is the privilege of mine honour,
	My oath, and my profession. I protest, 120
	Maugre[1] thy strength, place[2], youth, and eminence[3],
	Despite thy victor-sword and fire-new fortune[4],
	Thy valour and thy heart, thou art a traitor:
	False to thy gods, thy brother, and thy father,
	Conspirant 'gainst this high illustrious prince[5], 125
	And from th'extremest upward of thy head
	To the descent and dust below thy foot,
	A most toad-spotted[6] traitor. Say thou no,
	This sword, this arm, and my best spirits are bent[7]
	To prove upon thy heart, whereto I speak, 130
	Thou liest.
EDMOND	In wisdom I should ask thy name,
	But since thy outside looks so fair and warlike,
	And that thy tongue some say of breeding[8] breathes,
	What safe and nicely[9] I might well delay
	By rule of knighthood, I disdain and spurn. 135
	Back do I toss these treasons to thy head,
	With the hell-hated lie[10] o'erwhelm thy heart,
	Which, for they yet glance by and scarcely bruise,
	This sword of mine shall give them instant way[11]
	Where they shall rest for ever. Trumpets, speak! 140
	Alarums. [They] fight. [Edmond falls]
ALBANY	Save him, save him.
GONERILL	This is practice, Gloucester;
	By th'law of war thou wast not bound to answer
	An unknown opposite. Thou art not vanquished[12],
	But cozened and beguiled[13].
ALBANY	Shut your mouth, dame,
	Or with this paper shall I stop it. – Hold, sir. 145
	Thou worse than any name, read thine own evil. –
	No tearing, lady. I perceive you know it.
GONERILL	Say if I do; the laws are mine, not thine.
	Who can arraign[14] me for't? *Exit*
ALBANY	Most monstrous! O,
	Know'st thou this paper?

An Officer is sent to watch over Gonerill. The dying Edmond confesses his crimes. Edgar sheds his disguise and tells how, as Poor Tom, he helped Gloucester, only revealing his identity to his father afterwards.

剧情简介： 一位军官被派去看管高娜瑞尔。奄奄一息的爱德门承认了自己的罪行。爱德格卸掉了自己的伪装，说出了自己如何伪装成可怜的汤姆帮助格劳斯特，后来才在父亲那里表明了身份。

Suggest a line that could be used as a caption for this picture of Edmond and Edgar.

1	govern	看管
2	exchange charity	彼此宽容
3	of … us	把我们寻欢作乐的罪孽当作惩罚我们的工具
4	The dark … got	他在肮脏污秽的地方生下你（got = begot）
5	wheel	命运之轮
6	gait	步态
7	List	听
8	bloody proclamation	死刑通缉令
9	That we … once!	我们宁可时刻忍受死亡的恐惧，也不想立刻死去！
10	semblance	外表，样子
11	habit	装束，打扮
12	rings	眼窝
13	stones	眼睛

Themes 主题分析

'The wheel is come full circle' (in pairs)

The recurring theme of justice and injustice, frequently expressed in the play as the turning of Fortune's wheel, reappears when Edmond acknowledges that he is fatally wounded: ''Tis past, and so am I' (line 154). Edgar exchanges 'charity' with his brother before revealing his identity and affirming that the 'gods are just' in their punishment of both Edmond and Gloucester for their sins of pleasure. Edmond acknowledges the role of providence in his demise, returning him 'full circle' to the bottom of Fortune's wheel.

- Take parts and speak lines 152–64. Read the lines with Edgar standing formally over his wounded brother while making clear his stern moral judgements about him.
- Change the body language, with Edgar cradling and comforting his dying brother, and read the lines again with Edgar taking a more conciliatory, forgiving approach.
- Which interpretation works better, or do you feel the lines should be performed in some other way?
- Decide on a gesture Edmond could use to accompany his words 'I am here' (line 164).

King Lear Act 5 Scene 3
李尔王

| EDMOND | Ask me not what I know. | 150 |

ALBANY Go after her, she's desperate, govern[1] her.

[Exit an Officer]

EDMOND What you have charged me with, that have I done,
And more, much more; the time will bring it out.
'Tis past, and so am I. But what art thou
That hast this fortune on me? If thou'rt noble, 155
I do forgive thee.

EDGAR Let's exchange charity[2].
I am no less in blood than thou art, Edmond.
If more, the more th'hast wronged me.
My name is Edgar, and thy father's son.
The gods are just, and of our pleasant vices 160
Make instruments to plague us[3].
The dark and vicious place where thee he got[4]
Cost him his eyes.

EDMOND Th'hast spoken right; 'tis true.
The wheel[5] is come full circle; I am here.

ALBANY Methought thy very gait[6] did prophesy 165
A royal nobleness. I must embrace thee.
Let sorrow split my heart if ever I
Did hate thee or thy father.

EDGAR Worthy prince, I know't.

ALBANY Where have you hid yourself? 170
How have you known the miseries of your father?

EDGAR By nursing them, my lord. List[7] a brief tale,
And when 'tis told, O that my heart would burst!
The bloody proclamation[8] to escape
That followed me so near (O, our lives' sweetness, 175
That we the pain of death would hourly die
Rather than die at once![9]) taught me to shift
Into a madman's rags, t'assume a semblance[10]
That very dogs disdained; and in this habit[11]
Met I my father with his bleeding rings[12], 180
Their precious stones[13] new-lost; became his guide,
Led him, begged for him, saved him from despair,
Never – O fault! – revealed myself unto him
Until some half hour past, when I was armed.

191

Edgar reports that Gloucester died happily. News comes of Gonerill's suicide and Regan's poisoning. Kent arrives to bid farewell to Lear. Albany demands that Edmond reveal the whereabouts of Lear and Cordelia.

剧情简介：爱德格说格劳斯特在欣慰中死去。高娜瑞尔自杀和蕊根中毒的消息传来。肯特来和李尔告别。阿尔博尼命爱德门说出李尔和考蒂丽叶的下落。

Write about it 写作练习

Edgar and his father

In lines 172–90, Edgar describes how he helped Gloucester – practically and emotionally – by leading him and saving him 'from despair'. However, he blames himself for not shedding his disguise sooner ('O fault!' line 183).

- In role as Edgar, write an account of his final hours with his father and his actions on the day of the battle. Explain why he reproaches himself so bitterly for concealing his identity too long, even though he comforted his father tenderly in his last hours, and why he only revealed his identity to his father as he was about to fight Edmond.

Characters 人物分析

The dying brother (in pairs)

Edmond says he is affected by Edgar's words about their father but, although he claims it might move him to 'do good', he does nothing straight away to revoke the death sentences on Lear and Cordelia.

a Suggest a gesture an actor could use to remind the audience of Edmond's earlier instructions to the Captain.

b Both Gonerill and Regan die off stage. Edmond greets the news with what could be a grim joke about his own agreement to marry both of them (lines 202–3). If you were playing Edmond, decide if you would want to make the audience smile at this point. Would humour add to, or detract from, the horror of this death-ridden scene?

1 **'Produce the bodies'** (in small groups)

Albany orders the bodies of the dead sisters to be carried on. He echoes Edgar's and Edmond's lines 160–4 in affirming the all-powerful 'judgement of the heavens'.

a Decide how you would stage the bringing-in of the bodies: casually, with great ceremony, or in some other manner?

b How should Albany react to seeing his dead wife?

c In some productions line 204 is omitted and the bodies are not brought on stage. What are the advantages and the disadvantages of this?

1 good success 胜利的结局（指决斗胜利）
2 our pilgrimage 我们的旅途经历
3 flawed 碎裂
4 smilingly 含笑
5 dissolve 融化在泪水里
6 smokes 冒着热气
7 contracted 订婚
8 marry 结合
9 Produce the bodies 把尸体抬上来
10 The time … urges 这种场合就顾不上过分讲究礼仪了
11 aye 永远
12 object 情景，场面

	Not sure, though hoping of this good success¹,	185
	I asked his blessing, and from first to last	
	Told him our pilgrimage²; but his flawed³ heart –	
	Alack, too weak the conflict to support –	
	'Twixt two extremes of passion, joy and grief,	
	Burst smilingly⁴.	
EDMOND	This speech of yours hath moved me,	190
	And shall perchance do good. But speak you on,	
	You look as you had something more to say.	
ALBANY	If there be more, more woeful, hold it in,	
	For I am almost ready to dissolve⁵,	
	Hearing of this.	195

Enter a GENTLEMAN [*with a bloody knife*]

GENTLEMAN	Help, help, O help!	
EDGAR	What kind of help?	
ALBANY	Speak, man.	
EDGAR	What means this bloody knife?	
GENTLEMAN	'Tis hot, it smokes⁶.	
	It came even from the heart of – O, she's dead.	
ALBANY	Who dead? Speak, man.	
GENTLEMAN	Your lady, sir, your lady; and her sister	200
	By her is poisoned: she confesses it.	
EDMOND	I was contracted⁷ to them both; all three	
	Now marry⁸ in an instant.	
EDGAR	Here comes Kent.	

Enter KENT [*as himself*]

| ALBANY | Produce the bodies⁹, be they alive or dead. | |

Gonerill's and Regan's bodies brought out

	This judgement of the heavens, that makes us tremble,	205
	Touches us not with pity. – O, is this he?	
	[*To Kent*] The time will not allow the compliment	
	Which very manners urges¹⁰.	
KENT	I am come	
	To bid my king and master aye¹¹ good night.	
	Is he not here?	
ALBANY	Great thing of us forgot!	210
	Speak, Edmond; where's the king, and where's Cordelia?	
	Seest thou this object¹², Kent?	

Edmond urges that someone be sent to cancel his death warrant on Lear and Cordelia. She was to be hanged to give the appearance of suicide. Lear enters, carrying the dead Cordelia and grieving for her.

剧情简介：爱德门催促赶快派人去取消李尔和考蒂丽叶的死刑执行令。本来的计划是，考蒂丽叶将被绞死而给人的表象却是自杀。李尔入场，他抱着死去的考蒂丽叶悲痛欲绝。

1 'Unbearable' theatre

This scene often has a tremendous visual impact on an audience. They have known about the death sentence since line 29, but have had to wait until line 220 for Edmond to admit to it and try to rescind it. Then, before anyone on stage knows or is able to comment, the audience sees an old, frail man struggling to carry the body of his youngest child and to bear the grief of her loss. His words are not so much words as cries of inarticulate despair: 'Howl, howl, howl, howl!'

Lear's despairing certainty of Cordelia's death gives way to desperate and ill-founded hope, which can be as disturbing as his grief. Albany, Kent and Edgar respond in their three half lines at 237–8. All of them are struggling to articulate a sense of pity that they find beyond words. Their philosophies of endurance, stoicism and justice seem to have proved inadequate. Samuel Johnson, an eighteenth-century writer, said he felt this final scene in *King Lear* was 'unbearable' and the play at that time tended only to be produced in an adapted version with a happy ending.

- How do you feel an actor playing Lear should speak the four 'howls' in line 231 as he enters? Take turns to play the king and try out different ways of saying the words. Then try speaking the even more challenging five 'nevers' at line 282.

1	Be brief	赶快
2	writ	执行令
3	on	= against
4	office	（杀死李尔和考蒂丽叶的）任务
5	token of reprieve	赦免的金牌
6	commission	命令
7	fordid	杀死，毁灭
8	men of stones	石头人（铁石心肠）
9	promised end	世界末日，审判日
10	Fall and cease	让天塌下来，万物毁灭

▶ 'Howl, howl, howl, howl!' The entrance of Lear carrying the dead Cordelia is one of the most famous and heart-rending scenes in drama.

KENT   Alack, why thus?
EDMOND   Yet Edmond was beloved.
            The one the other poisoned for my sake,
            And after slew herself.   215
ALBANY   Even so. – Cover their faces.
EDMOND   I pant for life. Some good I mean to do,
            Despite of mine own nature. Quickly send –
            Be brief[1] in it – to th'castle; for my writ[2]
            Is on[3] the life of Lear and on Cordelia.   220
            Nay, send in time.
ALBANY   Run, run, O run!
EDGAR   To who, my lord? – Who has the office[4]? Send
            Thy token of reprieve[5].
EDMOND   Well thought on. Take my sword. The captain,
            Give it the captain.
EDGAR   Haste thee for thy life.   225

                        [*Exit an Officer*]

EDMOND   He hath commission[6] from thy wife and me
            To hang Cordelia in the prison and
            To lay the blame upon her own despair,
            That she fordid[7] herself.
ALBANY   The gods defend her. Bear him hence a while.   230

                        [*Edmond is borne off*]

Enter LEAR *with* CORDELIA *in his arms* [*and the* OFFICER *following*]

LEAR   Howl, howl, howl, howl! O, you are men of stones[8].
            Had I your tongues and eyes, I'd use them so,
            That heaven's vault should crack. She's gone for ever.
            I know when one is dead and when one lives.
            She's dead as earth.
                        [*He lays her down*]
                        Lend me a looking-glass;   235
            If that her breath will mist or stain the stone,
            Why then she lives.
KENT   Is this the promised end[9]?
EDGAR   Or image of that horror?
ALBANY   Fall and cease[10].

Lear desperately seeks for signs that Cordelia lives. He boasts that he killed her murderer. Filled with grief, he is unmoved by the reunion with Kent and by the deaths of his other daughters. Edmond is reported dead.

剧情简介：李尔绝望地想找到一丝考蒂丽叶活着的迹象。他吹嘘说他杀死了谋害她的人。由于满怀悲痛，李尔对于与肯特重逢和其他两个女儿的死无动于衷。有人报告说爱德门死了。

◀ Choose one of Lear's lines as a caption for this picture.

1 **redeem** 赎回
2 **biting falchion** 锋利的弯刃刀
3 **crosses spoil me** 磨难让我不中用了
4 **tell you straight** 很快认出您
5 **If … behold** 若是命运女神夸口说有两个人他爱到极致又恨到极致，我们看到的是其中一个（即李尔）
6 **dull sight** 令人忧伤的场景；老眼昏花
7 **I'll see that straight** 我马上看看（他的注意力还在考蒂丽叶身上）
8 **That … steps** 我从您开始经历变故和落难就跟随着您悲伤的脚步
9 **Nor no man else** 除了我也没别人了
10 **present us to him** 向他表明我们的身份
11 **bootless** 无用，枉然

1 Mourning Cordelia (whole class)

This activity may help you to share the intensity of Lear's words at the death of Cordelia. It could be staged in a hall or drama studio, but it can be just as effective in a classroom. Everyone in the class can be involved.

- Identify phrases or sentences in lines 230–69 that express grief or sympathy for Cordelia or Lear. Write them on slips of paper.
- Two people play Cordelia and Lear. Distribute the slips to everyone except these two. Each person memorises their phrase or sentence of mourning language.
- Make a tableau of Lear and the dead Cordelia surrounded by a circle of sympathetic onlookers, standing or kneeling. Then, in turn, speak the memorised words as a soundtrack to the picture. Use atmospheric lighting and, at low volume, play appropriate music.
- Try introducing movement. For example, each speaker in turn could step inside the circle, move close to Lear and Cordelia and add a gesture to emphasise their words, before returning to the circle.

2 'Where is your servant Caius?' (in pairs)

Lear recognises Kent, but does not identify him with Caius.

a Take parts as Lear and Kent. Read from 'Who are you?' in line 252 to line 266. Try to show Kent's desperation and Lear's detachment.

b Talk about reasons why Kent is so keen for the king to know who Caius was and the likely audience response to his situation.

King Lear Act 5 Scene 3
李尔王

LEAR	This feather stirs, she lives: if it be so,
	It is a chance which does redeem¹ all sorrows	240
	That ever I have felt.
KENT	O my good master!
LEAR	Prithee, away.
EDGAR	'Tis noble Kent, your friend.
LEAR	A plague upon you murderers, traitors all.
	I might have saved her; now she's gone for ever.
	Cordelia, Cordelia, stay a little. Ha?	245
	What is't thou sayst? – Her voice was ever soft,
	Gentle, and low, an excellent thing in woman. –
	I killed the slave that was a-hanging thee.
OFFICER	'Tis true, my lords, he did.
LEAR	Did I not, fellow?
	I have seen the day with my good biting falchion²	250
	I would have made them skip. I am old now,
	And these same crosses spoil me³. [*To Kent*] Who are you?
	Mine eyes are not o'th'best, I'll tell you straight⁴.
KENT	If fortune brag of two she loved and hated,
	One of them we behold⁵.	255
LEAR	This' a dull sight⁶. Are you not Kent?
KENT	The same,
	Your servant Kent. Where is your servant Caius?
LEAR	He's a good fellow, I can tell you that.
	He'll strike, and quickly too. He's dead and rotten.
KENT	No, my good lord, I am the very man –	260
LEAR	I'll see that straight⁷.
KENT	That from your first of difference and decay
	Have followed your sad steps⁸.
LEAR	You're welcome hither.
KENT	Nor no man else⁹. All's cheerless, dark, and deadly.
	Your eldest daughters have fordone themselves	265
	And desperately are dead.
LEAR	Ay, so I think.
ALBANY	He knows not what he says, and vain is it
	That we present us to him¹⁰.

Enter a MESSENGER

| EDGAR | Very bootless¹¹. |
| MESSENGER | Edmond is dead, my lord. |

197

Albany returns authority to Lear. Lear again grieves for Cordelia, then dies. Albany asks Edgar and Kent to share power. Kent hints that he has not long to live. Edgar urges plain speaking, not dishonest formality.

剧情简介：阿尔博尼把权力还给了李尔。李尔再次为考蒂丽叶的死悲痛欲绝，然后死去。阿尔博尼请爱德格和肯特共享权力。肯特暗示说他将不久于人世。爱德格要求人们说真话，不要拘泥于虚伪礼节。

Themes 主题分析

Albany tries to restore order (in groups of five or six)

Faced with these appalling events, Albany attempts to ensure that villains and victims are appropriately treated. An important theme in the play has been the disturbance of the natural order brought about by Lear's division of his kingdom, and the parallel disruption he creates within his own family. The chaos has caused these tragic events, and Albany's formal attempt to set things right seems almost irrelevant. In most productions his lines are merely a background to the central tableau of Lear cradling his dead daughter.

- Stage lines 269–78, taking a named part each. The person playing Albany speaks the lines. Decide on how Albany should behave and in particular why he says 'O see, see!' (line 278). Decide on the appropriate speed for his words and how Edgar and Kent might respond.

1 Final words

In the Quarto version of the play, lines 297–300 are given to Albany.

- Decide who you think should have the last word: Edgar, Albany, or one of the other survivors? Give reasons for your choice.

Stagecraft 导演技巧

'Exeunt with a dead march'

The way the final moments of a play are staged can have a powerful effect on the audience as the image lingers on in people's minds after the play is finished. Remember that Shakespeare's theatre needed the '*dead march*' to clear the stage of bodies. Modern productions often dim the lights or drop the curtain on a still tableau, allowing the actors to clear the stage unseen before returning for their bows.

- In your Director's Journal, note how you would conclude the play, what final image the audience would see in your production and what sort of music – if any – you would want at this moment.

1 our （本段话中阿尔博尼多处使用御用复数）
2 What ... applied 只要能给落难的国王（great decay）带来安慰的事，都尽全力去做
3 With boot, and such addition 加官晋爵（boot和addition同义）
4 wages 奖励
5 The cup of their deservings 饮下罪有应得的苦水
6 O see, see! 哦，看，看！（让大家将注意力再次放到李尔身上）
7 rack （拉伸犯人四肢的）刑架
8 usurped 偷盗
9 Bear them 抬他们的尸首
10 the gored state sustain 支撑破碎的国土
11 dead march 伴随葬礼的缓慢严肃的音乐

King Lear Act 5 Scene 3
李尔王

ALBANY   That's but a trifle here.
You lords and noble friends, know our[1] intent.   270
What comfort to this great decay may come
Shall be applied[2]. For us, we will resign
During the life of this old majesty
To him our absolute power; [*To Edgar and Kent*] you, to your rights,
With boot, and such addition[3] as your honours   275
Have more than merited. All friends shall taste
The wages[4] of their virtue, and all foes
The cup of their deservings[5]. O see, see![6]

LEAR   And my poor fool is hanged. No, no, no life?
Why should a dog, a horse, a rat have life,   280
And thou no breath at all? Thou'lt come no more,
Never, never, never, never, never.
Pray you, undo this button. Thank you, sir.
Do you see this? Look on her! Look, her lips.
Look there, look there.   *He dies*

EDGAR   He faints. My lord, my lord!   285

KENT   Break, heart, I prithee break.

EDGAR   Look up, my lord.

KENT   Vex not his ghost. O, let him pass. He hates him
That would upon the rack[7] of this tough world
Stretch him out longer.

EDGAR   He is gone indeed.

KENT   The wonder is he hath endured so long.   290
He but usurped[8] his life.

ALBANY   Bear them[9] from hence. Our present business
Is general woe. Friends of my soul, you twain
Rule in this realm and the gored state sustain[10].

KENT   I have a journey, sir, shortly to go: 295
My master calls me; I must not say no.

EDGAR   The weight of this sad time we must obey,
Speak what we feel, not what we ought to say.
The oldest hath borne most; we that are young
Shall never see so much, nor live so long.   300

                                Exeunt with a dead march[11]

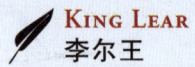
KING LEAR
李尔王

Looking back at the play 本剧回顾
Activities for groups or individuals

1 Recurring themes

Many of the principal themes of the play are touched on in its final moments. There are references to appearance and reality, vision and blindness, the natural order, justice and injustice, and compassion and reconciliation in the final scene.

- Select one of these themes and write about both its contribution to the final scene and to other parts of the play where it is referenced.
- Do you feel the play has conveyed a 'message' about your chosen theme?

2 The wheel of Fortune

- Draw, or mark out with ribbon/string, a circle to represent the wheel of Fortune, indicating in some way the top and bottom. Each of you takes the role of one of the principal characters in the play.
- Decide where each character is on the wheel at various points in the play: for example, just before and just after the love test in Act 1 Scene 1; during the terrible storm; just before the battle.
- Remember Edgar's words 'Who is't can say "I am at the worst"?' from Act 4 Scene 1, and decide where in the play you think each character is at the lowest point in their personal journey.

3 Timescale

Draw a timeline plotting the sequence of events from the division of the kingdom to the aftermath of the battle at Dover. Decide how much time could have passed between the start and end of the play and how much time has passed between the various acts. You could extend this to create 'back-stories' for the main characters that help to explain their behaviour in the play itself.

4 Enjoying tragedy?

In spite of all its cruelty and bleakness, *King Lear* is a popular play. It has been translated into many languages and is frequently performed. However, for about two hundred years between the late seventeenth century and the mid nineteenth century, the play was performed mainly in an adapted version that allowed Cordelia to survive and marry Edgar (this version also omitted the Fool). In small groups, discuss the following questions:

- How might the impact of the play have been altered by these changes?
- What do audiences gain from seeing the play in its original form? Do you think it is possible to enjoy *King Lear*?
- A practical problem that directors face when staging the play in a modern theatre is where to place the interval. Directors usually choose just before or just after Act 3 Scene 7 – the scene in which Gloucester is blinded. What do you think are the advantages and disadvantages of each choice?

5 The most interesting question

What is the question you would most like to ask of each of the following: Lear, Cordelia, Edmond, Edgar, the Fool?

- Write a separate question for each. Pool all your questions in the class. Decide which are the most interesting, and use them to hot-seat members of the class in role as the characters.
- Decide among yourselves which two or three characters have changed most or learned most during the play, then represent them with two class members seated back to back. One is the character early in the play and the other is the same character later in the play. Each should respond differently to hot-seat questions from the rest of the class.

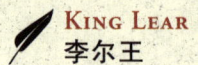

King Lear 李尔王

Perspectives and themes 视角与主题

What is the play about?

King Lear tells its audiences a story about families, about fathers and their children. In the main plot, King Lear makes the decision to give away his lands to his daughters; tragically, he ends up favouring Gonerill and Regan over the trustworthy Cordelia. In the sub-plot, Gloucester trusts the wrong son — he believes dishonest Edmond over loyal Edgar. These two interlocking narratives lie at the heart of the play, but *King Lear* is about more than just family relationships. Both Lear and Gloucester are powerful men, so the repercussions of their behaviour are widespread.

King Lear is also a play about a country being torn apart by terrible political decisions. It ends in an invasion, a battle and a bleak, dystopian (反乌托邦) conclusion that seems to offer no hope of redemption.

Despite its darkness and its tragedy, productions of *King Lear* are still very popular. Directors come back to it time and again because each production offers something new in and for each different age. Its themes and perspectives touch on what it means to be human, what it means to be a parent, a daughter, a son; what it means to love, to lose, to live and to die. Every time *King Lear* is performed it offers up new possibilities and reveals different shapes, patterns and meanings. For example, you can think about *King Lear* as:

- a tragedy in which an otherwise great man falls from power, and loses status and respect because of a tragic flaw in his character (you could argue that Lear's flaw is rashness)
- a moral tale about ageing and about the relationship between the old and the young in society
- a play of social realism about parents and their children, and about the terrible consequences of those relationships souring and breaking down
- a political play about decision-making, power and the relationship between the public and the private.

These and other perspectives might help us to construct various 'readings' of the play. Additionally, many people have interpreted *King Lear* according to a number of different critical perspectives. These include:

Feminist perspectives – by looking at the world from a woman's point of view, or from the perspective of the female characters in the play, we can offer different and challenging readings. For example, historically Cordelia and her sisters have been polarised and read as opposing female stereotypes: the passive archetypal 'good wife' (Cordelia) and the 'manipulative siren' (Gonerill and Regan). A feminist reading might challenge both of these positions, looking at the status of women within society and examining how gender has constructed both the power relations in the play and the resulting (male) readings of it. It might also focus on the absence of Lear's and Gloucester's wives or, indeed, any obvious mothers.

Cultural materialist perspectives – this is a perspective on the play that focuses on the ways in which politics, wealth and power influence relationships and behaviour. It can be used as a lens through which to regard the play as a critical response to the social and political norms of Shakespeare's own time or the time of any particular performance.

New historicist perspectives – these focus on the particular conditions of the time in which the play was written. Although the story is set at some undefined early period in British history, this approach can still be used as a framework to critique the attitudes towards women, old age, madness (and other subjects) that were common in Shakespeare's time.

Psychoanalytical perspectives – this standpoint looks at the unconscious desires of the various characters, often with a particular focus on the impact of repressed sexuality. The revelation of Edmond's and Gonerill's and Regan's mutual desires, for example, might be used as a starting point to explain their actions earlier on in the play.

Perspectives and Themes

Performance perspectives – this views the play through the history of its performance both on stage and, more recently, on film. The history of the performance of *King Lear* also reveals the prevailing social and political conditions at the time of each of those performances. For instance, *King Lear* was performed for a number of years during the seventeenth, eighteenth and nineteenth centuries with a rewritten ending, in which peace was restored and Edgar married Cordelia (see pp. 212–13 for more on this).

- In pairs, talk about which of the perspectives listed above you think would be most helpful in exploring *King Lear* further. Taking each perspective in turn, discuss its strengths and then possible weaknesses as an approach to reading the play. Then, either individually or in your pairs, write a dialogue between two people who favour taking different perspectives on the play. Try to show how their conversation develops and what arguments they make, both for using their particular perspective and against using the perspective being suggested by the other person.

Themes

Another way of answering the question 'What is *King Lear* about?' is to identify the themes of the play. Themes are key ideas or concepts that recur throughout a text. You might find it useful to think of a theme as a thread: on its own it is not necessarily particularly significant, but when woven together with the other themes and ideas and characters in the play, it helps to give colour, depth and strength to the whole story. In your writing, you should aim to explore the way these themes cross over and illuminate each other, rather than simply listing each of the themes. Some of the key themes of *King Lear* are discussed below.

Family relationships

At the beginning of the play, Lear and Gloucester both appear to believe that they head successful and happy families. However, their illusions do not last long. By the end of the first scene, Lear has torn his family apart. In the opening lines of the second scene, Edmond reveals the plot against his brother that will destroy Gloucester's family.

In this very political play, family problems have consequences beyond the immediate. Gloucester, troubled by the discovery of his son Edgar's supposed treachery, describes the conflict and friction that have arisen in Lear's kingdom:

> Love cools, friendship falls off, brothers divide. In cities, mutinies; in countries, discord; in palaces, treason; and the bond cracked 'twixt son and father.

In *King Lear*, a family problem is a sign of much wider national and cosmic disorder.

Fathers and their children

The riches of a kingdom and an earldom await the heirs of Lear and Gloucester. The issue of inheritance generates great resentment in some children on reaching adulthood. They must await the death of a parent before being able to acquire the family wealth. The letter that Edmond pretends has been written by Edgar makes this resentment clear:

> This policy and reverence of age makes the world bitter to the best of our times, keeps our fortunes from us till our oldness cannot relish them.

Gonerill and Regan also detest such 'aged tyranny', and want to take over the power, wealth and status of their father. Parents sometimes try to control children by manipulating their expectations of inheritance, and this is true when Lear makes the dangerous mistake of dividing his kingdom between his two ambitious daughters. Gonerill and Regan receive their inheritance and have nothing more to gain by tolerating their father's impulsive and erratic behaviour. Gloucester, however, does not choose to abdicate his role, so his ruthless son Edmond must scheme and plot to replace Edgar as heir, and then seek an opportunity to depose his father.

King Lear
李尔王

In the 'love test' in Act 1 Scene 1, Lear expects Cordelia to outdo her sisters in flattery but she says only that she loves him 'According to my bond', as a daughter ought to love a father. Lear finds this universal statement of family obligation 'untender'. He wants an elaborate and fawning expression of love. Failing to get it, he violently rejects the only one of his children who has real affection for him.

A major function of the family is to provide security for its members as they pass through childhood, sickness and old age. Indeed, it is sometimes claimed that one reason why people have children is in order to provide care for themselves in old age. Lear, over eighty years old ('Fourscore and upward, not an hour more nor less'), certainly expects to be cared for by his daughters after he has given up power. He had hoped to live with Cordelia: 'I loved her most, and thought to set my rest / On her kind nursery.' Lear later shows a calculating attitude towards love when he rates Regan's and Gonerill's affection according to the number of his servants they are willing to support. Whoever accepts the larger number must love him the most: 'Thy fifty yet doth double five and twenty, / And thou art twice her love.'

Daughters

Women often had powerful roles within their families, but the power they had outside the family was limited by the rules of inheritance, ingrained traditions, and the prejudiced attitudes of the state, the law and the Church. Nonetheless, powerful women were not unknown. King James's mother was Mary Stuart, Queen of Scots. His immediate predecessor on the English throne was Queen Elizabeth I.

Women in positions of authority caused much consternation in the sixteenth century. In 1558, the year of Elizabeth's accession, John Knox, a Scottish Protestant reformer, issued a pamphlet attacking female rulers. Entitled *First Blast of the Trumpet against the Monstrous Regiment of Women*, it argued that giving women, who are 'weak, frail, impatient, feeble and foolish creatures', any sort of authority was the 'subversion of good order, of all equity and justice'.

By the time *King Lear* was written, attitudes to women in power had been modified by Elizabeth I's success as monarch, but women still had relatively low status in society. In the play, although Lear's daughters are his heirs,

Perspectives and Themes

the power and authority of the crown is transferred to their husbands. Importantly, the daughters are not made queens regnant, monarchs in their own right. Regan and Gonerill are strong and influential figures, but they have to wield that influence through their husbands. Consequently, Gonerill has to goad Albany into action when he has doubts about how to react to the political crisis. She knows it would be difficult, if not impossible, for her to act alone.

Gonerill and Regan both want Edmond, not just as a lover but also as a consort. Their reasons may be entirely personal, or may be connected to their appraisal of his skills as a commander and ruler. Although all three princesses play authoritative roles in the preparations for battle, it is Albany and Edmond who lead the British army. Cordelia acts as commander-in-chief of the invading French army, but has been invested with that authority by her husband (Act 4 Scene 3, lines 25–6).

Mothers

Neither Lear's family nor Gloucester's family has a mother. Lear's wife, the mother of his daughters and the queen of Britain, is dead before the play begins. In the Gloucester family, too, both the mothers are absent from the play. Edmond's mother is mentioned only when he, or his father, refers lewdly to his conception, and there are no references to Edgar's.

Sons and brothers

The sub-plot of Gloucester and his two sons very obviously increases the dramatic effect of the main plot of Lear and his daughters. The good and evil qualities of the king's daughters are reflected in Edgar's struggles to protect his father, and Edmond's schemes to harm him. The play's exploration of family life offers every new production a challenge in how to portray the brothers.

Brothers can be remarkably similar or very different in appearance and character. There are obvious and stark contrasts between the Gloucester half-brothers. For example, Edgar plays a number of roles: a gullible dupe who believes his brother's false story; a madman, as Poor Tom; a choric commentator on suffering ('Ripeness is all'); a defender of right as he slays both Edmond and Oswald. In contrast, Edmond seems to be unremittingly devious, seeking whatever will serve his own interests. Only in the closing minutes of the play, near to death, is he prompted to do good, and unsuccessfully tries to prevent the deaths of Lear and Cordelia.

- ◆ Make a note of all of the characters whose role as a father, daughter or son is important in the play. For each character, find at least two quotations that reveal something of their attitudes to their family or their filial relationships. Write a paragraph on each character, using the quotations you have picked out, to show how each is presented in terms of family relationships in *King Lear*.

- ◆ In small groups, take it in turns to read out your paragraphs on each of the characters and discuss the different aspects you have chosen to draw attention to. Think about how each of the characters represents ideas about family.

Justice

At the end of *King Lear*, Albany confronts the bloody reality of the death and suffering caused by Lear's division of his kingdom and declares that both 'friends' and 'foes' will get what they deserve (Act 5 Scene 3, lines 276–8). But do they? It is true that Edmond has been killed by the brother he wronged, and the wicked Gonerill and Regan are dead. But the innocent Cordelia has died cruelly, hanged in prison, and Gloucester's blinding and mental suffering are hardly fit punishment for the 'crime' of fathering the bastard Edmond or being gullible. Does Lear, for all his flaws of character or judgement, deserve the agonies of madness he has undergone ('I am bound / Upon a wheel of fire'), or the twisted irony of being reconciled with Cordelia only to have her ruthlessly snatched away from him?

King Lear
李尔王

A belief in the power of divine justice runs through the play and is articulated through several characters. Lear strengthens his early displays of authority and paternal cursing by appealing to pagan deities. He swears by 'the sacred radiance of the sun', 'The mysteries of Hecate and the night', 'Apollo' and 'Jupiter'. Regan appeals to the 'blessed gods' when Lear turns his anger on her. Lear himself begs for help from the 'heavens': 'If you do love old men … send down and take my part', and acknowledges the authority of 'high-judging Jove'. Attitudes towards the gods in the play, however, are certainly not fixed. Sometimes characters see them as 'kind' and 'mighty', at other times arbitrary, indifferent and cruel. Albany finds them just: 'you are above / You justicers'. Gloucester thinks them spitefully unjust: 'As flies to wanton boys are we to th'gods; / They kill us for their sport'. But he then revises his opinion: 'You ever gentle gods'. To Cordelia the gods are benevolent: 'O you kind gods'. With his father dead and his brother dying, Edgar acknowledges a divine justice that watches over and judges all human actions: 'The gods are just, and of our pleasant vices / Make instruments to plague us.'

The play is also interested in the vagaries of human law and justice. Indeed, one way of thinking about the role of justice in the play is to consider the five different types of 'trial' that occur, in which one person judges another:

- Lear's 'love trial' of his three daughters (Act 1 Scene 1). Lear, as judge and jury, metes out the 'justice' he thinks is appropriate.
- Cornwall's 'trial' of Kent, whose bluntness earns him instant punishment in the stocks (Act 2 Scene 2).
- Cornwall and Regan's 'trial' of Gloucester (Act 3 Scene 7), at which the old man is not allowed any representation or defence.
- Lear's 'mock trial' of Gonerill and Regan (only in the Quarto edition, see p. 245) showing how his 'madness' craves justice against his ungrateful daughters.
- The trial by battle (Act 5 Scene 3). Edgar challenges Edmond to trial by combat on the charge of treason.

- The play clearly shows that when humans exercise justice, there is no guarantee that it will be fair, proper or right. Possession of power is more important than fairness. Gonerill sees herself as the queen – unchallengeable, controlling the law and yet beyond it: 'the laws are mine, not thine. / Who can arraign me for't?' In his madness, Lear damns the hypocrisy of the parish officer who lusts after the prostitute even as he is punishing her.

However, there are incidents in the play that suggest that a kind of natural justice is at work. A loyal servant protests about Gloucester's horrific treatment and mortally wounds Cornwall. Another helps his blinded master make his way to Dover. Oswald is killed by Edgar when he attempts to murder the old man.

◆ **Working in pairs, pick out between ten and twenty of your favourite quotations from the play that refer to justice or the law. Then select two of the following 'types' of justice: moral justice, legal justice, natural justice or religious justice. Take one idea each and work for a few minutes on your own. Using the quotations you sourced as evidence, write a paragraph arguing that the play shows that your type of justice prevails. Read your paragraphs to each other and continue to debate which holds sway.**

Madness

In Shakespeare's time, attitudes and responses to madness were harsh and unsympathetic. The 'mad' were thought to be possessed by devils and therefore had to be confined and whipped to expel the demonic spirits. Held in secure hospitals like Bethlem in London (from where we get the word 'bedlam'), the insane provided a grotesque form of entertainment for curious, well-to-do onlookers. Much of Edgar's language, as Poor Tom, is taken from a 1603 pamphlet describing how devils were 'cast out of lunatics' (see p. 212).

Shakespeare seems to have been particularly interested in madness as an agent of beneficial change. In his plays, suffering can transform characters' views of themselves and others. In the comedies, the 'madness' of love becomes an altered state of consciousness that produces sharper insight. The tragedies offer a more sombre perspective on the effects of madness, but its outcome is also clearer perception. For example, Hamlet (whether his madness be real or feigned) finds calm and understanding after his journey of mental suffering.

Madness in this play is most evident in the portrayal of Lear himself: his mind tormented and unsettled by his experience. But *King Lear* is not simply a psychological depiction of the insanity of an individual. Human madness is reflected in disturbance at two other levels – the natural and the social. The onset of the terrible storm in Act 3 suggests that tempests in nature mirror those in an individual's mind. Lear's abdication of power and the division of his kingdom would have been seen as acts of political madness by Shakespeare's contemporaries. By tearing up his country, Lear sets off a chain of social frenzy that results in cruelty, blindness, madness and death.

King Lear presents different types of mental instability. Lear's madness is that of a selfish, autocratic old man whose will is thwarted. His moral blindness, misjudgements and lack of understanding of himself and others inevitably lead to breakdown: 'O fool, I shall go mad.' As Poor Tom, Edgar puts on the madness of a Bedlam beggar. The Fool's 'madness' is professional, eccentric, witty, exposing weakness and folly: 'May not an ass know when the cart draws the horse?'

Lear's journey through madness to self-knowledge

Act 1 – Lear's tendency to mental instability is established; indeed, Regan tells us that 'he hath ever but slenderly known himself'. He subjects his daughters to a bizarre love trial, banishes his loyal adviser Kent and disowns Cordelia. He reacts with violent curses to Gonerill's challenge to his wilful behaviour.

Act 2 – Lear's sanity is undermined by his obsession with 'filial ingratitude', the 'unnatural' behaviour of Gonerill and Regan. Infuriated by Kent's punishment in the stocks, Regan's refusal to speak to him and Gonerill's alliance with her sister, Lear rants impotently about revenge. Fearing the onset of madness, he storms out of Gloucester's castle.

Act 3 – Lear's moods swing violently from raging in the storm to quieter sympathy for those less fortunate than himself: 'Poor naked wretches'. Lear's 'mad' companions, the Fool and Poor Tom, deepen the sense of his decline into insanity. He rips off his clothes ('Off, off you lendings!'), and hallucinates about devilish spirits.

Act 4 – a stage direction in Scene 5 indicates '*Enter* LEAR, [*mad*]'. Talking to the blinded Gloucester, Lear's language combines sexual loathing with hallucinations about hell and damnation: 'Let copulation thrive … there is the sulphurous pit, burning, scalding, stench, consumption'. Lear's disordered thoughts range over mortality, justice and authority, and erupt in savage emotion: 'And when I have stol'n upon these son-in-laws / Then kill, kill, kill, kill, kill, kill!' At last, reunited with Cordelia, Lear's mental torment ceases.

Act 5 – the cruel murder of Cordelia threatens Lear's wits once more: 'Howl, howl, howl, howl!' He dies, his final words suggesting that he is deluding himself with the thought that she lives.

Nature

The words 'nature', 'natural' and 'unnatural' occur more than forty times in the play. Almost every character appeals in some way to 'nature': to justify their actions or to help them, or to explain why things are as they are. Lear begins the 'love test' by inviting his daughters to compete for the largest share of his kingdom by combining their natural affection for their father with exaggerated statements of their love. But within minutes, he rejects Cordelia as 'a wretch whom nature is ashamed / Almost t'acknowledge hers'. Later, he will call Gonerill and Regan 'unnatural hags'.

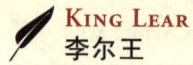

King Lear
李尔王

Why is 'nature' so important in the play? One major reason is that it is a powerful means of controlling people. Like all tyrants, Lear knows that if he can make everyone believe that it is 'natural' for him to rule and for his every wish to be obeyed, then he has power over them. They will think that what is 'natural' is right, and that it must not be challenged. If daughters think that it is natural to obey all their father's commands, or if people believe that society is naturally hierarchical, with a king at the top, then they are unlikely to challenge that 'natural' state of affairs.

For much of the play, Lear believes that everything he does is natural. Any person who frustrates his desires is unnatural, because it is natural that everyone should obey him without question. His view of his family is the same as his view of England: rigidly hierarchical with himself as father-king at the top, entitled to immediate and unstinting obedience. Nature herself is a goddess to whom he can appeal for revenge on his unnatural daughter Gonerill ('Hear, Nature, hear').

One way of understanding the play is to see it as the slow and agonising transformation of Lear's view of the natural order of things. Through his suffering, Lear's original view of nature is painfully stripped away.

Two views of nature

A traditional way of understanding the play has been to see it as depicting two different views of nature, malign or benign (bad or good). Characters are grouped according to their view of nature. That view defines their opinion of society, of what men and women are like, and of how they should behave. Although this two-fold view of nature is a simple stereotype, it can be a valuable step in developing your thinking about the significance of 'nature' in the play.

Nature as malign

The view of nature as malevolent links the ruthless individualism of Edmond, Gonerill and Regan. Nature is seen as a malign force that acts as a powerful motivator. It drives and feeds ruthless and selfish impulses. Humans behave like predatory animals, preying on the innocent and vulnerable. They lack conscience and moral sensitivity, and are concerned only with their own advancement and profit. Like Lear, Edmond thinks of nature as a deity, but sees her favouring the merciless, self-motivated individual. This 'natural' (illegitimate) son of Gloucester is coldly calculating and cunning. He mocks Gloucester's superstitions, and is scornful of any notion that his nature was determined by the stars. Gonerill and Regan flatter Lear shamelessly to gain a share of their father's wealth, but then renounce all 'natural' family bonds and duties. Hard-heartedly, they cast Lear out into the storm.

Nature as benign

Gloucester, Kent, Edgar and Cordelia are shaped by a benign vision of nature as a kind-hearted and benevolent force that strives for order, stability and harmony. Gloucester sees the world as orderly and hierarchical, valuing trust, loyalty and family bonds. His response to Edgar's apparent villainy is to proclaim him an 'unnatural, detested, brutish villain'. Kent's loyalty to his master, Lear, expresses itself in his unquestioning sympathy and concern for the king. Cordelia's nature is also truthful and honest. Her constancy and devotion to Lear act as healing forces. Edgar cloaks his true nature in the disguise of a mad beggar, but redeems, heals and restores his father, to whom he remains faithful.

◆ **Read the advice on writing about Shakespeare in general and about *King Lear* in particular on pages 240–3. Choose one of the essay questions on themes on page 242 and write about *King Lear* in response.**

The contexts of *King Lear* 《李尔王》的创作背景

When we watch *King Lear* on stage or read it in class, our experiences are always different; they are shaped by the context in which we watch or read the play. It is also important to realise that *King Lear* was written at a particular point in history, and in a particular place. These contexts inform how the play developed into the version you are studying today. No one can be certain why, in about 1605, Shakespeare chose to write a play with a storyline similar to 'Cinderella': a fairy-tale about a foolish father, a pair of ugly sisters and one loving but mistreated daughter. However, exploring various contexts for the play can help us to understand more and can reveal different ways of thinking about the play.

When considering contexts, it might help to think about two different types:

Contexts of production – these are the contexts of the historical moment of the writing of the play, in about 1605. These might include historical, social and economic contexts and various influences on the writer himself.

Contexts of reception – these are the various contexts that shape our experiences of watching or reading the play. They might include the decisions and attitudes of directors and actors, as well as the various assumptions, prejudices and norms of the time and place in which we are experiencing the play, either on the stage or on the page.

The key contexts of *King Lear* include:

- topical issues and contemporary power and politics
- historical sources for the play
- Shakespeare's reading
- some contexts of reception.

Topical issues and contemporary power and politics

Lurid real-life stories of greed and suffering among the moneyed classes were sensational and popular sources of gossip in the early seventeenth century. Sir William Allen, for example, a former lord mayor, in old age made the disastrous mistake of splitting his estate between his three daughters and arranging to live with them in turn. Once they had his money, the old man was treated with cruelty and disrespect. Unlike Lear's daughters, all three of Sir William's children mistreated him.

Sir Brian Annesley, however, did have one child who cared. She was Cordell, the youngest of his three daughters. In 1603, Sir Brian's eldest daughter tried to have him certified as infirm of mind and memory, and 'altogether unfit to govern himself or his estate'. Cordell challenged her sister in court, protesting that it was unjust to her elderly father 'at his last gasp to be registered a lunatic'.

Social and political issues

These very specific examples are emblematic of the wider social picture. For instance, inheritance in Elizabethan and Jacobean England was determined by male primogeniture (i.e. the first-born son inherits), and lack of sons was potentially dangerous for some families. At the start of the seventeenth century, as the childless Queen Elizabeth's life drew to a close, many feared a disputed succession and possible civil war.

The folly of deliberately dividing up a kingdom would have been obvious to Shakespeare's audience. They would have certainly understood Kent's outrage at Lear's carving up of Britain. English history had been traditionally seen as a steady movement towards the security, strength and cohesion of a single realm. The contrast between the recent peaceful succession of King James in 1603, which had united the crowns of England and Scotland, and Lear's unwise division of his kingdom, would have been all too clear to Shakespeare's audiences.

King Lear
李尔王

King Lear is firmly rooted in the political and social conditions of Shakespeare's times. The play reflects the political issues that were heatedly debated during this period: the divine right of kings, the unity of the kingdom, the changing social order that triggered a growth of conflicting factions and a threatening underclass. From this viewpoint, *King Lear* may be seen as a play about the struggle for power, property and inheritance in early seventeenth-century England.

The divine right of kings

The play opens with Lear portrayed as an absolute monarch who demands unquestioning obedience. In Shakespeare's time, monarchs believed that they ruled on God's behalf. When parliament attempted to go against her wishes, Queen Elizabeth I reminded its members that she was their anointed queen and God's representative on earth. Her successor, King James I (VI of Scotland), took this belief in the divine right of kings even further. He asserted that it was blasphemous and unlawful to question any action taken by a king. In 1610, he declared to parliament: 'The state of monarchy is the supremest thing upon the earth; for kings are not only God's lieutenants upon earth, and sit upon God's throne, but even by God himself they are called gods'.

However, such absolute rulers also acknowledged a God-given obligation. It was their sacred duty to keep their kingdom intact. Elizabeth emphasised that she had to answer to God for her government of the realm. She and James shared the conviction that it would be a sin against their divinely given authority to abdicate or to divide their country. This was an ideology embraced by most of their subjects. So the audience in 1605 probably shared Kent's horror at Lear's decision to throw off the responsibility of kingship and divide his kingdom. They probably also admired Kent's good sense in refusing to share power at the end of the play. To Shakespeare's contemporaries, therefore, *King Lear* was a play about how *not* to rule a country.

◆ In Act 1 Scene 1, Kent says to Lear: 'My life I never held but as a pawn / To wage against thine enemies, ne'er feared to lose it, / Thy safety being motive.' Working on your own, think about the way Kent is presented as a loyal and true subject to Lear, and a reliable and faithful upholder of the hierarchy. Making sure that you back up your arguments with carefully selected quotations from the play, write three or four paragraphs arguing that Kent is a model subject and a faultless servant of the king. Then write another paragraph arguing a different point of view about Kent.

Property and power

The England over which Elizabeth and James ruled was a society in transition. The feudal world of medieval times, with its strong allegiances and rigid hierarchy, had virtually collapsed. A newly prosperous gentry and commercial class challenged the power of the king and of an aristocracy divided among itself. Political factions abounded, strongly hinted at in the dangerous rivalry existing between Albany and Cornwall, and gossiped about by Kent and Gloucester as the play opens.

Newly acquired property gave power to a new kind of individual. Powerful men emerged, who felt no obligation to the old feudal loyalties. They were men on the make, filled with the spirit of radical individualism, driven by self-interest. Edmond, Gloucester's unscrupulous illegitimate son, refuses to 'Stand in the plague of custom'. In rejecting tradition he seeks to thrive by his own cunning, mocking the superstitious beliefs of his father, an upholder of the old feudal loyalty to the king. There is no place for an outdated system of chivalry in Edmond's moral scheme.

Shakespeare also gives expression to a dispossessed underclass who did not share in the affluence of the times. The enclosure of common fields (a topic you may want to research further) provoked protest and revolt. What the wealthy classes saw as necessary to more efficient farming, the poor saw as land-grabbing.

The contexts of King Lear

In the twenty years before the play was written, there were several food riots. Shortly after its first performance, serious riots against enclosures took place in the Midlands,

including Warwickshire, Shakespeare's home county. Bedlam beggars (the disguise adopted by Edgar as 'Poor Tom') were familiar and deeply worrying figures who roamed 'from low farms, / Poor pelting villages, sheep-cotes, and mills', pleading for charity.

In *King Lear*, Shakespeare gives expression to crucial political and social issues of his times. Some of these issues remain relevant today. In the twenty-first century the future of the British monarchy and of the union of the countries of the United Kingdom have again become subjects of political debate.

Historical sources for the play

Geoffrey of Monmouth wrote about King Lear and his three daughters in his *History of England*, over four hundred years before Shakespeare was born. The story was clearly a mixture of myth and legend, but many people in the seventeenth century regarded it as historical fact. In 1577, Raphael Holinshed retold the legend in his *Chronicles of England, Scotlande and Irelande*. Below is a summary of Holinshed's account of the King Lear story.

Leir, the ageing king of Britain, has three daughters, Gonorilla, Regan and Cordeilla, of whom his favourite is the youngest, Cordeilla. In order to help him to decide on the succession, he asks which of his daughters loves him best. Gonorilla and Regan speak extravagantly of the love they bear their father, but Cordeilla says that she loves him only according to his worth. Leir is furious and arranges for the two older daughters to marry the Dukes of Cornwall and Albany, between whom the kingdom will be divided after his death. The dukes are immediately given half of this inheritance. Cordeilla is to receive nothing, but the Prince of Gallia, who rules a part of France, chooses to marry her despite the fact that she has no dowry.

Cornwall and Albany resent having to wait for power. They rise against Leir, forcing him to give up all his authority. Leir's oldest daughters, with whom he has no choice but to live alternately, treat him unkindly and reduce the number of his servants.

Leir flees the kingdom, and travels to Gallia. Before he appears at court, Cordeilla gives her father money so he can arrive with clothes and servants befitting a king. Cordeilla and her husband make him welcome.

The Prince of Gallia raises an army to restore Leir to his throne. Cordeilla accompanies her father when he returns to his kingdom, and is named as his heir. The army of the Dukes of Cornwall and Albany is defeated, and the two dukes die in battle. Leir regains his throne and reigns for two years before he dies. Cordeilla succeeds him, but her reign is cut short by a rebellion led by her sisters' sons. She is imprisoned, despairs and commits suicide. Her nephews then make war against each other, and England is only restored to peace after one of them is killed and the other is able to rule uncontested.

King Lear
李尔王

Some of the alterations and additions that Shakespeare made to Holinshed's story include: adding the characters of the Fool, Kent and Oswald; inventing Lear's madness and the storm; inserting the entire sub-plot of Gloucester and his sons; having Cordelia die before her father and the play finish with the deaths of Lear's entire family; ending with the rightful king restored.

Shakespeare's reading

Shakespeare may have read or seen *The True Chronicle History of King Leir*, a play first performed in the 1590s but not published until 1605. In this dramatised version of the story, no characters die and Leir is restored to his realm at the end. It contains stage directions of 'thunder and lightning', which may have been Shakespeare's inspiration for the storm in Act 3.

Shakespeare certainly read Samuel Harsnett's *A Declaration of Egregious Popish Impostures* (1603). Much of the strange language used by Edgar when pretending to be the mad Poor Tom, especially the lists of demons' names (see page 114), is taken from this anti-Catholic pamphlet. It claimed to expose the evils of false exorcism (driving out devils from mad people), and quoted speeches supposedly made by people who pretended to be possessed by demons. By giving such evil language to Edgar, a 'good' character, Shakespeare increases the dramatic intensity of the play.

Shakespeare's most significant addition to the old legend is the story of Gloucester and his sons. This sub-plot mirrors the main plot of Lear and his daughters and is based on an episode in *Arcadia* (1590), a prose romance story by Sir Philip Sidney. Although in *Arcadia*, the main character is a king rather than an earl and the illegitimate son is directly responsible for blinding his own father after seizing his throne, the virtuous son (as in *King Lear*) is betrayed by his brother, loses his father's favour, and is driven into exile. The virtuous son then returns to protect his father but, while he guides his blinded father, he refuses to help him commit suicide. The blind king eventually crowns his virtuous son and dies happy.

Shakespeare's Gloucester sub-plot has many similarities with the main plot of *King Lear*. Both are about powerful men and their relationships with their grown-up children. Both involve the father's unjust rejection of a faithful child who continues to love and protect the father. Both show the fathers mistreated by the children whom they favour.

◆ Research at least one of the texts mentioned so far in this section. Read as much as you can of the text and make notes about how it helps you to understand *King Lear*. Organise your notes and offer feedback to the rest of the class.

Some contexts of reception

The context in which we 'receive' the text – the circumstances that surround our reading or watching of the play – can have a powerful bearing on how we think about it.

One such context is found in the performance history of the play. In 1681, Nahum Tate famously rewrote *King Lear*. Many of the productions of the play between that date and the beginning of the nineteenth century were, in fact, productions of Tate's version rather than Shakespeare's (although much of the text was the same). Tate made some crucial changes. Firstly, he gave this 'tragedy' a happy ending, where Lear is reinstated to the throne; secondly, Cordelia survives to marry Edgar (see p. 232 for more on this).

Many theatre-goers and critics (including Samuel Johnson) approved of the revision, arguing that *King Lear* was too terrible for the stage. However, what this means is that audiences for well over a hundred years of the play's history had a very different 'context of reception' or experience of watching the play from either Shakespeare's contemporaries or, indeed, an audience today.

Another interesting context of reception belongs in the realm of the intertextual. Jane Smiley's 1991 novel *One Thousand Acres* is a modern-day rendering of the *King Lear* story. The narrative has many points of intersection, tracing the basic plot and introducing many characters who are very similar to Shakespeare's. Indeed, some of them are even named to make the connections: Larry as Lear, Ginny as Gonerill, Rose as Regan, and

The contexts of King Lear

Caroline as Cordelia, for instance. There is also a sub-plot similar to the Gloucester narrative. The significance of the reception context is this: that having read this novel it reshapes our own attitudes to the human behaviours and betrayals in *King Lear* – and our experience of watching the original will always be slightly recalibrated by the experience of having read the novel.

Yet another interesting context is the success and performance history of Edward Bond's *Lear* from 1971. Working with the same story, Bond made much of the violence of the narrative and argued that 'an unjust society must be violent', re-casting Shakespeare's play for a different political, economic and social age.

Of course, perhaps the most powerful contexts of reception are the circumstances in which audiences see the plays performed. At different points in the history of the play and with different directors, different productions and different actors, the experience of watching Lear on stage has been vastly different. The section on *King Lear* in performance on pages 232–9 takes you through the performance history of the play in much more detail, but it is worth considering that each new performance or reading of the text established a brand new context.

- Working in pairs, choose a key scene from the play. Work through the scene and mark it up wherever there are moments when you think that having more knowledge about the context of the play would support your reading and understanding. Often these annotations will be in the form of questions. This will lead you to some further research: you will need to find out more about various contexts for the scene you have chosen.

- When you have completed the marking up and the research, work on your own to write a short essay with the title: 'How does an understanding of contexts help to shape a reading of a key scene from *King Lear*?'

King Lear
李尔王

Characters 人物分析

King Lear

Lear is a tragic hero very much in the mould of classical Greek tragedy: a powerful but fatally flawed ruler who, through hubris (excessive pride or arrogance), destroys both himself and those around him.

At the start of the play, Lear has clearly been accustomed to exercising absolute power for many years, but the old man's weaknesses quickly become apparent. His artificial 'love test' ('Which of you shall we say doth love us most …?') shows that he craves flattery rather than truth, inexplicably valuing Gonerill's and Regan's false and fawning declaration of love above the integrity of his youngest daughter's sincere expression of filial devotion and duty. Lear's angry disinheriting of Cordelia, and banishment of the loyal Kent, affirm the picture of a despotic monarch, unused to opposition. By the end of the first scene, Regan's comment about her father's sanity ('he hath ever but slenderly known himself') becomes increasingly relevant.

Once Lear has given away his kingdom, the play proceeds to chart his painful journey from pride and arrogance to self-knowledge and redemption. He rages at challenges to his wilful behaviour, finds his tenuous hold on sanity threatened by his daughters' 'filial ingratitude' and begins to question his identity ('Who is it that can tell me who I am?'). In the storm scenes, his mood oscillates between violent raging against the elements and quieter reflection on the state of his kingdom and the plight of the 'Poor naked wretches'. But he has yet to become fully self-aware; he rails against the elements: 'I am a man / More sinned against than sinning.'

CHARACTERS

Ironically, the further Lear descends into madness, the sharper his awareness of the world's evils becomes. His scathing attack on the hypocrisy of judges and the vulnerability of the poor reveals just how much he has learned through his suffering. Briefly, he emerges from his tortured madness to find some kind of peace and reconciliation with Cordelia, his youngest daughter – even contemplating the joy of their imprisonment together. But their period of happiness is all too short. The moment of peaceful self-knowledge captured in the lines 'I am a very foolish, fond old man … I fear I am not in my perfect mind', is soon destroyed by the tragic unfolding of Cordelia's hanging and Lear's subsequent death with his daughter in his arms.

Lear may be a flawed man, infuriatingly self-obsessed, morally blind, unjust and unfair, who acquires self-knowledge and sympathy for others only through suffering, but he is also a great man. Kent's faithful service bears testament to the qualities of loyalty and devotion that Lear – the king and the man – could inspire in others.

- Working on your own, note how Lear's language changes throughout the play. (Refer back to p. 207 for information on his descent into madness across the five acts, for example.) Different registers of his language might include: authoritative, regal, pleading, desperate, insane and regretful. The manner in which Lear speaks is a good indication of how his character is developing and changing.

- Choosing with care, select between eight and twelve lines that Lear says throughout the play that illustrate the very different types of language he uses at various points. Then write three or four paragraphs analysing the ways in which Lear's language reveals various facets of his character development at different points in the play.

King Lear
李尔王

Gonerill

Lear's eldest daughter speaks first in the 'love test', instantly displaying how devious and deceitful she is. Her words – slick, oily and probably rehearsed ('Sir, I love you more than word can wield the matter') – are clearly designed to appeal to her father's vanity. She knows Lear's weaknesses all too well – his volatile moods, poor judgement and lack of self-knowledge – and carries her ability for cold, objective assessment into her later dealings with him. Systematically she schemes with Regan to erode the last vestiges of the old king's power, to reduce the number of his followers and to make him homeless.

Gonerill has nothing but contempt for her 'Milk-livered' husband, openly plotting adultery with Edmond ('To thee a woman's services are due') and poisoning her sister to keep him for herself. In fact, Albany is a strange partner for Gonerill. He is uncertain about her motivations and her perceptiveness, commenting: 'How far your eyes may pierce I cannot tell; / Striving to better, oft we mar what's well.' Later on, however, his feelings about his wife are made much clearer when he tells her that she is 'not worth the dust which the rude wind / Blows in your face.' She refers to the 'hateful life' from which she hopes to escape with Edmond, and when Edmond is mortally wounded, Gonerill stabs herself through the heart. Is this an act of courage or merely perverse self-destruction?

Like her sister, Gonerill reveals herself to be monstrous during the scene where Gloucester is tortured. It is, in fact, Gonerill who first suggests that they ought to 'Pluck out his eyes'. Although it might be the case that what she has the imagination to conceive, her sister (and her husband, Cornwall) has the malign determination to carry out.

Regan

Lear's second daughter initially seems less spiteful and more restrained than her elder sister but, as the play unfolds, her sadistic disposition comes to the fore. It is Regan who proposes that Kent's punishment in the stocks be extended ('Till night, my lord, and all night too'), who wants to deny Lear even one follower ('What need one?') and who orders the castle gates to be locked against him as the storm rages outside. Most savagely of all, she participates fully in torturing Gloucester, urging Cornwall to take out both of the old man's eyes lest 'One side will mock another'. Like Gonerill, she is ambitious and keen to seek sexual pleasure, competing unashamedly for Edmond's favours. She is also confident and assertive, wilful and defiant. When she is poisoned by her sister, she meets what many see as a symbolically just demise.

Characters

Cordelia

Lear's youngest daughter speaks in only four scenes, yet her presence permeates much of the play. Her early exchanges with Lear show unnerving honesty in the face of so much that is false and contrived, her asides to the audience accentuating the integrity of what she says and feels. Although often played as more obviously feminine and gentle than her sisters, she is certainly not weak and vulnerable. It takes courage to stand up to her father, her candid assessments of her sisters' behaviour reveal great insight and perception ('I know you what you are') and she abhors deception and pretence ('Who covers faults, at last with shame derides').

When Cordelia returns to England, productions often stress her regal qualities, or emphasise the fact that she is commander of an invading army. However, her language resonates with words of healing and therapy, leading some to interpret her in a particularly Christian way. In displaying unconditional love and forgiveness for her father, she is a symbol of hope and goodness. That her life should be so pointlessly extinguished is perhaps the cruellest act of all in this bleakest of plays.

◆ Consider the female characters in the play. For each one, choose the three words that you feel best summarise the way in which the play constructs and represents these characters. For each of the words you choose, select at least one quotation to support this particular mode of representation.

◆ Working in groups, discuss the presentation of women throughout the play. Focus on gender stereotypes and how they are conformed to or broken, feminist representations and challenges to perceived gender power relations. See also the information about feminist perspectives on pages 202 and 204.

King Lear
李尔王

Gloucester

Gloucester is Lear's loyal and long-serving counsellor. Like his master, he is an elderly father who misjudges his children and who achieves self-knowledge and reconciliation with his virtuous child only after suffering extremes of pain and distress.

His flippant joking about his illegitimate son Edmond, and the ease with which the latter exploits his gullible and superstitious nature, do not create a good first impression. But that should not belie Gloucester's essential seriousness and sobriety as he muses on the troubling breakdown in society following Lear's abdication. Although he feels deeply divided loyalty between the new and the old regimes, he consistently sympathises with Lear and seeks to offer him solace when he is cast out into the storm. For this 'treachery' his eyes are plucked out. Yet ironically this barbaric blinding, like Lear's madness, leads to new insight and understanding. He admits his earlier follies ('I stumbled when I saw'), but has still to learn the priceless virtue of patience.

In deep despair he attempts to leap off the cliff at Dover, but is saved – and perhaps spiritually healed – by the disguised Edgar, who makes him realise that 'Men must endure / Their going hence even as their coming hither: / Ripeness is all.'

◆ Working on your own, record the key events involving Lear in the play and match these up with the key events involving Gloucester. You could do this by using two columns to note the main narrative moments for each character.

◆ Write two or three paragraphs to explain the ways in which Gloucester's and Lear's experiences mirror each other throughout the play.

Edgar

Edgar is Gloucester's legitimate and virtuous son. Like his father, he is easily duped by Edmond's scheming. Unfairly accused of plotting his father's murder, he is forced to disguise himself as the mad beggar Poor Tom to avoid capture. In this role, and as various peasant figures, he then helps both Lear and Gloucester attain self-knowledge and understanding. He also – as a kind of 'chorus' device – comments directly to the audience on the intensity of other characters' suffering. His philosophical commentary on his condition operates as a touchstone for the play's moral universe. When he sees his blind father led towards him, his response is simply: 'Who is't can say "I am at the worst"? / I am worse than e'er I was.'

In the later stages of the play, Edgar has more lines than Edmond. He speaks in asides, directly to the audience, but his soliloquies are more powerful and engaging than Edmond's. He becomes an overt force for good, killing Oswald after he is sent to murder Gloucester, and then mortally wounding Edmond in trial by combat.

When Edgar finally tells his father who he really is, Gloucester's heart "Twixt two extremes of passion, joy and grief, / Burst smilingly.' Neither Albany nor Kent has the heart to take over governance of England, so it is left to the young Edgar to try to pick up the pieces.

Edmond

Edmond, Gloucester's illegitimate son, is generally perceived to be a more dynamic and charismatic character, full of raw energy and desire. He is unabashed in his selfishness and he ruthlessly seeks to advance himself, using whatever means possible: 'All with me's meet that I can fashion fit'. His first appearance in the play is with a powerful soliloquy in which he claims: 'Thou, Nature, art my goddess; to thy law / My services are bound.' As a 'natural' son to Gloucester (i.e. not born within marriage), Edmond plays on the idea of nature being his ally and inspiration. His obsession with the way he is described as 'base' and as a 'bastard' seems to fuel his anger and resentment against the world. He remains confident, however, in his own abilities and strengths, describing how he has a 'mind as generous' and 'shape as true' as his 'legitimate' brother, Edgar.

Edmond cleverly discredits Edgar, betrays his father to gain favour with Cornwall, and exploits Gonerill's and Regan's sexual interest to strengthen his position further. He is ruthless and determined; in his opening soliloquy he is bluntly ambitious: 'Well then, / Legitimate Edgar, I must have your land.' There seems to be no pity or remorse in him: betraying his father 'must draw me / That which my father loses: no less than all.' Yet, close to death, he is strangely capable of one final gesture of decency in attempting to repeal Cordelia's death warrant: 'Some good I mean to do, / Despite of mine own nature.'

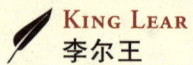

King Lear
李尔王

The Fool

Fools were popular well before Elizabethan times. In the Middle Ages, jesters were very common as household servants to the rich. They often wore the traditional costume of the coxcomb (jester's cap) with bells, and a motley (multicoloured) coat. Their role was to entertain with witty words and songs, and to make critical comment on contemporary behaviour. An 'allowed fool', such as Feste in *Twelfth Night*, was able to say what he thought without fear of punishment.

Lear's Fool is 'all-licensed', and so can speak frankly and critically about anything and anyone, especially his master, the king. He acts as a kind of dramatic chorus, an ironic commentator on the action he observes. Although he is threatened with whipping for impertinence, the Fool constantly reminds Lear of his folly. Lear is relentlessly used as the butt of the Fool's barbed comments: 'this fellow has banished two on's daughters and did the third a blessing against his will'; 'thou hast pared thy wit o'both sides and left nothing i'th'middle'; 'I am a fool, thou art nothing'.

The Fool moves easily between different styles of humour: stand-up comedy ('Thou hadst little wit in thy bald crown when thou gav'st thy golden one away'); song ('Fools had ne'er less grace in a year'); proverb ('Fathers that wear rags / Do make their children blind'); and sexual innuendo ('She that's a maid now').

The Fool's language seems to be a mixture of sense and nonsense. Attempting to analyse its exact meaning may destroy both its potential humour and its dramatic power. Some of the Fool's words may be puzzling, but all carry significance for Lear's plight. For example, 'So out went the candle, and we were left darkling', spoken as Gonerill begins to undermine Lear's sanity, is eerily prophetic of the blindness and confusion that will follow.

The Fool appears in only six scenes. From his very first appearance, his special relationship with Lear is evident. It allows him to escape punishment for his stinging criticisms, and sees him following Lear selflessly into the storm, almost as if he were Lear's alter ego, his second, more sane self.

This character disappears from the play in Act 3 Scene 6. When Lear says 'And my poor fool is hanged' just before he dies, he may be speaking of the dead Cordelia ('fool' could be a term of endearment). But his sorrowing words create echoes of the Fool (who had 'much pined away' for Cordelia). One production highlighted the relationship between Cordelia and the Fool by beginning the play with an ominous tableau of them with their heads linked by a hangman's noose.

◆ **Consider some of the critics' responses to the Fool (below) with a partner or in groups. For each idea, discuss how far you agree with the statement and how helpful it is in terms of understanding the role of the Fool in the world of *King Lear*.**

The Fool ... develops a dialect of folly and madness, to be heard in counterpoint with the language of an evil that remains horribly sane.

Frank Kermode

In an important sense the Fool is less an alter ego for Lear than for his daughters: like them he reminds Lear and the audience of the material basis for the change in the balance of power.

Kathleen McLuskie

The Fool is used as a chorus, pointing us to the absurdity of the situation. [He increases] our pain by his emphasis on a humour which yet will not serve to merge the incompatible in a unity of laughter.

G. Wilson Knight

[The Fool's jokes, riddles and scraps of rhyme] are like a trickle of sanity running through the play, a reminder that somewhere or other in spite of the injustices, cruelties, intrigues, deceptions and misunderstandings that are being enacted here, life is going on much as usual.

George Orwell

Kent

Kent is an important presence in *King Lear* for, although he does not speak a huge number of lines, he is on stage for almost half the play. Presented as Lear's loyal and devoted servant, he epitomises the kind of unconditional love that the old king could inspire. He is also the voice of unflagging honesty and plain speaking, challenging Lear in the love trial to 'check / This hideous rashness' and to 'See better'. In disguise as Caius he remains constant in his dedication to his master, following him through misfortune, storm and subsequent madness. He is never afraid to speak bluntly, disdaining pomposity and hypocrisy and defending truth. He also acts as a bridge with Cordelia, reminding the audience that she still keeps a watchful eye on her father. His selflessness is in marked contrast to the selfishness of others. Perhaps his ultimate act of loyalty to Lear is when he hints that he will follow his master into death: 'I have a journey, sir, shortly to go: / My master calls me; I must not say no.'

The role of Kent presents actors and directors with an interesting dilemma. He is fiercely loyal to the king, to whom he says: 'My life I never held but as a pawn / To wage against thine enemies.' But that loyalty arguably borders on blind, unthinking obedience: 'from your first of difference and decay / Have followed your sad steps'. Indeed, Kent can be seen as every bit as obsequious as Oswald, who so irritates him and whom he abuses with lines such as: 'A plague upon your epileptic visage.'

- ◆ Imagine that you are the director or the actor playing Kent. In your Director's Journal, make notes on how you will interpret this role. Will your Kent be a model subject and paragon of virtue, a relic of a failing hierarchical system, or something else?

- ◆ Write two paragraphs about what you think motivates Kent to feel such animosity towards Oswald and such deep loyalty to Lear.

King Lear 李尔王

The language of *King Lear*　《李尔王》的语言

Shakespeare's language is extraordinarily rich. It is textured and tapestried. The words are powerful, both on the page and in the hands of a skilled actor. As a student of the play, it can be enormously satisfying to spend time looking at the beautifully crafted language in detail. In terms of writing about the play, it is very helpful to have a good understanding of some of the ways in which the the words achieve their effects. Being able to employ technical language effectively and to write convincing analysis is a key skill. This section looks at some of the ways in which Shakespeare's language creates its particular effects in *King Lear*, and suggests some thematic language clusters that you might want to explore further.

Imagery

King Lear abounds in **imagery** (sometimes called 'figures' or 'figurative language'): vivid words and phrases that conjure up emotionally charged pictures in the imagination and help to create the atmosphere of the play ('I am bound / Upon a wheel of fire, that mine own tears / Do scald like molten lead.'). Shakespeare seems to have thought in images, and the whole play richly demonstrates his varied use of verbal illustration.

Shakespeare's imagery uses techniques such as simile, metaphor and personification. All are comparisons that substitute one thing (the image) for another (the thing described).

A **simile** (明喻) compares one thing to another using 'like' or 'as': 'We two alone will sing like birds i'th'cage'; 'My life I never held but as a pawn'.

A **metaphor** (隐喻) is a comparison, suggesting that two dissimilar things are similar. Metaphor is a process of 'carrying across' an idea associated with one concept and applying it to one that is not obviously related: 'Come not between the dragon and his wrath'; 'How sharper than a serpent's tooth it is / To have a thankless child'.

Personification (拟人) turns all kinds of things into persons, giving them human feelings or attributes: 'Thou, Nature, art my goddess'; 'Ingratitude! Thou marble-hearted fiend'.

◆ Identify three or four striking uses of imagery in the play. You could make sketches to create a powerful visual reminder of the ideas being suggested.

◆ Write an analytical paragraph on each of the images you chose in the activity above, explaining carefully how and why it achieves its effects.

The language of conflict

Antithesis (对偶) is the opposition of words or phrases against each other, as when Lear accuses Cordelia, 'so young, and so untender?' and when she replies: 'So young, my lord, and true.' This setting of word against word ('young' against 'untender' and then 'young' against 'true') is one of Shakespeare's favourite language devices. He uses it extensively in all his plays. Why? Because antithesis powerfully expresses conflict through its use of opposites – and conflict is the essence of all drama.

In *King Lear*, conflict occurs in many forms: father against daughter, son against father, brother against brother, sister against sister, wife against husband. The kingdom itself is divided, and is invaded by the foreign army of France. Thematically, sight works against blindness, nature against the 'unnatural', man against animal, rich against poor, truth against deception.

Shakespeare's dramatic style is characterised by his concern for comparison and contrast, opposition and juxtaposition (并置) : he sets character against character, scene against scene, word against word, phrase against phrase. For example, when Kent is banished in the first scene, he expresses the moral and social confusion stemming from Lear's impulsive decision in a series of antitheses. 'Freedom' pivots against 'banishment'; 'hence' against 'here'; Cordelia is praised whilst her sisters are scorned. And Kent's speech culminates with his promise to 'shape his old course in a country new'.

The language of *King Lear* is full of variety. What follows is a brief description of some key language features and image clusters that Shakespeare uses to provide insight into the play's crucial concerns.

The language of power

Shakespeare initially gives Lear an imperative style of speaking, which matches the old king's conviction at the play's outset that his every wish should be obeyed. His first words are an abrupt order to Gloucester: 'Attend the lords of France and Burgundy'. Throughout the opening scene his language bristles with the commands, imperious statements and questions of a king confident in his unshakeable authority: 'What can you say to draw / A third more opulent than your sisters? Speak.' Even in his madness Lear strives to dictate to the elements, instructing the storm: 'Blow, winds, and crack your cheeks!'

But when Lear is reconciled with Cordelia in Act 4, although he expresses himself in similarly direct language – 'Pray do not mock me', 'Do not laugh at me' – the tone is softer and more intimate. Even at the end of the play Lear still gives orders, but now they are radically changed into the style of polite request, 'Pray you, undo this button. Thank you, sir.' His final words, 'Look there, look there', are an impassioned plea for confirmation that Cordelia still lives. So, while Lear may speak the language of power, there is great variation in his speech. For example, his dialogues with the Fool are quite different from those with Gonerill and Regan. As the play progresses, he learns through his suffering that a king's role is not simply to command. By the time he is reunited with Cordelia, his language has changed completely.

- ◆ In pairs, take parts and speak the following dialogues aloud: a) Lear and Cordelia, Act 1 Scene 1, lines 77–114 (from 'Now our joy' to 'Good my liege'); b) Lear and Cordelia, Act 5 Scene 3, lines 3–26; c) all that Lear says in Act 5 Scene 3, lines 231–85. When you have spoken the lines, talk together about how you think Lear's language changes in these three scenes. When you have finished, working on your own, write several paragraphs about the way Lear speaks to two or three major characters; trace the interactions throughout the play, noting any changes in his manner of addressing them and suggesting reasons for these changes.

Sight and blindness

Another powerful theme in the play is the interplay between the ideas of sight and blindness. This is closely related to the themes of appearance and reality, which you may have looked at in other Shakespeare plays. Sight often operates as a metaphor for understanding.

When Lear banishes Kent with 'Out of my sight!', Kent's reply, beginning 'See better, Lear', highlights Lear's moral blindness, his lack of self-knowledge and understanding. The king is clearly unable to see through the falseness of Gonerill's claim to love him 'Dearer than eyesight'.

In contrast, there is a terrible literalness in Gonerill's Pluck out his eyes', and in Cornwall's brutal execution of that order, 'Upon these eyes of thine I'll set my foot.' The many images of sight and blindness that pervade the play sharply underscore and emphasise the dramatic effect of Gonerill's and Cornwall's horrifying words.

King Lear
李尔王

Gloucester talks ironically of not needing 'spectacles' to read Edgar's traitorous letter. The villainous Edmond can clearly 'see the business'. Lear speaks of 'Old fond eyes' that threaten to shed tears, and the physical pain and suffering experienced by Gloucester as a result of his blinding bring him insight into his past errors, 'I stumbled when I saw'. His new-found compassionate awareness of the nature of the world is vividly expressed: 'I see it feelingly'.

◆ Pick out at least six quotations that draw from the imagery of sight and blindness in the play. You might start with: 'For there was never yet fair woman but she made mouths in a glass' (a 'glass' is a mirror); 'How far your eyes may pierce I cannot tell'; and, 'Because I would not see / Thy cruel nails pluck out his poor old eyes'. Use the quotations either to write a couple of analytical paragraphs on the ways in which Shakespeare uses images of sight and blindness in *King Lear*, or prepare a presentation to the class on the same topic.

Animal imagery

King Lear resonates with the imagery of animals. Lear likens his daughters' cruelty to that of predatory birds and beasts. He calls Gonerill a 'Detested kite' whose ingratitude is 'sharper than a serpent's tooth'. Her face is 'wolvish', her tongue 'serpent-like'. In his madness he sees Gonerill and Regan as 'pelican daughters', cruelly feeding on his flesh and blood.

Disguised as 'Poor Tom', Edgar describes himself as 'hog in sloth, fox in stealth, wolf in greediness, dog in madness, lion in prey'. Gloucester's outburst 'As flies to wanton boys are we to the gods / They kill us for their sport' reduces humans to insignificant insects.

In his madness, Lear sees man without his fine clothes as little more than a 'poor, bare, forked animal' and howls like an animal himself over the dead Cordelia: 'Why should a dog, a horse, a rat have life, / And thou no breath at all?'

Disease and pain

The political and moral disruptions that result from Lear's division of his kingdom are echoed in recurring images of pain and disease, of bodies racked and tortured. Most obviously, Lear's madness and Gloucester's blinding illustrate the theme of mental and physical suffering.

The language of the play is studded with references to sickness and ailments. Kent identifies Lear's banishing of Cordelia as a 'foul disease'. Lear views the Fool's criticisms as a 'pestilent gall' (an infected irritant). On both his ungrateful daughters he wishes 'all the plagues that in the pendulous air / Hang'.

To Lear, Gonerill is 'a disease that's in my flesh', 'a boil / A plague-sore, or embossèd carbuncle'. In his madness, Lear's ravings trigger his disgust at the thought of sexually transmitted diseases, 'There's hell, there's darkness, there is the sulphurous pit, burning, scalding, stench, consumption'. But although disease imagery runs through the play, it is partly counterbalanced by the language of healing. Cordelia, grieving for her father's madness, urges that:

> All you unpublished virtues of the earth,
> Spring with my tears; be aidant and remediate
> In the good man's distress.

Reunited with Lear in Act 4, Cordelia seeks to return him to health, 'restoration hang / Thy medicine on my lips'.

Christian or pre-Christian?

There is much argument about whether *King Lear* is a Christian play. Those who regard it as Christian see Lear redeemed by the 'crucifixion' of his suffering. They identify Cordelia as a symbol of Christian redemption, almost Christ-like. She is a healer of suffering, a purger of ills and sins. Her reconciliation with her father helps to restore his wits. Her language affirms such Christian qualities as tolerance and understanding: 'blest', 'virtues', 'aidant', 'remediate', 'love', 'goodness', 'cure', 'restoration', 'repair', 'pity', 'benediction'. When she returns at the head of an army to aid Lear, her words echo those of Jesus, 'O dear father, / It is thy business that I go about' (Act 4 Scene 3, lines 23–4).

King Lear
李尔王

However, there is also much evidence in *King Lear* of a pre-Christian world. Characters do not appeal to a Christian god, but to the sun, Hecate, Apollo and Jupiter. Lear proclaims his faith in 'high-judging Jove'. Gloucester's world is beset by superstitious beliefs in the 'late eclipses in the sun and moon'. Edmond puts his faith in Nature as his goddess. Gloucester, Albany, Cordelia and Kent constantly appeal to the gods as they try to make sense of the apparently arbitrary nature of fortune and justice that they dispense, 'This shows you are above / You justicers'.

'Nothing'

The word 'nothing' resounds throughout the play. Cordelia uses it first, saying 'Nothing, my lord' in answer to Lear's love test. She has nothing to say, no flattering words to embellish the dutiful love she feels for her father. Lear's response adds a new meaning, 'Nothing will come of nothing'. If she does not declare her love, she will inherit nothing. The word will shift its meaning constantly in the mouth of each character: no words, no wealth, no meaning, no brains, no identity.

Gloucester will reward Edmond ('it shall lose thee nothing') for his false loyalty. Kent criticises the Fool's joking advice, 'This is nothing, fool'. Lear's criticism of the Fool is returned with a sharp twist of meaning, 'thou hast pared thy wit o'both sides and left nothing i'th'middle'. The Fool gives the word yet another interpretation – loss of identity: 'I am a fool, thou art nothing.' It is a meaning that is echoed as Edgar discards his true personality, 'Edgar I nothing am'.

Gonerill and Regan chillingly remind Lear that his former power will be reduced to nothing, 'What need you five and twenty? ten? or five? … What need one?' The consequences of Lear's rash act are devastatingly brought home to him, although 'nothing' remains unspoken.

Many of the characters are left with nothing at the play's end. In the most literal sense, they will be brought to nothing, losing life itself.

The language of King Lear

Plain speaking

King Lear strikingly explores the differences between speaking sincerely and insincerely. Some characters' private thoughts quite clearly do not match their public voices.

Cordelia recognises that her sisters speak untruthfully in Lear's love test, but she refuses to speak dishonestly: 'I want that glib and oily art, / To speak and purpose not'. Yet elsewhere, Gonerill and Regan's language is plain and direct, even though the duplicitous nature of their scheming pervades the play.

Kent is banished for his plain speaking, 'his offence, honesty' and returns as a character still committed to speaking candidly and bluntly.

Edmond, in contrast, uses lies to prey on a 'credulous father' and his 'foolish honesty' and later uses his cunning to 'stuff his [Cornwall's] suspicion more fully'.

The virtuous Edgar, disguised as Poor Tom, lies to his blinded father, but his motivation is benign and with almost the final words of the play he urges plain speaking: 'Speak what we feel, not what we ought to say.'

Blank verse or prose?

How did Shakespeare decide whether his characters should speak in **blank verse** or prose? His theatre audiences generally expected to hear plays in verse, but it was conventional for prose to be used by low-status characters, for comedy, to express madness and in letters. It is a popular belief today that Shakespeare's high-status characters speak verse because it is particularly appropriate to the noble, 'serious' thoughts of aristocrats, and his lower-status characters use prose to reflect the everyday or comic thoughts of 'ordinary' people.

Is this belief true of *King Lear*? Shakespeare never followed any convention slavishly, and there are plenty of exceptions in the play to these verse/prose conventions. Consider, for example, Gloucester and Edmond's conversation in Act 1 Scene 2, Lear's dialogues with the Fool, and Lear's conversations with Poor Tom and the blinded Gloucester.

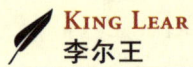

King Lear
李尔王

Critics' forum 评论家论坛

On these two pages you will find extracts from various influential critics, writing about *King Lear*. The readings are very different and, in some cases, contradictory.

◆ Working in small groups, read through each extract and try to summarise each position; you should then find evidence from the play to support the claims that are being made. Look back at pages 202–3 and decide whether you think any of these viewpoints fit in with the various critical approaches suggested there. While reading each extract, think about it very carefully in relation to the play as a whole. Make sure that you ask:

- What values, ideologies, attitudes or representations are evident in each of these extracts?
- Which quotations from the play would be most useful in supporting each of these readings?

But though this moral be incidentally enforced, Shakespeare has suffered the virtue of Cordelia to perish in a just cause, contrary to the natural ideas of justice, to the hope of the reader, and, what is yet more strange, to the faith of the chronicles … A play in which the wicked prosper and the virtuous miscarry may doubtless be good, because it is a just representation of the common events of human life; but since all reasonable beings naturally love justice, I cannot easily be persuaded that the observation of justice makes a play worse.

Samuel Johnson, 1765

This recurring and vivid stress on the incongruous and the fantastic is not a subsidiary element in King Lear: it is the very heart of the play. We watch humanity grotesquely tormented, cruelly and with mockery impaled: nearly all the persons suffer some form of crude indignity in the course of the play.

G. Wilson Knight, 1930

Apart from Lear, the protagonist, and Gloucester, his shadow, the subsidiary dramatic persons fall naturally into two parties, good and bad. First, we have Cordelia, France, Albany, Kent, the Fool, and Edgar. Second, Gonerill, Regan, Burgundy, Cornwall, Oswald, and Edmund. The exact balance is curious. It will scarcely be questioned that the first party tend to enlist, and the second to repel, our ethical sympathies insofar as ethical sympathies are being aroused in us. But none are wholly good or bad, excepting perhaps Cordelia and Cornwall.

G. Wilson Knight, 1930

The position of the hero in this tragedy is in one important respect peculiar. The reader of Hamlet, Othello, or Macbeth, is in no danger of forgetting, when the catastrophe is reached, the part played by the hero in bringing it on. His fatal weakness, error, wrong-doing, continues almost to the end. It is otherwise with King Lear. When the conclusion arrives, the old king has for a long while been passive. We have long regarded him not only as 'a man more sinned against than sinning', but almost wholly as a sufferer, hardly at all as an agent. His sufferings too have been so cruel, and our indignation against those who inflicted them has been so intense, that recollection of the wrong he did to Cordelia, to Kent, and to his realm, has been well-nigh effaced. Lastly, for nearly four Acts he has inspired in us, together with this pity, much admiration and affection.

A. C. Bradley, 1957

The close links between misogyny and patriarchy define the women in the play more precisely. Gonerill and Regan are not presented as archetypes of womanhood for the presence of Cordelia 'redeems nature from the general curse'. However, Cordelia's saving love, so admired by critics, works in the action less as a redemption for womankind than as an example of patriarchy restored.

Kathleen McLuskie, 1985

Critics' Forum

King Lear *wrests itself free of the presiding ideologies at war within its world, aligning itself instead with the mad, the blind, the beggared, the speechless, the powerless, the worthless: with all those 'Who with best meaning have incurr'd the worst' through their heroic failure to be 'as the time is', to think, feel and act as history dictates.*

Kiernan Ryan, 1989

King Lear *depicts something very much like such a world turned upside down: Lear, as the Fool says, has made his daughters his mothers, and they employ on him, as in a nightmare, those disciplinary techniques deemed appropriate for 'a slippery age, full of passion, rashness, wilfulness'. 'Old fools are babes again', says Gonerill ... In the carnival tradition, tolerated – if uneasily – by the medieval church and state, such reversals of role ... could be seen as restorative, renewing the proper order of society by releasing pent-up frustrations and potentially disruptive energies.*

Stephen Greenblatt, 1990

Our directors and actors are defeated by this play, and I begin sadly to agree with Charles Lamb that we ought to keep rereading King Lear *and avoid its staged travesties. That pits me against the scholarly criticism of our century, and against all the theatre people that I know, but in this matter opposition is true friendship.*

Harold Bloom, 1999

Edgar understands that as long as we are capable of saying we are 'at the worst' we have not yet reached the point: 'the worst is not / So long as we can say, "This is the worst"'. This might be the motto of the play, an unrelenting study in protraction; patience, which is continuallyrecommended, is defeated by fortune, by nature, by the indifference of heaven to justice.

Frank Kermode, 2000

- ◆ Imagine that *Forum* is a television discussion programme. In it, a group of professional critics, with differing views, is brought together for a discussion of a key literary text; tonight that text is *King Lear*. One student should chair the debate; the rest should take a critical stance based on one of the extracts on these two pages. The idea is that each student gives a considered and detailed reading of the play and continues to argue their case throughout the programme. In order to do this effectively, you will need to prepare very carefully and to select a number of relevant quotations from the play. This activity works well as part of a revision programme before an examination.

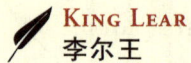

King Lear
李尔王

The truth and reconciliation commission
真相与调解委员会

A role-play activity for the whole class

Time: a month after Lear's death.
Place: a court-room somewhere in Britain.

This group activity will help you to revise and improve your knowledge of the play. The activity is designed to establish the facts of what happened in the final weeks of Lear's reign, to bring the truth to light and to learn lessons from the past. The focus is on understanding why characters behaved in the way they did, rather than to apportion blame. Each student will take the role of one person involved in some way with the play. Edgar and Albany would be obvious characters (as might be Kent – you could imagine he doesn't disappear); you might even invite the Fool and the King of France to return to give evidence). You will need to create other characters from various parts of the play. You could, for example, have servants from Gonerill's house, a knight who was one of Lear's retinue, a lord who was present in the court during the 'love test', and a farmer from Dover. Be creative with your choices. One student takes the role of lead investigator and invites each character in turn to give evidence and then to be questioned by other members of the commission. At the end of the hearing, the lead investigator (and assistants, depending on the size of your class) will give a summary of the events and their conclusions.

Each of the various characters might consider some of these questions and suggestions in preparing to make contributions:

Lead investigator

- Work in a small group with the assistant/usher(s), etc.
- What questions will you put to each character?
- What concrete evidence exists? Any exhibits to use in court (e.g. letters)?
- Consider how you will shape your questions to elicit full answers (as opposed to 'yes'/'no' replies).

Assistant(s) to the lead investigator

- Assist coroner in running the proceedings.
- Establish an order of events and present it on paper.
- Keep a record of the commissions' proceedings.

Edgar

- Why do you think things ended up as they did for you?
- What were you able to observe about the king from the perspective of being disguised?
- How do you feel about Edmond in retrospect?

Albany

- Had Gonerill's behaviour always been worrying?
- At what point did you realise that things were going wrong?
- Do you think you could have done anything differently to affect the course of the action?

The truth and reconciliation commission

Kent
- Is it true that the king had 'ever but slenderly known himself'?
- What do you think led Lear to behave in the way that he did?
- What do you identify as the main problems in society that led to the tragedy?

King of France
- What was your response to the initial 'love test' and Lear's behaviour in the court?
- How did you find Cordelia during her time with you in France?
- Why did you decide to invade Britain?

Gonerill's servants
- What did you think of Oswald's behaviour and attitude?
- Were you put under pressure to behave in a particular way?
- How would you describe the atmosphere in the household when Lear and his retinue were staying?

One of Lear's one hundred knights
- What was the atmosphere in the group like and how did the knights behave?
- How did King Lear treat his knights and what were his expectations?
- Could you see that things were going to go wrong?

A lord from Lear's court
- What did you think about the love test and was it in character for Lear?
- What did members of the court say about it in private?
- Could members of the court have done anything differently to avoid the tragedy?

A farmer from Dover
- What was the atmosphere like in preparation for the battle?
- What did you observe?
- What do ordinary people think about the events in the kingdom?

General questions for all to consider
- What relevant events were you present at?
- What contact did you have with the main characters?
- Did you witness any significant events first hand?
- How do you regard your position in this society?
- What eye-witness accounts can you offer the commission?
- Why do you think various characters behaved in the ways they did?
- What do you think their motivations were?
- Could the tragedy have been prevented?
- How might you speak when giving your evidence and how might this reflect your character and role?
- To what extent might we apportion blame to individuals?
- Going forward, how can we learn the lessons of history and ensure that nothing like this happens again?
- What systemic changes would need to take place to ensure that this never happened in future?

Other roles (if needed)
Jury members, ushers – could help others prepare their roles, or be responsible for creating exhibits (letters, etc.).

King Lear
李尔王

King Lear in performance 《李尔王》的演出

Shakespeare was himself an actor and we find references to the art of performance throughout his work. One powerful metaphor that recurs throughout his plays is that of the theatre as the world. Perhaps its most famous incarnation is in *As You Like It*, when Jaques tells his audience: 'All the world's a stage / And all the men and women merely players'. Those 'players' (or actors) charged with performing a Shakespeare play often find themselves meditating on life being like a play, and *King Lear* is no different. In Act 4 Lear tells us: 'When we are born, we cry that we are come / To this great stage of fools', reminding us that this is a play rooted in the traditions of the theatre and of performance. It is also a play with a diverse and sometimes surprising performance history.

Performances in Shakespeare's time

King Lear was probably performed many times during Shakespeare's lifetime. It is a play suited to the Globe Theatre's bare, unadorned stage since it demands little in the way of props and set. Although the play was most likely first performed in 1605 – probably the year of its creation – the first recorded performance is 'before the King's majesty at Whitehall' on 26 December 1606. What would King James have made of a Christmas entertainment showing the spectacle of a mad king who divided and gave away his kingdom? He probably enjoyed it, partly because it confirmed his view that a divided kingdom was the utmost political folly, and partly because 26 December was traditionally a day on which human foolishness and the virtues of enduring hardship with patience were celebrated.

How King James 'watched' *King Lear* would have been greatly affected by the factors that influenced Shakespeare as he wrote it, namely the prevailing political and cultural assumptions of the time (see pp. 209–13). Since those first performances, all subsequent productions have mirrored in some way the interests and anxieties, preoccupations, beliefs and values of their times. There is no one 'right way' to perform or interpret *King Lear*. Each performance reflects the current political, religious, literary or aesthetic ideologies of its audience and society.

We know very little about the play's early performance history. There is a record of a production in Yorkshire in 1610 but little else. The plague was rife during the play's early years, and the theatres were closed from 1642 until after the restoration of the monarchy in 1660. But perhaps it also fell victim to the vagaries of fashion and taste: *King Lear*, certainly in comparison with some of Shakespeare's other works, was not a heavily performed play in the fifty years or so after the playwright's death.

Performance after Shakespeare

A strange thing then happened. In 1681, the future poet laureate, Nahum Tate, rewrote the play to suit, as he (and many others) saw it, the prevailing mood and culture of the time. Tate's changes were extensive. He remodelled much of the structure of the play, cut the character of the Fool and gave Cordelia a confidante. Perhaps his most drastic action was the manner in which he reshaped the ending. Lear was restored to the throne and the happy conclusion was underlined by a marriage between Cordelia and Edgar – more in the tradition of Shakespearean comedy than tragedy.

For the best part of 150 years, Tate's version of *King Lear* was the one favoured by directors and actors – and was almost exclusively the one performed. Thus, in a strange quirk of performance history, the play that audiences would have seen for over a quarter of its performance life was not actually the one Shakespeare wrote but a hybrid of his lines and Tate's.

King Lear in performance

◆ Working in pairs, imagine a conversation between a contemporary director and theatre producer. Take one of the two roles each. The theatre producer should argue in favour of rewriting *King Lear*, just as Tate did, in order to give it a happy ending, to have a wedding at the end and to make it much more popular in theatres. The director should argue that the play should be left as close as we can get to the text that Shakespeare wrote. When you have practised your dialogue you could perform it in front of the class.

The famous eighteenth-century actor David Garrick played the role of Lear on several occasions. His style of acting was exaggerated and melodramatic, and well suited to Tate's version. During this period, although the text continued to alter, Tate's 'happy' conclusion remained the ending of choice. Both the Fool and the dystopian *denouement* were to remain absent from the stage for several years yet.

It was not until the nineteenth century that Shakespeare's original script of the play began to enjoy real stage success over Tate's happy-ending version. But even then the influence of political considerations on drama and theatre can be clearly seen. John Kemble played the role until 1810, but during the mental derangement of King George III, performances of *King Lear* were suspended because the sensibilities and politics of the time dictated against such productions – reminding us that the performance history of any play is also a history of contemporary values and political exigencies.

Nineteenth-century productions were increasingly concerned with spectacle. Large casts, lavish costumes and monumental sets were used in an attempt to give historical accuracy to the play. The problem was that historical accuracy is not a concept that lends itself happily to *King Lear*. Quite simply, no one knows where or when Shakespeare intended it to be set (and it is possible that he had no specific time or place in mind except 'long-ago England'). Famous productions have set the play in Saxon times, among the ancient Druids or, as Charles Kean did on the Victorian stage, at Stonehenge.

King Lear
李尔王

- Working on your own or in a pair, imagine that you are a designer for the stage production of *King Lear*. Note down what you would want on stage and what costumes you have in mind for some of the key characters in order to convey your own ideas about the mood and atmosphere of *King Lear*. Consider different possible historical or social settings for the play based on your own knowledge of world events, politics and history.

- When you have made these decisions you should either sketch a design for the set or write a production proposal suggesting what you would want in terms of set and costumes and giving reasons for your decisions.

At the end of the nineteenth century, a Henry Irving production (influenced by Ford Madox Brown) set the play in a Britain recently vacated by its Roman imperial occupiers – a world of decaying grandeur. The production was not considered a huge success. As the histrionics and lavish historical illustration of the nineteenth century drew to a close, the twentieth dawned with the promise of technical innovation and a 'purer' version of the text.

Lear in the twentieth century

The new century saw attempts to return – as closely as was possible given the problem of Quarto/Folio versions – to what Shakespeare originally wrote, and to face squarely the bleakness and horror of Shakespeare's vision. Although the tradition of extravagant productions lingered on, most no longer attempted to create an impression of realism. In a century that gave full expression to the terrors of mechanised warfare and human cruelty, *King Lear* became one of the most frequently performed of all Shakespeare's plays. Many people now argue that it is Shakespeare's greatest play.

Donald Wolfit's 1943 performance was praised from many quarters. However, the play was once again shaped by the context of reception – a wartime production was inevitably coloured by contemporary events.

▲ Komisarjevsky's Stratford production of 1936 focused (in those inter-war years) on power and made a huge spectacle of Lear's throne, which was the only item of furniture on stage.

The famous British actor John Gielgud played King Lear twice in the middle of the twentieth century, including in 1950 at Stratford. However, according to Gielgud's autobiography, his 1955 production was not a success, the acting being pushed into the background by the costumes and the sets.

Another great name of the British stage was Laurence Olivier. He played Lear on several occasions: the first time at the Old Vic in 1946 and, finally, in a television adaptation in 1983. You may be able to get hold of a extracts from the production to view yourself.

- See if you can gain access to an extract from a filmed version of the play. There are many clips available online and your school or library may have further access. Watch one scene from the film very carefully several times. Note the elements that come together in the production: look at the setting, the costumes, the lighting, the acting and the direction.

- Write two or three paragraphs analysing the effectiveness of the version of the production you have viewed. You should comment on and evaluate all the different aspects of direction, design and production.

Modern productions

Many more recent productions attempt to bring out the play's contemporary significance and relevance.

One of the most celebrated versions was Peter Brook's production at Stratford in 1962, which emphasised the bleakness of existence and its pain and suffering. For example, there was no help from servants for Gloucester after his blinding and Edmond's line 'Some good I mean to do' (Act 5 Scene 3, line 217) was cut.

Paul Scofield's austere version of the play seemed designed to resist audience sympathy and the hostile universe appeared indifferent to human suffering. The great theatre critic Kenneth Tynan said of Scofield's performance in Brook's production:

> *Instead of assuming that Lear is right, and therefore pitiable, we are forced to make judgements – to decide between his claims and those of his kin. And the balance, in this uniquely magnanimous production, is almost even ... [Lear] is wilfully arrogant, and deserves much of what he gets ... This production brings me closer to Lear than I have ever been; from now on, I not only know him but can place him in his harsh and forgiving world.*

Antony Sher's dazzling performance as a red-nosed Fool in 1982 (below) received great critical acclaim, especially in his riotous scenes with Michael Gambon's Lear. However, he perhaps unfortunately upstaged some of the other characters, especially the traditionally dynamic and energetic villain, Edmond.

King Lear
李尔王

Another maverick Fool was Linda Kerr Scott in the RSC's 1990 production featuring John Wood as Lear. Small, Scottish and a hyperactive presence on stage, the success of Scott's performance as the Fool was disagreed on by critics. The performance also saw a powerful young coupling of Ralph Fiennes and Linus Roache as Edmond and Edgar.

In 1997, the Young Vic Theatre cast a female Lear (Kathryn Hunter) as if the king were so old that he was virtually beyond gender. In a wheelchair, with bald, shrunken head, he was presented as an inhabitant of a nursing home in a set that was full of steel scaffolding and huge wooden doors (see p. 201).

In the same year, the Old Vic production was marked by a clever staging of the storm scene in which a jagged slash opened up at the back of the stage, through which Lear and the Fool stumbled, as if from another world.

The Royal Shakespeare Company (RSC) production in 1999 was directed by the renowned Japanese director Yukio Ninagawa, and its oriental soundscape and Japanese-costumed Fool (see p. 112) suggested the universality of the play's themes.

▼ This 1981 Hungarian production set the play on the site of an abandoned factory and railway. The loudspeakers and the stark set emphasise the director's intention to present the play as a political parable about authority in Eastern Europe in the 1980s.

King Lear in performance

▼ Shakespeare's plays are popular with audiences he could never have imagined. This is from the Japanese film *Ran*.

King Lear on film and television

Peter Brook's brooding 1971 film version emphasised the play's gory and brutal aspects, and almost entirely removed the character of Cordelia. It is an important milestone in the history of *King Lear* on film, and memorable, amongst much else for a scene between Lear and Gloucester that Robert Hapgood describes as revealing, 'the tender camaraderie of these two tough losers'.

The Russian director Grigori Kozintsev's 1971 Russian-language film (known as *Korol Lir*), with a translation by Boris Pasternak and with music by Dmitri Shostakovich, was austere, haunting and full of suffering although there are hints that Lear learns through that suffering, an interpretation which might have been influenced by the political conditions of contemporary Russian society.

Through film, Shakespeare's plays are popular with audiences he could never have imagined. The photograph above is a still from the Japanese film *Ran*, which sets *King Lear* in the traditional culture of Japan. This wildly violent production, with Buddhist influences, again demonstrates the way in which the play is so often adapted for the particular time and circumstances in which it is being performed.

Productions for television have included Jonathan Miller directing Michael Hordern in a BBC version of 1982 and the Olivier production, directed by Michael Elliott, from 1983.

Many other films, such as *A Thousand Acres*, *My Kingdom* and *King of Texas* are considered by many to be adaptations of the play.

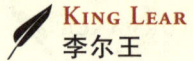

King Lear
李尔王

King Lear in the twenty-first century

Nigel Hawthorne's 1999 performance of the eponymous king was savaged by critics, not long after his hugely acclaimed role in the film of Alan Bennett's *The Madness of King George*, in which he quotes lines from *King Lear* (see page vi).

Julian Glover was the first Lear at the newly reopened Shakespeare's Globe in 2001 on the South Bank of London's River Thames. The bare stage was adorned with a post that was used for the delivery of some of the play's soliloquies (see pp. ix and 215). Shakespeare was back being performed in one of his original venues.

Declan Donnellan directed Nonso Anozie as Lear in Stratford in 2002 (see p. xi).

Christopher Plummer played the role in New York in 2004. Other 2004 productions saw Corin Redgrave taking on the part of the king for the RSC and Kenneth Albers being directed in the role by James Edmundson at the Shakespeare Festival in Ashland, Oregon.

Kevin Kline played Lear in New York in 2007. Reviewers largely praised this version, particularly the moments of high emotion, such as when Lear emerges from his period of insanity and is reunited with Cordelia.

Ian McKellen was also Lear in 2008, in a production that was later filmed for television (see p. viii).

Derek Jacobi, playing Lear in London at the Donmar Warehouse in 2010, was praised for his depiction of Lear's madness. Many critics considered this a classic production, believing it encouraged the audience to feel Lear's pain, as well as acknowledging the cruelty of some of his actions.

Jonathan Pryce played Lear at the Almeida in Islington, London, in a 2012 production directed by Michael Attenborough (see p. v). This was a relatively domestic Lear that proved very powerful in terms of portraying the effects of family breakdown and internal strife.

◆ Working on your own, conduct some research into the genre of theatre reviews. If you have online access, you will be able to find a wealth of material. Read a range of reviews, preferably from reputable sources such as mainstream newspapers and magazines. You may even be able to find reviews of productions of *King Lear*. If you have been able to watch a production, either in the theatre or on film, write your own review of that version of the play.

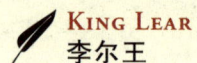

King Lear
李尔王

Writing about Shakespeare 笔论莎士比亚

The play as text

Shakespeare's plays have always been studied as literary works – as words on a page that need clarification, appreciation and discussion. When you write about the plays, you will be asked to compose short pieces and also longer, more reflective pieces like controlled assessments, examination scripts and coursework – often in the form of essays on themes and/or imagery, character studies, analyses of the structure of the play and on stagecraft. Imagery, stagecraft and character are dealt with elsewhere in this edition. Here, we concentrate on themes and structure. You might find it helpful to look at the 'Write about it' boxes on the left-hand pages throughout the play.

Themes

It is often tempting to say that the theme of a play is a single idea, like 'death' in *Hamlet*, or 'the supernatural' in *Macbeth*, or 'love' in *Romeo and Juliet*. The problem with such a simple approach is that you will miss the complexity of the plays. In *Romeo and Juliet*, for example, the play is about the relationship between love, family loyalty and constraint; it is also about the relationship of youth to age and experience; and the relationship between Romeo and Juliet is also played out against a background of enmity between two families. Between each of these ideas or concepts there are tensions. The tensions are the main focus of attention for Shakespeare and the audience; this is also how the best drama operates – by the presentation of and resolution of tension.

Look back at the 'Themes' boxes throughout the play to see if any of the activities there have given rise to information that you could use as a starting point for further writing about the themes of the specific play you are studying.

Structure

Most Shakespeare plays are in five acts, divided into scenes. These acts were not in the original scripts, but have been included in later editions to make the action more manageable, clearer and more like 'classical' structures. One way to get a sense of the structure of the whole play is to take a printed version (not this one!) and cut it up into scenes and acts, then display each scene and act, in sequence, on a wall, like this:

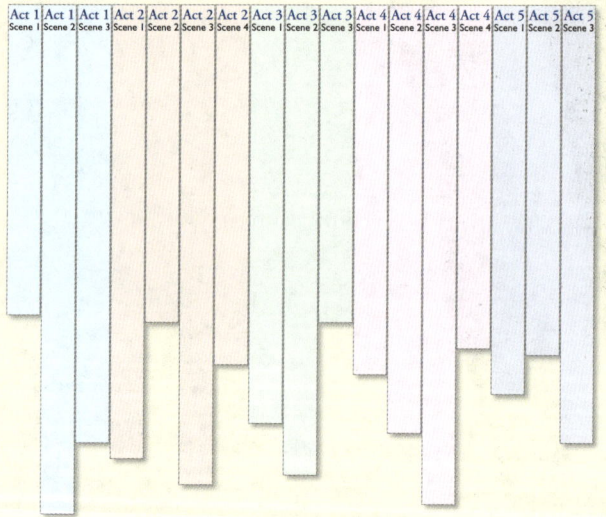

As you set out the whole play, you will be able to see the 'shape' of each act, the relative length of the scenes, and how the acts relate to each other (such as whether one act is shorter, and why that might be). You can annotate the text with comments, observations and questions. You can use a highlighter pen to mark the recurrence of certain words, images or metaphors to see at a glance where and how frequently they appear. You can also follow a particular character's progress through the play. Such an overview of the play gives you critical perspective: you will be able to see how the parts fit together, to stand back from the play and assess its shape, and to focus on particular parts within the context of the whole. Your writing will reflect a greater awareness of the overall context as a result.

The play as script

There are different, but related, categories when we think of the play as a script for performance. These include *stagecraft* (discussed elsewhere in this edition and throughout the left-hand pages), *lighting*, *focus* (who are we looking at? Where is the attention of the audience?), *music and sound*, *props and costumes*, *casting*, *make-up*, *pace and rhythm*, and other *spatial relationships* (e.g. how actors move around the stage in relation to each other). If you are writing about stagecraft or performance, use the notes you have made as a result of the 'Stagecraft' activities throughout this edition of the play, as well as any information you can find about the plays in performance.

What are the key points of dispute?

Shakespeare is brilliant at capturing a number of key points of dispute in each of his plays. These are the dramatic moments where he concentrates the focus of the audience on difficult (sometimes universal) problems that the characters are facing or embodying.

First, identify these key points in the play you are studying. You can do this as a class by debating what you consider to be the key points in small groups, then discussing the long-list as a whole class, and then coming up with a short-list of what the class thinks are the most significant. (This is a good opportunity for speaking and listening work.) They are likely to be places in the play where the action or reflection is at its most intense, and which capture the complexity of themes, character, structure and performance.

Second, drill down at one of the points of contention and tension. In other words, investigate the complexity of the problem that Shakespeare has presented. What is at stake? Why is it important? Is it a problem that can be resolved, or is it an insoluble one?

Key skills in writing about Shakespeare

Here are some suggestions to help you organise your notes and develop advanced writing skills when working on Shakespeare:

- Compose the title of your writing carefully to maximise your opportunities to be creative and critical about the play. Explore the key words in your title carefully. Decide which aspect of the play – or which combination of aspects – you are focusing on.
- Create a mind map of your ideas, making connections between them.
- If appropriate, arrange your ideas into a hierarchy that shows how some themes or features of the play are 'higher' than others and can incorporate other ideas.
- Sequence your ideas so that you have a plan for writing an essay, review, story – whichever genre you are using. You might like to think about whether to put your strongest points first, in the middle, or later.
- Collect key quotations (it might help to compile this list with a partner), which you can use as evidence to support your argument.
- Compose your first draft, embedding quotations in your text as you go along.
- Revise your draft in the light of your own critical reflections and/or those of others.

The following pages focus on writing about *King Lear* in particular.

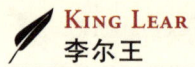

King Lear
李尔王

Writing about *King Lear* 笔论《李尔王》

The aim of this section is to help you to write well about *King Lear*. Your writing might take a number of different forms and respond not only to the text of the play, but also to different productions and performances on stage and on screen. Whatever form your writing takes, keep these two key considerations in mind:

- *King Lear* is a play. This means that your writing should reference the conventions of drama: you should be writing about acts, scenes, characters, stagecraft, speeches, soliloquies, asides, entrances and exits.
- The characters on stage are not real people. They are creations of the playwright, who have been realised by actors and directors on stage. Some critics find it helpful to think of characters as constructs. One easy way to remember to think in this way is to use phrases such as 'Shakespeare presents'. For example, rather than saying 'Edmond is evil', you might write, 'Shakespeare presents Edmond as evil'. This is a small but important distinction.

Different types of writing

Conventional essays

Many students follow courses that are assessed by writing a formal literary essay. When writing in this convention, it is usually a good idea to:

- set out a clear thesis in the introductory paragraph, which shows how you will answer the question in the essay
- quote frequently, making sure that quotations are relevant and succinct, and that you follow them with a clear analysis of how the language achieves its effects
- engage with critical voices by reading other views on the play and, where appropriate, quoting critics and agreeing or disagreeing with the views expressed (see also 'Critics' forum', pp. 228–9)
- organise and order your paragraphs with great care; first sentences of paragraphs, in particular, should be rigorously focused on answering the question
- make sure you are absolutely clear about the particular expectations of the assessment structure of the course or examination you are following.

Formal essays will often ask you to look at such areas as theme, character or different critical views. The following are examples of essay questions:

- How far would you agree that *King Lear* is a play that is primarily concerned with the relationship between parents and children?
- 'As flies to wanton boys are we to th'gods; / They kill us for their sport'. How far would you agree that *King Lear* is a play devoid of justice?
- How helpful is it to think of *King Lear* as a study in different types of madness?
- Edmond says: 'Thou, Nature, art my goddess'. What is the role of nature and the natural world in the play?
- To what extent would you agree that Cordelia is a two-dimensional and, therefore, rather uninteresting character?
- What do you think is the function and role of the Fool in *King Lear*?
- To what extent would you agree that Lear is 'more sinned against that sinning'?
- 'Kent's loyalty is sycophantic and unbelievable.' How do you consider the character of Kent in the light of this statement?
- 'Through a restless process of internal disruption and dislocation, *King Lear* wrests itself free of the presiding ideologies at war within its world, aligning itself instead with the mad, the blind, the beggared, the speechless, the powerless, the worthless'. How useful do you find this view as a commentary on the play?
- '*King Lear* depicts a world turned upside down'. How far would you agree with this view of the play?

◆ Choose at least one of these questions and write a detailed, developed and analytical essay in response to it. You should aim to write in a formal literary style, to include a clear thesis and to develop paragraphs in a logical, organised and persuasive manner.

Close analysis of a particular scene

Close reading is a key literary critical skill. One effective way of demonstrating and practising it is to look closely at a scene and to write several paragraphs analysing how it takes shape dramatically and how the playwright controls its language. If we were to take as an example Act 1 Scene 2 of *King Lear*, a detailed critical analysis of this scene would need to address the following questions:

- What is the effect of introducing Edmond to the audience through a soliloquy?
- What are the key features of the soliloquy?
- What are the dramatic effects of this, following straight on the departure of Cordelia?
- What are the dramatic effects of Gloucester entering at this point in the scene?
- What themes and ideas are introduced and developed in the dialogue between Edmond and Gloucester?
- What dramatic possibilities are explored with the use of the letter?
- What are the effects of Edmond's second 'soliloquy' and why do you think this time it is in prose?
- Why might Shakespeare have chosen to introduce Edgar at the end of this scene?
- What are the effects of Edmond's closing lines?

◆ Choose this (or another) scene from *King Lear* and write several paragraphs analysing the scene's particular dramatic and linguistic features. Give evidence from the script. You might find it helpful to start with a series of questions.

Creative writing

The possibilities for creative writing about *King Lear* are endless. For example, Jane Smiley's 1991 novel *A Thousand Acres* is an interesting contemporary take on the universal issues raised in *King Lear*. You might be interested in writing in one of the following genres or modes:

- a letter (perhaps one of the letters featured in the play)
- a newspaper account of some of the events of the play
- a poem in response to an aspect of the play
- an extra scene – perhaps an omitted scene or one that comes before or after the events of the play
- a film script for part of the play
- an interior monologue for one of the play's characters reflecting on their own behaviour and the behaviour of others.

And finally …

◆ Write a reflective account of your time spent studying *King Lear*. What did you initially expect the experience of studying Shakespeare to be like? Try to pinpoint where those assumptions came from. Were your expectations fulfilled – or challenged? What aspects of studying the play did you find most difficult and what helped you overcome them? What did you like best about the play? What was your favourite activity in this book? Did it change your understanding of an aspect of the play? If so, how?

KING LEAR
李尔王

The Quarto and Folio editions 四开本和对开本

None of Shakespeare's plays has survived in manuscript, so all modern editions are based on the early printed versions of the plays. Some plays were published during his lifetime in individual volumes usually called 'quartos'. Some of these quartos were authorised editions and some were pirated editions exploiting the popularity of the play. Most of these were very inaccurate. *King Lear* survives in an apparently official quarto of 1608 and in the version collected after Shakespeare's death and published along with thirty-five of his other plays in an edition called the 'Folio' in 1623.

'Folio' (from the Latin word for 'leaf') means a book made from folding a single large sheet of paper once to make two leaves or four pages. This large format was obviously appropriate for an expensive collection of plays running to 900 pages. 'Quarto' (from the Latin word for 'fourth') means a book made by folding a large sheet twice and making four leaves or eight pages; a smaller and more convenient size, suitable for a single play script.

The Folio version, on which this edition of the play is based, contains about 115 extra lines not found in the Quarto, and it is missing about 280 lines, which only appear in the Quarto. There are also hundreds of differences in punctuation, individual words and in who speaks specific lines. We do not know whether Shakespeare wrote two different versions of the play or whether it was frequently adapted and altered to suit different casts and situations, so what we have are two versions of what may have been several revisions.

Modern directors can choose which version to use, but most use a mixture, selecting lines and scenes that fit best with their view of the play. For example, the Folio version plays down the fact that Cordelia's intervention involves a foreign invasion, apparently focusing more on the moral rather than the political impact of her role. The Quarto can be seen to make the horror of Gloucester's blinding more bearable by showing the humanity and courage of two compassionate servants. Lear's death scene is changed substantially in the Folio by a line addition that makes his last thought about Cordelia rather than himself. The Folio also transfers the final lines of the play from Albany to Edgar – from someone politically powerful to someone who has suffered and could be seen as morally powerful.

What follows are selected lines from the Quarto version that do not appear in the Folio, the version used in this edition. There are also references to differences between the Quarto and Folio versions, sometimes including additional lines, on pages 12, 28, 30, 38, 72, 120, 132, 138, 142, 144 and 168.

THE QUARTO AND FOLIO EDITIONS

The mock trial of Gonerill (following line 14 in Act 3 Scene 6)

Lear conducts a trial to 'arraign' (bring before a court) Gonerill and Regan. He instructs Edgar to take the part of a judge in robes, the Fool to be his partner ('yoke-fellow') and Kent to join them as a member of the 'commission' (panel of judges). A 'joint-stool', a low stool made by a carpenter, stands in for Gonerill.

EDGAR	The foul fiend bites my back.
FOOL	He's mad that trusts in the tameness of a wolf, a horse's health, a boy's love, or a whore's oath.
LEAR	It shall be done; I will arraign them straight.
	[*To Edgar*] Come, sit thou here, most learnèd justicer.
	[*To the Fool*] Thou, sapient (聪明) sir, sit here. – No, you she-foxes –
EDGAR	Look where he stands and glares! Want'st thou eyes at trial, madam?
	[*Sings*] Come o'er the bourn, Bessy (英国传统舞蹈或戏剧中一个男扮女装的角色),
	to me.
FOOL	[*Sings*] Her boat hath a leak
	And she must not speak
	Why she dares not come over to thee.
EDGAR	The foul fiend haunts poor Tom in the voice of a nightingale.
	Hoppe-dance cries in Tom's belly for two white herring (鲱鱼, 一般是红色).
	Croak not, black angel! I have no food for thee.
KENT	How do you, Sir? Stand you not so amazed.
	Will you lie down and rest upon the cushions?
LEAR	I'll see their trial first. – Bring in their evidence.
	[*To Edgar*] Thou robed man of justice, take thy place.
	[*To the Fool*] And thou, his yoke-fellow of equity,
	Bench by his side. [*To Kent*] You are o'th' commission;
	Sit you too.
EDGAR	Let us deal justly.
	Sleepest or wakest thou, jolly shepherd?
	Thy sheep be in the corn;
	And for one blast of thy minikin (微小) mouth
	Thy sheep shall take no harm.
	Purr, the cat, is grey.
LEAR	Arraign her first; 'tis Gonerill. I here take my oath before this honourable assembly, she kicked the poor king her father.
FOOL	Come hither, mistress. Is your name Gonerill?
LEAR	She cannot deny it.
FOOL	Cry you mercy, I took you for a joint-stool (小方凳).
LEAR	And here's another whose warped (扭曲) looks proclaim
	What store her heart is made on. – Stop her there!
	Arms, arms, sword, fire! Corruption in the place!
	False justicer, why hast thou let her 'scape?

245

King Lear
李尔王

The lessons of suffering (following the last line in Act 3 Scene 6)

The Quarto includes a soliloquy for Edgar after Lear has been carried off to Dover. Edgar acknowledges that the king's suffering is far greater than his own. He plans to watch events and to reveal ('bewray') his true identity when the charges against him have been disproved.

> EDGAR　　When we our betters see bearing our woes,
> 　　　　　We scarcely think our miseries our foes.
> 　　　　　Who alone suffers, suffers most i'th'mind,
> 　　　　　Leaving free things (无忧无虑) and happy shows behind.
> 　　　　　But then the mind much sufferance doth o'erskip,
> 　　　　　When grief hath mates, and bearing, fellowship.
> 　　　　　How light and portable my pain seems now,
> 　　　　　When that which makes me bend makes the king bow (折腰).
> 　　　　　He childed as I fathered. Tom, away!
> 　　　　　Mark the high noises (流言), and thyself bewray
> 　　　　　When false opinion, whose wrong thoughts defile (玷污) thee,
> 　　　　　In thy just reproof repeals and reconciles thee.
> 　　　　　What will hap more tonight, safe 'scape the king!
> 　　　　　Lurk (潜伏起来), lurk!

Husband and wife hostility

Albany claims the sisters' cruel treatment of Lear will make them like 'monsters of the deep'. Gonerill replies by contemptuously, mocking his manhood. Extract (i) appears in Act 4 Scene 2, after line 33 ('Blows in your face'), and extract (ii) after line 38 ('So horrid as in woman').

> (i) ALBANY　　I fear your disposition:
> 　　　　　　　That nature which condemns its origin
> 　　　　　　　Cannot be bordered certain in itself (无法把自己牢牢束缚住).
> 　　　　　　　She that herself will sliver (割裂开) and disbranch
> 　　　　　　　From her material sap (汁液), perforce (势必) must wither
> 　　　　　　　And come to deadly use.
> 　　GONERILL　No more, the text is foolish.
> 　　ALBANY　　Wisdom and goodness to the vile seem vile;
> 　　　　　　　Filths savour but themselves (臭味相投). What have you done?
> 　　　　　　　Tigers, not daughters, what have you performed?
> 　　　　　　　A father, and a gracious aged man,
> 　　　　　　　Whose reverence even the head-lugged (被绳索牵头) bear would lick,
> 　　　　　　　Most barbarous, most degenerate, have you madded.
> 　　　　　　　Could my good brother suffer (容忍) you to do it?
> 　　　　　　　A man, a prince, by him so benefited (蒙受王恩)?
> 　　　　　　　If that the heavens do not stir their visible spirits
> 　　　　　　　Send quickly down to tame these vile offences,
> 　　　　　　　It will come.
> 　　　　　　　Humanity must perforce prey on itself
> 　　　　　　　Like monsters of the deep.

(II) ALBANY	Thou changed and self-covered thing, for shame
	Be-monster not thy feature (不要把自己变成魔鬼). Were't my fitness (合适)
	To let these hands obey my blood,
	They are apt enough to dislocate and tear
	Thy flesh and bones. Howe'er thou art a fiend,
	A woman's shape doth shield thee.
GONERILL	Marry, your manhood! Mew! (学猫叫，嘲讽阿尔博尼缺乏男人血性)

An additional scene

The Quarto includes a complete scene after Act 4 Scene 2, in which Kent and a Gentleman discuss the French invasion of Britain. The Gentleman describes Cordelia's compassionate reaction to news of her father's plight, and how Lear's sense of shame makes him unwilling to see her.

KENT	Why the King of France is so suddenly gone back, know you no reason?
GENTLEMAN	Something he left imperfect (未完成) in the state which since his coming forth is thought of, which imports (事关重大) to the kingdom so much fear and danger that his personal return was most required and necessary.
KENT	Who hath he left behind him general?
GENTLEMAN	The Marshal of France, Monsieur La Far.
KENT	Did your letters pierce the queen to any demonstration of grief?
GENTLEMAN	Ay, sir. She took them, read them in my presence,
	And now and then an ample tear trilled down (滚下)
	Her delicate cheek. It seemed she was a queen
	Over her passion, who most rebel-like
	Sought to be king o'er her.
KENT	O, then it moved her?
GENTLEMAN	Not to a rage. Patience and sorrow strove
	Who should express her goodliest. You have seen
	Sunshine and rain at once; her smiles and tears
	Were like a better way; those happy smilets (微笑)
	That played on her ripe lip seemed not to know
	What guests were in her eyes; which parted thence
	As pearls from diamonds dropped. In brief.
	Sorrow would be a rarity most beloved
	If all could so become it.
KENT	Made she no verbal question?
GENTLEMAN	Faith, once or twice she heaved the name of father
	Pantingly (喘息着) forth, as if it pressed her heart;
	Cried 'Sisters, sisters! Shame of ladies! Sisters!
	Kent! Father! Sisters! What, i'th'storm? i'th'night?

King Lear
李尔王

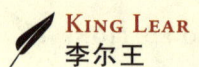

	Let pity not be believed!' There she shook
	The holy water from her heavenly eyes,
	And clamour moistened. Then away she started
	To deal with grief alone.
KENT	It is the stars,
	The stars above us, govern our conditions (品性),
	Else one self mate and make (同一对夫妇) could not beget
	Such different issues. You spoke not with her since?
GENTLEMAN	No.
KENT	Was this before the king (这里指法兰西王) returned?
GENTLEMAN	No, since.
KENT	Well, sir, the poor distressèd Lear's i'th'town,
	Who sometime in his better tune remembers
	What we are come about and by no means
	Will yield to see his daughter.
GENTLEMAN	Why, good sir?
KENT	A sovereign (天大的) shame so elbows (推搡) him: his own unkindness
	That stripped her from his benediction, turned her
	To foreign casualties (到异国他乡听天由命), gave her dear rights
	To his dog-hearted daughters – these things sting
	His mind so venomously that burning shame
	Detains him from Cordelia.
GENTLEMAN	Alack, poor gentleman!
KENT	Of Albany's and Cornwall's powers (军队) you heard not?
GENTLEMAN	'Tis so. They are afoot (行进).
KENT	Well, sir, I'll bring you to our master, Lear,
	And leave you to attend him. Some dear cause (某种重要原因)
	Will in concealment wrap me up awhile.
	When I am known aright, you shall not grieve
	Lending me this acquaintance. I pray you, go
	Along with me.

▶ The title page from a Quarto edition of the play. It refers to a performance staged for King James in 1606.

M. William Shak-speare:

HIS
True Chronicle Historie of the life and
death of King LEAR and his three
Daughters.

With the vnfortunate life of Edgar, sonne
and heire to the Earle of Gloster, and his
sullen and assumed humor of
TOM of Bedlam:

*As it was played before the Kings Maiestie at Whitehall
vpon S. Stephans night in Christmas Hollidayes.*

*By his Maiesties seruants playing vsually at the Gloabe
on the Bancke-side.*

LONDON,
Printed for *Nathaniel Butter*, and are to be sold at his shop in *Pauls*
Church-yard at the signe of the Pide Bull neere
St. *Austins* Gate. 1608.

King Lear
李尔王

William Shakespeare 莎翁年表
1564–1616

1564	Born Stratford-upon-Avon, eldest son of John and Mary Shakespeare.
1582	Marries Anne Hathaway of Shottery, near Stratford.
1583	Daughter Susanna born.
1585	Twins, son and daughter Hamnet and Judith, born.
1592	First mention of Shakespeare in London. Robert Greene, another playwright, described Shakespeare as 'an upstart crow beautified with our feathers'. Greene seems to have been jealous of Shakespeare. He mocked Shakespeare's name, calling him 'the only Shake-scene in a country' (presumably because Shakespeare was writing successful plays).
1595	Becomes a shareholder in The Lord Chamberlain's Men, an acting company that became extremely popular.
1596	Son, Hamnet, dies, aged eleven. Father, John, granted arms (acknowledged as a gentleman).
1597	Buys New Place, the grandest house in Stratford.
1598	Acts in Ben Jonson's *Every Man in His Humour*.
1599	Globe Theatre opens on Bankside. Performances in the open air.
1601	Father, John, dies.
1603	James I grants Shakespeare's company a royal patent: The Lord Chamberlain's Men become The King's Men and play about twelve performances each year at court.
1607	Daughter Susanna marries Dr John Hall.
1608	Mother, Mary, dies.
1609	The King's Men begin performing indoors at Blackfriars Theatre.
1610	Probably returns from London to live in Stratford.
1616	Daughter Judith marries Thomas Quiney. Dies. Buried in Holy Trinity Church, Stratford-upon-Avon.

The plays and poems

(no one knows exactly when he wrote each play)

1589–95	*The Two Gentlemen of Verona, The Taming of the Shrew, First, Second* and *Third Parts* of *King Henry VI, Titus Andronicus, King Richard III, The Comedy of Errors, Love's Labour's Lost, A Midsummer Night's Dream, Romeo and Juliet, King Richard II* (and the long poems *Venus and Adonis* and *The Rape of Lucrece*).
1596–99	*King John, The Merchant of Venice, First* and *Second Parts* of *King Henry IV, The Merry Wives of Windsor, Much Ado About Nothing, King Henry V, Julius Caesar* (and probably the Sonnets).
1600–05	*As You Like It, Hamlet, Twelfth Night, Troilus and Cressida, Measure for Measure, Othello, All's Well That Ends Well, Timon of Athens,* **King Lear**.
1606–11	*Macbeth, Antony and Cleopatra, Pericles, Coriolanus, The Winter's Tale, Cymbeline, The Tempest.*
1613	*King Henry VIII, The Two Noble Kinsmen* (both probably with John Fletcher).
1623	Shakespeare's plays published as a collection (now called the First Folio).

Acknowledgements 鸣谢

Cambridge University Press would like to acknowledge the contributions made to this work by Rex Gibson, Mike Clamp, Jonathan Morris and Rob Smith.

The authors and publishers acknowledge the following sources of copyright material and are grateful for the permissions granted. While every effort has been made, it has not always been possible to identify the sources of all the material used, or to trace all copyright holders. If any omissions are brought to our notice, we will be happy to include the appropriate acknowledgements on reprinting.

Extract from Kenneth Tynan's review of Peter Brook's Royal Shakespeare Company production of *King Lear* on p. 235 copyright © Guardian News and Media Ltd 1962.

Picture Credits

p. iii: RSC/Royal Shakespeare Theatre 1976, © Donald Cooper/Photostage; p. v top: Talawa Theatre Company / Cochrane Theatre 1994, © Donald Cooper/Photostage; p. v bottom: Almeida Theatre 2012, © Geraint Lewis; p. vi top: RSC/Barbican Theatre 1999, © Donald Cooper/Photostage; p. vi bottom: RSC Young People's Shakespeare/UK Tour 2012, © Donald Cooper/Photostage; p. vii top: RSC/Royal Shakespeare Theatre 1993, © Donald Cooper/Photostage; p. vii bottom: Lyttelton Theatre/National Theatre 1990, © Donald Cooper/Photostage; p. viii top: Maly Drama Theatre of St Petersburg/Barbican Theatre 2006, © Donald Cooper/Photostage; p. viii bottom: RSC/Courtyard Theatre 2007, © Donald Cooper/Photostage; p. ix top: Royal Court Theatre 1993, © Donald Cooper/Photostage; p. ix bottom: Tokyo Globe Company 1991, Robbie Jack/Corbis; p. x top: RSC/Royal Shakespeare Theatre 2004, © Donald Cooper/Photostage; p. x bottom: RSC/Royal Shakespeare Theatre 1982, © Donald Cooper/Photostage; p. xi: RSC Academy Company/Swan Theatre 2002, © Donald Cooper/Photostage; p. xii top: English Touring Theatre/The Old Vic 2003, © Donald Cooper/Photostage; p. xii bottom: West Yorkshire Playhouse/Leeds 1995, © Donald Cooper/Photostage; p. 6: RSC/Albery Theatre 2005, © Donald Cooper/Photostage; p. 10: Dennis Krausnick (Lear), Bill Watson (Cornwall), Jonathan Epstein (Kent) in a Shakespeare & Company production 2012. Photo by Kevin Sprague; p. 18: Theatre festival, Bangalore, © JAGADEESH NV/epa/Corbis; p. 22: Shakespeare's Globe 2001, © Donald Cooper/Photostage; p. 28: West Yorkshire Playhouse/Leeds 2011, © Donald Cooper/Photostage; p. 34: RSC Academy Company/Swan Theatre 2002, © Donald Cooper/Photostage; p. 38: RSC/Albery Theatre 2005, © Donald Cooper/Photostage; p. 46: Royal Court Theatre 1993, © Donald Cooper/Photostage; p. 52: RSC/Royal Shakespeare Theatre 1993, © Donald Cooper/Photostage; p. 55 top: The Donmar Warehouse 2010, © Johan Persson/ArenaPAL; p. 55 bottom: RSC/Royal Shakespeare Theatre 1976, © Donald Cooper/Photostage; p. 58: RSC/Royal Shakespeare Theatre 1993, © Donald Cooper/Photostage; p. 66: Lyttelton Theatre/National Theatre 1990, © Donald Cooper/Photostage; p. 72: Maly Drama Theatre of St Petersburg/Barbican Theatre 2006, © Donald Cooper/Photostage; p. 76: RSC/Royal Shakespeare Theatre 1982, © Donald Cooper/Photostage; p. 78: Contemporary Legend Theatre at the Royal Lyceum Theatre/Edinburgh International Festival 2011, © Clive Barda/ArenaPAL; p. 84: Theatre festival, Bangalore, © JAGADEESH NV/epa/Corbis; p. 97 top: London International Mime Festival/Shaw Theatre 1985, © Donald Cooper/Photostage; p. 97 bottom: RSC/Royal Shakespeare Theatre 2004, © Donald Cooper/Photostage; p. 100: RSC/Courtyard Theatre 2010, © Geraint Lewis; p. 112: RSC/Barbican Theatre 1999, © Donald Cooper/Photostage; p. 120: Shakespeare's Globe 2001, © Pete Jones/ArenaPAL; p. 128: West Yorkshire Playhouse/Leeds 2011, © Donald Cooper/Photostage; p. 130: Shakespeare's Globe 2001, © Donald Cooper/Photostage; p. 133: Theatre Royal/Bath 2013, © Nobby Clark/ArenaPAL; p. 136: Suzuki Company of Toga/Barbican Theatre 1994, © Donald Cooper/Photostage; p. 140: Peter Hall Company/The Old Vic 1997, © Donald Cooper/Photostage; p. 148: West Yorkshire Playhouse/Leeds 2011, © Donald Cooper/Photostage; p. 154: RSC/Courtyard Theatre 2010, © Donald Cooper/Photostage; RSC/Royal Shakespeare Theatre 1976, © Donald Cooper/Photostage; p. 164: The Donmar Warehouse 2010, © Johan Persson/ArenaPAL; p. 170: RSC/

King Lear
李尔王

Royal Shakespeare Theatre 1976, © Donald Cooper/Photostage; p. 173: Leicester Haymarket production/The Young Vic 1997, © Donald Cooper/Photostage; p. 180: *King Lear* directed by Grigori Kozintsev 1971, © Lenfilm/The Kobal Collection; p. 186: Shakespeare's Globe 2001, © Donald Cooper/Photostage; p. 190: RSC/Royal Shakespeare Theatre 1993, © Donald Cooper/Photostage; p. 194: The Old Vic Theatre 1989, © Donald Cooper/Photostage; p. 196: Shakespeare's Globe 2008, Marilyn Kingwill/ArenaPAL; p. 201 top: Leicester Haymarket production/The Young Vic 1997, © Donald Cooper/Photostage; p. 201 bottom: Theatre festival, Bangalore, © JAGADEESH NV/epa/Corbis; p. 204 Cast of *King Lear* in a Shakespeare & Company production 2012. Photo by Kevin Sprague; p. 211: RSC/Albery Theatre 2005, © Donald Cooper/Photostage; p. 213: RSC/Courtyard Theatre 2010, © Geraint Lewis; p. 214 left: Shakespeare's Globe 2001, © Donald Cooper/Photostage; p. 214 right: RSC/Courtyard Theatre 2007, © Geraint Lewis; p. 215 top: Jonathan Croy as Gloucester and Dennis Krausnick as Lear in a Shakespeare & Company production 2012. Photo by Kevin Sprague; p. 215 bottom: RSC/Royal Shakespeare Theatre 1982, © Donald Cooper/Photostage; p. 216: RSC/Courtyard Theatre 2007, © Geraint Lewis; p. 217: Almeida Theatre 2012, © Marilyn Kingwill/ArenaPAL; p. 218 left: Shakespeare's Globe 2008, © Elliott Franks/ArenaPAL; p. 218 right: West Yorkshire Playhouse/Leeds 2011, © Donald Cooper/Photostage; p. 219: RSC/Royal Shakespeare Theatre 1990, © Donald Cooper/Photostage; p. 221: West Yorkshire Playhouse/Leeds 2011, © Donald Cooper/Photostage; p. 223: Shakespeare's Globe 2001, © Donald Cooper/Photostage; p. 225: RSC/Royal Shakespeare Theatre 1990, © Donald Cooper/Photostage; p. 226: Shakespeare's Globe 2008, © Donald Cooper/Photostage; p. 227: RSC/Royal Shakespeare Theatre 1982, © Donald Cooper/Photostage; p. 233: engraving of David Garrick as King Lear, © Topfoto; p. 234: Royal Shakespeare Theatre 1936, © Topfoto; p. 235 top: *King Lear* directed by Peter Brook 1970, © Filmways/Athena/Lanterna/The Kobal Collection; p. 235 bottom: RSC/Royal Shakespeare Theatre 1982, © Donald Cooper/Photostage; p. 236 left: RSC/Royal Shakespeare Theatre 1990, © Donald Cooper/Photostage; p. 236 right: Miskolc National Theatre, Hungary 1981, © MTI Photo; p. 237: *Ran* directed by Akira Kurosawa 1985, © Herald Ace/Nippon Herald/Greenwich/The Kobal Collection; p. 238: The Donmar Warehouse 2010, © Johan Persson/ArenaPAL; p. 239: The Old Vic 2003, © Geraint Lewis; frontispiece for the Quarto edition of *King Lear* 1608, © The Granger Collection/Topfoto.

Produced for Cambridge University Press by
White-Thomson Publishing
+44 (0)843 208 7460
www.wtpub.co.uk

Managing editor: Sonya Newland
Designer: Clare Nicholas
Concept design: Jackie Hill